The Baptist – Part I: Judge's Genesis
Copyright © 2016 by Ryan Gerard
All rights reserved.
No part of this book may be used or reproduced in any manner whatsoever without written permission except in the case of brief quotations embodied in critical articles and reviews.
Registration No: 1135651
Literary.

Cover images Copyright © 2017 by Ryan Gerard

Gerard, Ryan David
'The Baptist' – Part I; Judge's Genesis / Ryan David Gerard—1st ed.

ISBN-13: 978-1534939431
ISBN-10: 1534939431

[1. Fiction. 2. Action. 3. Science—Fiction..]
Title ID: 6378744

www.baptistbookproject.com

"THE BAPTIST"
By Ryan David Gerard

!DISCLAIMER WARNING!

 The opinions expressed in the following are those of the author and are meant to be just that; *opinions*. This is a *fictional* story and is not meant to be taken as what I feel should be fact—nor does it mean that I believe in or condone any of the actions the characters may take. It is a vast array of flawed and *real* characters that don't have the luxury of being pruned, polished and edited to suit the image of what everyone wants to see. This is simply an account of how they live and act through the situations and what entails after. (similar to another book I know) This three part book series is simply designed to portray a series of 'what-ifs' for entertainments sake and food for thought.
 For the Christian reader; to avoid becoming a stumbling block to anyone, I should warn that this book may contain things that may be offensive. This is not a typical piece of Christian media! This is not meant to be the type of book that is used for 'in-church' bible studies or something that is solely for the believer. I wrote this for everyone on the outside of faith because there is a real world out there where these types of things take place. Even though it is potentially offensive at times, please give it a chance.
 On the flip side, this book does speak on spiritual issues and faith, in case that may offend you. I would also ask that you take a chance on my story. I promise you, this is unlike anything relating to the topic you have ever read before. I believe that if you see the entire series through to the end you will see the grand scheme of my intentions.

Thank you,
Happy reading!

Regards from the Author
-Ryan David Gerard.

For my wife and children;
My own personal connection back to everything good about life...

PROLOGUE
In the not too distant future...

War will end us.
Or plague.
Pollution.
Famine.
The means isn't certain, but...
The end.
The end *is* certain.

After decades of terrorism and violence,
   apathy was no longer a viable solution...our arrogance in proclaiming; there will never be another world war, was coming to an end...
One can only be pushed so far,
stretched so much until...it's time to push back.

Baltimore. Time; unknown. Irrelevant.

Baltimore standing free. Its citizens living their day to day lives. People going about their business and daily affairs.

I used to think there was something *I* could do to save us. To save the goodness of life for the innocent and repay every horrible thing that I learned to hate. For evil is a very real thing in this world and it needs to be dealt with.

For now,
   the morning sun crested, in between two sky scrapers, with that brilliant early morning orange and it glistened off the glass structures. People were off to work, sipping their coffee, flicking their cigarette butts, reading their newspapers and scrolling down their social media feeds. Bikes and cars filled the air with bell rings and horn honks. Friends were having conversations as they walked along or rode the bus. They shared ear buds and listened to their favorite music together. They took selfies.
But they all had something in common...
...life.
Behind the faces and the eyes of each person were thoughts about life. Some were thinking about money or marriage and others were thinking about the harsh words they had just spoken to someone, or had spoken to them. Some were thinking about how good life was and others, how dismal. Some people's heads were filled with epic and apocalyptic thoughts, while others thought about how mundane and dry life was.

A day in the life of the conflicting nature of our existence.
How can life be so horrible and amazing at the same time?
I learned that saving the world from the end is impossible. The damage has already been done. The world has been dying ever since its genesis. Decaying— A long, slow death.

Crime and injustice has ravaged our world. Like the pains of dying one feels as they slowly die from disease.

The streets bleed.

How, then, do we deal with this problem? The 'condition' that we call being human. Only thing left to do is save our souls.

The real war will be for our salvation,
and it's only a matter of time...

In the midst of all these people a man walked among the crowds, blending in, in the sea of dark colored clothing—a blackness that hides everything. He spied these faces as he walked among them, with a certain satisfaction. He especially took pride at the faces that bore the marks of a life of pain and anguish. The hardened faces of circumstance.

In a city park another man sat on a bench, waiting for His company. A simple looking man who you probably wouldn't be able to pick out of the crowd. There was nothing extra special about Him. He wore simple blue jeans and white t-shirt. No other distinct facial features really. He just sat there waiting, with nothing to do but sit and watch as the people passed Him by. People He loved so much, but who had no idea who they had just walked passed. He watched as a man played with his dog. A woman talked on the phone with her sweetheart and giggled and The Stranger, as this man was come to simply be called, smiled to himself.

Then the dark man arrived and He didn't even look up or over at him. The Stranger carried on watching people but He knew the man was there. The dark man sat beside Him and also didn't look at Him either. They both just stared ahead at the people in silence. The dark one noticed what The Stranger was looking at and started to watch it too. Two men sat at one of the chess tables having a match. An intense game of wits as they both stared at the board.

The dark man chuckled through his nose.

"Well," he said. "Isn't that ironic?" He asked, motioning to the game.

The Stranger said nothing and watched the contrasting black and white chess pieces as the two men playing moved them about the board.

Several moments passed before; finally, the dark man inhaled deeply and exhaled a long breath.

"It's been a while..." He spoke into the silence.

The Stranger hesitated before answering. "...too long." He said.

"Not long enough." The dark man scoffed.

"You know, sometimes I miss our little chats." The Stranger said.

"You know why I'm here." The dark one spat.

The Stranger stopped again. And then answered. "Yes..." He said grimly. "...I do. Your...proposition."

"You sound nervous..." The dark man said, with a certain mischievous delight in his voice.

The Stranger sighed. "Don't forget your place, or who you're talking to." He said, finally turning His head to glare at the dark man. "It's you who's required to come and ask me for permission."

The dark man now turned his head too, to meet The Stranger's gaze and they exchanged glares for a moment or two. Then the dark one smiled insecurely and laughed a breathy chuckle as he looked away again.

"I guess you read the outline I sent then?" He asked passively.

"Yes." The Stranger replied.

"So...do you accept?" The dark one asked.

The Stranger sighed again and returned His attention to the people walking around them.

"I think you're wrong." He said to the dark man, not looking at him. "About them." He added, admiring the people.

The dark man realized that He was referring to the citizens and he rolled his eyes.

"Oh, please!" He remarked. "These people?! You think the people of your original day hated you?! Pah! They're a treat compared to the people today." The dark man sighed and began to scan the park. "Look at them." He stated, shaking his head. "They have no idea what's coming do they? How can they walk their dogs, or go to work, love their spouses, play chess...when this world is so close?" He shook his head some more, still watching them all buzz about the park. Then he scoffed and chuckled. "They're so willfully ignorant." He asked. "And you think they'll care about you? Most of these people don't even know what they believe. Agnostic..." He chortled. "My favorite word. They're so saturated with technology and intelligent public figures who call the shots."

The Stranger just sighed, not quite able to disagree with these comments. "I know." He simply replied. "You've done quite well manipulating them haven't you?"

The dark man grinned slowly now.

"And you've been chipping away," The Stranger continued. "Building this war you speak of. Unleashing men like Joseph Kovacs and his 'Bears' onto the world. You'll probably get it too."

"You sound like you're giving up before it's even begun!" The dark one said.

The Stranger paused and lost his gaze into the chess board. His glare glazed over and He just stared at the moving pieces. "No." He said softly. "I accept your challenge."

The dark man scoffed. "Ha!" He laughed. "But if you think I'm pulling any punches this time around, you're sorely mistaken."

"Well then," The Stranger said. "I guess you won't have anything to worry about will you?" He asked, looking over at him again with a sarcastic and confident smirk on His face.

The dark man screwed his face up and scoffed some more.

"You sure you're ready to do this?" The Stranger pressed the dark one. "You already failed once to kill me. What you're asking for is ridicul—

"—What I'm asking for," the dark man cut in angrily. "Is a second shot at the title." He glared hatefully now into the face of his victor. The Stranger chuckled.

"Last chance..." He said. "...Are you sure you wanna do this?"

"Trust me, I'm positive! I won't make the same mistakes again."

The two men stared at each other for a while more, sizing the other one up.

"Okay..." The Stranger eventually said, turning back to watch the chess match. "But you'll have to wait a while."

"For what?"

"For me to set this up. To set the stage for you. Give me time while I organize a way to reset time."

"Why don't you just snap your fingers and zap us back there right now. I'm ready now!"

"No. I'd rather let this play out naturally and not force anything."

"What's the point of that?"

"Two words." The Stranger simply said. "...free will, my friend...free will."

The dark man stewed. "Fine!" He said. "It'll be more worth the wait, to see your blood again!" He stared fire into The Stranger's very soul.

"...so you have the board then..." The Stranger said. "...what's the first move?"

The dark one grew a most sinister grin across his face and clapped his hands together to rub them. "Well..." He said giddily. "It's funny you should ask."

"Really? Why's that?"

"Because my player is already here." He nodded towards the activity in the park ahead of them.

The Stranger looked to where he had motioned. Surprisingly, it was at the two men playing chess. One of them stood up and adjusted his glasses. He was a nervous looking man, about in his forties. He was staring at the board intently still, to the other player's dismay, and he patted down his beard with his hand.

"Him?" The Stranger asked.

"That's my guy..." The dark man replied.

"Huh..." The Stranger simply puffed. "Very interesting..." And the dark man didn't see it, but a subtle smirk appeared on The Stranger's lips.

After several moments, this awkward man they were both looking at suddenly moved his knight to a kill position on the chess board. He didn't even say it, but he just looked at his opponent and smiled arrogantly. Then he walked away, leaving the other guy frantically looking at the board trying to figure out the check mate.

"Very interesting indeed..." The Stranger said, looking at him as he went.

"Anything else?" The Stranger asked the dark man.

"I've interviewed for a position on staff with the guy who's running for president; Harold Kingston."

"Really...?" The Stranger asked.

"If you wanna look me up...I'll be taking on the name; Paul Ranston."

"That's it?"

"That's all you need to know for now." Ranston said. "And what name are you going to assume this time?"

The Stranger smiled softly. "My name..." He said. "...I am what I am. They will have to come to know my name in a whole new way, for themselves!"

"Hmm...How typical of you," Ranston said. "Now, let's hear it."

"Hear what?"

"I told you my first move...now you tell me yours."

The Stranger looked sullenly back to the people in the park. He scanned the crowd very intently until His eyes landed on His intended target. He stopped to watch her; this young girl with her back facing them.

"Hello?" Ranston asked. "I asked you a question."

The Stranger continued to watch the girl in the park, ignoring Ranston.

She suddenly turned as if to walk away, revealing her large pregnant belly. The young girl sighed and started to rub her tummy like a ball and wasn't really paying attention to her surroundings. She took a couple steps to go but—

Whoops! She collided with another man and they both let out startled yelps.

"Oh my goodness, I'm so sorry!" The man who ran in to her said frantically.

Ranston, when he realized that it was his player she had bumped into, looked over at The Stranger with confusion.

"It's okay, really." The young mother said, laughing it off.

The man, Ranston's chosen, glanced down and realized she was pregnant and his eyes went wide.

"Oh no!" He blurted, covering his mouth with his hands. "Oh no, I'm so sorry!" He said, slicking his long hair back.

The young woman chuckled warmly while caressing her belly. "It's really okay! I'm fine, I swear, don't worry!" She continued to smile kindly at him for reassurance.

The man saw compassion in her face which brought his emotions way down. He snapped out of his guilt and felt relieved when he finally realized she was okay. He laughed out loud and lowered his hand.

"Oh, wow!" He laughed. "I'm so clumsy, forgive me." He said a little more tranquil.

"It's fine!" She said.

As they talked, The Stranger looked over at Ranston with a stone cold look.

"That's not fair..." Ranston said. "He's my player..."

"I know..."

"You can't intervene!"

The Stranger cocked both His head and His eyebrow up inquisitively, as if to poke a bit of fun at Ranston. "Excuse me?" He asked.

A frustrated Ranston scoffed and rolled his eyes. "I mean...you can't...principally. You can't!"

"And I won't." The Stranger stated simply.

"Then what's with this?" Ranston motioned towards the two people.

The Stranger shrugged playfully. "You picked your player...this is mine..." He said.

"This woman?" Ranston laughed.

"Who said anything about the woman?" The Stranger asked.

"Anyways..." The socially awkward man said. "...thanks for being so nice, ma'am. Take care of that baby." And with that he began to walk past her as he spoke, acting nervous and jittery, not knowing what else to say.

"No problem." She replied, chuckling kindly at his social slights.

"Oh," The man said, turning quickly back towards her. "Boy or girl?"

"Oh, it's a boy." The mother replied with a smile.

"Great! Congratulations." He said, as he turned to walk a few more steps. He turned looking over his shoulder in stride at her. "Does he have a name?" He asked.

"John." The mother answered. "His name is John."

"Well, good luck to you and John!" He said, before turning away for good to go about his business.

"Thanks, you too!" She hollered back, laughing. She thought the middle aged man's lack of social cues was cute.

The Stranger...all the while was watching this interaction. He watched the mother smile to herself at the pleasant interaction. It was a simple moment that made her remember the goodness of humans. She smiled and looked down at her stomach with The Stranger's player inside, and she rubbed it.

The Stranger allowed a simple smirk to spread across His face.

"Hey!" Ranston urged. "So, what's your move?"

The Stranger still didn't answer as He began to piece together His plan, watching the two players walk in opposite directions.

"Do you even have one?" Ranston pried.

The Stranger smiled more. "Yah...you know me...Paul...I always have a plan!"

And He continued to watch the man and the baby go their separate ways...
...for now...

As she walked away, the young mother had to stop when she felt something. A strange twinge in her uterus. Soon her leg was soaked as the amniotic fluids all poured out of her. She gasped and snapped her head up with wide eyes!

Ranston though, still scheming, let his gaze drop back to the chess table. The awkward man's opponent was still trying to figure out his finishing move. After a few moments he finally figured out that he had in fact been beaten. He sighed and struck his king down with a wooden clank on the board.

Ranston stewed as he watched, thinking about his own game...

His was just beginning,

And now the board was set...

He looked down into his hand at what he had been playing with this whole time. He stared at the object intently, salivating now that his opponent had agreed to his plan.

With wide eyes he rolled it around with his fingers.

A shiny silver coin.

Then he flicked it into the air...

PART I
JUDGE'S GENESIS

CHAPTER ONE
Wooden Pieces

July 23. 2015.
It's funny that the first sounds we make are cries of anguish. I was brought into this world to the sounds of my mother's pain. Maybe it's engrained in us from our first breaths. The two toned nature of life, so perfectly reflected in hospital rooms every minute of the day. Pain, blood and horror, but glorious joy and marvel all at the same time.

My piercing cries followed my mother's and amidst all the chaos and tears, the muffled voices gave me my name...

"John...John...welcome to the world John..."

—"John..." The chaplain's voice said. "John? Are you with me?"
I snapped back into it. "Sorry?"
"Are you here?" The chaplain asked, chuckling. "I kinda lost ya there."
"Yah..." I said slowly. "I'm here, sorry...I—
—"*10-33 in progress, corner of Fayette and Eastern...*" The droning voice of the dispatcher was still echoing in my thoughts.
"John?" The chaplain pressed.
Though I was physically in his office, my brain was still out *there!*
The squelches of the police scanner flashed in my head as I stared blankly at the floor.

"*70 fox-hound, we have a domestic disturbance in progress. Male suspect is possibly armed.*"

I couldn't help it. It was like that feeling you get after playing a cell phone game all day or that job you had on an assembly line. Performing the same function over and over until that function just consumes your brain! I sat there in the chaplain's office, replaying the radio calls from my shift.

"*We need immediate assistance at Barnes and Long! Suspect is armed with a knife!*"

When it was silent, this was the only thing that I could ever hear.

"*Immediate medical assistance at location! Victim is a child! Repeat, the victim is a child!*"

Most nights, I would just sit there in the dark, in the police cruiser, allowing the calls to flood my ears.

I had to close my eyes in anguish. The horrible details of each call were overwhelming me.

"*Robbery in progress, all units in the area respond.*" The dispatcher went on.

"*Officer down! Send immediate medical, and we need back up out here!*"
All the calls were blending together in my mind. I sat there and recalled each one.

"Oh my god, he shot her! He did it, he shot her!"

I pressed my eyes tighter together.

"We have a jumper! Send in the negotiator to deal with this gu—no, don't!! Sir, no!! Dispatch he jumped! Oh, God, he jumped!"

—"John!!"

I blinked many times and looked around his office. He had yelled to get my attention.

"Are you alright John?" The chaplain pressed.

I cleared my throat. "Yah...I'm good. Good to go, sorry...just..."

"The feelings." He concluded.

I stopped fidgeting and peered up at him. He just stared back until I nodded in agreement.

"They're still there." I said. "The darkness is still there. I have to force myself to stop replaying the radio calls, but I feel like if I don't...if I don't give in to the darkness then I'll lose a piece of myself, you know?"

The chaplain just stared at me, waiting for me to go on.

"I've always been this way." I went on. "I've always felt like something is wrong with our world. Don't you ever get that nagging sense? You don't know what it is, but it's there...right?"

The chaplain nodded. "Yes, absolutely." He said. "And you think that if you don't adopt this darkness, then you'll...stop being a good cop?"

I sighed. "I dunno, I...I've been this way as long as I can remember..."

A memory flashed before my eyes. The same one that always did when I actually stopped to think about these things. My mother's crying face. Every boy remembers his mother.

"Is it bad if I like it?" I asked the chaplain in jest. "It's what makes me a good cop."

"But it's also the bane of your existence. You came to me remember?"

"I did."

"Look, John." He said. "You're not wrong for wanting to save the world. Trust me. But if you'll let me tell you a story—

—Suddenly there was a rap on his office door that broke our conversation.

"Come in!" He called.

The door opened and I turned to see another cop standing in the frame. I nodded to him, as I knew him.

"Oh." He said. "I'm sorry; I thought I had an appointment today."

The chaplain looked at his watch. "Um...I don't think so, excuse me a sec John." And he got up to attend to the other cop. "Let's go check the schedule." He said to him.

I watched them go and they left the door open so I could see into the busyness of my precinct at shift change. Then I sighed and faced the chaplain's desk where there hung a cross on the back wall. Staring at it now, had a new meaning to me at this point. I chuckled, under my breath, at the irony.

How did I get here? So much has happened. And now as I sat here at the end of my story, it's about to begin for you...This is all so magnificently insane! I'm still wrapping my own head around it to be honest.

I only had time now to wait for his return, so I began to look around the room. It was Christmas time and the chaplain had his office decorated for the season. I found myself always looking for a calendar lately. The one in the office read December 2041.

My eyes landed on the nativity scene he had set up. Again, these ancient symbols and stereotypes had new meaning to me after what I had just gone through. The scene made me think back and imagine what it would have been like that night...the night it all started and everything was changed.

My name is John Revele.

This is my story, but I am not the center of it.

Let me explain...

* * *

"*GASP!*"

His dream woke him with a startle and the old man shot up in his bed. He now sat, propped up on his hands, heaving in and out—it was a bad dream.

2015. Washington D.C.

He was disturbed by the vision he saw in his dream. *It can't be*, he thought, *I won't allow it!* All alone in his room; his luxurious suite, he sweat nervously in his king-sized bed. He sat there unbelieving and looked around through the gigantic bay window to his left at the heavy snowfall outside.

Leaning forward, he let out a long sigh. *No—it can't be—No—Never!* He flung off his silk duvet and sheets to swing his feet down to hit the floor. After he slipped his feet into a pair of suede slippers, he stood up to slip on his matching polyester house coat with a golden crest on the left-side; labelling and displaying his position of power over an entire nation. Not just a logo; the seal of the president of the United States. The head honcho, commander and chief, the big cheese—The King—warm in his palace tonight, polar opposite of the brutal weather on the other side of the walls,

Where tonight, the darkness waited,

crouching,

like a beast...

From his bay window he stared out of the White House and into the cold, brutal night, mulling over his premonition, re-assuring himself. *No—Never!*

Winter.

A deepening darkness where the only thing filling it is the harsh flakes of snow that are pushed around and tossed like nothing in the cold night. The kind you wouldn't ever want to go out in. Where the fierce, gusting wind is the only audible thing amidst the blowing snow.

You probably couldn't even imagine a warm feeling now.

So, imagine a coin...a cold metal coin, proverbial and hauntingly fighting over which side to land on.
Flipping through the air as it falls to the ground, turning side over side.
It fell to the ground amongst a whole handful of cold pocket change and a young girl made a desperate noise. A young man who was with her quickly bent over and scrambled over the mess of coins, barely able to salvage them all.
"Forget it!" The girl said hopelessly. "He said it's not enough anyways."
The young man stood up, with what he was able to pick up and looked kindly at her for a second before turning to the bus driver. The driver looked down at the pathetic pile of change in the young man's open palm.
"Please." He begged, as he advanced up the bus steps.
The bus driver sighed a long pitiful sigh. "I can take you to the edge of town." He said. "But I don't go any further than that." He warned. "Not into that infested part of town."
"That's fine." The young man answered. "Really! Thank you!"
He turned and helped the girl he travelled with up onto the bus. She grunted in discomfort, as she held her pregnant stomach.
From the increasing darkness, a shadowy figure now approached, watching the bus drive away carrying these two seemingly insignificant characters away from him. The faceless, nameless, darkness of a man, if you could even describe the 'it' like that, stood calmly in the snow, not at all bothered by the cold. Sent on a dark mission, by one darker than him. It crouched down in a morphing mass of black and scooped up a coin that the young man had missed. It rolled it around in its ghostly black extremities and smiled...if shadows could smile.

Like the weather, there was something else going on in that moment of history portrayed in that little wooden barn made of sticks and straw. Something else crouched outside that stable. Something that followed the woman there and waited to devour the package she was about to deliver to the world. The child...who this entire *epic* story is about...the centre.

The president, Harold Kingston, walked down the hallways of The White House, staring at the floor in a daze. With the dream so fresh in his memory he was thinking back to the beginning of his presidency...

...A mass of balloons all tumbled to the ground of the big banquet hall. Happy music played and the people were all laughing and cheering in celebration. The fancily clad guests were lifting champagne glasses off trays as the servers walked around offering it to everyone.
Through the thick of falling balloons Harold was walking through the crowd. They all smiled at him, shook his hand vigorously, embraced him and even kissed his cheek. So opposite to what was happening in his present.

It took him a while to get to his friend, our dark man; Paul Ranston, who just stood at the back of the room waiting patiently. Harold almost ran to him and they shared a big embrace. During this embrace, Ranston pulled his friend's ear close to his mouth and whispered;
"I've given them to you, Harold. This country is ready to believe in you." They released their embrace and turned for the photo-op but Ranston kept whispering. "Their weak. Ready to be molded into whatever we want them to be. Think of the possibilities. The country is ours!"...

...Paul Ranston. Harold's trusted friend now, and chief of staff—as he promised The Stranger. Harold was on his way to see him, after waking from his dream. Those happy days seemed so far away now. In his desperation he had called Ranston, who had defended Harold when voters called him a power-hungry dictator. In the end, it was Ranston who schemed up the marketing stunt that won Harold Kingston the presidency.

Ranston had received a frantic call that night and now he waited in the dark, like he preferred, on the edge of the desk in the famous Oval Office. He himself, thought back to election night as he waited...

..."Here's to fixing the world's problems!" Harold had said, and they clinked their glasses together. Harold drank quickly, where Paul slowly lifted the glass to his lips. He sipped, even though he couldn't taste anything and he stared at this idiot, Harold, with a grin behind the rim of his glass.
Paul Ranston had much *fixing* to do of his own. A lot of things had gone very badly for Paul and the 'circles' he and others like him travelled in. The stage was set now, for him. He was where he needed to be to begin trying to fix his problems.
A dark second chance,
 with a *dark* intent.
Paul sopped up the champagne left over in his black goatee with his bottom lip and swirled the glass around a bit, staring down into the funnel with those dark eyes. Then he met Harold's eyes.
"Congratulations...Mr. President." He said in a dark and sly voice.
"Well, my friend...I have many duties to attend too...but those can wait!" Harold laughed out loud. "Right now, I have to allow the server to fulfill his duty...my glass is empty! I need to fix that first!" He continued to laugh as he departed, giving Paul another few slaps on the back. Paul just smiled and then looked around at the big 'Kingston for president' campaign posters. He knew that he had orchestrated all of this and took a sense of pride in his work now that it was over.
"Yes...Fix." Paul said to himself, looking around still. "So many things to fix..." he went on. 'Kingston will deliver!' another poster displayed. Paul chuckled to himself when he remembered that slogan. He was trying to ap-

peal to people's need of being delivered from evil, in an evil time. The people needed someone raised up and Paul had given them Harold Kingston.

What the people didn't know was that Ranston was the ultimate man behind the curtain and by electing Kingston, they elected Ranston too.

"We'd better get started." Paul concluded to himself back then...

...and now, on this cold night...

It was 2:00 AM when Harold shoved the doors to the Oval Office open. He lifted his gaze to see Ranston sitting on the edge of the big oak desk, with his arms crossed, waiting for the president. Harold shut the doors behind him and turned to face his friend. The moonlight shone in through the big windows and in the soft glow Harold spoke out.

"We need to talk."

"So it seems" Ranston replied, with a certain sarcasm in his voice. "So talk." He continued.

"I can't shake the dreams." Harold began. "They're happening more and more now, every night. I'm haunted by the visions of it Paul, I—I can't—"

"Harold relax, let's just take this slow now...In the dreams...Is it like we thought?"

"Exactly how we thought Paul!"

"So take me through it." Ranston's voice stayed calm and methodical, unlike Harold's.

"They turn Paul, they turn against us!" Harold raved on. "I knew this would happen, I knew it, I knew it!"

Harold had had his doubts soon after the election. Ranston had assured him that everything would be fine. Harold was a proud man, arrogant, very self-involved which also made him very insecure. At the slightest hint of someone disagreeing with him he would get completely bent out of shape and lose sleep over it. He wouldn't be able to rest knowing that there was someone out there challenging his word. He would fester and stew every time he had a doubt. He was a power hungry man but with insecurities that caused him great paranoia. He was a conniving man who would confide in people like Paul Ranston to force people, or trick them, into going along with his ideas; like he had done so well during the campaign.

Right now he was crying and carrying on about a fear that he got into his mind the first week in office. *What if they find out? What if I'm exposed? What if people start to regret their decision to elect me? What if there is a revolt?*

Harold had not been hiding in a cave his whole life; He had seen how mostly every political figure had been treated before and after elections were won. Most of the time politicians were held in public contempt, and scrutinized on every decision they made. He was terrified of a bad image and couldn't stand the idea of the public not agreeing with him. Every time his name went in the paper, or Ranston told him about some press conference, Harold would get all paranoid and have delusions of the *hostile takeover* he was so sure was going to happen. More and more the paranoia grew until the dreams started happening.

"Harold, listen to me." Ranston began.

"But—"

"No, Harold, Stop!" Ranston became fiercer, showing his 'daddy-like' control over Harold; because he obediently stopped and lowered his head in frustration. "We can fix this" Ranston continued. "We can fix anything; remember what I told you in the beginning."

Harold sighed deeply as Ranston's words came to his mind again. *"Think of the possibilities. The country is ours!"*

"Together," Ranston started. "We've built an empire! Of gold..."

"And of blood!" Harold added. And he lowered his head in shame, anguish in his face. "They're going to find out, Paul!" He continued.

"Harold...Harold..." Ranston got up off the desk and walked over to him. "Sshhh..." He said, patting his back. "Blood is not a problem." He said. "This whole country is built with blood. You're no more guilty then the forefathers."

Harold sighed with deep grief.

"We can make this go away..." Ranston said. *"We can fix this."* His favorite line. "There is a way..."

Meanwhile, the 14 year old girl trudged along painfully through the snow, looking for shelter. She stopped to rest a minute against the wall of some back alley. They were in the slums of the city, where the bus had dropped them off as promised. It was a place no one in her condition would hope to end up. She rested a hand on her bloated stomach and winced in pain. Another hand came along side it for support and she looked back at the young man travelling with her. They shared a look of hopelessness before they heard something in the shadows behind them. It startled the man enough to press them forward. It wasn't only shelter they were seeking but a place to have this baby...

Harold raised his head methodically to meet Ranston's gaze. After much conversation and scheming, he had had enough of talk, enough of the dreams and was ready to put an end to whatever threat he felt was coming. If there was to be some sort of uprising, Ranston had him convinced that it needed to be 'fixed' immediately and drastically. In the dreams, Harold had seen a boy born. A boy who would grow up to—

—"Dad?"

A timid voice snuck in the question, too afraid to interrupt the conspiring pair of schemers. Harold turned around to see his 37 year old son who was visiting for the holidays. He was already in Washington, as the apple didn't fall far from the tree in politics. He was a young congressman, on business in D.C.

"Junior?" Harold greeted him. "What are you doing up son? Can't sleep?"

"I was already up, getting a snack from the kitchen. I bumped into Janice; she told me she saw you romping down the hallway in a hurry. She said you seemed worried."

"Oh." Harold laughed a little pathetic laugh. "I'm fine Junior, just had some urgent president business to attend to...the glory of it all!" Harold waved his hand around. Behind him, Ranston rolled his eyes and steamed with annoyance.

"I'm worried about you dad," Harold Junior went on. "You've been getting worse every time I see you. At Thanksgiving I noticed it."

"Son...son...I'm fine, really. Just the craziness of the holidays, a lot of concerned taxpayers out there this time of year." Harold lied. He knew his son was on to him, but couldn't admit his weakness to him. Not when his next stop, after D.C., was his mother's house. All the more reason to wrap up this little situation he and Ranston were trying to discuss. He couldn't fail. He wouldn't.

His son waited impatiently while Ranston brewed with his arms folded, waiting for the president to dismiss him. Harold on the other hand, walked over to his son and placed his hands on his shoulders.

"Junior. You don't need to worry about me. You don't need to worry about anything. If this is to all be yours one day, and you want to move in to my room, instead of staying in the guest room, then we can't afford this...weakness. You are going to be president just like me, if you want it. We are Kings, Junior. It's in your name...it's in your blood." Harold thought about what he had just told his son. Images of his dreams popped in and out of his thoughts. His resolve strengthened and he took a long look back at Ranston. Turning back to his son, he tightened his grip on his shoulders.

"So help me...no one is going to stand in your way once it's your turn. No one is going to take our kingdom from our family."

CLOMP!
Boots.
CLOMP!
Marching in unison through the cold streets. Hard, black boots. On a terrible mission this hallowed eve. As a rendition of the 'Carol of the Bells' played at some evening mass, these deadly agents made their way down the alleyways, sidewalks, and streets to deliver their blow on the city.

Ding...Dong. The bells carry out their haunting tune.
Orders. Just following orders.

Ding...Dong, ding...dong.
The young girl and man still travelled in secret, through the same alleys. Still on the run, still looking for a place to have the baby she carried. To deliver her package.

But that dark and ghostly shadow pursued them as well. A dark and terrible force that followed, waited, and crouched in anticipation of the package. It moved through the dark alleys and narrow back streets of the hidden places of the city. The perfect place to conceal itself in the shadows. It slithered around every corner after the pair as they desperately tried to find a place to stay.

They had had no luck so far and had been at it all night. The girl couldn't help but think that they had tried every place in town, but the man hadn't given up. Since they started, they moved progressively into murkier waters so to speak. From travel lodges, to hotels, to motels...but nothing came up.

Ding...Dong, ding...dong!

Now, they were in the slums of the slums; the wrong side of the tracks. They searched and they searched and found nothing! The man had given up on the inside, but for the sake of the girl and baby she carried, he forgot about himself and pressed on, more determined than ever.

Ding...Dong. The beast still following behind.

They reached their complete desperation and the girl had long since begun her labor when they came to the back door of some crummy-old-run-down apartment building, with what seemed like a thousand stories. The perfect place to cram all the low-lives, degenerates and misfits. The losers...

Ding...Dong.

Slam! The sound of doors to hundreds of homes being smashed in by the dark militia, hired to do Harold Kingston's dirty work. Peaceful, happy homes, where an innocent little girl heard her mother and father screaming in terror as they ripped her little brother away from them. The evil of this night strengthened and backed by some dark and terrible force too unimaginable. The militia continued all night, searching...

Ding...Dong.

The Carol of the Bells kept playing as they tore through house after house, brutally killing all of the cities little boys. Mothers wept and fathers raged in an attempt to fight off the militia from getting into the house, only to be dragged away, beaten, or killed. Babies...slammed on the ground, thrown out of second-story windows, suffocated...shot...killed...fixed.

Ding...Dong...

Slam! The door hit the wall with force, after the young, desperate man kicked it in to gain entry to this dilapidated building.

As the forces of evil made their way through the city, searching for babies to kill, these two misfits stumbled their way through floor after floor of apartments. The man was yelling the entire time; *Help! Somebody please help!* He banged on every door. No one opened up to for them. As little brothers, cousins, nephews, potential doctors, firemen, writers, musicians, friends, and fathers all over the city were being taken from the earth, the girl screamed in pain as she fell to the floor. She couldn't take it anymore. The contractions were too great now to ignore. The baby was coming...now!

Ding...Dong!

The man pleaded with everyone who poked their heads out to see what the commotion was, but nobody would help. Instead, at the sign of him paying attention to them they slammed their doors in fear, wanting no part of this mess. The girl had no choice but to lie there in the middle of the floor and groan in pain as the birthing process begun.

Ding...Dong.

The formless, shadowy beast had entered the building as well, following them up every floor until now. Now, when the girl was subdued by her pains, would be the perfect moment to strike. It approached her as she was helpless there, unseen to the man. Closer, closer...closer...

Ding...Dong.

Suddenly, as if opened by force, the fire exit door behind the man smashed open with such force it seemed that some great figure must have done it. In the last fleeting seconds, as the beast grew closer to them, the man spun around to look out of the fire exit and noticed something. A far better place to deliver the baby then here in some hallway. Not too far away, only a few floors down on the ground outside, behind the apartment building was a maintenance shed. Surely there, he could find some blankets maybe, towels, sheets, coverings, water!

Ding...Dong.

As the man asked the poor, tired young girl if she could make it, the beast was almost upon them. The man looked up when he thought he heard something, or saw something out of the corner of his eye. But he couldn't have seen what he thought he saw...that sort of thing doesn't exist...does it? He looked back and met the girl's gaze and he allowed himself a brief moment to consider what he saw.

What he thought he saw, was a dark figure approaching fast and another figure, dressed in white, moving in the way to block the dark one. That's it. Another contraction began to come on and as the girl groaned through clenched teeth, the thought of that supernatural event immediately left the man's mind.

Racing now, down the elevator and out the door, around the back to where he saw that shed, the couple was almost done their insane journey. This night was almost over. As he got the shed open and lay the girl down to rest on the floor the thoughts returned to him. He began to look over his shoulder in paranoia. What happened with those two figures he saw? Did they fight some glorious battle? Who won? Did the dark figure win, and is he now poised outside of this shed, waiting for us yet again? The idea was so absurd and the man was letting his imagination wander. Focus, he needed to focus.

The man became increasingly frustrated as he failed to find any of the things he had hoped for. No water, no sheets, barely anything useful. A broken apart tool shed mostly. He slammed a few things around until he leaned against the wall and gained a glance over a shelf where he didn't see before. Towels! A pile of towels. He rummaged them up and quickly made good use of them. He rolled one up for the girls head and laid her down on it, another one he placed rolled up under her back. The third he tossed aside for now.

    As she screamed and the mangy dogs and alley cats made their sounds, the militia carried out the rest of their orders. No more baby boys. No more little boys from this city who would grow up to play baseball with their dads or learn how to ride a bike or fall in love. But another little boy...one who would rip the kingdom away from the one who did this and change the face of our planet forever, made his first noise. On this cold, fateful night, in the place where you would never want to end up, among all of the rejected in society, including the animals, the man used the third towel to wrap the baby up and present him to his mother. She held him tight. The ordeal was over. The greatest story ever told was about to begin, but that didn't matter now. How could she have known? That this baby was the greatest gift the world would ever know. For now, she just held him and rocked him. As all of the rest of the noise in the city seemed to fade away for him, the baby made his first cry.

    Not such a silent night after all...

CHAPTER TWO
Time Frame

The great pendulum of time swings back and forth. Each sweep of it has kept track of time through the ages, telling stories...
In this case, two stories.
Two lives.
Two pieces.

It was a memory that always drifted past my mind's eye. Like a reoccurring dream that I couldn't forget. My mother. A vivid memory of her crying face when we were out driving one day. I was still a little boy and didn't understand the world yet. We came across a homeless man on the street corner and she began to urge my father to give him some money. I don't know if it was because she saw the same look of utter despair in his eyes that I saw, rocking me to my inner core, that she became so full of sorrow. I watched her begin to sob as we drove away, saying; *that poor man!* Over and over. *That poor, poor man!* I couldn't stop thinking about that for days and it still haunts me.

A seed was planted that day.

A dark and terrible seed that would only grow the more it was watered by the world we live in.

When it first happened, I didn't want to believe it.

The big 'time shift', that only a select handful of people would come to understand. The shift that brought about the new First Noel.

How could anyone believe it?

But before it did happen, a whole lot of other things needed to happen first...

* * *

The pendulum moves back.
To 1977.
The *real* 1977.
Day 1...
A Star Wars poster hung on the wall of little Jason Richter's room. Comic books about space and books on the paranormal were strewn about as well. Among other literature, there were books on Tesla and Einstein's theories. A chess game, in progress, was set up on his desk, while the boy himself sat staring out his bedroom window. This was the life of Ranston's chosen chess piece, long before that day in the park.

His mother crept in, past the gaudy picture of Christ hanging in their hallway. She prayed for her son daily. "Are you going to go and play today, Jason?" She asked.

Jason turned and saw her clutching her rosary beads again and looking worried.

Jason just shrugged. "I dunno, mom."

His mother smiled sweetly at him and then began to cough. She walked off and Jason heard the sounds of her violent coughing echo down the hall as he turned back to the window.

I'm sure you can imagine a story of a kid who wasn't into sports and didn't excel in the area of *recess*. Why would he? He never saw the point, knowing he was no good...even though people always say *it's about having fun,* we all know it's not. It can be fun; when you're winning!

On this particular day, Jason watched a group of kids on their way back from a baseball game at the park. All of them giving each other high fives and compliments; good *hit!* Or *nice catch out there! Did you see that dive that Bobby took?* Jason didn't see anyone get credit for simply trying, and he would see the disappointed looks on the faces of the kids who did lose. Bottom line was that he knew the truth about humans, about boys—about men...men as creatures, who's only goal it's ever been to *win*. Even though he wasn't caught up in sports, Jason understood the fundamental issue that sports teaches; competition, goals...victory. Just think about how disappointed you are when the high school team loses at the end of the movie...and the movie is trying to teach some fluffy message about winning and losing, *there are no losers, everyone is special,* but really—the viewers are upset.

He was sitting at his window staring, but he didn't care that he wasn't involved; he just sometimes did this to pass the time.

"He just doesn't seem to care at all about other kids!" His teacher's words echoed in his thoughts. He was remembering a time when he was sitting in on a parent/teacher interview.

"Is that true?" His mother had asked him that day.

"I...just...don't like other people." Little Jason answered.

After spouting out numerous teaching degrees and diplomas, certificates and other pieces of paper that somehow qualified her, Jason's teacher informed his parents that "In all her years" she had never seen a kid like him. More comments like this were said after the parents had inquired what she meant, and after somewhat of a runaround, she finally made a point stating that "something was different" about their son. The teacher's words rung out in his head and he watched his mother grip her rosary beads that she always clutched when she was stressed. He was surprised that she never cut her palms open, how tightly she gripped those things.

As time went on from there; what the teacher was trying to deem as "something different" in a negative way, developed into more of a gift in Jason. Although the teacher wasn't able to explain it properly, it was clear that he was just keen and extremely bright all throughout his school days. Jason proved over and over again that he had a great intelligence and could always figure problems out. He remained the top mind in his class through every grade. But something like this doesn't happen without consequences.

In these days autism, or the milder forms of it; what they call Asperger's, was not as easily diagnosed as it is in modern day medicine. That, or ADD, ADHD, ABCDEFG, whatever...back then you were just a weirdo...and poor Jason Richter's social awkwardness didn't help him much.

Jason turned from his window and went back to his other desk which was littered with parts of the old television set. He loved to take things apart and see how they worked. He knew the television had something to do with the glass tube he found inside, but as he examined it in his hands through his thick glasses he was still wondering. He put it aside for a second just to his left, and tinkered away at some other sections of it, using his screwdriver and his magnet...

It was a long rod style magnet that was designed to get down into places where little fingers couldn't reach and get loosened screws out of the way.

He carefully,

meticulously,

worked away...removing the casing surrounding the power unit attached to the cord, which wasn't plugged in.

On the radio, the singer sang;

"Time has come today,
Young hearts can go their way.
Can't put it off another day."

Jason worked away, in the same calm fashion that he always did, breathing slowly through his nose and moving very carefully. He put the magnet and the handful of screws he had removed down then took a sip of his juice box. Jason liked to peel the corners of the tin foil boxes up like wings, and then actually rip the top open to make accessing the juice easier—so he wouldn't have to squeeze the box for those last satisfying drops.

He lifted the lose power unit out to inspect it but the large TV shell was right in the middle of the desk and in the way. His dad had lifted the TV up into his room in the first place, but Jason was figuring that since it was all in pieces, maybe it wouldn't be as heavy as before. He stood up and wrapped his arms around the set like a hug, and his face scrunched up as he began to lift...

It was one of those moments,

He knew he shouldn't be trying this, but once he started, that sense of pride came flooding in; he wasn't going to *lose* this battle.

Time has come today...

The radio played on.

Time has come today...

With his glasses all pushed up to his forehead, crooked and not helping him see, Jason struggled with the TV and began to stumble backward. In a desperate attempt to save it, he lunged forward and forcefully shifted his body weight so that his chest launched it back onto the desk with a crash!
Time has come today...
—ZZZZZAAPP!!
Jason didn't really have time to see what exactly happened because he had immediately closed his eyes and curled into a ball. But he heard the calamity. After some crashing noises, there was a buzz, a zap, and some scraping metal sounds. He opened his eyes just in time to see a bright light flash and some kind of electric arc. He had left his screwdriver and a ruler sitting together on the desk so that the ruler was lying horizontally across it. The screwdriver was resting at the far left end of the ruler near the zero inches mark. Jason watched in amazement as the screwdriver was whipped thirty inches across to the other end of it!

"Oh, the rules have changed today..."

As the flash this whole incident had created faded away, Jason was left standing there in shock. He was still thinking about how lucky he was that the TV hadn't broken, or he hadn't tripped and made this whole mess worse! But as he stood there thinking about that, and his heart rate decreased, he couldn't help but be a little perplexed.
After he snapped out of it he began to look around the table and piece together what had just happened.
How did that screwdriver move by itself?
That's what he was going to find out.

* * *

The pendulum moves forward.
2022.
My eyes, stared into Big Gary's, who stood about five feet tall. This goliath of a boy was huge for his age!
A gladiator's arena of the other kids had formed around the two of us--all chanting;
"Fight! Fight! Fight!"
I can tell you, I still remember those chants. But because I'm so dramatic, I remember them as the sounds of a thousand blood thirsty Romans!
Big Gary stood across from me, angry as all hell for what I did to him.
Most other kids in our school feared Big Gary and avoided eye contact with him. He loved to lord his size and so called power over everyone smaller than him.
One really small kid in particular was just running to class from recess with his oversized backpack bouncing up and down and every which way, adjusting

his glasses. He didn't see Big Gary standing there and slammed into him. Gary spilled his drink all over himself and the floor.

"Watch where you're going you little geek!"

He grabbed the little guy by the straps of his backpack and lifted him up to slam him on the wall at eye level.

"Put him down Gary!" a voice called from behind him. He glanced over his left shoulder, without lowering the kid. Then he turned and gave me a long menacing stare while trying to screw his face all up in an attempt to be scary. But I wasn't scared of him.

When recess hit, Big Gary shoved me from behind. I tumbled a bit and then spun to face my assailant. My eyes burned into Big Gary's, who I could tell was on fire with rage and fury. The look on his face was screaming: *Why aren't you afraid of me!? You're ruining me!*

Finally, Big Gary charged at me in a frenzy. I moved out of the way, dodging his attack and was able to shove him into the chain-link fence. When he tried to lash at me again—

POW!

I socked him right in the face. It was beautiful. All the other kids cheered my name.

"John-ny, John-ny, John-ny..."

I had never felt so alive!

Stopping this bully and helping the kids he preyed on felt amazing!

Even as I sat in the principal's office waiting, I thought about how Big Gary wouldn't be bothering anyone again. He was so embarrassed. The look on his punk face was priceless.

My school had one of those resource police officers and he usually made stops by the office. Good ol' Officer Mac. McNeil actually. He had obviously been called for this little dust up and he sat in between me and Big Gary with his arms crossed. Mac seemed massive when I looked up at him. Big Gary was called in first and that left me and Mac alone.

After a few awkward moments of silence he peered down at me and I froze.

"So what did he do?" Mac asked in a deep intimidating voice.

"He...um...he was bugging another kid." I stammered in my little voice.

"Just the one?" He asked.

I furrowed my brow. "No...He bugs all of us."

Silence from Mac. He just grunted and looked ahead again.

I felt compelled to say more all of a sudden. "He's a bully. He thinks because he's big he can push us around. He's always pushing little kids and yelling, taking kids' stuff, staring at everyone..."

I looked up at Mac again but he wasn't responding. I sighed and looked at my hands.

"Well..." His deep voice finally said.

I looked up at him sheepishly and he looked down at me smiling.

"I guess it's a good thing you stopped him then." He said.

I chuckled. "Uh...yah!"
Mac reached into his pocket. "Here," he said. "I have something for you..."
I waited anxiously to see what it would be. Mac produced a small little piece of silver colored plastic and placed it in my hand.
"You can be my deputy here at the school." He said.
I looked down at the fake sheriff's badge he gave me in awe.
"What's your name kid?"
"Uh...John. John Revele."
"Well, John Revele...You let me know if you see anything else, okay?"
"Okay! Sure!"
The door to the principal's office opened, breaking our conversation.
"You got what it takes kid." Mac whispered to me, while getting up.
"To what?" I whispered innocently back.
Big Gary was being ushered out while the officer got in between us. He turned to me again and answered.
"To be a cop." He whispered.
My eyes lit up and then I glanced at Big Gary. He was trying to glare at me but I stared back menacingly. He couldn't hold the gaze and he looked away. The principal came up behind him in the door frame and then Gary stormed off.
"John?" The principal called me. "Come in please."
It was my turn. I walked past Mac towards the office. It didn't matter what the principal said in there. Nothing he could say could tear down what Mac just did to me. I looked back at him before I stepped in the office and he winked at me.
From that day on, I knew what I wanted to do for the rest of my life.

* * *

The pendulum moves back.
Swoosh.
1977.
Day 15.
In church, one fine Sunday morning. Little Jason Richter sat, in between his parents, listening to the preachers words. He could hear him speaking but only caught that Charlie Brown adult noise. It had been two weeks since his little electromagnetic accident in his room.
He sat here, doodling these thoughts on a ripped open offertory envelope from the back of the pew. He drew a child's sketch of what happened on his desk that day, with a magnet on the right and the screwdriver clinging to it. There were little lightning bolts around the whole picture, and he scribbled the words electro-magnetism beside his sketch. He had also drawn a spilled juice box to the left and labeled it: 'conductor', and the glass tube out of the TV labelled: 'vacuum effect'.

His mother coughed beside him, breaking Jason's concentration. He looked up and saw his father reaching over to make sure she was alright. He could read the concern on his face.

To distract himself, he doodled on the back of the offertory envelope.
He drew circles.
Never ending lines.
Loops.
Over and over, until one word the preacher said, resonated.
"Time!" His voice echoed down. Jason lifted his head up at the mention of time.

"There is a time for everything, and a season for everything under the sun..." The preacher went on. "A time to be born and a time to die, a time to plant and a time to uproot, a time to kill and a time to heal...a time to love and time to hate, a time for war and a time for peace..."

Ain't that the truth...?

Little Jason looked down to his doodles again and it was his lightbulb moment. He looked back up excitedly.

Days 21 through 42 were very busy times for young Jason.

A dog eared copy of *A Wrinkle in Time* lay split open on his desk, almost near the end. After trying to generate the shock again and again with numerous experiments, the most he could do was cause the screwdriver to slightly rumble from the current running through it, and on one occasion jump up off the table...but he couldn't get it to propel across the line again.

On day 63, his experiment expanded down to his parent's basement and here he was now, with a copy of Tesla's book: *Wonders of the Future* open beside him, as he tried feverishly to recreate what had happened with that screwdriver. Armed with the knowledge that electro-magnetism plus a third unknown component, possibly chemical, had been the cause of this particular 'moving screwdriver' effect; he set out on what would become his life's work. After every moment of his spare time, in between science fairs and actual school homework, family stuff, eating, sleeping (which he did little of now), he was always rushing to his desk to do calculations, notes, and studies to figure this out. His mom would chuckle warmly as he scurried from the dinner table with a mouth full of food still. Dad would call after him to wait but his Mom would just laugh and tell him to let it be. When she started to cough, Dad would get up to help her. Jason was missing all of this unfold as he obsessed in the basement. Seeing as how he was a busy young boy, more than a year had passed by.

By day 437 of this journey, the basement lab was filled up with tables, lamps, science tools; microscopes, and chemistry sets. Mom and Dad would watch this from a distance and watch his obsession grow.

* * *

Swoosh.
2032...I was 17 years old and doing my own form of research.
For my world history class I needed to write a paper on the world wars. As I researched the topic I stumbled across numerous video clips and articles explaining the horrors of what people had done. I read about the Germans; Nazis...The holocaust. I saw pictures of people's flesh burnt away from Hiroshima, images of nuclear bombs detonating. I listened to Hitler's speeches, Stalin. Going back further; I read about slavery, and the civil wars. Vietnam, Afghanistan...Saddam, Osama—I watched the plane crash into the tower over and over, I just couldn't believe it. Genocide, torture and murder. Stemmed from greed and corruption—

What is this?
I kept a journal of my thoughts;
This feeling I have?...

Those were the first words I wrote down and it was a long time before I put pen to paper again.
I started to live my life in a different way. I was sad most of the time and just kind of walked around watching everybody. I would watch television and get even more depressed when I saw all the terrible things happening in the world. I would watch movies about war and cry during the death scenes. I can't explain it...it just started happening more and more and I was depressed—I thought the world 'sucked'. I went back to my journal:

Even though I'm privileged, I still feel this way. I've hit a wall. I've stopped to smell the roses—only I don't like the smell! It's a foul stench of hatred, bitterness, and decay...death. I know I'm not exposed directly to the horrors of the world, but I am starting to see them for the first time. I can't whine about neglecting parents. They've done the best they can raising me. My only problems have been stupid girl problems, which...aren't really problems at all? Are they? My childhood was average at best. I crawled, then walked, played with toys, went to school, then I grew up. My story doesn't involve tragic events and let downs. I'm not going to pretend like these things haven't happened to everyone else. In the long run...who really cares? These are trivial things that make no difference at all. No one should feel sorry for me...

That dark seed that was panted inside of me as a boy had begun to sprout.

* * *

Swoosh.
Day 1,472.

Jason's Mom gripped her rosary tightly as always. Her optimism, regarding her son, had faded and Dad just let it be, like she asked him to. She turned from the TV where they were watching Ronald Reagan being inaugurated as the president. She heard the front door. Little Jason tromped in, pulling a wagon full of various things right through the main hallway; scrap metal and old junk he had found. He didn't even say hi and he just rushed past the living room as his mother just watched. She tapped her husband on the arm and he looked to see the tail end of Jason run past. They looked at each other with an odd look.

Day 1,503...
A haunting day finally came. Jason had been so busy that he wasn't expecting it. His father walked up behind him and waited for Jason to turn around. When he finally did, he saw the grief on his dad's face...

...The funeral for his mother was long and confusing. He just wanted to go home and cry.
When his dad tried to comfort him he brushed his hand off and ran for it! He ran out of the cemetery and collapsed behind a mausoleum. He cried, clutching his mother's rosary beads in his hand. Trying to find comfort.
"Why did you take her from me?" He asked God, in a little pathetic voice that was cracking from the onset of puberty.
"Because He's cruel!" A harsh voice said.
Jason startled up with a gasp and saw a shadowy man standing before him. He was afraid.
"Who are you?" He asked the man.
The sinister man grinned. "I'm the caretaker." He said darkly. He looked around to seem like he worked here. "Being surrounded by death makes you kinda cynical." He went on. "The only thing that's certain in this world is what we can make for ourselves." The man said, gesturing at Jason's hands. Jason looked down at the beads and then back up at the man.
The 'caretaker' as he called himself this time, shook his head. "Tisk, Tisk, Tisk..." He clicked his tongue. "If only we could turn back time eh boy?"
Richter stopped and stared at the ground. He slowly lifted his gaze to the caretaker's and his face was full of wonder. "That's it..." His little voice whispered.
Then he got up and ran off, leaving the rosary beads on the ground.
The sinister caretaker, who hadn't named himself Paul Ranston yet, smiled to himself.
The seed had been planted...

If he wasn't obsessed already, Jason worked feverishly now, down in that basement. Upstairs, his dad moped on the couch and drank.

At night time, Jason lay in bed, with his mind racing and he stared out the window and up to the stars. He got an old feeling that he always got. That feeling that something just isn't right with the world.
"If you won't help us..." Jason spoke to the stars. "...then I'll have to do it."

* * *

Swoosh!
2034.
The acceptance letter welcomed me into police foundations. I was packing up for college, leaving behind my childhood bedroom of superhero paraphernalia. Still infused with these dark feelings; I began throwing out the knickknacks and the junk I had collected over the years. I tossed a snow globe, a bunch of old toys, and my old cell phones, but I kept my favorite stuff--A Captain America figure that I smirked at nostalgically, a miniature Thor hammer, things like that. While I was rummaging around and tossing things out, a glimmer on my desk caught my eye. A silver point poked from underneath some pages. I chortled because I knew exactly what it was. I dusted off the plastic sheriff's badge Mac gave me and spent a while staring at it. The picture that it was hiding behind was significant actually. I took the time now to reminisce. It was a picture taken for the high school year book. My best friend Ridley was beside me and our older buddy Dave who had a kid. She was in the picture as well. The little blonde haired sweetie, Maggie, was leaning off of Ridley's shoulders trying to get to her favorite uncle John. I chuckled warmly at the memory. So much life had happened in between to cause me to forget my passion. I set packing aside and lay in my bed still clutching the little badge. Then I remembered my passion and suddenly it became so clear...
I could change the world!

* * *

Swoosh!
Months went by, and Jason's father listened to the banging and crashing his son's experiments created down there.
Eventually, by day 1,604, Dad started to feel well enough to get off the couch and try moving on.
He tried reaching out to his son, but most often the awkwardness of silence screamed louder than ever at the dinner table where just the two of them sat.

Because his room was so often empty, Dad would creep in periodically, if only to see the mess and tidy it up for him. He picked up the books Jason was reading and sighed. Encyclopedias, text books, science fiction books by all the greats. He shook his head wondering how his brain was comprehending these things at such a young age. He picked up one in particular; another Tesla. *A Machine to End War* it was called. He stacked these carefully on the shelves in his room and went about cleaning. He found comic books about space monsters and pseudo reality, paranormal activity and space time continuum, and he tried to understand the things his son was into. He stumbled across his scribblings and his notes. On one sheet of paper he found a note written in big bold letters: *I WILL INVENT TIME TRAVEL!!!*

His father crept to the basement to speak with his son. When he reached the bottom he saw his son's laboratory and couldn't help but be impressed. His main desk lay across the far wall and it was the cleanest section of his workspace. Everywhere else there were papers and notes, as well as dirty dishes, pop cans and other tools and gadgets. Jason had long since neglected keeping anything neat or tidy and was focusing all his efforts on this new big machine he was making.
Dad approached to speak with his son, but was drawn in by his work. I guess they had just assumed this was a child being a child and that it would pass...but this...
This was different!
Now his dad knew what that teacher meant!
He realized the potential in Jason and he suddenly felt a great swell of pride within himself.
Jay turned to see his dad and was almost embarrassed until Dad smiled at him. He crouched down to his level and placed his hands on his shoulders. He just looked at him with awe and in that moment they shared an emotional connection deeper than words would ever say. They had the conversation they needed to have about their grief, with just their eyes! Dad fully understood what Jason was trying to do and he decided to encourage it, even if he thought it was preposterous.

Soon, Dad was going with him to the junk yard, in the rain no less; eager and full of childlike excitement as they loaded his pickup truck with whatever Jay said he needed. Dad would even stop by on the side of the road on his way home from work to pick up an old car battery he saw, or other pieces of junk he saw.
More months passed as he worked away until he finally had put something together he was certain would work.
"Day seventeen, twenty." He spoke into a video camera.
It was a very, sort of haphazardly put together, jumbled up piece of equipment built with all spare parts and recycled items. It started on the right with a rather large magnet; one of those big horseshoe industrial ones. He fastened it down with his Dad's clamps. He had a car battery as a power source with jumper cables. Instead of grape juice as a conductor; he had found a whole lot of copper wire which he twisted into long cables and connected

them to some aluminum pop cans that were fastened together with duct tape. A long copper pipe was laid out horizontally across the bottom of the table that stretched 12 feet across with a 15lb weight at the other end of it. When he finally figured out that the television tube created a vacuum effect of electrons, he soon figured out that when the glass was broken this vacuum had obviously reversed, propelling these chemically charged electrons forward.

This was the key...

His mom's old vacuum cleaner was on the left and he was boiling a liquid compound of the same compound within the color tube in order to change its properties into gas form. The gas was sucked into the basin of the vacuum cleaner as Jason scurried over to check the connection on the car battery.

It was good to go.

He and his dad looked at each other excitedly.

His mind was spinning! His brain was going a mile a minute now.

He motioned for his dad to back up which he did, and strapped on his ridiculously large safety glasses.

Jason had Mcgiuvered a little rig, sort of like a hammer that would drop and land on the button to reverse the vacuum and propel the particles.

He took a deep breath...

He closed his eyes...

He took one last look around at all the components of his machine,

And...

*"One point twenty one
Jig-o-watts!"*

He hit the device to drop the hammer, and it fell; barreling towards its destiny. It crashed into the button and released the contents out through the same hose.

Jason connected the end of the jumper cables to the iron weight and the electric current ran directly through the cables. Dad cringed.

The charge ran down into the pop cans and then—

POP!

There was a bright flash and a louder crackling noise to go with it...Jason and his dad both had to cover their faces and close their eyes tight as they turned their backs to the table and crouched down for cover.

They heard the sound of scraping metal and a growing hum or buzz; then a loud

CLANG!

Jason stood slowly, afraid to turn around. But he had to know...When he turned he stared in disbelief. He saw the 15lb-er attached to the magnet!

He did it!

Dad stood slowly behind him as he lifted his safety glasses up.

The thoughts started flooding in. Jason didn't expect it would actually work, but now that it had...his ideas were becoming a reality. The note he had written himself could possibly come true. The opportunities this would open up in science were unimaginable in other groups. Depending on what circles you travel in, the kind of thing Jason Richter had in mind were deemed as *impossible*.

If Jason could figure out how to change the molecular make up of an object, making it able to move across the other side of a *physical* line...than he wanted to speed up this process so that the object moved even faster...

And faster,

And faster,

And faster...

Jason was as smart as they come. If he could somehow generate speeds of this magnitude, than he thought, or rather—he dreamed...that he could move them across more than a physical line...

He could move things across *time*...

Outside of the small basement window, a dark man stood on the curb and he had watched the blue electric zaps emanate from the basement.

He was dressed in an all-black suit and had a black goatee. Much more than just a caretaker.

Ranston, the old schemer, had had his eye on little Jason Richter for a while now.

He reached into his pocket and walked to the end of the street where he disappeared out of sight.

"So?" Someone to the side of Ranston asked him.

Ranston met with a friend who stayed in the shadows. He spoke towards the dark shaded area in the bushes where the voice was coming from.

"So what?" He asked.

"Is he ready?" The voice hissed.

"He's well on his way." Ranston said, removing his silver coin from his pocket. "He's still a boy W..."

The voice groaned. "When will you make your proposition to...to...?" 'W' asked, struggling to say the name.

"Don't say His name!" Ranston hissed. "I despise the name!"

"When will you take your plan to Him?" W asked.

"In time, my dear W...in time. You'll have your chance to wreak havoc..." Ranston rolled the coin around in his fingers and stared at it.

"And you'll have your revenge...master!"

Ranston let a slow grin appear on his lips. "In time..."

CHAPTER THREE
Living the Dream

A simple man, that you've already met, stood at an urban corner, leaning on the light post. He wore His usual white t-shirt and His hands were stuck in the pockets of His simple faded blue jeans. He chewed on a tooth pick and watched the people in the streets. Apparently this was His favorite pastime.

The other side of Ranston's coin—The Stranger, a long time after their meeting in the park, stood here now looking out into the street.

His face was a simple looking face, hair was simple hair, stubble; five-o-clock shadow, all dark in color. I wish I could describe Him to you better, but there really wasn't much to distinguish. No big nose or uni-brow or anything. But He looked like any other unassuming guy you might pass on the street. He was handsome, I guess. A very average man.

As He watched everyone go about their days, one guy in particular passed His field of vision right in front of Him. The motion blur caused Him to now follow this guy along his path. He watched the guy walk a little ways and then quickly slip a black ski mask over his head. The Stranger raised an inquisitive eyebrow. The guy then rushed into the convenience store he was standing in front of.

The Stranger then turned His gaze and began to scan the crowd. Across the street, past the rush of cars, He saw who He was looking for and grinned.

A peppy young guy trotted along the sidewalk and entered the diner there. I was out of the academy now and all grown up...

"This coffee has sugar in it." I said to the girl inside.
I have this weird thing, about my coffee. I can't have sugar.
It needs to be *honey*.
"I'm sorry sir?" The cashier was confused.
"Sugar, you guys put sugar in my coffee. I asked for honey."
I stopped into this coffee shop on my way to work. I was running late and since I had just started this job I didn't quite know all the routes yet. I walked to work most days and this morning there was a sidewalk closure on my usual route; *which*...had a coffee shop. *My* coffee shop, where they knew me and knew that I liked honey. It was a rare place that fortunately accommodated my needs. But this place was the only place on my detour that served coffee.
"Sir, we don't normally have honey back here."
"You don't have honey in the back? This is a diner."
An awkward silence, and then she retreated to the back room, rolling her eyes.
"Thank you." I said.

2037.

The cashier came back out with my coffee, now properly flavoured with honey, and I stepped out into the streets. I was hit with the refreshing 'aroma' if you will, of the city; people chattering, the dull roar of car's engines, horns honking, sirens blaring, down to the jackhammers bouncing. I loved this 'scent' the city gave off. I came to a stop on the sidewalk to take a sip of my honey coffee, and I had to let out an *'Ah'* of satisfaction. That was the stuff. Now my morning could start.

As I smacked my lips and surveyed the area, my eyes took notice to something. Across the street, at the little convenience store, a guy ran out. I just happened to catch him as he was peeling a ski mask off his face. I noticed he had a hand stuffed in the inside of his jacket and he was looking all around. Well my eyes locked onto this guy now and I tracked him as he travelled down the sidewalk. I pulled my phone out to make the call.

I tracked this guy all the way to a cross walk and there was a number of people waiting there. I stood behind the crowd, sipping my coffee. The little walking guy hadn't appeared on the sign yet but this guy went anyways. He was all thugged out, the whole nine (which I couldn't believe was *still* a style). I watched him go, with his stupid over exaggerated swagger and how he kept touching the brim of his hat and constantly looking from side to side. He was making a stupid screw face as well.

Our light changed, a few moments later and this dude wasn't even half way through the intersection. I was able to catch up to him and as I passed him, I don't know what came over me. I improvised. "Think you're cool, eh buddy?" I blurted out.

"Say what?" The thug replied.

"You couldn't wait about seven seconds like the rest of us?" I said.

"Boy, you best watch yourself! Who you think you talkin' to?" He was flashing his attitude card now, thinking I would back down like everyone else he victimized on a day to day basis.

"You think you're *hard* man?" I continued as we all reached the other side of the street. "I bet you don't know the first thing there is to know about the hard side of life."

"Fool, whatchyou know about life, punk!? Man, get outta my face!"

"Yaah, you think you're hard. I know you do. You think you're baaaaad." I scoffed. "You think because you don't care about traffic lights, that makes you a bad-ass?"

"Hey, yo...step off man!" He was getting angry now and he started to walk away. But I wasn't done yet so I followed him.

"Here, can you hold that for a second?" I asked a lady as I passed her my coffee. She was too flustered to refuse and she just took it as I turned my focus to my perpetrator.

"If you were a bad-ass," I said. "You'd knock me out right here and now. What else do you know about being hard man? Just because you dress like a thug and listen to their music doesn't mean you are one." I was trying to push his buttons. My hope was to get him to stop which he did. He was trying to walk away but I wouldn't let him. I needed him to come close to me. I needed it to be his choice to come close to me, or I would miss my chance.

"Alright 'G', you go get em'" I said.

He turned. I pissed him off. He started towards me and I smiled. He got right in my face. Perfect.

"What's yo problem 'cuz? You better get steppin before I box yo ass all over the—."

CLICK.

The ratcheting sound made his eyes bug out and the sounds of sirens were approaching louder. He glared at me and I smirked back at him. I didn't feel like chasing anyone today which is why I flushed him out and made him come in such close proximity to me.

"You're under arrest." I stated as the sirens blared from just around the corner. I stood there with this thug holding one cuff on his left hand and he wasn't struggling at all. I guess I was right in what I said about him. "I saw you about two blocks back." I said. "Turn around, man."

The thug made a horrible sucking noise with his lips against his teeth and stomped his foot. Like a baby. He complied and turned around and I applied the other cuff. "Don't move." I told him, and I patted him down right there in the street. The uniform officers approached the scene just as I was taking out the gun from in front of his pants. I knew the key words to say next. "Gun." And the cops ripped this guy to the ground to secure him. He was barely struggling, but now he was all charged up.

"I should have shot you fool! I shoulda' killed yo ass!"

"If you had a *real gun* in the first place and not an air-soft, you would have shot me in the street when I first approached you. Like I said kid...you ain't hard. You robbed a convenience store with a toy gun." I bent down on one knee beside the thug and put my hand in his jacket pocket. "If you're not prepared to take a life...then don't be a coward and intimidate people with this crap." I said holding up the pellet gun. "Do you know what you put that poor old man and his wife through now?" I pulled a big stack of bills out of the pocket and handed it and the toy pistol over to one of the uniforms and stood up. The thug made that awful noise again, louder this time, and as I retrieved my coffee from the nice lady the other officer assisted my new friend to his feet and started walking him over to the cruiser. I took a sip of my drink as they marched him past me. He tried to stare me down but he couldn't maintain eye contact. He was pushed into the back seat and the other officer approached me.

"Nice work." He said.

"Thanks. I was just on my way to the precinct. Do you think Sarge will be mad?"

"Well, you know how he feels about rookies Revele..."

"Hot-heads!" Sarge screamed. "All you damn rookies are a bunch of hot-heads!" He paced back and forth in his office with me standing there, now in my uniform. "How am I gonna' explain this to the Captain?" I couldn't help but smile, because I felt like a movie star. He continued to berate me about civilian complaints and the 'mayors' office, and how there's a proper police procedure for arrests. I just stood there taking it. I felt like Bruce Willis in Die Hard. I loved this job.

"You're lucky there's good news Revele!" Sarge continued. "This punk you arrested was heavily involved in gang activity. He has no priors, no record, but only because he's never been picked up on anything yet. He was very fortunate until today...until he met you."

"Thank you sir." I said and my sergeant stopped to shoot me the evil eye.

"You're still on probation rookie. Now, you came highly recommended by good friends of mine at the academy. All you're training officers gave you excellent reviews. You're lucky Mac is at this division, pulling strings for you."

I smiled.

"I myself can see your potential." Sarge said. "But don't get cocky on me Revele!"

We stood there with me looking straight ahead and him right up beside my face.

"You're dismissed officer." He said.

I was 22 years old at this point. A naive and fresh-faced young pup out of the academy. I had been a police officer for about nine months now.

As I stepped out into the hallway from my sergeant's office and removed my forage cap from my head, many other officers were passing me. Some of them just smirked, others gave me a pat on the shoulder and some actually shook my hand with an encouraging comment. There were some that were shooting me dirty looks and grumpy comments.

I looked across the floor to the other side of the precinct and saw him. He was already grinning at me in approval. Officer Mac. The grey had crept into the roots of his hair now but he was still a big brute. A tough old bastard who had mentored me through the whole process. He flicked two fingers off the top of his head at me and winked. I chuckled to myself.

"Hey buddy." A pat on the shoulder came from the side with a greeting from my friend and partner, Ridley.

"Hey Rid'." We slapped hands and locked them together in our usual way.

"How's your ass feeling?" Ridley said, motioning his head towards the sergeant's office.

"Haw...Haw..." I mocked. "It wasn't too bad."

We began to walk down the hallway.

"Is buddy gonna' complain about you?"

"Who knows man? Let him...what's he gonna' say Rid?"

"You're a crazy son-of-a-bitch John. You know that?"

"Ah...He wouldn't have shot me, even if it was a real gun. I know his type man. Trust me."

"John Revele 'the invincible'." Ridley mocked me. I just rolled my eyes and we kept walking. Ridley and I were at the academy together. In fact, we were boys together. We met in high school and remained friends ever since. We both shared a passion for being police officers and we knew everything there was to know about each other. He was just as *zealous* as I was for doing police work.

"You're one to talk man." I said to him. "What about that crazy guy wielding the knife in the bus station?"

"Hey, that woman was pregnant...and there were kids around! I wasn't about to take the chance."

"I'm just saying." I laughed. "Where do you think I get it from?" I winked at Ridley as we came out of the hallway into the main lobby area of our station.

I took a second to look around. I still couldn't believe I was here. I was like a goofy kid taking in all this police culture. The epicentre of crime fighting. The superhero headquarters.

"Hey." Ridley said, trying to get my attention.

I was standing beside a police slogan poster, letting the words written on it sink in. An American flag was draped on a pole beside it. I came out of my daydream and looked at Ridley. "Huh?"

"You with me partner?" He asked.

"Yah man." I replied.

"Good." He said. "Look at this." He lifted up a newspaper.

I sighed at the sight of the headline. "Kovacs." I said. "Again?"

"This asshole's gotta go down man."

"What did they attack this time?"

"The Golden Gate Bridge."

"Geez!" I said, snatching the paper out of his hands. I lifted the paper up to see the front page photo. A shot down the famous red landmark with hundreds of cars in a horrific pile up. Burnt metal frames, only skeletons of the cars they used to be. The headline read: *THE BEARS STRIKE AGAIN.*

"Man," I said. "Not even the transportation is safe. What is this? Like the fifteenth major attack?"

Ridley snatched the paper back from me. "This guy is changing the world man." He said. "They're saying he—The Bears—is the most successful terrorist organization the world has ever known."

I shot him a look. "How's that?"

Ridley just returned the look. "Are you scared, John?" He asked. "Have you taken a look at the streets we police? C'mon Captain America, come down to earth." He slapped the paper with the back of his other hand. "It ain't safe out here anymore. People are scared. Kovacs has done that."

I took a long look at the carnage in San Francisco. Then I let out a regretful sigh. I looked back up to my partner and smirked.

"Well, we better go make a difference then." I stated, motioning back towards the slogan on the police poster behind us.

Ridley began to chuckle and he shook his head.

"It's your turn to buy coffees, asshole." He joked.

I laughed and we moved on from where we were standing.

I swung around the corner and my eyes were taken hostage.

"Hey." Ridley slapped my arm with the back of his hand. "There she is man."

"Ssshh. Shut up Rid!" I whispered.

Officer C. Mash.

C. for Clare.

I pretended to act cool as we headed towards the briefing room.

I had noticed this girl right away when Ridley and I were transferred to this station after our training was over.

"You know her dad is the mayor right?" Ridley said to me.

I didn't care. She caught me looking at her all the time. But I loved it when she smiled back at me every time.

After our morning huddle, we were headed out to the garage to get in our squad cars. We weren't out of the doors yet and I noticed 'Mash' as I called her back then, was carrying a bunch of files and a few boxed up long guns on her way to court. She had been on for some time before my class got on. She was a more senior officer than I was. She was struggling with the door so I rushed in to 'save the day'.

"Here let me get that for you." I said in the sexiest voice I could pull off.

"No, it's alright I got it." Clare said.

"No really, please...allow me." I was trying to get around her to the door handle but she wouldn't accept the help.

"I'm fine man, it's ok." She said. Now I was a little annoyed, offended even.

"No please. I'll get it...what are you? One of these independent woman; I can do this on my own; I don't need a man's help kind of thing, or what? C'mon...Please...let me get the door for you."

Clare shot me a funny look. I didn't know how to take it...it was hard to tell if she was pissed off or intrigued. She would later tell me, it was a bit of both. I had never really talked to her before, but she knew me. We had worked out of the same station for months now and there was always a little spark when we passed each other in the hallways. I guess she was just surprised that a rookie officer would talk to her like that. She had been used to people tiptoeing around her because she was the mayor's daughter.

I sneaked around her and pulled the door open for her with a goofy grin on my face. She stared at me for a while but then her hard exterior turned to a grin and she shook her head, chuckling to herself as she walked out the door.

"You're welcome." I said.

CHAPTER FOUR
The Human Condition

4 years later. 2041. Present day.

Her alarm went off at 5:00am, and she searched around aimlessly, smacking everything but the snooze button. Her fingers eventually found the alarm clock and she slapped the top of it, hoping she would hit the button. Once the noise had gone away, she lay there with her head facing the opposite side of the bedroom, but all she could see was her husband's back, dressed in a white sleeveless undershirt. Clare was half awake and the fog of sleep still clouded her thoughts. It was like this every morning as she felt a sense of happiness when she saw her husband beside her in the bed.

But it only lasted a few brief seconds each time, because she was only feeling the remnants of happier memories, from a long time before this. Every morning she almost reached out to him, to rub his back or run her fingers through his hair—but, she couldn't...even though she knew he would like it, and even though she wanted to...she couldn't—doesn't make sense does it? But who said relationships did?

Once she had remembered how things really were, she sighed, with her arm still stretched out onto the alarm clock and she rolled onto her back to stare at the ceiling for a while. She looked over to spy the time written on the face of the clock but her eyes flicked to a picture on the night stand.

Her and I.

I was secretly awake beside her but didn't turn around either. I just lay in bed with my eyes open, staring at a picture that I had on my own night stand of the two of us. During much happier times.

Clare peeled her gaze away from the picture to look at the clock: 5:04am. Her office was about a half hour from home; which was a loft apartment on the fourth floor of their building. She rolled out of bed and stepped out of the bedroom out into the large open space of the loft, leaving me in the bed. I waited to see if she would say good morning or give my head a rub or a kiss. I was delusional.

It was pretty much all one big room, the loft; with really high ceilings. It was all concrete and metal, very industrial looking, but we had spruced it up and gave it more style. Clare and I were pretty well off, so we had trendy leather furniture and glass coffee tables, with trees in planters and other plants in the corners. Our colour scheme was a dark chocolate brown contrasted with beige and a deep crimson red thrown in the mix. There was a big set of metal winding steps that ran up the centre to another level, which was more of a big platform suspended above the rest of the loft. This second floor was open and balconied so you could see the whole loft standing on it.

Our bedroom was on this platform and right next to it was a small personal gym we had set up. Clare began her morning routine by lifting some weights and doing some chin-ups, for about an hour.

Clare had always wanted a big kitchen and she had one in this loft, which was right at the bottom of the stair case; you pretty much walked right into the kitchen from the last step. It was her dream kitchen; lots of cupboard space and dark tiles on the floor, stainless steel appliances and a big island in the middle of the kitchen; her favourite part.

She enjoyed her kitchen so much that she liked to give herself time in the morning, after her work out, to just sit there and enjoy a cup of coffee—

Or she used to, back before the stress of her job had got to her. Back in those *happier times* mentioned earlier...

Now—things were different and what originally started as some quiet time for Clare, had become more time to review her case files. She put the coffee on and then pulled over the open files which were left there from last night. A box labelled 'KOVACS' in black marker, lay open and files were spread across the table; photos of the many attacks carried out by the terrorist gang The Bears:

Bombings on Russian parliament; Moscow city hall, St. Petersburg, even an anthrax attack on the Kremlin. Hostage situations in Poland, chemical attacks in the U.K., attacks in some of the Asian countries on their borders. France. Germany. Rio De Janeiro, where they had brought down the big statue of Jesus Christ, sending it barreling down the mountain into the buildings below it. Hollywood. Wall St. Ottawa and Toronto, Canada. Worst of all, or at least what was the most memorable for the citizens of North America, was when; on the twentieth anniversary of 9-11, Kovacs sent a missile screaming into the statue of liberty, obliterating it; and this, in Kovacs words, was to let the people of the new world know that their very *freedom* should feel threatened.

She studied a series of photographs and then placed them down on the table to rub her temple. Sighing, she looked over at a second cardboard box on the table. This one was labelled 'THE BAPTIST' and the lid was still on it.

Clare tried to return to her work but soon flopped the pictures down again. She couldn't focus. She flipped her long brown hair out of her face and tucked it behind her ear with her fingers. With a sigh, she looked over to the Baptist box again. Then she gave in and reached over to grab it. She dragged it over and flipped the lid off. She pulled out a case file and began going through it.

Pulling one out one photo in particular, she lifted it up to give it a good long stare.

"Who are you?"

She asked the ghost in the picture, out loud.

"Whatever it takes, no matter what...I'm going to find you."

Clare glanced up at the time displayed on the microwave: 6:35am...she better get moving.

While she showered, I got up and sat on the edge of the bed for a while. As I stared at the steam pouring out of the open bathroom door I thought about how things were between her and I. Then I looked back down to the picture that stood beside my wallet, cigarettes and badge. The squeak of the taps signaled it was my turn to use the bathroom. I took a smoke from the pack and lit it. After my first drag I exhaled the smoke as Clare came out of the bathroom in a towel. I hated how good she looked. I ran my fingers through my hair as she rounded the bed behind me to her side and I finished another drag. While looking at the picture again I placed the cigarette in my lips and got up to go the bathroom. Behind me, Clare looked down to my night stand where she saw me looking and sighed, realizing it was the picture that I was looking at. She watched me go into the bathroom and shut the door. Then the sound of my piss splashing into the bowl echoed from behind the door. She didn't realize it but she had been holding her hand against her belly and when she looked down and noticed she felt a pang of pain begin to build. Then she sat on the edge of the bed and looked at her picture of us.

Suddenly the door was opened and she walked in on me as I was putting my cigarette out in an ashtray on the bathroom counter. I accidentally caught her glare when I didn't mean to and I couldn't look away. Those big green eyes always got me, even now.

We looked at each other for a while until she spoke.

"Please talk to me." She pleaded sadly and almost inaudible.

I sighed and broke her gaze to look down at the counter.

"I can't..."

"Why not?"

"Because, Clare, there's...there's too much to say."

I sighed. There was a long silence that seemed would never end.

Then Clare left the room and she went about getting dressed, leaving me in the bathroom to stare at the fizzling cigarette butt. I raised my eyes up to look at myself in the mirror. It was a harder face then I remembered from even a few years ago. My usually clean shaven face was now thicker with scruff and even my eyes looked different.

Then I sighed and tapped the mirror lightly. Television channels appeared on the surface of the glass and I began to distract myself with the daily news.

"C'mon, John." I told myself. "Get it together man! Get it together."

The catchy little news tune came on as I turned and peeled my tank top off. I threw it aside and Clare heard the shower turn on from the room.

She had been staring at the picture of us again but now she sighed. She grabbed the top of the frame and flipped the picture down on its face.

In the bathroom I let the hot water cascade down my face and chest. I placed my hands on the tiles and hung my head down so the water poured over my neck. Somehow this relieved the stress I had been feeling...if only for a short while.

Soon Clare was dressed and she was in the kitchen pouring her coffee into her trendy star bucks travel mug. She was staring up at a big painting on the wall. The living room space was to the left of the stair case, right across from the bar counter Clare was standing at and on the far wall there hung a big painting. When she looked at this painting, a longing always started to grow in her. Old emotions sparked and it made her feel nostalgic for days gone by.

The classic and familiar words of the news anchor filled my ears.
"*In other news...*" They started, as I rubbed the suds into my face.
"*...renowned physicist, Dr. Jason Richter has announced there has been a major breakthrough in his controversial time project.*"
I stopped scrubbing and bent an ear. I let the water run down my face and clean the soap off.
"*Richter has not yet said what the breakthrough has been, but Globe-X has announced they will hold a press conference later this morning to inform the public.*"
I wiped the excess water and soap off my face as I moved my head out of the water and I shut the water off as the news anchor continued.
I quickly pushed my head out of the shower to see the screen.
The TV showed footage of a now older Richter as news crews followed him around.
I grabbed a towel and dried off as the news continued the coverage.
"*We don't know for sure, but some followers are speculating that an imminent test at one of the sites is a given, while others say he's cancelling the whole project that Globe-X has pulled funding...pardon my pun, but only time will tell! Stay with us for continued coverage this morning. Rick Brennan, WPN news.*"
I finished wiping my face and stared at the screen as the story ended.

Downstairs, Clare heard the sound of clanging metal as my feet rushed down the staircase...
Here he comes, she thought.
I was frantically grabbing my stuff and looking for my keys.
I was *late* again...
He didn't even say *good morning*...Clare's thoughts continued.
I put my shoes on, threw on my reddish-brown leather jacket and headed towards the door; which was a good twenty to thirty feet away from the kitchen in this giant *empty space*...which was feeling emptier every day.
Clare stood there, with her back to the door, pretending to be pouring her coffee still.
Maybe he'll stop,
Maybe this time he'll do it.
But she heard the noise of the big metal door—CLUNK!—and the soft squeal of the hinges opening and her eyes shut...

It was a couple of minutes before she shook it off and tightened the lid onto her mug. As she packed away her papers into the boxes, she thought back to how things used to be. As much as Clare pretended to be a tough girl, this bothered her. Even though her job demanded a certain level of confidence and assertion...she was still a woman...

He didn't even say good morning...he didn't even say *goodbye*...

But most of the time, Clare was able to brush it off. She buried it inside—again—because now, it was 7:07am, and if she didn't get going she'd be late.

She padded her pockets, double checking to see if she had everything, but something was missing. She looked all around until she remember she had put what she was looking for down beside her coffee mug. She walked back over to the counter and picked up a simple, black leather wallet, with a long metal bathtub chain attached to it. Across the top of the golden shield was written; 'federal bureau of investigation.' FBI.

She slung the chain over her neck so that her badge hung down her torso and then she pulled her glock out of its shoulder holster to inspect it. She slipped the magazine out to check the rounds and then pushed it back in to the handle of her service pistol. She racked the slide and clicked the safety on before slipping the gun back into its holster under her blazer.

There was no time to think about her problems now...

No place for them in her line of work.

Now, it was time for *action!*

She packed up the files she was looking at; those pictures of the man she vowed to catch, into the box, she stacked it on top of the 'KOVACS' box and marched forward, carrying both, to start her day.

On my way out of the front door of our building I stepped into our little bohemian section of the city. Graffitied walls and faded brick. The aura of the city hit me and I somehow felt more at home out here than in there. I adjusted my jacket and the way it fell on my shoulders and then I pulled out my bad habit again. I lit up a smoke and snapped the zippo shut. I took one last look around before stepping off and my eyes stopped when I saw Him across the street.

The most unordinary ordinary man.

"You again..." I whispered under my breath.

He was wearing the same outfit that I usually saw Him in. He was standing there with His hands in His pockets as if He was waiting for the bus, but those eyes. Those eyes locked onto mine once more and burned into my soul. Especially now, after what I done...

What I had done...I was trying not to think about that.

He was still smiling though. A quaint little smirk on His lips to suggest that He was on my side. I stared back wanting to berate Him, but I was frozen. I was usually not scared of any man, but I was very apprehensive with this guy.

I blew out my drag and then finally walked off.

The Stranger just watched me as I went.

* * *

The music blared in our police cruiser.

The sun had risen over the horizon and was still a visible round orange shape.

It was at perfect eye level through the cracks in the concrete jungle we drove through. I watched it as my partner drove and we played hide and seek. It ducked behind buildings and then popped back out as the buildings zipped by.

Baltimore. I loved this city.

I softly nodded my head to the beat of the music as we drove around looking for trouble. A new unlit cigarette dangled from the corner of my mouth and I kept my eye on the streets, window down.

Ridley drove.

I read the graffiti sprayed on the walls. Urban art. I watched the people of my city. There was always just something about the city that I loved. Even though it was grungy and rough, there was something *beautiful* about that *grit.*

"Are you gonna light that thing or what man?" Ridley asked.

I smirked and removed it from my mouth. I closed my eyes and took a big breath in through my nose. Then I exhaled with satisfaction.

"Just gotta get that last aroma of the city in Rid." I said.

Ridley chuckled and shook his head.

"C'mon Rid, you gotta try it sometime!" I said, looking at him. "You gotta *feel* the city man! Don't ya' feel it?" I looked back out the window. "That rushing sound that cars make..." I went on. "...live a river. The sound of distant horns honking, sirens wailing, jackhammers. Low bass beats from cars as they pass by. There's a..." I sniffed in dramatically. "...ahh, there's an aroma that seeps out of the ground, out of the sewers." I was getting carried away. I placed the smoke back in my mouth and dug into my pocket to look for a lighter.

"Yah, man that's the subway system." Ridley laughed.

"There's another good smell!" I exclaimed, taking the smoke out of my mouth to speak. "That and the smell of a hot summer day man! That scent that the heat gives off somehow" I put my smoke back in and kept talking. "I love that shit!" I muttered out of the corner of my mouth, bouncing the cigarette around. I clinked open the top of the zippo and flicked on the flame. "That's the grittiness of these streets my man!" I went on, staring into the flame. "Where real life happens..."

"You're crazy, John..." Ridley said as I raised the flame to touch the cigarette. "I do hope you realize that. Please tell me you at least know how crazy you are." And he laughed.

I snapped the lighter shut as I took my first drag and looked into the glorious sun as it travelled beside us. I took the smoke out and exhaled the drag dramatically.

"Yah..." Is all I said. He didn't know it, but Ridley's words struck a chord there and made me think about recent events.

"How's Holly man?" I asked to quickly change the subject, before Ridley noticed.

"Uh...She's good buddy." Ridley said, shortly, with a hint of guilt in his voice. He didn't look at me.

I blew another drag out. "And the kids?" I pressed.

Ridley nodded awkwardly. "They're good too."

I stared at my partner. I could tell I was making him feel uncomfortable.

"Rid..." I said. "I've known you and Holly since high school! What are you hiding? Just because your marriage is perfect, doesn't mean I don't like hearing about it man, c'mon."

He sighed. "I know dude...it's just...I feel for ya!"

I scoffed. "Hell, Rid, I feel for me too but I ain't cryin'"

There was a bit of a silence and then Ridley replied. "Maybe you should, John." He said.

I was taking a drag from my smoke and I stopped suddenly. "What?" I muttered with smoke pouring out my mouth. "Cry?" I asked. Then I blew the rest out the window and coughed a little.

"I dunno what I'm saying man." Ridley went on. "You've just been this friggen' robot the last little while. You haven't been yourself. I want you to feel something!"

"Trust me, Rid." I said, looking out the window. "I feel plenty." And I took another drag.

"How's things with Clare anyways?" He asked. "When's the funeral?"

I didn't answer. Something crept in but not guilt. Fear maybe...

"Saturday." I said gruffly, still staring out the window. And I fidgeted in my seat. I could feel Ridley's eyes on the back of my head but I didn't want to look at him as these certain thoughts were in my head.

"And how are you man?" He asked.

"I'm fine."

Another long pause. "C'mon, John..." He broke. "This'll be the second funeral in the month for you guys. And it can't be easy losing a—"

"—I don't wanna talk about it, Rid!" I snapped, looking at him now.

Ridley sighed and stared straight ahead. I glared at him from the side, feeling guilty that I snapped on him, hovering my cigarette in one hand, propped up on my elbow out the window. I sighed and shook my head, looking ahead now too and I took another drag.

"I'm sorry, Rid." I said, not looking at him. "I got a lot on my mind man..."

After a while Ridley sighed and gave in too. "I know buddy." He said nodding. He reached over and hit me with the outside of his fist, pumping me in the chest a couple of times. "I know..." He repeated.

I stared out the window for a few moments, feeling comforted by my friend. I felt a surge suddenly to confess to him what I had recently done.

"Rid, I..." I trailed off as soon as the words left my mouth. I looked up into his eyes and he was waiting for the rest of the sentence.

"What?" He asked.

I couldn't. Not yet.

I exhaled through my nose and dropped his gaze. "Nothing..." I said. "Never mind."

I looked back out the window for a while, as Ridley drove silently. He turned the music back up and I rested the back of my head on the seat. I took the last long drag from my cigarette and flicked it out the window.

We drove around our assigned blocks for most of the morning. We stopped in for a coffee at my favourite little diner. Stepping out of the cruiser, I slipped my aviators on. As we walked towards the shop, people recognized us.

"Oh, here comes trouble." One of the regulars said. He was just stepping out of diner with his breakfast in a to-go bag.

"What's goin' on Frank?" I said, lifting my hand up.

We completed a slapping handshake.

"Stayin' out of trouble?" I went on with him.

"Of course man!"

"Good, good." I said. "I'll catch you later."

Frank went about his business and Ridley went in first, dinging the little bell on the door.

Every face in the shop turned to us and the place stirred with welcomes.

"They love us, Rid." I whispered to him, peeling off my shades.

Ridley rolled his eyes. "What do you want?" He asked in annoyance, half laughing.

"What I always get."

"K, cool."

"Hey don't forget the honey!"

"Yah, yah, whatever."

I smiled and turned to the people.

"Ken!" I said to the first guy I saw. Ken was a big tall guy. Strong and silent type though. He never said much, but he was a nice guy.

"Hey John." He said grumbly. He sat there sipping his coffee black and mowing down his big breakfast western sandwich, wearing worn out construction clothes.

He was sitting next to a little wiry guy and a few others. All the regular guys were here. Including this weird quiet guy who always sat in the shadows. I never quite saw his face, the amount of times we came in here. Longer, shaggy hair and a scruffy beard. He came in with the wiry guy all the time but always sat in the back unseen. I never spoke to him.

"Finding any work big guy?" I asked Ken, leaning on the high table he was sitting at.

"Nah, man..." Ken said. "Odd jobs here and there...nothing steady."

"Yah," said the little wiry guy next him. "That tends to happen when you punch people in the face!" He jabbed.

"You wanna be next little man?" Ken threatened.

The little guy laughed.

"I think you'd better be careful there Bart!" I said to the guy. "Ken could kick your ass seven times before you even knew it...I wouldn't want to piss him off." I laughed along with them. Even Ken was smiling.

Maybe skittish is a better word for Bart. Not much to the guy really...the clothes he wore were always way too big for him and hung off his skinny frame. He was always very talkative and excitable.

"What's the word on the street boys?" I asked them.

"Nothing much man." Bart said. "Sexrex is up to his old tricks. He's hosting a string of parties coming up."

I looked over to see if Ridley was listening or watching. "When?" I asked quietly. "And where?"

"Tonight there's one". Bart said. "At his club."

I nodded along. "Cool, cool." I kept looking at Ridley to see if he was coming back.

"What are people saying about the Mayor?" I asked even quieter.

"Same...nothing." Bart said. "No one knows who this Baptist guy is."

I remained staring and nodded along.

"You hear about this time travel stuff?" Bart asked me.

"Yah actually, I did. Something's up...they haven't announced it yet."

"Friggen time travel man!" Bart exclaimed. "Think of the possibilities. I mean Ken here—"

He said slapping his back. "—he could go back and fix his drinking problem."

"You'll have to go back and fix your face!" Ken warned.

Bart laughed. "Pretty wild though isn't it?"

"Yah totally." I said. "I've been watching this Richter guy since I was a kid! It'll be exciting to see what he says." The conversation stopped and my eyes found the weird guy at the back again. He was staring at me. I stared back for a bit until Ridley came up with the coffee.

"Here you go, man."

"There he is!" Bart said.

"How you doin' Bart?" Ridley asked.

"Good, man!" He replied, looking goofily back and forth at both of us. "The damn Goon Squad, watching over our district!" He said grinning like an idiot.

"Please..." Ridley said.

"Ah c'mon Rid." I said. "I like the name. We've earned it."

"Damn right!" Bart said. "You guys are good cops man. Honestly. It's hard to find."

"Hey listen man," I started. "The age of YouTube made this world a different place. Even we wear these." I said, pointing at my shirt camera.

"How does that work?" Ken asked.

"Yah, now you can't even talk smack about your bosses." Bart said, laughing.

"Ah, we log them in at the end of the day." Ridley said, still holding both coffees. "The cool techs will edit it out for you." And he winked at them.

We all shared a laugh and I turned to get my coffee from Ridley.

"But listen boys..." I said, cracking open the plastic lid. "I didn't sign up for just a paycheck like some other cops. This is gonna sound cheesy as hell, but I wanted to help those who couldn't help themselves. Be a protector of those who don't have the means you know? I love this city! That's why we signed up. We've seen a lot of stuff. Gang busts and robbery calls. I can't stand the whole gang scene. Most of the time when we roll up on a call, say; a domestic or a dispute, I can be fairly reasonable. The laws, obviously, only allow me to do a certain amount, and the law actually stipulates a minimum of what I must do in order to keep the peace. A lot of arrests we make have been of people in the wrong place at the wrong time; in bad places of their life...which I came to understand is most of the people we deal with. The public on their worst days, right? I understand that for the most part the people are just reacting to bad things happening in their life and we have a job to do to protect people. But these assholes who purposely victimize everyone they encounter; walking around with a scowl and an attitude...trying to intimidate others on purpose. Carrying guns, because they don't know how to deal with their conflicts like men. They usually end up killing people who had nothing to do with their rival beef. Innocent kids and women. They wouldn't give a second thought to sticking a loaded gun in someone's face, forever ruining their lives, making victims of everyone around them to hide their own insecurities. I can't stand that! The kind of people who think they are invincible and talk to everyone who disagrees with them with vicious anger. The kind of guys who beat the snot out of people for saying 'no', shoot people who piss them off, kill other men for something as stupid as embarrassing them in front of their friends. *Do these types of people deserve a chance?"*

I was holding the room. Even the weird guy at the back was hanging on my words as I monologued. I took a second to blow my coffee and take a tiny sip.

"Basically, you hate bullies." Ken said.

"Exactly right, big guy." I said, tipping my coffee towards him. "Listen, I don't think I'm above the law by any means. Rid and I make decisions the best we can." I motioned to my partner and he nodded along. "But we're not above human emotion. I too feel things; anger...hate...vengeance. There's guys that we work with who are the exact same description I made of gang members, just on the other side of things. We go in and out of the courthouse and experience stuff that makes you get more and more lost in the grey cloud of the law. Some lawyers are honestly defending innocent clients and doing amazing work absolving people who don't deserve to be victimized, where other lawyers just do it because they wanted to win; and whether the guy was red with guilt didn't matter. Even prosecutors flop back and forth and either vigorously pursue a criminal who needs to be convicted, or I've also seen ones who just had a previous beef with the defense lawyer and do things just to piss them off. Judges who accept bribes or make deals with guys who don't deserve the deals, or just lazy ones who are too scared to handle the power given to them to make these kinds of decisions. *Who are the bad-guys and who are the good guys?*" I looked over to Ridley again who was in a somber mood listening to my rant. "We're faced with this question everyday guys." I went on. "And I can only hope...that I won't become one of the bad-guys myself."

As I finished those words I felt a conviction because of recent events. I kind of glazed over and stared out the window for a few moments.

"That's deep man..." Bart joked. Then he laughed.

Everyone started chuckling.

"Hey you asked, man." I said, laughing at myself. In between chuckles I took another sip of coffee.

"We gotta go partner." Ridley said, already heading towards the door.

"Alright guys." I said turning to leave myself. "Take care of yourselves." I snuck another glance at the weirdo in the back then looked back to the boys. "Thanks for the Intel boys." I said under my breath. "Stay safe!"

As we drove around again, I felt a new zeal for my love of the city streets, stemmed from my speech I just gave and fresh on my soul. I let the city air hit my face and enjoyed it.

"I love you, John." Ridley said out of nowhere.

I furrowed my brow and looked at him, wondering where that came from. Then he broke out smiling and I realized he was making fun of me. I sighed and rolled my eyes, laughing at myself now too. "Shut up, man!" I said and I shook my head. Ridley laughed out loud and kept driving. I took a sip from my coffee and licked my lips. And our morning carried on.

My friend the sun had risen higher to the peaks of the skyscrapers now and turned from orange to yellow. It was a radiant splotch on the surface of my sunglasses as I stared up at the concrete monuments. My city reflected in the lenses. An image of man's achievements and the greatness of the city.

"What's with this?" Ridley asked, rubbing a hand on his own face.

"What? This?" I asked back running a hand over my jawline.

"You growing a beard buddy?"

"Just trying something new."

"I think I like you more clean shaven dude." Ridley answered. "You're letting yourself go man, what gives?"

I didn't say anything. I just laughed and looked out the window.

"You go to the club last night buddy?" He asked abruptly.

"Hhmm?" is all I could come up with.

"Either that, or you and Clare were having a bangin' party last night in the loft?" He joked. "It sounded like you were at the club when I called you."

I didn't say anything and just looked out the window. I could feel his expecting glare burning me.

"What were the guys at the diner saying about Sexrex?" He asked me.
He took me off guard and I froze. I didn't realize he had heard that. "
"Sexrex?" I asked stupidly.
"Yah, I thought I heard Bart say something about him." Ridley said.
"Oh...Well you know Bart." I began. "He wants to help us out all the time...I think he was just saying something about a big party he's hosting tonight at his club...giving us the heads up to be on the lookout." I lied.
"But we're on the day shift, man."
I laughed nervously. "Well, Bart doesn't know that."
Ridley was giving me a suspicious look. He had been on to me lately. He wasn't an idiot.
"You planning on going or something?" He asked me.
I gave him an 'as if' look. "Are you kidding?" I started. "Me...partying with Sexrex. The seedy underboss of all the sex trafficking and sex trade industry in town, and I'm gonna go hang out at his club?"
Ridley sighed while he stared ahead to drive.
"What are you doing going to clubs John?" He asked. "That's completely not your scene."
I figured I should give him something. He was my best friend that I trusted completely. I mean, I knew he wasn't an idiot and he would figure it out eventually. I didn't want to put our friendship in jeopardy.
"I saw Maggie, man." I answered.
"What?"
"She's selling herself on the street Rid!"
"John..."
"That little punk, Megga is pimping her out...he must have been recruited by Sexrex."
"Megga? That two timing piece-a-garbage? John, what are you up to man?"
I bit my lip and stared out the window, not wanting to say anything else, but Ridley knew me well enough to know what was going on.
"John. Sexrex...you can't just go up against a guy like that single handedly. We're cops man, you understand? There's a whole task force trying to bring him down—legally."
"They're moving too slow." I finally said. "I can't wait around...how'd you like to be the one pulling Maggie's body out of the bay?"
"I wouldn't man, but think about what you're doing...whatever it is you have planned..."
"How'd you like to face Dave when you die...if you see him again...and tell him you just stood by and let his little girl be killed by some drug addict or pimp? Or some old business man who snapped and strangled her for not performing properly?" I was getting angry now.
"John...Mags' has to make her own choices man. No one can force her."
I screamed and punched the roof of our cruiser. Ridley stopped talking and we both just stared out the windows for a good long while.

"Look man." He started up again. "I'm your friend. I meant what I said and I love you. I know you better than you think and I have a good idea what it is you're thinking about. We've had each other's back and you've saved my ass a lot of times, and vica-verca. We don't owe each other a damn thing. Now...I won't patronize you and I won't stop you...but I'll ask you...brother...please..."

I was waiting for him to tell me to give it up again and stop, but I guess he saw in my eyes how serious I was about it. He breathed out slowly. "...just be careful man." He simply said. I didn't look at him, but out of the corner of my eye I could see him shaking his head.

"*I'm here with Dr. Jason Richter,*" a voice out of the radio said. "*A man who's success in time experimentation has driven him to be one of the most interesting and controversial men in history, how are you Doctor?*"

"What is this?" I asked. "Is this it?"

"No, not yet." Ridley replied. "This is an old broadcast. Haven't you been paying attention to the radio? The media has been recapping all his interviews and stuff all morning."

I listened to the interview proceed.

"*Why time travel?*" The TV talk show host asked.

"*Why not time travel?*" Richter asked back. "*I mean, think about it Bill. The state the world is in now. America is not the greatest country in the world anymore! The world is on the brink of a Third World War! Joseph Kovacs? The Bears? Pah! They're just the start. And, not to mention, Bill...You've got to have things in your own life you're not proud of am I right? All of the mistakes we've made as a species. The wars, the violence, the injustice. The crime we see unfold in front of our eyes every day.*"

Richter's words hit home for me then. I just sat and stared out to the people I kept safe and let the words sink in. I especially related to what he was saying about the state we were in and the crime I was getting used to as a cop. The way I had been feeling my entire young life was coming out through Richter's mouth. Ridley looked at me funny when I reached over and turned up the volume.

"*Humanity would benefit from this discovery.*" Richter went on in the interview. "*We could go back and stop Hitler before he went nuts, or go even further back and change his influence that made him like that in the first place! Fix the weaknesses in the Titanic and save all those lives. Save Kennedy. Stop nine-eleven...every single mistake, Bill. All of it...*"

My heart almost start to hurt from the truth of his words. I pulled out my cigarette pack as he went on. "I need to meet this guy!" I said rhetorically, shaking my head.

"*Every single bad decision!*"

I lifted the pack up and pulled one out with my mouth.

"*Every bad thing ever in human history could be corrected.*"

I clinked the zippo open and scratched the wheel to light it.

"*And the struggle's on a personal level too! How many of us, would love the chance to go back and change things.*"

I leaned my head back and let out my first drag.
"*Some aspect of our lives.*" Richter went on. "*Make a different decision, fix our mistakes. We could live in a world with no regrets. Essentially...we could finally live in a perfect world...*"

CHAPTER FIVE
There's Always a Girl

He didn't even kiss me...he used to kiss me.
Clare thought as she drove down the highway towards work, on that same day. The country and the world awaited Richter's big announcement. As the radio broadcast Ridley and I were hearing ended, she pulled up to the security gate and smiled at the guard on duty.
"Hi Mike"
"Good morning special agent Mash, how was the drive in?"
"It was alright." She shrugged. "Traffic wasn't bad."
They usually had this type of chit-chat while Mike checked her I.D.
"Thank you special agent Mash." Mike said, as he handed it back to her.
The gate buzzed and Clare drove through to go past the sign labeled 'Federal Bureau of Investigation; Baltimore Field Office'.

Clare thudded the two file boxes down on her desk. A small desk among other ones, grouped together in a large room. Most of the room was the giant screen on the far wall that they used for monitoring, tracking, accessing data bases, satellite imaging...etc. She took a sip of her coffee as the projection system powered on and the logo for her unit faded into view; 'F.B.I. Anti-Terrorism Unit, Baltimore Division.' Behind her was a glass wall that looked out into the rest of the building and the entrance into their office.
Clare was the first one there this morning, as usual. She took another sip of coffee before making a twirling motion with her finger signaling the program to begin accessing files. The technology in *2041* had gotten pretty neat. A digital sensor; like an infra-red, scanned her body and was reading her every movement which controlled the program. A roster of photos were projected in 3D; as if they were hovering in the air in front of Clare, with a message stating; 'incoming updates'.
She made a pushing motion with her hand and the floating images moved away from her. She snapped and a second square appeared hovering in front of her. She used her index finger and moved it downwards in the air so that a keyboard scrolled out. Clare typed in; 'access mainframe database.' Then she hesitated, and began to chew her bottom lip like she did when she was second guessing herself. She shouldn't be doing what she was doing...but she typed in: 'intelligence department' anyways. When the next screen popped up, she typed: 'locate case file' and Clare looked back at the glass wall to see if anyone was around. She was clear to type: 'The Baptist'.
Right away the files began to pop up in separate little squares all around her. An image of a handwritten note floated there. Evidence from the scene, crime scene photos, ballistics, a close up of a pencil drawn symbol. A circle with a cross in the centre. She found the file she was looking for; a video file.

65

She took a deep breath and sighed. She rubbed her temple and closed her eyes for a second before she hit play. The video played out the scene that was causing her so much grief and she watched intently with her hand covering her mouth, eyes wide. No matter how many times she watched this it didn't get easier—

An older gentleman was walking out of a local bar in the CCTV camera footage from above. The nicely dressed man began to walk to the right of the shot with two other large men escorting him. Clare watched as they turned around suddenly, as something got their attention. Before they could react, the video showed a faint red mist pop out of one of the larger men's back, as he jerked and his body went limp and crumbled to the ground. Just out of the left side of the screen, there was a white flash and the second large man dropped to the ground in a heap, leaving the older man in the middle covering his head and crouching.

But then, Clare watched in horror, as this cowering man suddenly stopped covering when he allowed himself a glance up. His hands lowered and his body straightened up, as a dark figure walked into the shot with his arm outstretched. He was holding a gun and he was wearing all dark clothing, with a hood covering his head and face. But obviously it was enough for his victim to see the face. Clare could tell that the old man *knew* his shooter.

It seemed, in the video that the man tried to say something, but before he finished—another white flash out of the muzzle of the gun and the old man dropped to his face.

Clare watched as several more flashes came and the unknown shooter walked forward towards the man—emptying his clip—

—"Good morning special agent."

Clare quickly waved her hand in the air to make the files disappear off the screen and then she took a sip of her coffee as another member of her team was arriving for work.

"Hi, Ray." She said awkwardly after she swallowed her mouthful.

"How's it going?" Ray asked.

"Fine...I'm fine..." She lied. Seeing it again made her jumpy. The adrenaline coursing through her made her hand shake and the mug rattled against the desk as she put it down.

"How about you?" She went on. "Traffic was pretty good today eh?"

"Yah, I was surprised."

More usual chit-chat as Clare wondered if Ray had seen what she was doing. Ray put his stuff down and sauntered over to Clare's desk which was right beside his. Clare was trying not to look at him. She sat down at her desk now and she took another shaky sip from her mug. She began to look through the dailies on the big screen. Ray stopped to Clare's right with his hands in his pockets. He wasn't a dumb guy...he had seen the video playing, but he always tried to give Clare the benefit of the doubt. He glanced over and saw the boxes on her desk, scratching his head as he noticed 'The Baptist' case files.

"How you doing?" He asked.

Clare pretended not to notice the concern in his voice. "I'm fine Ray." She said, annoyed. "You already asked me that." She glanced up and met his gaze by accident and then couldn't break it. She let out her tension by sighing and shaking her head.

"What?" she asked.

"C'mon Clare. It's only been a week. You shouldn't even be back at work yet, Mark said—".

"I don't care what Mark said, Ray! I need to get my mind off of it."

"Is that why you take home the case files? To get your mind off it?" Ray motioned to the box on her desk, and Clare reactively spun the box around so that the writing on it couldn't be seen.

"What are you doing partner?"

"I need to find him."

"Find who? The Baptist? Why?" Ray's voice became a little more convicting. "What's it going to change?"

Clare stewed in her chair and her face tightened up. Her jaw muscles bulged as she clenched her teeth behind a closed mouth. She wished Ray would just go away...*how could he understand?*

"I need to know why." She replied.

"Again...why do you? Just leave it alone."

"You don't understand, Ray..."

"What don't I understand? You're obsessed!" He was raising his voice now. He stopped and looked around the room. He turned and sat on the edge of her desk with his arms crossed and there was a few moments of silence. Clare sat back in her chair and put her hand over her mouth again.

"Look..." He began. "I'm worried about you okay?" His voice lowered now and returned to the concerning kind he had before. "That's all it is...listen, there's stress and there's something else. I know you okay? Stress was when you got on board with Kovacs." He motioned over to the two boxes on her desk. "Stress you can handle. This...Baptist case, this is something else. All of us can see the difference."

"What's that Ray?"

He stopped for a breath and answered. "Sadness, Clare..."

"Don't I have a right to be on this one?" She asked.

"Of course."

Clare sighed and looked at the ground.

"But that's not why you're sad."

"What?"

"You're sad because things were almost better at home and this new case ruined it."

The truth made Clare stew some more and she bit her bottom lip again as she looked away. But then she had a thought and she turned back to him.

"Since when do you care about the quality of my relationship?" She asked him.

Ray sighed now. "I care about you, Clare. When we're working on cases you're different than this. I know the timing of all this hasn't exactly worked out in your favour."

"—please don't give me marriage advice now."

"I'm just saying...not the best way to start your new life, with a big case like Kovacs."

Clare looked over at both boxes with regret then fixed on the Kovacs one. "Yah..." She started. "Well...terrorists don't really give a shit do they?"

"No but you should...usually once one chapter closes you take a break."

"No, usually, the next one starts right away and doesn't give you a chance." Clare snapped, looking back to Ray.

"C'mon partner..." He said. "Look, I get it okay? I know it's hard to stay away, but this new one's kicking your ass before we've even put Kovacs to bed fully."

"Well that's why I came in today isn't it?" Clare replied.

"K, fine..." Ray said standing up off the desk. "Come to the debrief, close this case and go home."

She sighed at the word and there was silence between them. Ray took this time to secretly look at her with longing eyes now.

"If you're better I'm better." He stated. "I need you better."

Clare breathed out again, wiping the hair from her brow and looking to the case files again, this time fixating on the Baptist one. "I was almost better." She said. "Being here has put me and John in this position. I spend too much time at work, I know that. But..."

"But you can't stop."

"How can I stop?" Clare asked turning back to him. "Especially now"

"Because this one's too personal!" Another male's voice cut in.

They both turned and saw their boss; Mark, standing at the top of the small steps at the entrance of the room.

"Morning sir." Ray greeting him.

"Mark, Hi." Clare said.

"Good morning agents." He said. "Ray is right Clare. And you need to take some time to decide."

Clare furrowed her brow. "Decided what sir?" She asked.

"Which person you're gonna be." He replied. "We can't have a dual minded agent on our team. I recruited you onto my team because of the potential I saw in you at the time. The fact that you're still here after..." He trailed off and Clare lowered her head. "That takes guts kid." He said looking at Ray to correct his critique of Clare's character. "But Ray is right, that the rest of us see this...other thing going on. It's not you."

"Sir, I—"

"I don't wanna hear about your marriage problems." Mark cut in. "Those are your problems. Not for work. But if you want my opinion you're not the typical house wife type."

"And what type am I then?"

68

"The kick the bad guy's ass type! That's who!"

Clare chuckled awkwardly. "What if I don't wanna be that person anymore?"

"I don't think you'd survive." Ray cut back into the conversation. "You need to be busting "punks" as you love to call them. Hell, Clare, I thought that guy we interrogated was gonna crap himself the way you got in his face."

Again Clare tried to deny her identity and shrugged humbly.

"That's the you we need back!" Ray said. "The you I need."

Clare didn't respond. She just sat there rubbing her top lip with her index finger.

"I'll be ok, Ray." She said somberly. "I just need some time. Being here is gonna help me."

"Then you better stick with that decision, Agent." Mark said.

"Sir..." Ray began.

"Nope." Mark said sharply. "That's the end of it. She's here...she's gonna work." He said looking at Clare. "I'll see both of you in the briefing room in ten minutes!"

"Yessir." They both said and then Mark walked out.

Ray looked one last time at Clare and knew there was nothing else he could say. He sighed and followed Mark out.

"Cya in there, Clare." He muttered.

Ray then left and Clare heard the gentle thud of the glass door closing. She looked at the box for a long time and then she looked back at the big screen...the video file was still minimized in the bottom right corner of it...She glanced back to make sure he was gone and then opened up the file again.

Ray's words rang in her head and she wondered why she tortured herself this way.

He was right,

What good would come of it?

She didn't know...

She didn't care.

She rewound the video over and over again, watching the same scene and she relived the pain each time she watched the old man die.

* * *

Clare entered the debriefing room where Ray and the other members of her team were waiting and they all looked right at her. She only made eye contact with Ray, who gave her a little smile. But she could feel all the eyes on her.

Pity.

That's all she could feel from them. They were all wondering if she was okay, or wanted to say something, but didn't know what to say...and she hated that feeling.

"Good morning Mrs. Mash" Mark said.

There was also an unknown male and female in the room; agents, she figured, from higher up...here to hear the debrief that was about to commence.

"Sorry everyone, I wasn't sure if I was coming in today. But I guess I should be here for this."

"It's up to you Clare." Mark said. "I think we would all understand if you didn't feel like coming in. "

Clare glanced around the room at her teammates who were, no doubt, waiting to watch her break down and say *'oh thank god, what a relief, thanks for understanding, I'll go home.'* and at the two high class agents, staring at her, clipboards in hand.

"It's my case sir." She spoke up with a determination in her voice that made Mark, and everyone else in the room, realized that there wasn't anything they could say to make her go home.

"I need to be here." Clare nodded her head slowly to everyone and she caught Ray's eye. Ray gave her a reassuring look and she smiled back awkwardly. Mark was staring at her, trying to think of what to say.

"Okay." He simply said, as he turned to push a button on his little hand held clicker remote. "Let's get started then."

Clare gave a final head nod and breathed in through her nose, as the lights were dimmed.

The screen at the end of the long table displayed the Anti-Terrorism logo again, and then a picture of a man popped up—glaring into Clare's eyes. She stared right back with conviction.

"This," Mark started. "The whole world knows, is Joseph Kovacs."

Clare locked eyes with the image on the screen; as if the man was in the room with her. His eyes burned back at her. She knew that Joseph Kovacs, when he was brought in, and when he was sat in front of a camera for his mug shot; the look he gave into the lens was for her. Kovacs had imagined that lens was Clare's eyes and he leered into it, just for her.

"Kovacs is an international terrorist" Mark continued, and he glanced at Clare with a slight smirk. "This is the man responsible for the state of the planet right now. For our guests, as a recap; Russian national, born in 1989, mother raised him after his father, who was part of the Russian military and a communist, went nuts and murdered his whole platoon..."

Mark's voice began to soften in Clare's ears as he continued. Her eyes fixed onto the image of Kovacs and she tuned her boss out. He was only a dull mumble as she just glared into Kovacs' face. The rivalry still drew her in.

Her mind flashed back to the incident that started their grudge.

Mark's voice was replaced with sounds of gunfire and shouting. Rapid, automatic rifle fire, all around her like a war zone. Kovacs' face grinning at her. They were in the woods and she had she had him at gunpoint—

—Clare blinked herself back into her reality and gave her head a shake. She rubbed her eyes to push that stress back in. Ray kept a concerned eye on her from across the table.

Mark droned on with his presentation but Clare couldn't stop herself from recapping the history in her own head—

Kovacs' face wouldn't leave her mind's eye: Very Slavic facial features, rigid bone structure; large protruding forehead, large nose, square jaw and he had a military haircut with a big bushy beard. The most distinguishing feature Kovacs had, was the *eyes*; dark eyes that almost sunk into his skull, making dark shadows all around them. His protruding forehead created an awning type effect, casting more darkness over his eyes. The brow furrowed, no matter what emotion he was feeling and formed a 'V' shape, making him look furious all the time.

He glared back at her in the woods that day.

"Don't move Kovacs!" Clare told him. "You're under arrest you son-of-a-bitch!"

She breathed slowly through her nose to counteract her adrenaline and she burned holes in Kovacs with her furious stare. She could see now that what lay behind his eyes wasn't just madness...

It was *pure evil*.

"For what?" He asked, in his thick Russian accent.

"For what?!" Clare asked rhetorically. "How 'bout murder? How 'bout genocide?"

Kovacs laughed out loud; a deep throaty laugh that threw his head back.

Clare's breath was quick with stress and her eyes burned. She blinked rapidly—

—she snapped back into reality with the sound of Kovacs' laughter in her mind. His dark voice, playing from a video, drew her back into the debrief going on:

"People of the world." His voice began. An old propaganda message was playing on the screen.

"If two dogs pass each other in the wild," he went on. "and they have never met. They will bare their teeth at one another. They will growl, they will snarl, and they will defend their territory. They will fight! There will be blood! The time has come. The time to tear down your governments. For too long I have watched as nations leaders *bully* its citizens! Long ago I learned about life...about death...and everything in between. We are dogs! Animals! That's all we are. Instinct drives me, fuels me. And it's a dog eat dog world! Do not pretend that you are above this, that you do not have these carnal instincts as well. When a man passes another man in the street...and they have never met, will they not stare each other down? You are dogs too! And we are all trapped, by our governments! Governments who are trying to train us...*tame us*—but...no more!"

As Kovacs' old broadcast went on, Clare remembered all of the carnage The Bears had unleashed on the world. Images of burning fields flashed in her memory. The fields in Gettysburg where thousands of soldier's bodies, who fought and died for freedom, were laid to rest. An absolutely visceral attack, when Bear soldiers cut the hearts out of greedy traders on Wall Street.

Clare shut her eyes tight and her memory took her back to that day in the woods again...

..."I may be a murderer agent." Kovacs had said to her that day. "But so are you." and he paused for effect. "You want to kill me right now...don't you?"

Clare's finger was all the way on the trigger now almost squeezing it.

"You have murder in your heart agent. Hatred, vengeance...judgment."—

—"last but not least!" Mark's voice broke into her thoughts.

Clare looked up to see Ray still looking at with concern.

"The Bears most recent attack," Mark went on. "Fresh in all our memories, I'm sure."

An image popped up on the screen. An arial view of Vatican City—or what was left of it. Everyone in the room was looking at a black crater where the world's most powerful religious influence once stood so proud.

"Using strategically placed martyrs," Mark said. "All over the religious city; he destroyed it, sending all of Rome, and everywhere in the world into massive panic. This is why they say he's the most successful terrorist. Joseph Kovacs successfully brought down everyone's rock. Where their eyes and hearts turn in times of crisis. What once stood as a super power over the entire free world is now in ashes. Folks, this has always been the Bear's mission. For the world to see and know what hopelessness meant..."

The room was silent and mournful in memory of all the victims.

Clare allowed her eyes to fall on Ray once again, who was still shooting her worried looks. But a dark voice crept back into her thoughts.

"You and I are the same..." Kovacs' voice echoed in her brain.

Clare was holding Kovacs at gun point again, back in the woods that day.

"We're all the same." He said to her. "The only difference is that I'm not afraid to act, and you are!"

Clare burned with anger and she could feel the hotness creeping up the back of her neck and reaching her ears. She breathed through her nose, and her nostrils blew hot smoke; like a dragon.

Her mind flipped and flittered, like a rolodex, rewinding this whole scene to the action that led her here.

The sounds of shouts and gunfire were all around her and she was standing in the midst of whizzing bullets and chaos. Gunfire was raining down from the windows above them and the tactical team was pinned down at the front of the house.

WHIZ...POP! POP!

The snipers took out the threats.

BAM!

The tact team slammed the door open with a breach tool and the wood-splintering sound filled the air. The front line guys all chucked flash bangs through the frame and seconds later the light from their pops flooded the house.

"Go, Go, Go!"

"Move in!"

The voices all erupted.

"We're moving in!" Ray shouted to their team. "We're gonna back em up!"

Tunnel vision. Clare focused her eagle eye gaze right into the broken door frame. Soon all she could hear was the thuds in her ears as her feet hit the ground. She felt like a first-person-shooter video game.

RATTA-TATTA!

Machine gun fire erupted inside the house. It was the last thing Clare saw before...

BOOOOOM!

A wall of dirt and debris appeared in front of them, like a wave rising out of the ocean, and Clare shielded her face as she dove backwards. This wave circled the entire perimeter of the house.

Kovacs had this place well protected and chocked full of traps. Some kind of remotely detonated explosive had been set off, devastating most of the team in all directions. Clare felt the sharpness of the high pressured dirt that exploded scraping her arms and face. Bodies of her teammates crashed into her and she was pinned.

Clare opened her eyes and all she saw was a face full of leaves on a white back drop, as her vision focused again. The white became the day light, as she was looking into the sky. She looked around in a panic and noticed the shrapnel filled bodies of a couple of her team mates littered around her. One was right on top of her and she shoved him off. As she began to sit up she saw Ray's body lying lifeless about ten feet away.

But when Clare stumbled back up the second time she noticed several of the S.W.A.T. team guys still standing and helping the injured ones. Clare made it to her feet again and choked through the dust and smoke, trying to get a glimpse of the scene. She stood there in the fray thinking; *we've lost it. None of my team is probably even alive. I wonder if Kovacs is even here!*

She was looking all around and she didn't even know her bearings anymore. She couldn't see Ray and she spun in circles trying to find out where she was.

"R...Ra—" She couldn't breathe. She could barely even open her mouth. She coughed violently and spit out blood onto the leaves. The sound of machine-gun fire broke through the ringing in her ears and she rolled into the fetal position for whatever cover that offered.

"Team two, moving in!" Clare heard more voices coming from the other tact team sweeping forward.

RATTA-RATTA-BBRRATTA!!

They opened fire on the Bears thugs who were shooting. Their gun fire got louder as they approached behind Clare and she watched as their boots scurried past her face. Once the fire was in front of her she got up to run to Ray, but as she staggered to her feet—

"Medic!" one of the tact guys screamed. "Take care of her!" one of the team members rushed to her side and began helping her back towards the road where medic teams were waiting. "C'mon let's go! You're gonna be alright!"

"No!" Clare cried. "We have to get the rest of my team!" She looked back at Ray as she continued to be led away from the scene.

"You need to get away from the gunfire! You need a medic!"

"No, I'm fine—Ray!" Clare began to resist the tact guys pull on her now, and he started to pull her more forcefully now. He was only trying to help.

Clare struck him hard in the stomach with a solid left knee and he released his control on her.

Clare had obviously found her strength again, and the adrenaline was flowing through her veins now. She turned to run towards Ray as the tact guy came after her.

"Agent!" He screamed.

"Ray!"

BLAM!

A single shot. Clare felt the bullet just barely graze her left cheek and the gust of wind that moved her hair slightly. In a simultaneous motion she dove to the ground and looked back over her left shoulder. The bullet had already slammed into the neck of the tact team guy, just sneaking in under his face mask and above his body armour.

He was only trying to help.

A wide-eyed Clare watched in horror as he hit the ground and then she snapped her gaze to the house where one of the members of the Bears was emerging through the door jamb. Team two continued their fire fight with the Bears in the house.

Clare rolled over onto her stomach and crawled the rest of the way to Ray. When she made it, she propped herself up beside Ray.

"Ray!"

She shook him, and she heard a faint groan. She sighed, knowing now that he was alive but she noticed his bleeding ears and he was still unconscious.

More Bears emerged and began to overpower the tact team. Clare was able to locate her pistol and she grabbed it. As she was checking her mag there was a loud gun shot that seemed closer than the others. A body of one of the tact guys thudded beside them.

Clare quickly holstered her pistol and then grabbed his assault rifle. She sat up angrily. She squeezed that trigger and felt the rumbling of the rifle butt as it thudded into her shoulder.

RATTA-TATTA-RATTA-TATTA-RATTA-TATTA-RATTA-TATTA!

She guided the bullets at the Bears, mowing them down to create enough of a delay in the firing, for the team leader of two. He didn't miss his opportunity.

"MOVE!" He shouted. His team all rushed the house.

Clare fired until the slide clicked back on empty. As she breathed out her stress, she lowered the gun as the tactical team past her line of sight. As they did, she saw a motion blur through the dust. Two or three figures, sneaking through the smoke, away from the house. They were going towards the wooded area behind it.

Kovacs.

She turned quickly to signal her team...or anyone who was left.

"HE'S ON THE MOVE!! I GOT HIM OVER HERE!! C'MON!!"

But as she ran she didn't notice them get gunned down by the last remaining few Bears who kept the fire fight alive with whoever was left.

Clare was empty. She tossed the rifle down and she retrieved her side arm. The look on Kovacs face reminded her of the *punks* she used to bust for stealing at the mall. Happy and cocky that they were getting away. But Clare never lost a man.

The snaps and cracks of the branches filled the air as she maneuvered her away through the forest; jumping, leaping, dodging tree limbs, hurdling logs on her mission towards Kovacs. The international terrorist, responsible for so much death and destruction...and here she was chasing him. *Was this real? How am I the one now responsible for him?* None of that mattered as she chased him.

He was thirty feet ahead of her now. "Freeze!" She screamed. "F.B.I. freeze!" she hadn't noticed that the other men with him had disappeared. She began to close in.

Closer,

Closer,

Closer...

Kovacs tripped, and fell on his face.

"Don't move!" Clare shouted and she closed in on his position. Then she was eating a mouthful of leaves that Kovacs had thrown when he rolled over, and as she was spitting the leaves out and trying to focus—WHAP!—Kovacs swung a thick tree limb at her and whacked her on her left side in the ribs. The body armour softened the blow, but it was still enough force to make her stumble. But Clare counteracted quickly with a distractionary knee strike to his stomach. She then slammed him under the chin with the side of her gun. He flung his head back but before he could fall, Clare struck him across the side of the head with the gun one more time; *hard*, and Kovacs crashed to the ground forcefully.

She did it.

She caught him.

She had him there now and she rose her gun up and now held him at gunpoint. Kovacs groaned and rolled around.

"You're under arrest you son-of-a-bitch!" She shouted.

And you know the rest from here...

After their conversation, Clare's finger grazed the trigger.

Clare began to squirm. He was right. She *did* want to kill him. All those people he killed...thousands. She had him here, in her sights. She *could* pull the trigger and no one would know the difference. *It was self-defense.* He *was resistant.* Nobody would care if she did kill him—they would understand why she did it.

"Everyone in the world wants to kill me agent" He stated. "And that's good. Look at what I've bred. Vengeance is in all of us. We all want justice."

She wanted to kill him, but something about having this truth spoken back to her stopped her.

Suddenly she caught Kovacs break his gaze and look past her. A menacing grin crept across his face now and Clare's heart began to pound when she heard a twig snap behind her.

She wanted to turn around and see who it was, but she couldn't. Kovacs could get away or try something else. An impending sense of doom fell over her; because she knew that whoever was behind her was probably going to kill her...so she waited...

Her last thought was that at least she could take out the world's most dangerous man before she died, go out a hero. Death behind her and a *choice* in front.

"You lose." Kovacs gloated and he began to stand up slowly.

Clare raised her gun up and was about to fire—

But then the rustle of leaves came around to her left and in her peripheral she noticed that this other man was not alone. He was a large man. One of The Bears' thugs named 'Grizzly'. Clare saw that his big forearm was wrapped around the torso of another member of her team; Jill. Jill was the rookie before Clare joined their unit. The Grizzly had a very large hunting knife, with the edge of the blade pressed against Jill's neck and He was smiling at Clare. She moved her aim at him now. She looked Jill in the eye and saw her terrified expression. She could see that Jill was trying to be strong by not crying, but there were very real tears running down her face.

"Drop the gun." The Grizzly said.

Clare breathed *fire.* She was going to lose. She was a pretty good shot, but Jill's head was so close to his, that even the slightest miscalculation could end up blowing her head off. Kovacs was chuckling.

"Enough of this!" The grizzly shouted. "We don't have time for this toying, Joseph!"

Clare's eyes darted back and forth. Kovacs grinned as he stared back at her.

"Okay." He gave the order.

"Clare!" Jill cried in desperation.

"No!" Clare screamed.

Kovacs raised his hand and a disappointed Grizzly stopped putting pressure on the knife. Jill's neck had started bleeding now and she was wincing and craning her neck in an attempt to get away from the blade. Clare didn't lower her gun...she couldn't do it.

"Clare..." Kovacs repeated.

Oh no, she thought. Her eyes went wide. Now he knows my name—

—"Over here!" a loud voice echoed down the hills and rang through the trees. Right away, Clare, Kovacs, Grizzly and Jill all knew what it was. The cavalry was on their way!

For a few brief moments time seemed to stop and Clare and Kovacs both gave each other a panicked look—stale mate—*now what?*

As the sounds of feet rushing through leaves thundered towards them, the Grizzly made a decision of his own. As Clare was looking around, her hope was interrupted by the piercing scream Jill made. Clare snapped her attention back and watched in horror as the Grizzly was living up to his nickname. He was digging the blade into Jill's neck—the blood was horrific.

Now, her choice was simple.

BLAM BLAM BLAM BLAM BLAM!

The bullets ripped through Jill and she stopped screaming. Grizzly was hit but not enough times before—

—*CRUNCH!*

Kovacs tackled her, like a missile, and they hit the ground hard. Clare's gun went flying and Kovacs struck her in the face. He raised his fist for another blow, but Clare used her forearm to block it and rammed her knee into his groin.

While they fought, Grizzly swung his own assault rifle off his shoulder and threw a barrage of bullet spray towards the incoming troops.

Where was the cavalry? They had sounded close but Clare didn't realize how far into the woods she had chased him.

She rolled over and stood up to run, but felt a painful tug on the back of her head. Kovacs swung her, like a pendulum, by her pony tail and tossed her into the trunk of a tree. Before she could turn around she felt a push on the back of her head and she grunted through the pain as her face was pressed into the tree bark.

Behind them, Grizzly pulled the pin on two grenades and tossed them quickly one after the other in two different directions towards the troops.

"DOWN!" Clare heard them call before the blasts went off, followed by more burst of rifle fire.

She struggled but couldn't move as he was holding her against the tree. Then she felt a hot steamy breath on the back of her neck and she closed her eyes. She knew Kovacs was there and she told herself that this was it. She felt the hairs of his beard on her ears and he whispered.

"You should have let me go Clare..."

Clare was horrified and opened her eyes when she felt a long thin object slide between her legs. She knew that Kovacs was holding the hunting knife, blade-side-up on her crotch. Her eyes went wide and her breathing quickened. She began to struggle and Kovacs spun her around to face him. He wrapped his hand around her neck and squeezed so that Clare began to grab at his hand trying to pry it off of her. The echoing voices of back up were still too distant and Grizzly continued to hold them at bay with his fire. With his other hand Kovacs produced the blade in front her face. Clare saw that it was still covered in Jill's blood.

Her nostrils flared and she stared into his eyes when he brought his face close to hers. Her eyes darted to her left back and forth to see if she could see the back up yet.

Kovacs pressed her head further towards the tree and forced her to look at him. "I was wrong about you Clare." Clare was trying to burn holes through his skull with her blazing stare. "You're not afraid of me at all are you?" He asked.

PA-TOOIE!

Kovacs received a red mist on his face; Clare's spit, mixed with her blood. When he opened his eyes she was nose to nose with him and they saw into each other's eyes.

"You're a punk!" She hoarsely managed to force out. Kovacs saw her determination and willingness to do what it takes to stop men like him. If he admitted it, he began to feel a small amount of fear of Clare. But then he smirked and he lowered the knife down her body, dragging the tip softly down her face, following the curve of her neck around the chin and he scraped it down. He stopped at her sternum just above her breasts and he allowed himself a perverted glance at her. He met her gaze again and she just breathed her dragon fire, nostrils flaring…waiting for it. She wouldn't let him see her fear—

RATTATATTATATTATATTA!!!

A closer sound of gunfire interrupted and Clare watched Grizzly get riddled behind Kovacs and fall to the ground.

— "CLARE!" The voices shouted down the hill.

Kovacs snapped his head to the left. The sound of branches breaking and rustling of the team thundering down the hill towards their location erupted. Clare couldn't move…but it happened so fast. She felt the blood flowing through her neck veins again when Kovacs let go. She watched hazily while she slid down the tree, as he retreated. She heard several gun shots ring through the air and Kovacs was running.

There he went,

Despite everything that had just happened…she still cared about him getting away.

She should have been grateful to be *free* from him, that he was *leaving*…she was *safe*.

But she still felt the shame of defeat as she watched him disappear into the forest.

She had met Joseph Kovacs and the legend of their history together began. Clare's head was fuzzy and she just lay there on her side staring after Kovacs who got smaller and smaller as he ran. As her vision focused and the noise of footsteps grew louder towards her, she breathed for the first time, it seemed, since this whole ordeal started. Her breath was steady and her blood pressure seemed to normalize as she shook the trauma off. She sat up and looked around as the surviving members of the tactical teams and medics rushed onto the scene.

As they were all attending to her, assessing her, asking her a million questions she peered through the crowd and caught a glimpse of a man standing there with his gun still pointed.

Ray lowered his weapon in a sigh of relief and smiled at Clare.

* * *

"Agent Mash?"

Clare raised her head up and snapped out of her daydream as Mark called her name. She had been recounting her whole history while Mark recapped for the high class agents at the debrief. She was back in the present now.

"Agent Mash," Mark repeated. "If you could fill the team in on the details regarding the capture of Mr. Kovacs."

"Of course." She said quietly, and she cleared her throat.

She glanced at Ray while she walked by who gave her that old reassuring look he always gave her. All eyes were still on her as she came to the front.

A surreal feeling suddenly swelled up inside of her. That her saga with Kovacs, what had become the crown jewel of her career, was actually ending.

Was this real?

How many times had she beat her frustrations out on our punching bag? With each step towards the front of the room, she remembered her furious blows. Those nights, after the Boston incident, where I had been kept awake by the hard packing sounds of her fists and grunts.

"Finish this Clare." My voice echoed in her head. She was remembering a fight we had about the whole subject. "Please...Just finish it."

"Good morning." She began, to the group. They all stared back. Clare knew what she was supposed to say but the words wouldn't come. The shock of this all being over was still surreal.

"I wish I could go back to the beginning!" She had said desperately to me that night. "It's not like I'm ever going to catch Kovacs!"

Ironic that she recalled these words as she stood in her position now.

"You're too good at this." My voice crept back into her mind.

"Besides...we both know that you wouldn't ever be done. You wouldn't be the same. And—." I stopped to swallow a big sob, before continuing. "—and I wouldn't have you...the full you. I would only have half. Because you need to finish this. You're whole career has been leading to this."

Clare listened to me, knowing I was right.

"But then again..." I continued. "I only have half of you now don't I?"

Clare's eyes closed and her eyelid hit the puddle of tears that had pooled at the base of her eye causing a single tear to roll down her cheek.

"Agent Mash?" Mark's voice snapped her back.

"Uh...Joseph 'the Kodiak' Kovacs," she forced herself to just start talking. "Was apprehended roughly two weeks ago in a high risk operation. Our team led a raid on the last known hideout of the Kodiak, in Mongolia. Kovacs and a number of the Bears members were located in the mountains of Khovd. I'm pleased to announce that, with the cooperation of our military and our president's decision to attack this site, we successfully infiltrated the hideout and using sheer presence of force, we outnumbered the gang of terrorists. The military tact team had all the areas closed off making it impossible for anyone inside to escape." Clare carried on through her speech as images of the mountain village and helmet cam images from the tact team flashed across the screen.

It felt good for her to be saying these words. She breathed a little easier and the room began to feel less tense.

"After a full sweep of the hideaway," Clare went on. "Teams located Kovacs and executed the arrest of the world's most ruthless and dangerous terrorist."

A light clapping started, which stopped Clare in the middle of her debrief. The applause grew until everyone in the room was clapping and Clare let an awkward smile appear on her lips. She looked around and saw that Mark was grinning at her while clapping. They all were looking at her and aiming the applause at her. She caught Ray's eye and he was smiling warmly at her while clapping his congratulations.

The applause faded and she continued. "Most of the other Bear's members were killed during the raid," she said. "But the ones who weren't were also arrested as war criminals and brought back state side with Kovacs. They are all being held in separate maximum security facilities all over the country, in segregation from the general population, under guard twenty-four-seven. To be frank agents...and excuse my crudeness...Kovacs doesn't even piss without somebody at his side. They are all awaiting justice hearings in the near future, and I'm assured that they will be prosecuted with extreme prejudice for their crimes against this country, and humanity."

As Clare was saying all of this, she could feel a sense of closure coming over her. All of the time of her life she had put in to this finally paid off. But as the presentation ended, she still felt a darkness in the pit of her stomach. As the people in the room cleared out, gathering their papers and shuffling out, she was surprisingly not even thinking about Joseph Kovacs and all the stress he had caused in her life.

She was still replaying the images of the old man dying in the video through her head. This is what was *now* consuming her mind. Mark and Ray had remained behind while everyone else left. Mark was seeing the higher class agents out, exchanging all the appropriate pleasantries and goodbyes, and Ray approached Clare while he could.

"You did good." He said to her.

"Thanks Ray." She was still acting awkward, not knowing how Ray was feeling about what had *really* happened out there.

"It's alright Clare." He started. "You did good out there...and no one will find out. It was only me and you—."

"My all-stars!" Mark shouted, and he walked up behind them. "You did great Clare, thanks for that. How does it feel?"

Clare smiled at him. "It feels good Mark. I can't really put words to it. I guess I don't really feel any different. It's almost like life is just picking up again from where it left off...'on to the next' kind of thing." She lied and chuckled a nervous chuckle.

Mark smiled back. "Good work." He said and he placed himself in between both of them with a hand on each shoulder. He looked back and forth at the two of them. "Both of you, really...great work."

"Hey guys?" The voice of another team member broke in.

The three of them turned to see him leaning through the door frame.

"Richter...that scientist guy?...He's on TV now..."

CHAPTER SIX
I'm NOT Sorry I Spilled the Juice

Day 23,475
64 years in the making.
Jason Richter thought about every day since the one in his bedroom, as he stepped up to the podium. The bright flashes of the cameras hurt his eyes and he squinted and shielded his face. He adjusted his glasses and just waited for the commotion to die down.

Behind him stood his two lab partners and a host of other stakeholders. An annoying little lawyer who represented the company that funded Richter's machine and some other people from the legal team at Globe-X.

It had certainly been a long road for all of them to get here this morning...

* * *

...Cairo, Egypt.
The desert sands were suddenly disturbed on a desert road. The two black SUV's bumped and rolled in the night. They used to be bright, shiny looking cars but now they were covered in dust as they travelled. It had been a long journey from the city out here into the desert. They rose and fell with all the hills and the people in them bumped along with their movements.

Inside, the annoying little lawyer sat. He didn't belong out here in the desert. He was a middle aged man who spent most of his time in an office somewhere. He sat here uncomfortably, as the SUV bounced around, looking out the window.

"Where are we going?" He asked, looking now to the back seat of the car, where another man sat silently. It was dark out, but the moonlight highlighted his profile.

"What's the matter Mr. Kitch?" The mystery man asked. "Can't handle the suspense?"

"The suspense I can handle...It's the smoke screens and all this cloak and dagger stuff that's bothering me." He replied. Then he adjusted his trench coat and shifted in his seat uncomfortably. The man in the back was so still and unshaken that it bothered him. "You told us that you were taking us out here to show us something. The client I represent will be greatly disappointed if all I have to show for it is some sand in my underwear." He said, getting a little annoyed now.

"Patience is a virtue Mr. Kitch..." The man in the back replied. His voice was dark along with his appearance.

"Hmm. More smoke screens. Why am I not surprised?"

"Your client will not be disappointed. You're here to represent their legal interests. If it was up to me...you wouldn't have been invited on this little excursion. But the men in the other car up there insisted you see this for yourself. So please, Mr. Kitch...consider yourself lucky to be here...and—shut up please."

The stuffy lawyer bit his tongue and clenched his jaw in annoyance as he turned back to the window. The man in the back seat looked ahead out the front window.

"Ah." He said. "You see Mr. Kitch? Patience..."

Mr. Kitch looked ahead to see what he was talking about. The other SUV in front of them disappeared over the ridge ahead of them. Kitch could see a bright glow rising over the hill as they approached. When they rose over the ridge he saw their destination. One of the world's most famous landmarks—one of the wonders of the world was just ahead—the pyramids of Giza...

But, not only the pyramids. The entire site was lit up by big industrial work lamps and busy with activity. A few hundred yards to the right of them was why they were really here;

"This, Mr. Kitch..." the old man in the back began. "Is what makes this site a true wonder of the world!"

Kitch's jaw was on the floor when he saw the size of it!

It was a giant metal ring. Spotlights illuminated it in the night. A huge donut shaped circle that towered hundreds of feet above the apexes of the pyramids.

"It's gargantuan!" Kitch proclaimed.

The old man in the back chuckled. "Yes, it is quite something. It doesn't even look real does it?"

Kitch just shook his head in amazement.

The ring had other metals coiled around the entire structure. If Kitch could minimize it, it would be like coiling a spring from your pen around a key ring. Only the coils seemed to be very tightly wound and sturdy. Kitch could see they were copper. All around the ring were large metal binders fastening the coils in place. The ring itself was resting in a half moon shaped metal base...

...Back in present day Kitch squirmed up on the stage behind Richter as the press all took photos.

The media circus.

All around the city, people were stopping in their workplaces to tune in to the TV.

Watch on their smartphones.

Listen to the radio.

Ridley and I had just booked a guy we arrested that morning into the division. The cell door wasn't even closed yet before I noticed the commotion of officers scrambling towards the parade room. I looked around too and noticed other officers staring at their phones.

"What the hell is going on?" Ridley asked me.

The clunk of the cell door echoed and then I hustled over to join the crowd.

"Jimenez." I grabbed this new kid's attention. "What's up?"
"That time travel Doctor is doing that press conference now." Young Jimenez replied.

I stopped and grabbed Ridley. I looked at my watch, not remembering the time.

"Let's go, Rid."

Clare joined the rest of her team in their big mission room where a TV was always set up to keep them current. Mark and Ray joined her as well. Everyone was stopped and looking at the screen...

...In Egypt that night; the SUVs descended down the hill towards the pyramids and Kitch looked around to all the commotion surrounding them. Other vehicles were parked all around; big military style cargo trucks and personal vehicles. There were military personnel, in full tactical gear who were armed and patrolling all over the place. *What were they guarding?* He wondered. They entered through a set of wire fences guarded by more militia.

A big plaque tied to the fence displayed that Globe-X was in charge of the site.

He also observed a number of what he assumed were scientists or engineers; men in lab coats. Some were hunched over tables reading notes, others were examining blue prints. In addition to these men, there were workers as well; wearing those bright orange vests with the neon 'X' stripes. They were carrying pipes, wood, tools, setting up scaffolding, climbing scaffolding to elevated positions on the pyramids. The site was alive with people clamouring over each other. One scientist was shouting orders at a group of workers who, as they approached closer, appeared to Kitch to be Egyptian nationals...slave labourers...

...In my own present day; I felt my heart beat increasing as I grew excited to hear what Richter had to say. We entered the parade room and saw the host of officers all gathered to watch the TV. Ridley and I remained at the back of the crowd looking on.

"Uh...G-G...Good afternoon." Richter's voice squealed in the microphone with a slight blast of feedback.

The crowd of reporters went quiet.

All of the cops were chattering until big officer Mac, the gruff old bastard, turned and hollered.

"Quiet down you numbskulls!!"

We all shut right up, and Ridley and I shared a chuckle.

Then we turned to the TV set.

It was eerily quiet on the real life side of that broadcast. Richter was not much for public speaking, given his lack of empathy for *anyone*. He stood there staring out at the press, with Kitch and his two lab partners behind him. He swallowed a lump in his throat...

...The first SUV came to a stop in the desert that night in Egypt. A man placed his feet on the ground and got out of the rear passenger side door. He looked around the worksite curiously and he smiled. This man was the first of Richter's lab partners who would soon be standing behind him at the press conference, after this evening. Behind him, on the other side of the SUV, the other lab partner exited. The two men caught each other's eye in the midst of looking around and the first man smiled at the second, who just stared blankly. He was a bit more skeptical. They turned towards the second SUV which pulled in behind them. The passenger side door opened immediately and Mr. Kitch exited. He was a weaseling little man with a sour look on his face. He adjusted his trench coat like he always did and walked towards them. The back driver's side door of his SUV opened behind him, but he didn't wait for the mysterious man he travelled with to approach the other men.

"This is it!?" He yelled, pointing to the ring.

"Mr. Kitch..." The first lab partner said. "This is what's paying your bills!" He laughed.

A cane hit the desert sand and the dark man in the back seat of the second SUV placed his feet on the ground. He leaned on his cane and stood up out of the car.

He was an old man now. He placed his fedora cap on his head, adjusted the brim and then he began to make his way towards the other three men.

"Don't patronize me Ernest!" Kitch yelled at the man who made the comment. "I'm here to assess if what you're doing here is legit!" He continued.

The man, whose name was Ernest, just smiled and chuckled as Kitch spun around to see the old mystery man approaching.

"I hope you brought us out here for more than a little sightseeing!"

"No, Mr. Kitch..." The old man said, as he looked up. The brim of his fedora cleared his face and revealed it into the light. Paul Ranston, the old schemer looked up at the ring. They were all a good distance back from it still. "...as you can see, this is so much more than a tourist attraction now."

"Let's get started!" Ernest shouted, with a big grin still on his face. "I've been waiting a long time to see this!"...

"Let's get you boys suited up!" One of the technicians hollered at them...

...At the press conference;

"I, uh...I've called the attention of the media today..." Richter finally began. "...not on my own, but, um...by the request of Globe-X corporation."

A slight rise in the chatter broke out.

Richter nervously looked back at his two lab partners. Ernest, the more outgoing one, urged him in gesture, while the other more solemn one just stared blankly.

"Um..." He went on. "...they asked that I address you myself in regards to our project in time experimentation." Richter paused, played with his glasses and rested his hands up on the podium with his elbows locked. He took a long look out towards the reporters and scanned the crowd. "I am pleased to announce..." He continued. "...that we recently scheduled a private test of the machin—"

The room chatter rose higher among the reporters and held the attention of everyone watching. Richter looked around the room and noticed the change in the atmosphere. These people were so hungry for what Jason had to offer and he could tell...

...As they walked towards the entrance, in Egypt, Mr. Kitch looked through his face-mask at the worksite. All he could hear was the sound of his own breath as it fogged up the piece of glass covering his face now. They passed more scientists and construction grunts. In the distance he saw the door to the plastic tunnel leading out towards the ring. The one with the radiation symbol on it...He saw the old man Ranston in front of him, limping without his cane. The physical body he had manifested for himself had grown old now. All part of the facade.

Seven men approached the doors; Mr. Kitch, Ranston, Ernest, the other lab partner, plus the henchman they brought and the two drivers of the SUVs. All of them were wearing white radiation suits and they came to a stop at the airlock.

PPSSSHH!!!

The airlock startled Kitch as it opened. The team of seven entered and began down the long tunnel.

"This was the first one built?" Kitch's muffled voice asked from behind the mask.

"Correct Mr. Kitch." Ranston answered him. "Before these guys came on board." He motioned towards the other two lab partners.

Ernest chuckled. "Impressive isn't it Kitch?" He slapped him on the back and Kitch flinched.

Ernest laughed a little louder. "Easy!" He said.

"How you've managed this far, Mr. Lawrence, is beyond me." Kitch whined, while inspecting his suit for rips.

"Well they haven't managed alone." Ranston said.

"Oh yes." Kitch relied sourly. "I met your prize pony once. In Washington."

"My prize pony?" Ranston scoffed. "I don't know if I'd be calling him that."

"Oh really? The way you go on about him is ridiculous."

Ernest laughed heartily again. "He's got you there, Ranston!" He said. "I don't usually agree with Kitch here, but..."

"Well why wouldn't I?" Ranston chortled. "Mr. Richter has helped me achieve my goals!"

Ernest looked at the other lab partner and they gave each other apprehensive look, while Ranston smirked to himself ahead of them.

"Hmm." Kitch grumbled. "Well, I can't say I was very fond of Mr. Richter."

"He probably wasn't fond of you either." The other lab partner said.

Ernest laughed. "But I wouldn't take offence, Kitch." He said. "He's not too fond of very many."

"So, how many more of these giant air purifiers are there going to be?" Kitch asked rudely.

"Let's just worry about this one for now, Mr. Kitch."

"But, there will be more...right?"...

...the mic squealed at the press conference. "...Uh..." Richter went on. "...we have multiple sites, but...using two in particular we have successfully moved a man across the globe at alarming rate of speed!"

Then the chatter broke into incoherence and Richter was taken a little aback.

At the station; Ridley and I looked at each other with excited grins.

"When was this test?!" One question stood out from the commotion. "Which two sites!?"

"What happened to the man?! Is he alright!?"

Ernest, who was there that day, rushed in front of the mic. "Uh...Dr. Richter will take your questions one at a time, please!!" He said loudly.

Ernest stepped away as the crowd died down a bit and Richter looked out into the crowd. He pointed at one reporter.

"Dr. Richter, you've just told the world that teleportation is possible, how—"

"—uh," Richter cut in. "Not teleportation...actually. We're not stepping through big fields of energy and walking through on the other side..." Richter began defending his work. "This is more exact science. The subject is actually physically moved from point A to B—"

"Where did the subject come and go to?" Another reporter asked out of turn. "How long does it take for the subject to get there?"

"Seconds..." Richter said with a proud little chuckle. "...Is the answer to the second part. And he wasn't just moved a few feet or anything. It was continents. Across the sea! Africa to North America in mere seconds!"

Before he was barely past saying 'North America', the reporters roared into a frenzy of questions.

My eyebrows raised involuntarily and I twerked my neck back. I looked to Ridley who was shaking his head in awe.

"That's crazy, man..." He said...

...In Egypt that evening, Richter's lab partners exchanged a glance at each other. Ernest was beaming with excitement and the other one, simply remained his neutral self. Kitch fidgeted with his suit as the big set of doors opened up. He glanced at the other two who obviously knew what this thing was. He could hear a very loud buzz or humming that began as soon as they had entered the doors.

The team was at the base of the ring they had seen from afar, now looking up at it. Way up. Kitch couldn't even guess how many hundreds of feet the span of the diameter and height was.

"A long time ago!..." Ranston began shouting. "...A great architect named; Imhotep built this place. This place was designed for the pharaohs! Kings of men! The pyramids were designed to be steps...steps—in order that the souls of the dead kings could ascend into the heavens!"

"That's incredible!" Ernest shouted, staring in amazement. "Jay did it...He actually did it!"

"Yes..." the monotone voice of the other partner said in agreement. "It seems he has. Why isn't he here?"

Ranston stood there and marveled at the giant object he was looking up at.

"And now we will use this place," He continued, in a softer tone. "To ascend ourselves—to the apex." He said, as he gazed up at the ring. "And we will be like the great kings..." He finished his speech and looked back at Kitch.

"So Mr. Kitch..." He began. "Do you think your client will be willing to fund us now?"

Ernest and Ranston shared a laugh at his expense while Kitch just stood there in amazement of this thing.

"Th...This is incredible!" He gasped. "Donald's right though, why is Mr. Richter not here?"

"He's working off site." Ranston answered sharply. "In Canada."

Then he gazed up at the ring and smiled. His plans were finally coming to fruition. This was the beginning of what he had come to realize long ago was his chance...

...his chance to *fix* his problems.

The old man sighed a deep breath.

He was darkly invigorated.

Excited,

This was it.

Now it was starting...

..."How do we know you're not just saying this to deter our attention for a while?!" One reporter at the press conference was able to get out amidst the chattering. That was enough to grab Richter's attention and he raised his hand up to quell the crowd.

"I'm glad you asked!" He shouted. He looked behind him as a projected image appeared, floating in the air. It was the logo for the Globe-X Corporation, spinning and it quickly turned into a video clip. "Because we happened to document the testing." Richter added.

A hush fell over everyone who was watching.

The video showed a split screen of the two different places. These two big metal rings were in both images. One was labeled 'Giza' and in the other one, the ring was gargantuan and towering above the Horseshoe Falls in Niagara. They had built it right in the middle of the Niagara River and the waters rushed around the base of it to pour over the edge. Both were humming loudly and there were teams of scientists wearing radiation suits all over. There was a small little metal pod in the centre of the Giza image. It was open and there was a man getting strapped into this thing.

I myself watched intently at the station as they closed the canister and prepped the pod.

Richter had now stepped away from the podium and he joined his colleagues off to the side, where he watched his creation exhibited to the world.

"What's the matter, Jay?" Ernest asked him.

"Haven't you ever showed off your work to anyone?" Richter asked back. "This is my baby, Ernest. And the whole world is watching this..."

"Since when do you care about when anyone in the world thinks?" His other lab partner, Donald, asked in jest.

Ernest gave Donald a little nudge and he shrugged. Richter ignored the comment and watched the reaction of the press in anticipation.

On the video, a scientist pulled down on a lever and the big clamps holding the pod in place were released. It almost looked as if the pod just disappeared. It became a fast motion blur on the screen as it zipped away.

On the left screen only several seconds passed, as Richter promised, before a huge splash exploded out of the water at the base of the falls. The humming stopped immediately and began to wind down to a duller and slower sound.

"The magnet was turned off at this point!" Richter announced, stepping back towards the podium. "We're still trying to develop a better way to slow down the object!" He went on. "But for a first trial, as you can see, we were able to achieve the amazing task of moving our subject from A to B. Note the date and time stamps on both images. Same day...same time...minus the time-zone difference."

"That's friggen' wild!" I said out loud, shaking my head.

The next shot was a rescue operation, pulling the pod out of the water down the Niagara River somewhere and the human subject giving a thumbs up to the cameras.

I let out a slight chuckle. A puff of air more than anything and I shook my head again in amazement.

Clare laughed and looked at Ray.

The reporters all went crazy with questions.
"What's the next steps!?" One asked.
"Uh...well!..." Richter began. "...now we start vigorous testing at the other sites and we get this thing off the ground!"
"Are you saying your close?" A reporter shouted.
"I'm saying..." Richter hesitated. "Yes! Yes we are..."
The press all erupted yet again. It grew too much for Jason so he gave them a wave and walked off with the rest of his team following.

Amidst the crowd; Paul Ranston, the sinister old man, stood and watched his chess piece.
He wore an all-black suit as usual, with his black fedora cap. His goatee was no longer black but grey. He grinned at Richter as he walked off stage with Ernest, Donald, Kitch, and the rest of the group. Something was about to happen, and Paul Ranston was salivating for it!
He couldn't wait.
But he would still have to bide his time.
His phone sounded off and he raised it up to see.
New message from 'W'. It read.
Ranston clicked on the notification and W's message popped up.
'S' watching the conference. Things look good master.
Ranston smiled and typed: ONE STEP CLOSER, W. Then he sent the message and smiled.

CHAPTER SEVEN
Man and Wife

At nightfall that day, I set out on the tip that Bart, the wiry guy from the diner, had given me. In the industrial section of town, amidst warehouses and factories, the mammoth haven of night life stood. The big neon sign flashed: *The Sexrex.*

Bass pumped out of the club as I approached it. I stood across the street, smoking a cigarette and I watched the bouncers let pretty girls in. A buzz rumbled in my pocket and I took out my phone to read the message. Ridley was texting me:

'Hey man. How's everything going? Still thinking about what we talked about in the car. Just checking in dude. Let me know.'

I stared down at my screen and sighed. I almost texted him back but instead slipped my phone back in my pocket and lifted the object in my other hand. I looked down to the gun and just glared at it. I felt the cold steel as I gripped it. I took a long drag off my smoke as it burnt down to the filter, and then I reached behind me and tucked the gun in my waist band. I flicked the nub away and blew the smoke out, and then I stepped off the curb towards the club.

The bouncer put his hand up to stop me but I showed my badge. He looked me up and down like a tough guy then gave me the nod to go past him.

I entered the club and the bass filled my ears. It thumped in my chest as I pushed myself towards the bar.

"You again!?" The bartender playfully hollered at me.

I nodded. "I'll take a beer!"

"What kind?" He asked.

As I sat down on the stool I glanced up and shot him a sarcastic look.

He threw his hands up in jest. "Of course..." He said. "How silly of me!"

A moment later he was slamming my usual honey brewed lager down on the counter and I paid him.

I sipped away on my beer and began scanning the club. I turned my back to the bar and rested on it.

Then I looked up and spotted him.

He was hard to miss.

Sexrex, the man himself, who this club was named after, was towering over everyone else he was with as he appeared at the railing of the balcony.

He placed his large hands to rest on it, and he gave his usual cursory search of the dance floor from behind his sunglasses. I thought he looked right at me and I just stared back.

A tap on the shoulder got my attention. I turned to see the bartender placing a shot down in front of me.

"On the house man!" He said with a smile.

I placed my beer down and took the shot.

"Thanks!"

When I turned again to the balcony, Sexrex was gone. I took a deep breath and then downed my shot. I wiped the drops from my mouth with the shot glass still in my hand, and then I slammed it back onto the bar.

"You want another!?" The bartender asked with a laugh.

I furrowed my brow this time. "You trying to get me drunk!?" I hollered back.

He chuckled. "I see you coming in here!" He said as he walked back over. "You look stressed buddy!" He grabbed the bottle and began to refill my shot. "Cmon! This is Sexrex! Loosen up my friend!"

I chuckled and lifted the shot. I saluted the man and downed it.

Then I returned to my beer and took a long thirst quenching sip. I rested on the bar and began to scan the crowds. His large frame caught my eye again. Now Sexrex was walking the floor with his entourage. I kept my gaze on him and just followed his movements.

The dinosaur part of his name derived from the fact that he was a beastly seven feet tall and he was thick. He wasn't chiseled muscular but you wouldn't want to take a swipe from one of his paws. He was a half black, half Irish mix—an odd combination; that gave him mocha skin with lots of freckles; afro-centric hair, but red. He usually wore flashy three piece suits. Green was his favourite colour and he sported it most of the time. He wore lots of jewelry around his wrist and neck, as well as Celtic rings and a charm bracelet. His face was a hard looking face; protruding jaw, crooked nose from being broken many times and he grew a pointy red goatee. His face was very scarred from all the years of trouble he'd been through and he wore sunglasses all the time which covered a glass eye. The right one got torn out during a bar fight when he was young back in Ireland. He was probably roughly 45-50 years old now.

I took another big swig from my beer and continued to watch him.

Nobody knew his real name; 'Sexrex' was what everybody knew him as. He appeared on the scene a while ago in the entertainment district. He opened up a few night clubs and strip joints in town and he used them to run his other businesses out of; prostitution being the main one. Sexrex dabbled in a bit of everything; drugs, fraud, extortion, you name it. We had busted a few of his little massage parlours but he just opened more once the charges were dealt with. Underbosses and a lot of minions had taken the fall for him on these occasions and he didn't care about them. He always found more pawns to use and more businesses were established quickly. He even provided services to guys who wanted to use the date rape drug against girls. We cracked a place one time, where guys would come in and pay a fee. The waiters at this place would slip the drug in her drink for you and then give you keys to a room. Sexrex was the ultimate pimp. Hence his name, as in Tyrannosaurus Rex; king of the dinosaurs. This guy was king of the seedy underworld and it was his mission to take over the entire city and rule it one district at a time to build his empire.

Watching him, I reached for my gun in my waistband. My anger had grown enough just thinking about what I knew about him—

—"Hey!" The voice of the bartender cut in.

I was jumpy and I snapped my attention to him with wide eyes. My hand quickly slipped back into my lap.

"I thought I told you to start having fun, huh!?" He asked me with a big grin.

I just stared back blankly, still in a bit of an emotional frenzy.

The bartender's face dropped out of a smile. "Holy shit..." He whispered. "I don't envy you cops, pal."

"How did you know I was...?"

"I see everything, pal. All kinds of people. If you ain't a typical Irish flat foot then I'm Santa Claus!"

I sighed and looked down to my drink.

"It's a shitty world my friend!" Said the bartender, throwing up his hands to put the club on display. "Look at where we are here...both of us, ya know what I mean? You look like you've seen a lot of shit."

I looked up at him now with more ferocity. "What would you know about it?" I curled my lip at him.

He sneered back and squinted his eyes. "You judging me?" He asked. "Look, bud, this is a job but it don't mean I like it. You think I like half the shit I see in this place? You of all people must know the kind of person the big guy is. Don't you look at me like that! You're the one who's in here by choice!"

With a grunt I shoved the stool out, and stood to grab him. I clutched his shirt and brought his face to my snarling teeth. I seethed at him.

"You have no idea why I'm here!" I growled. "The things I've done! The things I will do! I'm telling you how it is...pal! You don't look at me like that..."

He stared back at me with wide eyes and swallowed a lump in his throat. "Okay, man, just...take it easy."

I held him in place and reached behind me...

But a moment later I only slapped more money down onto the bar.

"Leave the bottle." I whispered. Then I let him go and slunk back onto my stool. I watched him walk away and I guzzled down the last of my beer. My pocket buzzed with new messages from Ridley but I ignored them and poured myself another shot. Sighing, I lifted the small glass up to my eyes and glared at it.

"What the hell." I stated, and then I downed it, slammed the glass down and began pouring another.

I sucked that one back with eyes shut tight and grunted after it went down. Then I needed to take my phone out to remind myself of something. I scrolled down the messages and read:

'What's going on John?'

'Where are you man?'

'What are you doing?'

I closed the texts and started into my photo gallery. The pictures I was thinking about popped up and I swiped through them obsessively.

A young blonde haired girl was in the picture. She was standing on the street corner where I had taken the pictures in secret. I swiped through a whole series of these, where she stood in scandalous clothes. Soon the pictures got closer in on her face and I cringed again. No matter how many times I looked at these, the condition of her face got me.

I had to put the phone down and I buried my face in my hand. I remembered that year book photo of my high school years. Ridley and I, plus our other buddy Dave, and his little blonde haired daughter; the result of a teenage pregnancy. I ran my fingers through my hair and reached for the bottle again. I poured another shot and gulped it with a grimace, then I picked up my phone.

I swiped past the pictures of this little girl I used to know to see others I had taken that same night. In these pictures she was talking with her handler. Megga, a young wannabe thug who, in the photos, appeared to yell at her, take her money, slap her, and send her back to work. Again my emotions boiled and I looked up from my phone to start scanning the club once more.

I found Sexrex again, standing in the corner with his entourage. He was talking to someone else and when the crowd parted I could see who it was. The girl's handler from the pictures. Megga, the guy I had told Ridley about. He and Sexrex exchanged words and he handed Sexrex a wad of cash. I glared at them both and suddenly remembered the weight of the gun tucked behind my pants. I downed another shot for courage and wiped my lips. My head was starting to feel heavy now. I continued to glare at the two scumbags, trying to build my courage.

I took another shot.

I thought of the blonde girl's face.

I took another shot.

Gunshots filled my memory and I remembered the last face.

I took another shot.

And another.

And another.

With each one my head grew fuzzier and I got woozier. The weight of all my problems consumed me until—

...my eyes slowly opened and the soft orange light of morning poured in through the slivers. My head was pounding though it was quiet where I was now. My whole body ached from the contorted way I was sleeping. I was in my car and once my eyes opened I focused on the Thor hammer dangling from my mirror. The familiar sight of this keepsake snapped me into my surroundings and I sat up with a groan. I rubbed my eyes while I got myself into a half seated position, and then I stopped once I looked into my lap and saw my gun. I jumped a little at the sight of it and just stared for a few moments. I couldn't remember if I had used it, but was horrified at the idea. I grabbed it and hurriedly crammed into the driver's seat. I tossed the gun onto the passenger seat and went to start my car. I stopped though, when I looked through the windshield. Across the street, just outside the club, there was yellow tape and dozens of cops. Media had gathered as well. My heart stopped at the immediate thought that me and my gun might have something to do with this. A loud buzz in my pocket made me jump. Then I realized it was just my phone. I took a breath and sighed it out as it buzzed some more. Then I shakily slid it out to check.

'Seriously, John. Where are you man? What happened last night?'

Ridley was texting me again. I couldn't answer the question, even in my own mind.

I looked back up to the crime scene and knew I had to satisfy myself. After all, I was a cop. I put my gun in the glovebox and stepped out of the car.

I approached the crime scene cautiously, and reached for my badge in my back pocket. As I was taking it out, scanning the crowd of people, another set of eyes caught my attention. A couple of cops were questioning witnesses. The once friendly eyes of the bartender were staring back at me and they were filled with conviction. I slowed my pace down and proceeded with more caution. Then before I could react the bartender was pointing me out.

My heart skipped and I instinctively spun around before the other cops could see my face. I shoved my badge back in my pocket and started to walk away. My heart was pounding and I felt full of guilt without even knowing why! The flush started creeping up my neck and hot blood boiled to the surface. I was in a panicked walk, thinking I was okay until—

—"Hey!!" A voice bellowed behind me.

My pace quickened.

"Excuse me!!" The voice shouted again, and I heard the scraping of jogging feet on pavement.

I walked even faster, if I could, and I pulled my hood onto my head and stuffed my hands in my pockets.

"Sir! Please stop!" The officer shouted, and their pace quickened as well.

I kept walking.

"You! In the hoody!"

"Shit!" I whispered to myself. I dodged around a corner and broke into a sprint.

The two officers began shouting and they started running too. When they turned the corner they saw me taking off down the alley and they began pursuit.

Huffing and puffing, I zoomed past patrons on the street. They were mere *whooshes* in my ear or close calls of collisions. I knocked a few guys cell phones out of their hands when I shoulder checked them and I almost fell when I tried to dodge a mother pushing a stroller with her baby in it.

My heart was certainly beating now; to the point where I thought it would break out of my chest. My muscles screamed and ached and felt as if they were on fire. But police officers are human beings as well, thankfully. They too are subject to the science of human weakness and suffer the same burning of hell fire on their muscles. Amidst my aching gasps for air, I saw an alley up ahead and thought that'd be a good place to duck into. If I was caught, I would have to face my realities, which I imagined now as I ran. I would end up in some court room facing a judge and social workers who plead my case as a sad story. I would be forced to either stay in jail, or take some diversion course involving counselling and therapy. Therapy I didn't want. Through my heaving breaths and gasps I told myself to keep running. *Just keep running John!*

I took a final few glances behind me and the cops were right on me! I dodged left down the alley. I wasn't going to let them get me.

I couldn't stop, I wouldn't...

—*SMACK!!*

The skin on my face felt like a fire! There was pain in my chest and the breath was gone out of my lungs. I had tripped and I rolled over to gasp for air. I knew this was it. I was expecting to hear the shouts of police getting closer to me and see blurry figures appear over me as I stared up into the overcast sky.

I closed my eyes awaiting my pursuers. But they never came.

After several moments had passed, in which those cops should have closed in, I opened my eyes and sat up. The alley way I had turned down was empty; just dumpsters and fire escapes.

Where did they go?

All I could stare at was the opening into the street, backlit by the morning shine. A light at the end of the tunnel. My freedom awaited through that light but...all I could do was sit there, propped up on my elbows, staring at it.

CRASH!

I snapped my gaze up as, through the silence, something had caused a noise at the end of the alley. I looked to see a garbage can knocked over and the round lid rolling towards me. It stopped at my feet as I continued to try and see who did that. I was frozen until I was certain it wasn't the cops.

A figure appeared, silhouetted by the light. He was average height, average build and obviously not a police officer.

Did he see anything? Is he going to alert the police?

As these thoughts rushed in, he began to lean over and pick up the trash off of the ground. In the midst of all that was happening, I couldn't help but think; *what is he doing?* Why would he bother to pick up trash out of the alley? Some of it was dripping wet; that brownish, orange garbage juice leaking off of most of it.

Disgusting.

But there He was, cleaning it all up.

I came to the conclusion that He hadn't seen anything. He must have been some bum just passing through. As I winced through the pain in my body from the fall, and examined my scrapes, I glanced up one more time. I met the gaze of this Stranger and I was able to make out His face. Enough for me to realize I had seen him before. I had seen Him a day earlier when I left my building. I had seen Him many times before as well. He had stepped back into the light more and I caught a glimpse. His face still appeared dark and shaded, but like a film noire shot, the eyes were highlighted now. There they were staring back at me. This *bum*, who I just assumed was passing through, was now staring at me, and I started to think that maybe He did know what was going on here. For the first time over our many encounters, I began to get a weird feeling that this guy was following me around. Our eyes remained locked, even after I tried to peel my gaze away and nothing broke the moment. He straightened up and placed a piece of trash back in the bin, and to my surprise He finally broke the stare and went about picking up more garbage. I tried to move but winced in pain when I felt the sharp pain in my twisted ankle. I glanced around quickly at the alley and then back out to end of my tunnel where The Stranger was still cleaning up. He was just finishing up and He moved the trash bin back into the alley, placing it just inside the corner so that it wasn't sticking out anymore. He placed the lid back on and wiped His hands together with that certain satisfaction of a job well done, and then rested His hands on His hips. Now that He had stepped into the alley a little bit, the way the light was hitting Him was different. He was no longer a silhouette and I could see that He didn't really look like a bum at all. He looked comfortable in His clothes; faded, well-worn jeans but not all torn up or dirty, work boots, white t-shirt, and a simple looking work jacket; displaying marks, stains, and little tears here and there. He appeared to be some sort of worker; not adding 'garbage man' to His resume, I assumed that maybe He was a tradesman...electrician, plumber...carpenter?

    Maybe I was over exaggerating this whole encounter with my own dramatic thoughts. But still...something about this moment wasn't ordinary at all. It never quite was with this guy. Our eyes met again as I limped towards the street. This time I averted my gaze back and forth; down towards the ground as I walked, and then up quickly several times to check if He was still looking at me. I wanted to ask Him; *what's your problem? Why are you staring at me?*

    But I knew.

    Somehow I knew.

    I knew that He knew...

    I knew exactly why He was staring at me; He was able to see through all of my nonsense and fronts, as if He knew every wrong thing I'd ever done. But He was staring at me, with a smirk on His face that wasn't smug at all—no—He wasn't judging me, or mocking me...I got the sense that He was saying *you're welcome*. I'll never know for sure what He did, but this whole moment in history, as time stood still for the two of us, and as I passed Him in imagined slow motion—I knew that He had seen me running from the police, He had seen that they were falling behind, that I was getting tired and couldn't keep it up anymore, He was watching as I entered the alley—and that thud or tug on my ankle; what was that? Was that Him? He somehow diverted the police, that much was clear. But why trip me? If He was going to lead the cops astray and me getting arrested wasn't His intention...then why stop me and send me barreling into the concrete?

Then...I had no idea.

Thinking back on it now, I know He was trying to show me; I can stop you...or, I could let you get caught, whatever variation of that you can muster. He wanted me to know that He could and had the option of doing both; turning me in, or letting me go.

He chose to let me go.

And how do I know all of this? How was I certain that my suspicions were true? Just before I departed from that fork in the road, I had stepped out into the light of the street. I stood there staring at this Stranger. I was cautiously looking around for police but there were none to be found. But when I looked back to The Stranger He didn't say anything. It was obvious to Him that I was searching the area for cops, and He was almost kind of half laughing at me. A final gentle look He gave me made me think He was saying; *relax, I took care of it*. The kindness in His eyes is what I couldn't get over...*why did He help me?* I looked down at my hands again and clenched them trying to stretch the skin back to normal and relieve some of the pain from the scrapes. When I touched my tender cheek I flinched because it was still on fire. I looked once again to the man who had saved my life.

I nodded at Him and I took a chance. I said: "thanks." And I stared at Him awaiting a response.

He just nodded at me and winked. "You're welcome." He said gently, confirming everything.

Quickly, I looked forward out into my city. I reached into my pants pocket and dug out a squished pack of cigarettes. I sighed, realizing they were all ruined and broken from falling on them. I heard a slight chuckle from behind me and I looked back to see The Stranger smirking. I gave Him an unimpressed look and pulled out the only undamaged cigarette in the pack and placed it in my mouth. I would normally toss the garbage away but my arm stopped short. I looked back at Him with the pack still in my hand. He chuckled and then He lifted the trash can lid and gave me an inviting look. I sighed and walked over to toss the garbage in the bin, with the smoke still hanging out of my mouth. I looked at Him with a cheeky grin and He placed the lid back on. Then I walked away, to avoid the awkward truth of this moment. I walked back to the edge of the sidewalk and reached for my lighter. I clinked open the zippo top and flicked the wheel several times before the flame appeared. I cupped the smoke and flame to light it and then snapped the zippo shut. I held on to the lighter and looked up to be met with a big bill board. It was advertising some new lifestyle product. All I remember was the words that popped out;

THIS IS NOT YOUR LIFE

I pulled in a deep drag off the smoke as I stared at those words. I blew the smoke out and then looked back towards The Stranger...

He was gone...

Another drag off the smoke and I chuckled. I tried to shove the lighter in my pocket but dropped it. I bent over to pick it up but had to do double take when I saw something on the ground. A small item was left behind from the tipped over trash. With a furrowed brow I placed the smoke in my mouth and reached across to snatch up the item. I rolled it around in my fingers and brought it to my field of vision. It was a small wooden chess piece. The knight.

"Hhmm." I murmured past the cigarette. Then I rose into a stand again and palmed the knight in my fist. I blew my drag out and turned around, only to be met by a sight that startled me.

The Stranger was still standing at the end of the sidewalk, making sure I found that token. Once He saw that I had it he raised His eyebrows at me and then he took off for good.

That was it. Little did I know; that day forever changed the course of the future—

And the present—

And the past...

CHAPTER EIGHT
Strange Sights

Meanwhile that morning,
Clare lifted her eyes to the sky when she heard the Celtic hum begin.
The bagpipes rose, lifting their song to the sky.
She stared at the coffin, remembering a very different ceremony a mere week prior to the one she sat in now.

In the other one, Clare was standing at attention, up on a stage with Ray standing beside her. They were standing in front of the White House. A sea of onlookers gathered in the grass and beyond the fence.

Ray was sitting beside her in the other. They were both wearing black, to match what the rest of the attendees had on, and they all formed a big dark splotch on a backdrop of dying grass and falling leaves.

The bagpipes sang, filling Clare with pride...

...Filling her with Sadness, and regret. But she didn't cry. She listened to the priest give a eulogy about a great man; a *leader*. It was a small ceremony, family and close friends only at the cemetery, compared to the massive turn out at the public viewing earlier, which gave a city the chance to say goodbye to its mayor.

Clare and Ray watched as the pipe band marched down the aisle towards the stage they stood on and Ray was nudging Clare's arm with his elbow. Clare was trying to look serious, but she couldn't help but smirk.

Clare was frowning at the other ceremony. She was staring at the coffin.

Ray was marching to centre stage. Clare was at attention and had to keep her eyes forward. Out of the corner of her eye she watched Ray bow towards the president who wreathed his neck with a medal of honour. Clare was getting goose bumps, along with her butterflies. She couldn't believe this was happening.

"Sean A. Mash. A beloved Mayor, in this great city of Baltimore. Your deeds, spoke louder than your words. You will be missed greatly." The priest closed.

"Agent Clare Mash." The announcer said. "For your hard work, for your determination, for your bravery, and your courage. This medal of honour is presented to you, on behalf of every American citizen, and on behalf of all nations!"

The president of the United States stepped in front of her, and smiled at her. She beamed back, not able to contain herself.

"Your country owes you a debt Mrs. Mash." He said. "Your country, and the world."

"Thank you sir." She said, very professionally, and she saluted the president.

Clare remained sitting there, staring at the coffin. Replaying the video clips over in her head of the old man being shot. Another twenty-one gun salute for the Mayor began.

BANG!...

The first shot thundered making her jump. Clare began to think about her father and when she first heard the news.

After their award ceremony, the team had gone out for drinks to celebrate. As Clare watched the faces of her teammates smiling, she remembered what having a normal life felt like.

*BANG!...BANG!...*the shots at the funeral interrupted her thoughts.

But she still remembered that night at the bar. It carried on and Clare felt an ever growing sense of relief that Joseph Kovacs was out of her life for good. She kept thinking about how she could work on our marriage now; get it back to the way it used to be.

BANG!...

I was working the overnight shift tonight, but she couldn't wait to see me the next day. She was happy.

BANG!...

The soldier's guns shot into the air as Clare continued to recount the video over and over.

BANG!...

Each time the twenty-one guns fired she imagined the bullets hitting the old man and his body crumpling to the ground.

BANG!...

The celebration was over. The team all exchanged handshakes, high-fives, and embraces for a job well done. One by one they started to leave and go home, leaving Mark, Ray and Clare to walk out together.

BANG!...

Clare couldn't shake the images from the video and she just stared at the coffin.
BANG!...

The three agents were leaving the bar in a happy state. They were laughing at something completely unrelated to Kovacs, because they could now. As they went their separate ways to their vehicles they too embraced; especially Ray and Clare.

BANG!...

Clare turned towards her car and stopped, startled. There were two men standing by her car in long trench coats and hats. Clare knew these guys...they were cops and longtime family friends. Clare had known them long enough to know that the looks on their faces were saying; 'bad news' and her smile faded.

BANG!...
Clare still watching the old man die in her head.

After they had delivered the terrible news to Clare she shook her head *no*. As they were celebrating; other things were going on in the city.

That night,
In another bar,
Three men, including the Mayor, exited and were headed home...
They were ambushed, and they were all shot...

Ray and Mark returned to Clare's side after the men gave her the news.

BANG!
The final shot rang out at the funeral, echoing through the air.
"Clare?" Ray said.
Clare came too and looked around. All the guests were standing and she was the only one still sitting.
"You ok?" Ray asked.
Clare gazed at the coffin for several moments, and then shook her head silently. She stood slowly and walked over to the coffin. Placing her hand on it and pausing for a moment's silence, she closed her eyes to say a little prayer. Then she opened her eyes and remained looking down at the coffin.
"Bye Dad."
Clare glanced at the priest and gave him the go ahead. The people closest to Clare's father, the Mayor of Baltimore, watched as the coffin was lowered into the earth to the tune of *Amazing Grace* on the bagpipes.

As the band played and the city said goodbye to its leader, Clare glanced, probably to look for me and if I was going to show up.

But...In the distance,
On top of a hill,
He was standing there...
There He was, 'that guy'.

Clare had seen him before, several times throughout her life. He was a simple looking man, though it was hard to tell what He was wearing; a pair of slacks and a *blue collared* shirt tucked into them. In fact He looked like any other average Joe you might see walking down the street.

But she didn't know who He was,
What His name was,
Where He came from...nothing.
A Stranger...

Clare could never pin point where she knew Him from, but He did have something very familiar about Him. *What was He doing here?* She thought. *Maybe He just knows my Dad and came to pay His respects?* She told herself...anything to divert how weird it was to think that maybe this guy was watching her. But she didn't think it was coincidence...especially when the man smiled at her. She looked away immediately, pretending she didn't see that. But her curiosity made her look back several moments later.

He was *gone*.

* * *

Clare sat on our couch in the dark, with only a glass of wine and a notepad journal. She turned to this journal every time she saw The Stranger...at the top of the journal she had made a heading; STRANGER SIGHTINGS, and there was an extensive list of the many times He had popped up in her life too—

—The big door of our loft squealed open, and Clare quickly hid the journal. Light poured in from the hallway into the dark living space, glistening a deep red off of Clare's wine glass. She swirled it around and took a sip. She had turned the lights off and was lying on the couch to wind down after the funeral. I had just opened the door and was entering the loft. She lay there listening to my footsteps and keys jingling.

The lights popped on and I saw her on the couch.

"Oh. Sorry." I dimmed the lights down duller. "I didn't know you were home."

"Where were you today?" Clare asked, with an annoyed tone.

A rush of doom came over me when I remembered the funeral. The little noises that I was making stopped, and there was silence. I had my back to her in the living room and I was in the kitchen.

"I was at work."

"You couldn't get the day off?" She asked. "Today, of all days."

I shook my head and sighed a deep breath out through my nose.

"C'mon Clare." I started. "You know why I didn't come...Your father—."

"Your feelings about my father have nothing to do with it." Clare began to raise her voice. "I had to rely on Ray to comfort me."

A stab of anger cut into my guilty feelings. Now I spun around to face her. "Are you sure you didn't enjoy that?"

"Ray's my partner—."

"I'm your partner!" I said, now raising my voice. "At least...I was, I...When did we stop trusting each other?"

"You're never around!"

"Me?! Before last week all you could say was Kovacs, Kovacs, Kovacs!"

"He was an international terrorist! It's my job!"

"And I supported that! But don't spout off speeches about 'not being around' Clare! You know as well as I do how that case consumed you...but I understood...I knew why you needed to catch him."

"That's not the point. I needed you today."

There was a pause in the dialogue.

"Ok..." I started. "But what about when you don't need me Clare?"

She lowered her gaze and fidgeted with her wine glass, swirling the liquid around, hypnotizing herself with the red whirlpool.

"What about when I need you?" I continued. "I have needed you Clare...for a long time now. I've been going through things too. Things that I haven't been able to talk to you about. I'm sorry I didn't show up to your Dad's funeral. But I wasn't the man's favourite person, you know that. I couldn't—."

"You're being selfish." Clare cut in. "Whatever's happened in the past...Kovacs is behind bars now...he'll be executed after his hearing. I was going to come home the night my dad died...the night he was murdered, and I was going to apologize for everything. I was—am willing to make this work again."

"But now you have a new 'bad-guy' to catch." I replied. "You don't think I've seen that other box of files you bring home? 'The Baptist'?" I swallowed a nervous lump when I said that. Clare couldn't make eye contact with me now. She knew I was right. She thought she could carry on, but secretly hunt down her father's killer. But hearing my words, she realized that she would get just as obsessed, if not more with this new case.

"I could take a cushier assignment." She offered. "I could go behind a desk, or back to watching surveillance tapes."

"I'm not asking you to do that."

"I didn't say you did. I want that."

"But that's not you Clare. We've been through this. You tried that, but you couldn't resist. Ever since I've known you, you've been doing this sort of work."

"I could paint again. We could go back to the beginning."

"Clare...you will always want to catch the bad-guys. You don't think I get it? Me of all people; the talks we've had...the things we've shared. Believe it or not, I'm probably the only one who understands you. No matter how hard you try, you can't help it."

There was a long silence.

"What are we supposed to do now then?" Clare asked me.

I stood there with nothing to say. As much as I was right, she was right too. All of the points I was making were hitting home, but this comment from her hit me hard back. What *were* we supposed to do? After a marriage and everything we'd been through. After Kovacs, and now her father's murder. *How do you just forget about everything and go back to life before?* I had been struggling with lots of things while Clare went through her own struggles. Things she had no idea about, that I wanted to share with her...but couldn't.

"I don't know." I stated. Then I decided to go out on a limb and do something crazy. "I love you." Something we hadn't said to each other in a long time. Clare perked up and met my eyes with hers.

"I—." She did love me. I knew it. She did. But the words seemed so surreal now. "I love you too." She said.

I released my breath that I was holding and a smile appeared on my lips. It was a relief to hear her say that.

There was nothing really else to say and a deep silence rang very loudly. Clare sipped away on her wine and just stared at her old painting on the wall. I stared around the loft while my mind wandered to things I had been hiding from her lately. From Ridley too. From everyone...my mind was still racing, trying to remember what I had gotten involved in last night at the Sexrex. As much as I really loved having this rare moment with my wife, my life events were consuming my mind—

—the sharp clink of her wine glass snapped me back when she put it down. When I looked over she was getting up off the couch and she walked over to me and stopped.

We stared at each other awkwardly for a few moments and we actually cracked warm, remorseful smiles at one another. I knew she meant it when she said she loved me.

But I was afraid.

"Goodnight, John." She said softly.

I sighed. "Goodnight."

She reached for my hand as she walked past me and only the tips of our fingers brushed gently when I reached apprehensively back. After she was gone I longed to hold her hand tight, but it was too late and I heard the metal sounds of her feet climbing to stairs to our room.

I stood there for another few moments until I forced myself to move. I went to the living room and folded the blanket Clare was using. I straightened the throw pillows and picked up her wine glass.

At the right moment, I glanced to the left and caught a glimpse under the couch. I stopped when I saw the note book Clare had hid under there.

I reached under and fished it out.

I looked up to the upper balcony in the loft and saw Clare getting ready for bed.
I knew I shouldn't.
I sat down on the couch with the notebook in hand and I just stared at it.
Then after a few moments I cracked it open anyways and my eyes feasted on what was in it.
I read all the notes written about this strange man Clare had kept seeing. I stopped with a gasp and looked up with my mouth open.
"No..." I whispered in awe. "There's no way..."
I turned greedily back to the book and began reading all of the dates she had written. I turned page after page, unfathomably. My heart was racing and my brain was ready to explode.
Is it possible? I thought.
Then I turned the last page I needed to.
My heart skipped and my stomach flipped.
I was now looking at the sketch of The Stranger Clare had drawn.
His simple and friendly face had been perfectly captured, enough for me to recognize Him as the same man I had been seeing too! In big bold letters above her sketch, Clare had scratched the name we all came to adopt for Him. After this day I just started referring to Him according to how she had named Him: THE STRANGER.
I suddenly reached into my pocket and pulled out the thing The Stranger had made sure I found. I rolled the little wooden knight around in my fingers, and I read the other statement Clare had written:
WHO ARE YOU????...

* * *

1987.
Roll back the numbers to day 3,441.
Jason Richter was 20 years old.

"You will be amazed!" The young Jason declared to the gathering crowd. "As I make that metal weight..." He pointed dramatically to the other end of the copper piping he was standing at. "30 feet away...to instantaneously whip across this line and make contact with these magnets!"
Jason had been entering science fairs and expos ever since he spawned his amateur machine in the basement. Now he pointed behind him at a larger and improved design.
He turned on his amplifier; capable of producing higher voltage than his previous car battery and turned each knob up to 'MAX'. He could hear the buzz of electricity, and he smiled at his audience, raising his eye brows up and down.

Everyone watched in amazement as Jason flicked the on switch which turned everything on at once.

ZZZZZZAAP!! SSSSHING!! CLAAANG!!

Applause followed the successful experiment, and Jason took a bow. He began to answer many questions about how it worked.

"Folks." He began. "I've shown you that it's very possible to move an object from point 'A' to point 'B' using this technology...which, isn't really technology at all is it? This is just simple physics people! Modified, amplified...its true potential tapped into! I believe it's very possible to extend this principal across vast amounts of not only physical space...but across space...and time!"

Pause for effect.

Crickets.

This is where Jason usually lost people, and the crowd started to dissipate.

* * *

Frustrated, Jason usually ended up behind a table at every fair. He stewed about why the people wouldn't just hear him out.

"Hello there." A man said, interrupting his thoughts. He startled Jason and his pencil snapped.

Jason looked up from his notes to see a Strange man standing on the other side of the display table.

"Hi." He replied. The Stranger was a simple and ordinary looking man to Jason, wearing a plain suit to blend in.

"That was a very interesting presentation Mr. Richter." The Stranger said.

"Thank you. I usually lose everybody when I get to the time travelling part." Jason laughed a little embarrassed chuckle.

"This is quite something." The man said, motioning to Jason's machine behind him.

"Oh...thanks." Jason said looking down at his notes.

"People are funny aren't they?" The Stranger asked.

"I'm sorry?" Richter queried back.

"People...they will only believe something up to a certain point won't they?"

Richter chuckled nervously. "Well...I don't particularly care for people all that much to be honest."

"I've had many conversations with people in my years." The Stranger went on. "For example, people will watch a television show and get heavily involved in its plot-line."

Richter started to get rather intrigued by this man.

"I hear ya." He said excitedly. "There's been so many sci-fi shows in which, at the start, the audience knows something is going on...something beyond the norm. This is the kind of stuff that makes it interesting and gets you hooked isn't it? In fact, I'm of the view that it's potentially *more* of a let-down when the explanation is too simple!"

The Stranger smiled. "The man behind the curtain theory..." He said.

"We want to be perplexed." Richter continued. "I mean...why else do these people come to these science fairs? We need the explanation of something to be *para*-normal...but only up to a certain point, am I right?"

The Stranger smiled again. "Absolutely." He said. "I've seen dedicated viewers of TV shows get all bent out of shape when the explanation to the mysteries were something supernatural or even spiritual for that matter."

"But wait a minute—" Jason cut in eagerly. "Didn't they know it was something beyond normal realms driving the plot? So what gives?"

They both shared a laugh until it died down.

"How old are you son?" The Stranger asked.

"Uh...I'm twenty."

"Just twenty? How long have you been doing this now?"

"Um...let's see...since I was about ten."

"My goodness! Most other kids your age are out playing sports or something. And here you are!"

Jason chuckled nervously and pushed up his glasses. "Well," he began. "I uh...I never saw the point to be honest. I mean, I did go through a stage at first where I tried to do the whole scene and 'be cool' but after not really doing well I uh... just stopped."

The Stranger nodded along and smiled. He opened his mouth to speak but Richter had the urge to keep talking.

"And it wasn't even really because of the fact that other kids would laugh and point, or because girls wouldn't pay attention to me, you know? I just didn't like that feeling of losing. I hate it actually." And he chuckled nervously again. He hadn't been looking at the man this whole time but he raised his eyes now to see him smiling.

"Uh...sorry, sir..."

"No, it's ok," The Stranger said. "I get it. I mean, it's a bit warped, but it makes sense why you wouldn't involve yourself in it."

Jason shrugged and pushed his glasses up again.

"You're something special Jason." The Stranger told him. "I think your work is going to be quite important in the future."

He was so pleasant to Jason. He really liked The Stranger's honesty and gentleness. Most of all He made him feel proud when He acknowledged his specific skills and gifts. Having someone affirm his worth meant a lot to Jason.

"Jason." The man went on. "My name is Gerald Feinberg."

Gerald Feinberg? Richter thought in his head. *That sounds made up to me...*

"I represent a group of people from...well; to be frank...I work for the government..." The Stranger said. "A very special group of the government that is researching things that are right up your alley. It's part of my job to travel the country in search of new...talent."

Jason's heart was pounding. He couldn't believe what he was hearing.

"Jason, I'd like to go back to my superior and tell him; that I've found someone very special. Someone who could change the way the world sees things."

Jason was beside himself. He didn't know what to do. He'd been planning something with these tests but he was never really sure what to do with it when it came. Here it was right in front of him for the taking.

"Are you interested in a job son?" The Stranger asked.

"I...I...uh...I'd...have to think about it sir." He got out.

The Stranger smiled. "Ok...if you think about it, here's my card." He placed it down in front of him on the table and they exchanged a glare. "I think you could do some real good Jason...It's your choice."

Jason was in shock. He couldn't move his mouth to say anything. He picked up the card and stared at it. A simple white card with the logo for a company named *'GLOBE-X'*.

"How am I supposed to find you?" He asked, not looking up. "There's no name on..."

When he looked up, The Stranger was gone...

His eyes then dropped down to the table and he furrowed his brow.

The Stranger had left Jason something too.

A small token.

Jason put the card down and reached for it with his other hand.

He brought the little piece of carved wood in front of his face.

A chess piece.

The bishop...

CHAPTER NINE
Those Happier Times

"Saddle up!" Ridley hollered as I shut my door and put my seatbelt on. "You ready partner?" He asked.
I turned my fresh face towards him with a goofy smile. My goofy, still new on the job smile. Before the world had broken me.
2037. Reset my clock back now.
Let me go back now and tell you how I got the way I did—well...how the feelings that were always there grew and how I was pushed over the edge.
"What's on tap for today?" Ridley asked me as we pulled out of the garage.
"Well, let me see here, partner." I clicked on the in car projection system.
The technology had come a long way since 2015 when I was born. We weren't quite at flying cars, power laces, or hover boards yet...but whoever comes up with this stuff had given mankind some pretty cool new stuff. The same tech from Clare's office but miniaturized. To give you an example; the lens was facing Ridley (he must have been the last one to look at it) so I raised up my hand and made a pinching motion with my fingers, as if I was grabbing the corner of the 'monitor' and I was able to turn the images towards me.
I looked up from the monitor to see the other squads leaving. I flung two fingers off the top of my head in a casual salute as we left the station to start our watch.
"What time is that detail?" Ridley asked.
"Not till eleven. So...we have time to clear a few of these calls." I began to scroll through the list on my screen.

Ridley and I went about our morning clearing a few simple calls, no arrests. We just cruised around for a while chatting.
"Did you see the price of gas this morning?" Ridley asked.
"Yah man, that's crazy...good thing I walk to work." I laughed.
"Oh yah, lucky you! I can't imagine what our parents had to go through buddy. Back before they came up with these new machines. Can you fathom having to fill your entire tank with gasoline? Psh! I'm so glad they figured out the triune system. I remember sitting in the back seat of our van as a kid and watching my dad put like ninety bucks in! Ninety bucks!"
"You get all upset when we fill the cruiser up to twenty." I cut in.
"Well yah, dude! Of course I do! You don't think they could perfect this system and make the entire car run on fusion instead of thirty percent? They need us to keep buying gas so they can keep drilling for oil man!"
I chuckled to myself and shook my head. Ridley was a bit of a conspiracy theorist. He was a very intelligent guy and he knew his stuff so I rarely got drawn in to *political* debates with him.

As I stared out my window, watching the streets of my city, my mind wandered, like it usually did, back to thoughts of the world as a whole and the state it was in. It started in my teens like I already told you at the beginning. But as much of an eager young man I was at this time; thinking *I* could change the world by becoming a police officer, *being* a cop opened my eyes to things. That seed was being watered more and more.

We stopped at a light and I heard the faint and muffled sound of a male's voice bellowing. I looked around and quickly noticed a wild looking man on the street corner. His hair was a mess and he was wearing ratty clothes. He was draped with two pieces of plywood. A sandwich board sign that had those old fashion apocalyptic words written on it, in big black letters;

THE END IS NIGH!

He was ringing a big bell in his hand and shouting.

"Check this guy out." I said as I rolled the window down to hear him.

"Behold!" He raved. "The word of God!"

"Why are these guys always so crazy?" I asked Ridley. "They're not all like this are they?"

"Thus saith Jehovah," the fanatic went on. "Behold, I will raise up against Babylon, and against them that dwell there, a destroying wind."

"And why do they always talk about Babylon?" I asked. "I thought Babylon was destroyed already, isn't it Iraq now?"

"Holly goes to church." Ridley said. "Babylon was responsible for obliterating the Jews and hauling them all away from their home country. But when these guys say Babylon they mean it more as a metaphor or something. Like it's a symbol for the state of the world. It represents the age of evil and corruption, something like that."

That little history lesson actually intrigued me and I gave a little impressed nod as I continued to watch the street preacher.

The light changed and Ridley pressed on the gas. I watched the crazy street preacher as we drove off. He saw me and stared right at me as he yelled;

"Babylon will fall! Babylon the great! Babylon will fall!"

As we got far enough that it hurt my neck to crane it anymore, I looked back to the front and gave my head a shake.

"Joseph Kovacs sure made this world a different place eh?" I stated.

"A scary place." Ridley said.

"The world was always a scary place, Rid. People just felt safer before."

"People were always scared, man."

"Not like this, dude. I think the Bear's attack on the Vatican a few years ago changed the game. The church was a symbol of hope and faith for so many, and this *man* has crumbled the religious power to a pile of rubble. Where do they turn to now? This guy!?" I asked dramatically, pointing back with my thumb in the direction of the street preacher.

"The world goes through periods of extremes though, John." Ridley said. "This is just ours. I mean c'mon, remember in school learning about September 11th 2001...it was no more impacting on our lives as World War II would have impacted our parents' life. I'm not trying to lessen the seriousness of these events in any way. I'm just saying that people very quickly move on to the next event of the week."

Ridley looked at me with a goofy grin. "You should be back there with that guy, man!" He jabbed.

I laughed out loud. "Yah right!" I said. "Can you imagine me...preaching from street corners?"

"I just know that you've got a real hate on for this world." Ridley said.

"I don't hate the world, man!"

"Sure you do! Ever since high school you've had these...feelings, or...whatever they are."

"Yah but that doesn't mean I hate everything!"

"Hello darkness my oooooold frieeeeeend..." Ridley sang to mock me.

"Stop! I'm not depressed! Maybe I was in high school, but I'm a grown ass man now. I've gotten my shit together. I'm not some gothic, emo kid who talks in a monotone voice and combs his hair in his face and stuff, and wears all black..." I trailed off as I looked down to my uniform.

Ridley noticed too and made a sarcastic face looking at my uniform too.

I laughed out loud again. "You know what I mean!" I scoffed. "I love life Rid...you know I do. Just because I'm angry with the way the world is doesn't mean I'm a pessimist. I'm a normal guy just like you. Look at that girl over there!" I said pointing to one that caught my eye. "I think she's hot! She tempts my loins if you know what I mean..."

Ridley laughed.

"I like beer, I like sex, I like my coffee with honey." I said holding up the cup that I had in the car. "I like singing in the car when I'm by myself. I belt it! I like driving with the windows down, I like hamburgers...I like this!" I said, slapping Ridley in the arm. "I like driving around and talking about life with my friend. I love life, dude!"

Ridley smiled and nodded along as he started to understand.

"I just get pissed off when crime and...the selfishness...the evil of other's interferes with these simple things that...whoever the hell is up there, gave us to enjoy. It's because I love life so much that I'm so passionate about it."

"I know, man." Ridley said. "I get you. Buddy, you have a Thor hammer hanging from your mirror in your car for god sakes! I get it man. You wanna save the world...I wouldn't have hung around you so much if I wasn't of similar thinking, dude."

"Exactly!" I exclaimed. "Don't you remember when we were kids buddy? Sitting around, talking about how we were gonna change the world?"

"And here we are..." Ridley said in an over exaggerated voice.

"Yes! Here we are!"

Ridley sighed and dropped his sarcastic face. He thought for a brief second. "You've heard of this Dr. Richter guy?" He asked.

"Yah. Of course. I follow his hashtag!" I laughed.

"*That* guy is gonna change the world, dude! All the stuff we never dreamed was possible... he's gonna do it..."

"See, there's the difference...I'm not willing to sit around and wait for him to do it."

"John...you are much more of an extremist, but..." He trailed off, chuckling.

I chuckled too. "I'm just saying Rid...these are dangerous times we live in. It feels like we're standing on a knife's edge, man! Who's gonna do something about all of it?"

"And lucky us..." Ridley said looking at me. "These are the streets you and I get to police every day."

I looked at him and smirked. "Well it's a good thing we're the goon squad then!" I said.

Ridley laughed. "You just want people to call us that." He said.

"It'll stick." I said. "You'll see."

We pulled our car into city hall and I threw my head back to finish off my second coffee of the day.

"I'm not looking forward to this." I told Ridley. "I can't wait until we're not the rookies anymore, and we stop getting these stupid assignments."

"You're just nervous because of your little office crush." Ridley made fun of me.

"Aw, shut up man!" I told him, and I threw my empty cup at him. He laughed out loud.

"Hey, Hey, Hey man! Watch it, you're gonna get honey all over me." Ridley said as he picked up the cup out of his lap and looked in it. "You and your weird coffee."

We parked our cruiser and approached in front of city hall where a crowd of people were busy setting up for the day. An audio visual team was laying down cables and running wires for microphones and speakers. We looked around and saw a protective fence, blocking a small group of protesters that would soon grow. Ridley and I walked up to a man who looked like he was in charge of something; he was holding a clipboard. People with clipboards always know what they are doing.

"Uh, excuse me?" I asked.

The man with the clipboards turned around and saw us.

"Ah!" he said. "There you are officers. They need you in the mayor's office."

"Thank you." I told him, and Ridley and I walked up the stairs inside city hall.

I knocked on the door to the mayor's office and we poked our heads in slowly.

"Ah! Come in constables!" He boomed, getting up from his desk.

Sean Ahab Mash.

Mayor of Baltimore

He was a large man. Not tall, but wide. Not fat, just...large, and not muscular. He had light hair that he parted to the side and wore glasses that rested on his large nose. They were covering his small beady eyes that almost closed shut when he laughed. He was laughing now when we walked in. A deep bellowing laugh that we could hear all the way down the hallway as we approached his office. He reminded me of the way the ghost of Christmas present is always portrayed in movies.

Who knows what he was laughing at, but everyone else in the room, his staff, was laughing along with him, as most people did. His large mouth was open, baring his perfect teeth, as he finished his laughter with a few more bursts of ha's. He motioned for us to enter and we stepped in.

"Morning officers." Another voice said. I looked over and saw a man who we didn't notice at first slide past us and smile politely. He was on his way out as we came in, then he was gone down the hallway. Something about that guy seemed so familiar but I didn't pick up on it then.

"Come in, Come in." The mayor stood up from his desk and walked around it, extending his hand to Ridley.

"Welcome officers!" He bellowed as Ridley returned his handshake. "It's always nice to see fresh new faces in my office. I get a new crew of you guys every day!" He was still smiling. He usually looked like he was smiling or about to break out in laughter.

He turned my way and extended his hand.

I reached out and grasped it, feeling his firm grip. "Good morning Mr. Mayor." I said as we shook.

"Good morning, officer...Revele." He glanced at my name tag, placed his other big mitt on top of our handshake and gave it a final shake.

"And officer...Simmons" He said to Ridley, glancing at his name tag. "You guys are from the same station as my daughter." He continued loudly, pointing his sausage finger back and forth between us.

"Yes sir" I said, nervously smirking. He didn't even say her name and I got all shy about it. This is what she did to me. I could see Ridley, out of the corner of my eye, laughing at me silently.

"It should be an easy morning sir." He said to change the subject and rescue me from my awkwardness.

"Oh, yes! I'm not worried about them." He bellowed motioning outside with his mitts. "It was their idea." He said, motioning to the other staff in the room, which I began to notice now.

Especially these two big guys who stood at either side of his desk. They looked familiar to me too. I think I had seen them on TV, escorting the mayor. But seeing them in the office and the way they were smirking at Ridley and I was weird. They were too well dressed to be from a hired security company, plus they were acting too casual. One was half sitting on the corner of the desk with his hands folded in his lap and the other one was standing with his hands in his pockets and one of his legs slacked so he was leaning a bit. I began to get an awkward feeling being in this office.

"I guess you guys will be escorting me around today huh?" Mayor Mash laughed. "Should be fun!" He raised his eyebrows and looked right at me. I wasn't sure, at the time, what he was suggesting. "I always have a good time with you guys." More laughing. He didn't stop. One might get the impression he was jolly.

"Can I trouble you guys for a drink?" He asked as he made his way back to his desk. Ridley and I looked at each other. "I like to have a little liquid courage before these things." He said, followed with a belly laugh. He leaned down and opened a drawer in his desk, and he placed three glass cups on the desk with a clink. He was looking at us, trying to read our reactions I assume. I can't speak for Ridley, but I tried to look as neutral as possible. I didn't need the attention of being involved in a scandal (not that this was that big a deal, after all; it's not like I didn't drink…I could see his point as he was about to give a big speech…I could let this one go). He thudded the bottle of scotch onto the desk and straightened up.

"No thank you sir." Ridley said for us. "We're on duty."

He looked at us for a moment and smiled. I don't know if Ridley saw it—but I noticed that he very slightly glanced at our shirt cameras. Then he twisted the cap off the bottle and broke his gaze with us.

"So, how long have you boys been on then?" He asked with a smile.

"Uh…just nine months sir." I replied.

He pointed the now open bottle our way. "Nine months! Pretty fresh eh? Hwah! Hwah! Hwah!" He laughed as he poured the alcohol into a glass.

I laughed along nervously. "Yes sir. But Ridley and I, we love it so far."

"Pretty good payout huh boys?" He laughed louder now…if that was possible, and he placed the bottle back onto the desk.

Ridley and I glanced at each other. "Yes sir, it's not bad." Ridley said to him. Picking up his glass he said "I bet your ladies are happier, am I right?"

"Yes sir." Ridley said with a smile.

"Ah…I don't really do it for the pay sir." I blurted out.

"No girlfriend then eh?" The mayor deduced, taking a swig from his glass. He stared at me with a mouthful of scotch and he swallowed. "What *do* you do it for then son?"

I hesitated and cocked my head to the side a little, pondering if I should bore this public official with my story. He didn't really care. But something told me, in his tone of voice, that he *was* fishing for something. "Well, sir. I guess I hit a point in my life where I was well aware of the world's problems and finally wanted to do something about it instead of complaining from the sidelines."

The mayor's face changed somehow. He was still smiling, but he was speechless and there was a long pause. "Oh." He finally said. He took another sip of his scotch. "Folks! I guess the old west ain't dead after all!" He said, piping back up to his usual self. He looked at me, and I dare say he looked a tad bit worried. He was staring, as if he was trying to size me up.

I just stared back,

I didn't want to be rude.

"We got ourselves a cowboy here." He said with a flashy grin. "That'll change son." He slapped my shoulder. "Hwahahaha!! That'll change!" He was still chuckling as he drank more from his glass, and turned away.

"No sir. I doubt that."

I had managed to make him stop laughing *two* times now, and he turned towards me again with a stare. I think he wanted to tell me off but he gave us one more flash of his pearly whites and asked "How 'bout some coffee boys?"

Ridley and I looked at each other and he shrugged.

"Do you have any honey?"

I stood there at the podium on the mayor's right hand side, Ridley was on his left. I watched the now massive group of protestors behind the security fence. Other officers were on standby to control the crowd. The mayor went through his speech as we stood watch from the stage. The crowd loved him when he spoke and he delivered a pretty good speech. I must admit that he even had me convinced that he actually would solve the city's debt problems.

The whole ordeal, including a question and answer period, was over by 12:30pm and we were escorting Mr. Mash back to his office through a secure path created; deemed no media or public presence.

Inside his office again, Ridley and I were allowed to catch up with each other. I had been eyeing his two henchmen since I saw them and thinking about the other guy who had hurried out of there at first.

"Rid." I whispered.

"Yah John what's up?"

"You getting a weird vibe from this place too?"

"You mean the ghost of Christmas present?"

I laughed. "You thought that too eh?""

"What are you thinking about John?"

I shook my head and sighed. Ridley and I didn't make eye contact as we spoke. We just scanned the room and carried on our conversation.

"I 'dunno man. You remember that guy who left in hurry when we got here?"

"I didn't really get a chance to see him...why?"

"I didn't recognize him at first...but I figured it out."

"Ok...so? Are you gonna' be making a point sometime in the near future?"

"It was Jimmy Olive"

"Jimmy Olive? As in, Bay Brook construction Jimmy Olive?

"Yah."

"Are you sure? John, what would Jimmy Olive be doing in the mayor's office?"

"I dunno' man. I mean, I was under the impression the mo—."

"—Boys!" A bellowing voice thundered, followed by that ol' Hwah! laughter.

"I want to thank you boys!" The mayor said as he slapped us both on the back. The blows were softened by our bullet proof vests but I cringed, more out of annoyance. I was beginning to dislike this guy. I looked up to the sky as if to ask whatever I thought was up there for patience.

"Always a pleasure working with Baltimore's finest! Hwah! Hwah! Hwah!"

The room was full of more people now, all laughing and shaking hands. Sean walked past us laughing and joined in on the merriment. He had another scotch in his hand.

"How long do we have to stay?" Ridley asked me.

"Sarge said to escort him around until we see the crowd out there dissipate...the other unit will radio us when it has."

"Great..."

I watched a pretty young girl from his office walk by him, and as she did; his big mitt slapped her on the butt. She jumped a little then turned to give him an awkward smile. I started to dislike the guy even more.

The day went on some more. Ridley and I had to escort him everywhere; the washroom, down the hall, a few little meetings with various other council members. He answered his phone during one of the meetings and told whoever was on the other end to "Just send them to my office."

When we got back to his office, he entered, giving us a big grin and the two lurches returned. They stepped in and blocked entry for us. One of them put up his hand.

"This is the mayor's private time." He said.

"Excuse me?" I asked.

"Well my lads!" Sean boomed as he stopped to look back at us. "It's been fun...usually I invite the cops in. The other guys they sent seemed more interested in sticking around, But—." And he looked at me. "You guys seem like you're all business! I'd hate to keep you back from your other 'more important duties' as it were."

He was brushing us off now. He was trying to sound polite but he was asking us to *go away*.

"Of course sir." I said, nonchalantly trying to peek into his office. I heard a faint giggling noise come from inside, and Sean pretended that he didn't hear it. He stood there, grinning like an idiot with his eyes squinted shut, waiting for us to leave. I looked over at Ridley for support. He shook his head at me because he knew what I was thinking.

I happened to glance down and see that the big guy in front of me had his shoelace undone. I looked up at him and smiled.

"Adios cowboy." Sean said in a softer voice.

"Ok sir, we'll see you later." I shifted my body weight and placed my foot on the shoe lace to trap it.

"Good luck." The mayor chuckled some more, under his breath for once, and turned to go in his office. The big lurches gave us a final stare down and then turned to follow him in.

The tug on his lace caused him to stumble and when I released it at the right moment his feet couldn't catch up with each other. He lunged forward and hit the door with a big thud. All of his mass made the door swing wide open. I had to hold in a smile as I pretended to show concern, rushing to his side.

"Oh my goodness, sir...I'm sorry!" I laughed as I patted him on the back. "You really should tie your shoelaces man. It's dangerous..."

The look on Sean's face was priceless. It was the first time I had seen a smile-less expression on him. He was really scared for a moment there, as he whipped his head around to see what happened...

And I looked past him,

To the three hookers he had sitting on a leather couch against the far wall. They too were shocked. Before I could react—*SLAM!* The door was shut in my face.

* * *

That night I didn't sleep well. Ridley and I had talked about turning him in but decided against it. It still bothered me though. The mobster, Jimmy Olive being there bothered me. I tossed and turned in my bed until I wasn't sure if I was asleep or awake. The whole night was blurry and seemed so long.

The naive part of me had always just assumed that public officials and the system were all in automatic balance. We were supposed to be the good guys! Everything was black and white. It bothered me that this was revealing to not be the case.

That seed inside of me was now sprouted and growing.

I had been staring at the clock, watching it turn from 2:00 to 3:30 to 4:15.

Suddenly I looked around and I was in the middle of a dream. And I knew it was a dream.

"Behold!" The man's voice bellowed. The street preacher was there, raving about Babylon falling some more. Sean Ahab Mash's obnoxious laugh echoed throughout the dream.

"There will always be someone left to fight!" He bellowed at me.

"There will always be someone left to fight!"

I heard someone whisper "*This is not your life!*"...

And then my eyes opened in the real world.

Slowly and silently.

The clock read 5:07. It was time for me to get up for work. I sighed and rolled over onto my back. My apartment was quiet but I could hear the faint noise of the city through the walls. It was still dawn and the dull blue light was just coming through my bedroom window. I grunted and rubbed my eyes.

"John!" A voice suddenly cried out in the darkness.
I was extremely startled and I shot up in my bed to look around the room. Nothing was there.
I heard the faint sound of a buzz or electric hum begin to rise and rise until there was a loud electric snap and the voice calling again.
"John!!" Louder this time.
I again was startled and I looked all over my room.
"John! Don't!"
I flung the covers off and got out of bed quickly. I grabbed a bat I had next to my bed and held it firmly.
"Who's there!?" I yelled.
The buzzing and humming rose and fell like someone was turning the volume up and down, and it was always followed and mingled with the sounds of the voice.
"John! Don't do it! Don't kill him!"
I crept through my apartment searching for the sounds of this voice and those were the phrases it repeated. It wasn't until I stopped and really listened that I realized something terrifying.
It was *my* voice!
"John!" The voice yelled. It sounded closer than before—right behind me and I whipped around. The buzzing and humming stopped dead and my eyes went wide at what I saw.
It *was* me!
But after my heart skipped a beat, I realized it was only my reflection in the closet mirror. I sighed and lowered the bat. I stared at myself and after a while I chuckled and shook my head.
Then I turned to walk away...
The buzzing sound got turned up quickly and filled the room again and I whipped around to the mirror. It was still me but something else extraordinary was happening now.
The reflection was acting on it's own accord and not reflecting what I was doing in real life. It was glitching in and out like a digital image with blue and white electric energy all around it. There were two versions of myself glitching back and forth between one another. One was a calm me, standing still and one was raising my arms up and screaming! The two different voices; calm and slow, and frantic and loud clashed as they both said;
"THis is NOt yoUR LIfe!!..."
A loud crash pushed me back and I got that feeling of falling.
"Aah!" I startled awake in my bed again and immediately sat up. I was sweating.
But...that felt so real. I had been back and forth between dreaming and awake all night that I still wasn't sure. I looked to the side of the bed to where I usually kept the bat, and it was gone...
I looked around and stopped when I saw the bat beside me in bed. I just stared wide eyed at it and I couldn't move.

Eventually I came to and I realized that the colour outside was more than the dull colour of dawn that I was used to waking up to. I zipped around to look at my clock and it said: 6:02!

"Damnit!" I yelled and I jumped out of bed. My shift started at 6:30...

I was rushing out of the locker room at 6:36, not fully dressed. I was still wrapping my gun belt around my waste and fastening it, when Ridley came running up.

"John!" He said. "You missed parade, man, c'mon. You know Sarge just takes it out on me."

"I know dude I'm sorry, I'm sorry." I replied, buttoning up the last few buttons of my police shirt.

"You're welcome." Ridley said, handing me a coffee.

"Ah." I said, clipping on my badge. "Thanks man." I took the coffee and we began to walk towards the garage. "What do we got today?" I asked.

"We're back on patrol." Ridley replied. "There's been a lot of robberies the last few nights so we gotta pay close attention to certain areas."

"Sounds good, buddy."

"K, you better report in, I'll sign out the sock gun and meet you in the car."

"Cool, man." I sighed. "Sarge is gonna be pissed."

"Good luck."

I turned away from Ridley and walked a bit until I was stopped again.

"Revele." The voice said.

I turned around to see the head detective of organized crime. Kang.

"You got a sec?" He asked.

"Uh...not really." I replied, walking backwards.

"K, I need to talk to you about yesterday, when you can...alright?"

I was confused. "How did you?..."

He cocked his head realizing I didn't know how he knew about yesterday. I didn't talk to this guy very often. "Go speak to Sarge." He said.

"Um...ok..." I furrowed my brow and turned around again.

As I made my way towards Sarge's office I thought I could hear the sound of raised voices, muffled by the walls of the office, so I approached with caution.

"You assured me this division wasn't going to be a problem!" Is what I thought I made out as I knocked on the door.

"And it won't be." Sarge's voice.

"Who is this guy?" The other voice bellowed. I knew who it was now, and my heart raced.

"Come in!" A muffled sounding Sarge said.

When I entered the room he flashed his big winning grin at me. "Howdy!" The mayor boomed before chuckling his obnoxious laugh. I didn't know what to say.

"Hi sir." I said.

"Revele, take a seat." Sarge told me.

What was all this about? I began to think, as I readjusted my tie clip and sat down. I was looking at Sarge waiting for something, anything. I could feel the mayor's gaze on the side of my face and I could see his big smile without even looking at him.

"Revele." Sarge began. "The mayor and I were just talking about yesterday's address, and the security we provided."

"Yes." I replied.

They were both starting to give me a really strange vibe. I allowed myself to look over at the mayor while Sarge continued.

"The mayor is very pleased with you and officer Simmons' performance."

I was still staring at Sean now, still a little confused. He just grinned back at me.

"He'd like to recommend you for a commendation in your file." Sarge said.

"Yes sir." Sean blared. "I was extremely pleased with you and your partner's services yesterday officer Revele. You know sometimes it's pretty stressful running a city—heck—I know you know what I'm talking about. You put your life on the line every day! Hwah! Hwah! I'm sure in your nine-months of service you can relate can't you?" He was laying it on thick. The sarcasm when he said 'nine-months' was obvious, though I don't think Sarge clued in.

But I knew what he was doing,

What he was trying to do...

I stared back at him, with a smirk of my own now. I was aware of his little tricks and I entertained him for now.

"Anyways," he went on. "With all the stress I'm under...I'm sure you can appreciate my situation. I'm just glad there's officers like you standing watch over my city." He said, with a special emphasis on the *'my'*. "I can sleep a little better at night, knowing I can trust the Baltimore police department, and all its officers to keep not only me safe, but the great citizens of this city." The two of us were in a locked gaze. I think we both completely forgot about Sarge.

"Well I'm happy to oblige mayor." I said with a dark tone in my voice. I made sure to emphasize the *'oblige'* to remind Sean that I *was* a cowboy.

Truth be told I was relieved. I was glad that it was being resolved this way, instead of a big scandal and media frenzy, which I was sure he would get out of somehow. The people loved him and he would win them back.

This way, he would fall harder,

When the time came...

CHAPTER TEN
The Missing Ingredient

He worked so meticulously, as he always did, hunkered over his project and focusing intently. What he was working on now was a smaller device, a handheld piece belonging to a much larger machine.

This time he took a sip from his coffee mug instead of a juice box.

He placed his mug down with a clunk and sopped up the droplets from his beard with his bottom lip. Adjusting his glasses and with his finished device in hand, his tinkering with the small part was done. He walked over to a platform and stepped on. As he did he was interrupted by a voice calling to him.

"Mr. Richter!" He called.

The now older Jason Richter stopped with a bit of a cringe and he sighed, closing his eyes. He wasn't particularly fond of this guy. He wasn't particularly fond of anyone, as you know.

"Yes Mr. Kitch?" Jason said, turning to greet him. He was 67 years old now in 2038.

"I've spoken with corporate." Kitch began, causing Jason's eyes to roll.

"And?..." He asked, exasperated.

"And...I know you don't care what corporate says. But they are paying for all of this, in case you haven't forgotten." Kitch whined on, driving Jason nuts.

"What's your point Mr. Kitch?" He said, in a raised voice, adjusting his glasses and fidgeting impatiently on the platform.

"They've paid for all of your progress so far Mr. Richter...you wouldn't even be standing there if it wasn't for them."

Jason ran his fingers through his long hair trying to hide his annoyance.

"I'm well aware of corporate's involvement...again, I ask, what do you want?"

"You asked me to bring your plans for yet another ring to them...they said no."

"Bah!" Jason shouted, not surprised. "Of course they did! Blind fools." Jason turned to go, but Kitch stopped him.

"They aren't impressed with the results they've seen thus far!"

"Oh no?!" Jason shot back sarcastically, and whipping back around.

"They're saying it's taking too long."

"Ha!" Jason laughed. "Isn't that ironic, in the line of work we are doing here?"

"They say if you can show them results by the end of the next two months then they will reconsider."

"Will they now?" Jason smirked and stewed in his disdain for these people. "And how is the ex-chief of staff?" He asked.

"Mr. Richter, Paul Ranston is just as keen as you are to see this project through, trust me. I was with him in Cairo. Besides, you know he has nothing to do with corporate funding. Any financial help he's offered has been out of his own pocket."

"Hmm. So he says. I still don't fully trust him...anyways—if you'll excuse me, I have to get back to work here." Jason replied pointing *up* at his project. "I wouldn't want to keep the good people of Globe-X in the dark now would I?"

"No...you wouldn't."

"Kitch, please. You're just a middle man, at best...handling the legal issues of your client...don't threaten me on behalf of a company who would just as soon throw you to the dogs as much as they would me."

"You disapprove of Globe-X?"

"No...I disapprove of you."

Kitch sighed a miserable sigh, realizing he had no come back for this remark, and he squirmed in his suit, looking away from Jason down to the floor as he grumbled under his breath.

"Mr. Richter." He began again, pushing his glasses up the bridge of his nose. "Here at home, Globe-X has invested a lot into your little experiments—"

"—Mr. Kitch..." Jason had to interrupt. "I really must be going." He continued, as he pushed a button on a control panel attached to the platform he was on. A loud metallic clunk startled Kitch.

"All I'm saying—" Kitch tried to spurt out. He was cut off again by the sound of gears grinding and chains rattling. Jason started to go up on the platform. It was a lift platform and he began to ascend away from a frustrated Kitch.

"—You're almost out of time!" He cried out.

Jason's smile broke into a laugh. "Time will soon be on our side!" He shouted down to Kitch. "Let me assure you Kitch, that there's nothing little about my experiments!"

Kitch stood there, glaring at Jason as he rose up and up on the lift.

It took him up towards the roof of the facility where a section of it opened up and revealed the moonlight of the night. The lift went through the hole and now Jason ascended up into a scene of green and palm branches. He felt the humidity over him like a wave and the sounds of jungle animals flooded his ears. The lift kept going and rose him above the palm trees where his eyes finally beheld his marvelous machine. Another enormous metal ring stood towering over the treetops, in the jungles of Madagascar. It was built on the beach and back dropped by the Indian Ocean which reflected the moonbeams.

There was a raised platform to access the ring and the lift thudded to a stop by it. Jason stepped off and he began down the metal walkway, looking down through the meshed steel to see the top of the Forrest. When he peered over the edge of the railing he saw the vague glimpses of the lab's roof, through the trees.

"Jason!" A man's voice said. Jason stopped, not seeing him, just short of the man. "Nice of you to join us." Ernest Lawrence said sarcastically before chuckling. "Did you finish it?"

"Yah Ernest..." Jason sighed. He wasn't particularly fond of Ernest either, but he could put up with him better than he could with Kitch. They had been working together on this thing for many years.

"Well, good, good...let's try it out." Ernest said. Jason fiddled with the device in his hand as he walked over to a section of the ring beside the platform.

"So did you talk to Kitch?" Ernest asked.

"Ugh!" Jason scoffed under his breath. "He's so...Kitch!"

Ernest laughed. "You should have seen him in Cairo."

Jason pushed a button and a compartment opened up. He paused and turned to Ernest. "Ranston was there too?" He asked slowly.

"Yah, he was there."

"How did he seem to you?"

"He...seemed like Paul Ranston." Ernest shrugged.

"Hmm." Jason turned back to the machine and slid the device in his hand into the slot.

"You don't trust him do you Jay?" Ernest asked from behind him. Jason paused again and sighed, glancing back at Ernest.

"No." Jason simply said. "No, I don't." And he quickly went back to work pushing some buttons and adjusting some levels on an instrument panel beside the device.

"Truth be told..." Ernest began reluctantly. "He kinda creeps me out too."

Jason perked his ears up for listening, but he continued working away, pretending to ignore Ernest.

"I mean...an ex-staff member of the White House cabinet surfaces and becomes involved with an international organization like Globe-X...What stake could he possibly have in your project?"

"I always wondered what politicians do after their terms are done." Jason remarked sarcastically. "Maybe he's trying to fix some past mistakes in history?" He laughed to himself.

"Isn't that what you're doing Jay?" Ernest asked boldly.

Jason stopped what he was doing and turned. "You're a scientist too Ernest...look at what we've built." He said, gesturing upwards to the ring beside them. "You and Donald have been with me since almost the beginning of this thing. We were young men when we started this. I'm an old man now."

"This all came from your brain though Jay. Donald and I have just helped."

"It's not just what I'm trying to do...it's why we're all here. Imagine the possibilities this could create. Time travel Ernest! You're not getting second thoughts are you?"

"No Jay. I'm not...but I think other people are." Ernest said, motioning down to the ground.

Back down in the lab, Kitch was talking to another man. Donald, the other man from the Egypt excursion...

"Mr. Kerst." Kitch began. "What is he doing up there?"

"The device?" Donald asked in his usual quiet way. "It's a small radiation device." He said monotoned

"And it's safe? In Cairo we had to wear radiation suits."

"It's contained...like in a microwave. The whole machine requires several of them. Plus...this machine isn't turned on yet. Once each of the sites get turned on, then we need to protect ourselves, but for now we're okay. We're only here for another couple days, then we're down under. That's when the technicians come and take over. They'll turn it on after we're gone."

Up top, Ernest was looking down at their lab, imagining them argue. He chuckled. "Little twerp." He said. "You know Kitch wants to see you lose right Jay?"

"Let him try." Richter said. "You should know me better than that by now, Ernest."

"Yah, I do...you always win."

"I don't think anybody alive enjoys losing." Richter announced. "It's why we speed up on the highway when someone passes us."

Ernest laughed. "Even though we were perfectly comfortable going the speed we were going..." he completed Richter's lesson.

"just another car passing us sparks something inside doesn't it?" Richter went on. "and people would be lying if they said they've never done this. Humans are pathetic."

"And yet you want this achievement for them." Ernest suggested.

Richter paused. "I want this for me! I'm tired of being a spectator...with this machine we can make this world the way we want instead of just wishing for it!"

He clicked that last switch into place and shut the compartment door.

"The missing ingredient." He said to himself, smiling.

"That's it." Ernest said proudly. "Now we can turn it on."

Jason took a huge breath and sighed out slowly. He looked up at the ring to admire it some more. "I'm doing it myself." He whispered to the sky—or rather, the being he thought was there. The one he made a vow against through his bedroom window as a boy.

"I often wonder..." Kitch went on, down below. "If all this radiation will be harmful."

He and Donald began to walk towards the base of the lift.

"I mean once the rings are all turned on." Kitch continued. "Couldn't it be damaging?"

Up top, Richter and Ernest were stepping onto the lift. The motor purred and chains rattled as they began to descend.

"What's the matter Jay?" Ernest asked, when he noticed his silence. Jason was staring up at the ring through the trees as they neared the ground. The roof hatch began to close.

"I was just thinking about when Gerald Fienberg approached me at a science fair. I never imagined that I would be here." He said, reminiscently.

"Who's Gerald Fienberg?" Ernest asked.

Jason began to look at Ernest with a furrowed brow—

—"Ah! Mr. Lawrence." Kitch shouted to interrupt the conversation.

"Kitch." Ernest said, acknowledging him.

"I trust you and Donald here are reminding Mr. Richter of my client's deadlines...he doesn't seem to listen to me..."

"Shut up Kitch." Ernest said. Donald chuckled as he joined up with his other two colleagues. "We're going as fast as we can here."

"Seems like the ring is ready to be turned on anyways." Donald pointed out.

"Yes." Jason replied. "It is..."

"Yah, and I have some questions." Kitch spoke up.

Donald sighed and rolled his eyes as Richter looked at him for clarification. "He thinks that all the radiation will damage something." Donald explained.

Richter looked at Kitch. "What do you mean?" He asked.

"I don't know." Kitch started. "Like, once we actually, you know...time travel, won't all the radiation cause some kind of damage to the...the...the thing...what's it called?"

"The space, time continuum?" Richter asked with an annoyed tone.

Kitch dropped his eyes. "Yah...that."

"What are you going on about, Kitch!?" Richter scoffed. "Are you the scientist or the lawyer?" He turned passively to Ernest. "Where did we find this guy?" He asked him. "I need to get some sleep."

Ernest chuckled. "Who's gonna keep Mr. Kitch here company?"

Richter looked at Kitch from under his glasses and scoffed. "He's not my problem." He said. "You guys can...make him a sandwich...or get him on the chopper and get him off site. Who cares?"

"Anyways..." Kitch sighed. "The chopper won't be picking me up until late morning, so...where shall I sleep?"

Donald and Ernest looked at each other once again and smiled. "Well..." Ernest began. "...your friends at Globe-X, the generous company they are, only really designed this facility for a team of three. Looks like you get the couch over there." He finished, motioning to another room.

Kitch looked over into another section of the lab at an uncomfortable looking couch. He let out a frustrated sigh and then tromped off towards it.

Ernest and Donald looked goofily at him as he left the project room.

"He's such a dick!" Kitch whined under his breath as he left.

Donald and Ernest looked at each other now and chuckled. Then they turned to Richter who had sauntered over to a big table filled with spare parts and tools. He was sifting through things and cleaning up for the night.

"You could stand to take it a little easy on him you know." Ernest said to him.

Richter chuckled. "Please, Ernest. His only interest is to shut us down."

"He's not right is he?"

Richter stopped what he was doing and sighed. He turned to face his lab partners and saw their curious faces.

"About what?"

"About the radiation. Is it possible to damage the continuum?"

"Ernest. Donald. You're scientists. You've seen the reports. You've seen the calculations."

"Well...yah." Donald said. "We have. You keep telling us about the...ramifications of time travel."

"The loops." Ernest said. "Isn't that what you called them?"

"The alternate timelines, yes..."

"You said, that if enough alternate realities were created, then a—"

"—then a radioactive spike could be like an atom bomb going off within the confines of space and time! Yes!"

Everyone stopped at this confession. Donald and Ernest looked at each other and Richter looked nervously towards the direction Kitch had gone. Luckily, it appeared that he didn't hear anything and he just grumpily made his bed. Richter sighed, half in relief, half in frustration.

"An atom bomb, Jay?" Ernest asked.

"Not a *real* atomic bomb. I said it would be *like* an atom bomb. The equivalent type of devastation. And yes, it would be catastrophic to the fabric of what we call the space time continuum."

Ernest and Donald fidgeted nervously. "Well, you better not let Kitch find out that little nugget." Ernest said.

"It doesn't matter." Richter said. "We're the ones in control. We're the ones with our finger on the button. We control the radiation. That's what the stabilizer we've built is for."

"And what if that does happen?" Donald asked.

Richter stopped and shot him a look. Both Ernest and Donald both waited for an answer. Richter shrugged. "I don't know, exactly. From all of my calculations...there's only been one conclusion."

"Which is what?" Ernest asked.

"Basically...the continuum will be broken."

"Broken?"

"Time will stop."

Ernest and Donald looked down at the ground and both exhaled intensely.

"Guys." Richter said. "You sound like Kitch! I told you, it's not gonna happen. Especially not before we even use the machine. Why don't we just worry about that first?"

Richter looked at his lab partners anxiously. A long tenuous moment passed until everyone relaxed.

Donald just walked away.

Ernest sighed again. "Ok, Jay." He said. "You're the boss."
The two of them remained in a stare down. It lasted a while until Ernest backed away, still staring at Richter. Then he smirked at him, turned and walked away.

"He certainly has his ways with people." Kitch called out.
Ernest and Donald were passing the couch where he was setting up his bed. They looked at each other and then stopped walking to speak with him.
"You learn to love him." Donald said.
"He's got no people skills at all!" Kitch carried on. "How he got this far is beyond me!"
Ernest chuckled. "I'm pretty sure he got here because of his genius mind and determination, Kitch...the fact that he doesn't like people doesn't matter...he doesn't need to like anyone...he's gonna change the world regardless."
"Hhmmppff!" Kitch made an unimpressed and nasally noise.
Behind all 3 of them, Richter rushed past on his way to bed. Kitch looked passed the other 2 and watched him. "He's still a dick." Kitch went on, adjusting his glasses.
Richter, meanwhile, passed through the facility's kitchenette and up the metal stairs to his living quarters. He shut the door and sighed. Being an introvert, all that people talking was hard. He peeled off his lab coat and tossed it aside. He flopped off his suspenders to let them hang down at his sides. Soon he was in just his underwear and a white tank top. He sat on the edge of his bed and ran his fingers through his hair while he let out a long sigh...
This whole project was getting the better of him lately.
Richter sat there for a good long while without even moving.
Then,
A noise that Richter knew began to rise in his ears...
He twitched his head up a bit at the sound of it...
A slow building electric hum or buzz.
He lifted his head slowly and stared at the door to his room.
"What on earth?" He said quietly to himself.
All of a sudden the buzzing stopped and a louder crack thundered into the room.
"Richter!!" A voice screamed, and then all noise stopped dead.
He whipped around to look all around the room. Whooshes began to zip behind him,
Beside him,
Behind him again....
"Richter!!" The distant voice called again. "RICHTER!" The voice was right behind him now! He whipped around and his heart leapt in his chest when he saw...
...*Me!*
...

I had a blueish energy surrounding me and I didn't stay there long. The image of me suddenly flashed and then I was on the other side of the room. Richter followed me as I jumped around sporadically.

"Richt..." My voice cut in and out. "...don't...help...m...do...Richt..." On one of my sudden jolts, I banged into a table and Richter's things fell off of it. A chess board he had on there crashed on the ground and the pieces scattered.

"Who are you!!??" Richter screamed.

Then a huge snap of electricity blew him back onto his bed—

—"*Gasp!*" His old lungs gasped for air as he suddenly sat up in his bed, with the covers on. Richter breathed in and out rapidly. He touched his head and looked around the room.

Empty....had I been dreaming? He thought.

Then he looked around and stopped. He didn't want to believe it, but his eyes locked onto to the scattered chess pieces and fallen table. He stared at it wide eyed for a moment and then he flung the covers off.

He went to the window of his living quarters and stared out into the night thick jungle that surrounded the lab.

The animals living in the heat and swinging the vines around them had no idea what was happening in there.

They were all alone and remote on this tropical island.

CHAPTER ELEVEN
Yippee Kiyay

"What?" Ridley asked, with disgust in his voice.
"Yah man, I was watching it last night on the retro channel." I replied. Continuing in our flashback to my happier days...
2037.
Ridley and I were at the police station, getting dressed in the locker room before our shift started.
"There's no way it's better than 'Way Too Fast'."
"Dude, I'm telling you...you only think that's good because that's all we grew up on. You should check out the stuff from back in the day—I mean, if you're looking for just some solid action movies for entertainment sake..."
"You're crazy man."
"Rid, I mean it. Some of these movies I've watched on there are amazing! There's this guy named Tarrantini—or something like that...I only caught a bit of his stuff, I'm actually watching the rest of this one called Reservoir Dogs tonight. You'd like it man! Cops, bank robbers, undercover, mob guys...and they don't know who the real bad guy is the whole time!"
"Reservoir Dogs?"
"Yah man, and the whole movie is dialogue driven, it's all set in a warehouse for pretty much the entire thing."
"Sounds dumb to me John."
"Nah it's great! I'm telling you, watch retro Hollywood tonight it's full of great stuff."
"Alright I'll take your word for it. But I still say Jayden Smith is the best action hero ever."
"Now, there's where I'd have to disagree Rid."
"What about Schwarzenegger?" Another voice said. My old mentor, Mac was walking by us on his way out of the shower.
"Schwarz-a-who??" Ridley asked.
I laughed out loud as I pulled my white undershirt on and adjusted the way it fell on my waste. I grabbed my bulletproof vest and began to inspect it.
"You young guys don't know anything anymore." Mac said as he rounded the corner to go to his locker.
"Hasta-la-vista!" He shouted from behind the next row of lockers, and his voice echoed through the tile locker room as he left.
"What is he talking about man?" Ridley said as he propped his foot up to tie his boots.
"Hasta-la-vista...baby. Didn't your parents ever let you watch the terminator movies?" I replied, slipping my vest over my head and letting it fall on my torso.

"Those ones with that Tatum guy playing a robot from the future or something?"

"Ugh! No man! Those were the stupid remakes. The original ones were starring possibly the greatest action hero Hollywood ever saw...cheesy as he was..."

"And what's this whole Hasta-le-pasta crap?"

"Hasta-la-vista! It's what Arnold says to the T-1000 before he shoots him at the end of the movie."

Ridley finished up tying up his boots and stood up to grab his gear out of his locker.

"I don't get it." He said, shaking his head.

"'Of course you don't man. 'cuz you keep watching all the new 'films'" I said, making quotations with my fingers, in between fastening the straps on my vest to fit my body. "A lot of this crap is either rehashed ideas; TV shows, books, remakes of old movies. Hollywood is out of ideas. Which wouldn't be so bad if they weren't trying to make things so believable."

"Meaning what?" Ridley asked, throwing his black uniform shirt over his vest.

"Meaning, people forgot why they went to the movies in the first place. CGI made people so desensitized, that it's become so hard to believe what they see on the screen. And now the fans just demand more and more, criticizing everything." I began buttoning up my shirt.

"You're rambling again buddy."

"I know, sorry...I just get upset. What happened to just going to the movies to be entertained? People like a good story, and they will accept it if you tell it right. I mean think about it Rid. We all know, whether you choose to acknowledge it or not, that there is some other force out there bigger than us."

"Here we go." Rid said as he finished tucking his shirt in to his pants.

"No, C'mon man. Seriously, don't do that...don't dismiss it...you know it's true."

"So what are you talking about here John? Aliens?...God?"

"Maybe...I don't know! I really don't...but I can't rule it out. There's got to be something else out here than me. That's what I'm saying; we fantasize about it through books and movies because we want it to be real. I think because we know it's real."

"You don't think it's just because deep down all of us are just bored of our own futile existence and use it as an escape?"

I finished fastening up my duty belt and reached for my service weapon. I pushed the clip into the bottom of it and racked the slide, and then I looked at Ridley.

"My life isn't boring Rid. Neither is yours." I said with conviction in my voice.

"You know you're not supposed to do that in the locker room." Ridley said.

I smirked and put the safety on my gun and then holstered it. I turned to my locker, grabbing a few more little items out of it; my blade, my pens, my flashlight and I inspected my face in my locker mirror to make sure it was clean shaven and ready for inspection. Then I slammed the door to my locker.

Ridley and I were all dressed for duty and walking down the hallway towards the parade room to get our morning assignments from Sarge.
"So, I still don't get this whole Hasta-le...v—vis—"
"—La-vista Rid."
"Right, why would you say that to somebody before you shoot them."
"Because man, that's what John Conner told him to say earlier on in the movie. It's called foreshadowing Rid."
"I still don't get it...why would Joh—."
"Because the terminator was a robot man. He didn't know how to give a little bit of attitude to a bad-guy and the kid was teaching him about being human...about emotion."
"So, Hasta-la-vista?"
"It's Spanish. It means see ya' later. He was teaching him how to really stick it to a villain, in style. He told him that at the beginning, before their bond is made during the rest of the movie. At the end, before blowing up the bad-guy, Arnold says; 'Hasta-la-vista, baby' and then pulls the trigger. It's that moment that makes the audience cheer. They've been waiting for the climax of the movie, when the bad-guy they really hate finally goes down. Then— BAM! Nobody does this anymore. The old movies used to be full of these little catch phrases...and Arnold was the king."
"I'm lost man."
"The catch phrases always had something to do with how he was killing the person, or who he was killing. He would say 'You're fired' before firing a missile with the bad-guy attached to it, or 'You're luggage' before killing an alligator, 'Stick around' after throwing a knife at a guy making him stick to the wall...get it?"
"Yah I guess so, that's actually kind of cool."
"Of course it is. They stopped doing it."
"Yippee-Kiyay!" Mac passed us in the hallway, saying that as he passed.
"That's Bruce Willis man!" I laughed.
"Who's Bruce Willis?"

We sat down at the big table in the parade room with all of the other officers, waiting for Sarge. Our conversation continued through the whole morning.
"That was from the Die Hard movies." I told Ridley.
"Die-hard? Isn't there like eight of those movies now?" Ridley asked.
"Again...stupid remakes. The original 'John McLane' was Bruce Willis."
"That really old dude? I think I do know who that is. Wait, isn't he dead?"

"Yah that's him...and yes, he is...back in his day he was up there with the Shwarz."

"The Shwarz?"

"Arnold. The terminator, Rid. C'mon man, keep up."

"Sorry."

"Anyways...Yippee-Kiyay was something Brucey said to Hans, the bad guy, very early on in the movie. Hans had been jeering him and insulting him, asking if he really expected to stop him. They had a cavalier conversation about their favourite movie heroes. Hans was comparing Bruce to an overzealous police movie hero, and Bruce confirmed that he was more of a cowboy."

"Where's this going John, Sarge is gonna be here soon."

"The point is...The bad guy was saying...'you'll never stop me' and Bruce put the fear in him by saying 'Yippee-Kiyay'; a famous saying from the TV show he was referencing. Letting the bad-guy know he was *going* to stop him."

"You guys still talking about this?" Mac asked as he sat down behind us.

"Yah man...John 'McLane' here was just educating me on the movies." Ridley replied.

"How did you guys get on this topic anyways?" He asked.

"John was telling me this morning how badly he wanted the chance to say a catchy phrase to a bad-guy."

"Oh-yah?" Mac asked.

"Yah man!" I said to him.

"See, at the end of Die-Hard he says 'happy trails Hans!'" Mac said.

"I know, but in the second one he says it before he shoots the broken phone lines—."

"No, No, No, John. That was the third one."

"You guys are messed up." Ridley said, shaking his head.

"I thought that was the fourth one." I asked Mac.

"No, in the fourth one he shoots himself through the shoulder to kill the bad-guy, saying his tombstone should read 'Yippee-Kiyay'"

"So what was the second one again?"

"In the second one, he's fighting the bad-guy on the wing of the plane—."

"—Oh yah! And he pulls the fuel dump—."

"—and then he falls off the wing and lights the trail of gas?"

And we both shouted "Yippee-Kiyay!" in unison.

As the three of us were laughing, Sarge finally came in.

"You school girls done giggling!?" He yelled, and I smiled, sitting back in my chair. Nothing like a good screaming from Sarge to start your day off right. I loved this job.

* * *

"You get your paycheck Rid?" I asked him as we drove.

"Yah man. Friggen' tax man took his usual slice of the pie. I swear that gets bigger every time." Ridley said. "I worked like a hundred and twenty hours last pay period, and I got the equivalent of what must be sixty!"

"Sixty?"

"I'm sick of it dude! I swear I'm gonna snap one day. When the revolution happens I'll be at the front-lines against these bastards!"

I just chuckled to myself when Ridley went on these little rants. We'd been through a lot so far and with our history we were more than partners. He was a *loyal* friend. I always knew I could count on him to have my back. Even if I didn't need him at the moment he was at my side ready to fight for me.

"Hey we got Mayor duty tomorrow?" He said.

"Yep."

"I thought you hated that guy? Or are you trying to get in good with your crush's daddy?"

"Something like that..."

"Well don't make it too obvious man...I'm surprised Sarge lets you switch your shift so much."

"I'm making it as random as possible, so that he doesn't notice, Rid."

Ridley laughed about it, not realizing my true intentions for requesting the mayor detail...he didn't need to know...

* * *

He didn't know about officer Kang from the organized crime unit and how he had approached me with his proposition. He eagerly came to me and pressed me to work for him. He tapped into my gung-ho side and to be honest; the thought of bringing a dirty mayor down, after he had tried to intimidate me, threaten me, and after observing his blatant abuse of his position, seemed excellent to me. I joined up, without the prospect of soon becoming closer with his daughter and I began to gather intel on Sean right away. Since then, I had been able to inform Kang of the numerous times I had had dealings with him.

The first time I showed my face at City Hall again, I saw that look of fear in Sean Mash's eyes. He was loudly chuckling with some of his other colleagues and when he turned to see me approaching with Ridley, his smile faded quickly. I could see the smugness drain from his face. I got to know his routine; who spoke with him at what times of the day, who travelled with him, who he walked the halls with, who he ate with, who his drivers were. Those two large body guards were always around and they were watching me too. I didn't care though. I just smiled and waved at them. This went on for a few months, and I stayed out of the way. Sean didn't have any reason to come back to the station and complain to Sarge again and I wasn't going to give him one. I smiled at him and he always pretended not to be worried, but it was written all over him.

During my observations of him, I had seen him refuse to talk to people who approached him. Certain people, because he knew I was there watching, he would turn them away or pretend he didn't see them. Then I would relay that information back to Kang, who then had that specific person investigated. A lot of them turned up dirty—no surprise there...and Kang deployed surveillance teams on them. They were all traced back to the mob in some way—another shocker. But no arrests were made. Kang needed to build a case. I was able to give Kang confirmation of a few hand to hands I did happen to see between Sean and some of these other men who otherwise had no business at City Hall. I guess Sean figured he could hide in plain sight and invite all of these mobsters to come and take care of a little business. Kang never could bust any of these guys, because then he would give away his informant...me. He laid low for a while, but not unlike other people, he got sloppy again. Ridley and I would periodically walk past his office doors, which remained closed with the two big oafs guarding it. I could always hear the faint sounds of ladies giggling and bursts of arrogant laughter from behind it.

What bothered me one day was when I saw a girl who worked for him. She was leaving his office crying. This was the same girl I had seen Sean grab her butt, the first time Ridley and I were in his office. She was smiling then, but now she wasn't. I had assumed that maybe she was another one of his bimbos he took advantage of at the time. Sean, I guess, didn't expect me that day because he came out of his office shortly after, looking at the woman as she stormed down the hallway. He didn't see me standing at the corner eating my lunch with Ridley. When he did see me his face went white briefly, and then he shrugged it off and kept walking. I think he pretended not to see me, but I looked right at him as I took a big bite out of my cheeseburger and smiled as I chewed it, raising a hand to wave at him as he walked the other way. I reported it to Kang, who didn't say much. A week later she was found dead...murdered...bludgeoned to death. Kang reviewed the case files with me, and all the evidence led them to some no name mob thug—a nobody in the crime world. Some higher wise-guy's second cousin or something. A young wannabe mobster who they got to do their dirty work. Kang explained it to me—it was most likely his initiation...if he kept his mouth shut and took the rap for this murder, did his time like a man...he would be a made man when he got out. This guy was smiling when they arrested him and he didn't make a peep to implement the mayor. But a frustrated Kang and myself knew it was him.

I was furious the next shift I took at City Hall. I almost wanted to barge into his office and arrest the pompous prick, or *worse*...But I didn't.

We saw each other in the hallway that day. This time, he was smug and I was fuming. We both secretly knew what was on the other's mind. He knew I wanted to come at him, but he knew that I couldn't, and I knew it too. I glared at him behind red eyes and this time he was smirking at me.

He was walking towards me, straightening up his suit jacket as he did. He gave an 'everything's ok' signal to the big oafs and approached me. I had to hide my anger and change the look on my face.

"Mr. Mayor." I said politely.

"Officer Revele." He boomed. He was beaming in arrogance with those beady little eyes squinting at me and his mouth half open baring his pearly whites. He laughed that big dumb laugh I grew to hate. "My daughter told me that you guys have started seeing each other." He caught me off guard, and I didn't know what to say.

"Uh—yah." I stammered, and I smiled at him through my anger.

"Well, well..." He went out loudly. "Isn't that something?" He glanced back at his body guards who smiled at me and then he looked back to me with a grin. "Isn't that just something?" He repeated.

I could pick up on his cues and could tell he was trying to threaten me, which normalized the situation and brought me back to my confidence in hating him. I smirked now and replied;

"Yah...Clare's really great." I nodded my head as I said it and his smile faded slightly when he realized I wasn't backing down.

"She's my special girl cowboy...I hope you know what you're doing." He said.

"Don't worry sir. I know exactly what I'm doing."

We weren't talking about Clare anymore...and we both just stared at each other for a moment. He obviously wasn't happy that Clare and I were together but I wanted to call him on the fact that it had nothing to do with caring about his daughter's wellbeing, and everything to do with the fact that it was *me* who was now more closely linked to his life. But I left it alone and just glared at him.

"Here." He said. "Let me buy you lunch." And he cracked open his wallet. As he pulled out a bill, something fell from his wallet that he didn't notice. He shoved the bill in my hand and smiled. "Good day to you..." He said with a dark tone. "...officer."

"Mr. Mayor." I replied calmly.

And he walked past me down the hall. His guards followed and they tried to stare me down. I just smiled at them until they passed and then I let my face drop when they were all gone.

My eyes found what he had dropped and I quickly bent to retrieve the possible lead. I lifted what appeared to be a business card. It was all black and glossy. Only an embossed logo in the centre. A black four leaf clover. On the back side there was a phone number.

Ridley met me a moment after and he handed me a coffee.

"Extra honey buddy." He said with a smile.

I didn't say anything and took the coffee, while slipping the business card into my pocket.

"What was all that about?" Ridley asked.

"Nothing man."

* * *

We cruised around for the morning and, as I sipped my coffee with honey, I kept my eye out the window in between conversations with Ridley.

I flipped the card around in my hand and just stared at it with my head resting on the seat. I was trying to remember where I knew this clover logo from.

Soon enough, that day, we were parked on a side road enjoying a tasty burger on Sean's dime.

"Mmhmm!" I said, Sam L. Jackson style. "Damn that's good!" I wiped the grease off my chin and chewed the juicy bite. It was quiet in the car as Ridley and I mowed down. The only thing heard would have been our chewing and deep nose breaths.

Ridley burped after a sip of his drink. "So how's it going buddy?" He asked me casually.

"Same old, man." I replied, reaching for my fries.

"Still having those...feelings?" He said sarcastically.

I shot him a look, holding my finger-pinch of fries in midair. "Shut up man, you're really still gonna harp on me about that?"

He laughed.

"Huh?" I pressed, sincerely annoyed, but still smiling. "After all the talks we have." I shook my head and fit the fries in my mouth. "My friend..." I joked with a mouthful.

"Buddy, we're jaded on this job, you know that." Ridley said. "I get it man, I do...I'm just messing with you." He shoved some fries in his mouth too.

"Well mess all you want, Rid." I said, chewing the last little bit of my bite. "I'm seriously getting pissed off out here on these streets."

"Aw, c'mon man! What about Clare?"

I swallowed my bite and got my soda. I raised it to my lips but paused and sighed. "Honestly, she's the only thing keeping me from taking to these streets outside the law, I swear." I took a sip from the straw.

Ridley laughed out loud.

"I'm serious, man." I said. "I'm twenty-five years old now and those...feelings...grow the more time I spend out here. We've seen the public do horrible things to each other over nothing, haven't we? Families ripped apart, lives lost. Young people's chances ruined from one bad decision. Custody battles in courtrooms, domestic violence, murders, prostitution, the list goes on and on...I'm really starting to see how awful humans can be."

There was a pause, while Ridley took a sip from his pop and I went in for another bite of the burger. Ridley jimmied his cup back into the holder and shook his head.

"Damn, John..." He said. "you're so passionate about this stuff!"

"Mmph." I forced out, unable to actually make words. With a furrowed brow I chewed quicker and moved the food to the side of my mouth. "What about you?" I mumbled. "All your political stuff! You're just as passionate about that aren't you?"

Ridley didn't say anything but he just nodded in agreement and fit more fries in his mouth.

"This is all that action movie stuff you were talking about earlier." Ridley said with a mouthful of food.

"I'm not saying I want to be a super hero or anything, Rid, I...I dunno..." I shook my head and kept chewing and I reached for my pop and drank.

"So you don't wanna be Batman?" Ridley made fun of me.

I swallowed my drink and raised my pointer finger into the air to wag it. "Batman." I said. "There's a friggen hero, man."

"So there's the answer, John! We'll just call Batman!"

"Batman doesn't exist, Rid...I wish he did...he needs to exist."

"Of course you do." Another sip of pop.

"F'n 'A, I do!" More fries. "I have a permanent musical score in my head. I walk around humming epic notes and battle drums." I washed the fries down with more pop.

"You have an apocalyptic mind, dude!"

I slurped the last drops up through my straw as I looked out the window. I sipped away until those last drops and my cup started making that sucking air noise. Something caught my eye, but Ridley kept talking.

"What about those messed up dreams you said you were having?" He asked me. He was chewing a bite and staring out his window. He didn't realize I wasn't paying attention to him. "The one where you appear to yourself and—"

"—Whoa, whoa, whoa." I suddenly cut in when I saw something. "Pull over there, Rid...it's Maggie!"

Ridley shoved the last bite of his burger into his mouth, crumpled up the wrapper and turned the cruiser on.

We rolled to a stop at the corner where she was hanging out with a bunch of other hoodlums.

"What's up Maggie?" I asked.

She didn't answer. She pretended she didn't see me and took another drag from her smoke. She was standing with her head lowered and a big hooded sweat-shirt that didn't fit. She was wearing the hood over her face so her blonde hair was coming out of the sides. The other guys she was with were all trying to stare us down. Ridley and I waved.

"What's goin' on boys?" Ridley shouted.

"Maggie." I said. "Come here."

"Hey what-ch-you want pig?" One of these losers shouted at me.

"I want to talk to Maggie, if that's okay with you chief."

"She ain't talkin' to no fuzz 'B. Man, we ain't doin' nothin' here...you guys are harassing us."

I scratched my eye brow with my thumb and looked over at Ridley.

"What? You see a couple of black guys in the hood and you figure we must be breakin' the law huh?" He said.

"I didn't say anything like that bro' I'm not bothering you, I just want to talk to Maggie."

"It's like I said 'B...she ain't talkin' right now."

Maggie wouldn't look at me. She had her back facing us and she wouldn't turn for more than a second to look at us.

"Maggie!" I shouted.

"You deaf pig?" the thug asked.

"Shut-up man!" Ridley yelled.

"Maggie!" I repeated.

The guys in the pack started shifting their body weight around.

"John." Ridley warned me.

"Maggie, C'mon, turn around. Let me talk to you."

She turned around very slowly to make eye contact with me and I gasped. Her face was still so young and innocent. The eyes looked broken and sad and they reminded me of her dad's. She also had a huge black eye which she was hiding on the right side of her face.

"John, don't." Ridley said.

I looked over at him and he shook his head no.

"Raisin?" I asked him.

He stared at me for a moment and then he sighed. He slowly nodded his head. "Raisin." Our code word to get the hell out if things went south.

I pulled the door handle and got out of the car quickly. Ridley sighed and paused a moment, lowering his head. He breathed out through his pursed lips and then he got out of the car too.

I started towards the group with a hand on my gun. Ridley was close behind with a hand on his. The guys in the group were local cronies...street punks...hood rats...take your pick. Most of them were known to Ridley and I as having some sort of gang affiliation, but nobody big in the bunch. The guy yelling at us; his name was 'Megga'. This passé just ran errands for bigger guys. I didn't like Maggie hanging out with them.

"How'd that happen Maggie?" I asked.

"John, I—."

"How!?" I repeated.

"I—I—I fell."

"Don't do that, don't cover for these losers."

"What'd you call me pig?" one of them asked.

"You heard me." I said, looking right at him. All of them were shifting and swaying, and making screw faces at us, buffing themselves up for intimidation. Ridley was on point, watching these guys. I turned back to Maggie and examined her face. I had to remove her hood.

"Hey, don't touch her 'cuz." Another crony said, as he actually took steps towards us.

"Back off!" I told him, with my finger right in his face, almost touching his nose. He just stopped and scoffed, eyeing me up and down, sizing me up. I turned back to Maggie and moved the hair away from her face.

"What happened Mags?" I asked again.

"John, please..." she said. Her eyes were glassing over and she looked so desperate.

"Who did this Mags?" I asked.

She wouldn't say. She paused for a long time but I wouldn't break eye contact with her. She shot her eyes over, quickly to her right and then back at me. She did it again several times. I caught her hint and I slowly looked to where she was aiming her eyes. Megga. When I looked at him his swagger got bigger and he rubbed his nose with his fingers, looking away for a moment and then back at me. He had already been making a screw face but he sniffed the air loudly and it scrunched his nose up even further. I don't even know if he had his eyes open they were so tightly squinted and he postured himself, slanting to the side and cocking his head the same way. I wanted so badly to walk over there and hit him, making a similar bruise on his face. She grabbed my hand and tugged on it and I looked back at her. The look on her face said; *'Please don't'*. I realized that she was right. Doing anything would just make them beat her again. Or worse. Plus, I didn't have just cause to prove that it was them. A motion of Maggie's eyes wouldn't stand up in court.

"What are you doing out here Maggie?" I asked her quietly.

She wouldn't answer. Not with these guys around.

"Go home Mags...please." I said. She stared at me for a long time and then glanced at Megga and back to me. I made a motion with my head to the right for her to leave and she started to walk away.

Megga started to walk towards us.

"Hey, Hey, where you think you're goin' bit—?"

I got in his way and stood my ground in front of him.

"Move, bitch!" He said, bringing his face close to mine. I could feel his breath on my face and our eyes were locked. Ridley was still watching the other guys and I could feel his presence at my side now, hand on his gun.

"Make a move Megga." I said to him.

Our stare continued for a while.

"She safe Rid?" I asked my partner, still staring at Megga.

There was a moment's pause while Ridley made sure the group was at bay, and he quickly glanced around the corner, then back.

"She's gone man." He reported.

Megga and I continued to stare at each other and I could tell he was getting uncomfortable. He was swaying and sort of bouncing now and a defensive smile broke out over his face. He flashed his dumb looking chrome grill at me, making that awful teeth sucking noise.

"Let's bounce!" He shouted to the rest of his friends, still looking at me, and they all started to dissipate behind him, with nothing to do but shake their heads and mimic that teeth suck as they left. Some of them made a gun shape with their fingers and aimed them at me, but I kept my gaze on Megga as he looked me up and down and shook his head as he retreated. Just before he left, he too made a gun shape with his hands and aimed it my head. I looked at it and something caught my eye to make me snap out of the stare down. A tattoo on Megga's hand that matched the black clover on the business card the mayor dropped.

Then Megga stepped off. Ridley came up close to me and we watched them leave down the sidewalk.

"Let's go man." He said.

I sighed and then walked in front of him towards the car, while he continued to watch the group of guys leave. His hand was still on the grip of his gun and he finally released it, clicked the safety back on and secured the holster before returning to the cruiser.

Ridley spun the car around and we were following after Maggie now, trying to find her.

"You okay man?" He asked me.

"I'm fine Rid." I answered, examining the card. "Make a right here." I confirmed that the logo on this card was the tattoo on Megga's hand.

"Look…John." Ridley said. "I know you have a special attachment to her—."

"I watched her grow up Rid. I can't just do nothing while she ruins her life like this."

"What are you going to do for her man? Is she gonna' to come live with you? She has a home."

"The orphanage is not a home man."

"Ok fine…but what else are you gonna' do for her? You're doing all you can as a cop."

"As I cop…" I whispered, under my breath.

"What was that John?"

"There she is." I shouted, changing the subject. Maggie was a few blocks away, but we could catch up. "Let's give her a ride back to the orphanage." I said.

"Okay." Ridley simply said. "I just don't see why you think you can do anything else for her."

"I have to try man. I owe it to Dave."

"Her parent's made their choices John."

"I know. But they were good people once, don't you remember that Rid? They were your friends too."

"People change when they get older buddy. They went their way into all the drugs…and Dave with his gambling debts. What did you expect?"

"Dave was always good to you Rid. Me too…we can't just let his kid run rampant on the streets without trying to steer her back on the right path."

There was a silence as we grew closer to Maggie, and I rolled down my window.

"Ah..." Ridley began. He was talking mostly to himself now. "There you go again. John Revele; defender of the widows and orphans."
I leaned out of the window and called Maggie into our car.

After we dropped her off, the social worker thanked us at the door and we were on our way, back on patrol. I was getting back into the cruiser and Ridley's words about my limitations wouldn't leave my head. They caused me to pause at the open door of the cruiser before I got in. I stood there and took a look into the sky. The sun was going down now and I scanned the cityscape. I sighed deep and got in the car. I was staring out the window again keeping an eye on my streets. They were getting worse the more I patrolled them with Ridley. Or maybe,
    they were always this way,
    and I was just starting to see it the more time I spent out here.

* * *

The days passed. Ridley and I continued to patrol the city, making arrests, stopping crime, preventing bad things from happening. I was back at the station filling out a report of a guy we arrested a day ago.
"Revele!" Sarge shouted.
"Yah Sarge?" I replied.
"The detective's office is asking for your report on her desk! Finish it up A.S.A.P. and get your ass up there!"
"Ok sir. I'm just finishing up."

I made my way up the stairs to the third floor, where the detective's offices were, report in hand. I was happy to go, because then I got to see *her*.
I knocked on a foggy glass window of a door that read: 'Detective C. Mash 9429'
"Come in!" Clare shouted.
I opened the door and stepped into Clare's office and shut the door. She was stone cold and barely even looked up at me.
"Hi Detective." I said with a smile.
In the two years Ridley and I had been patrolling around together, Clare had moved up the ranks. When I met her she was a first class constable and she had now made detective.
She looked up at me with a serious look. "Do you have my report Revele?"
"Yes Ma'am." I said, stepping forward with a goofy grin still on my face. "But you might be mad at me...it's not completely filled out."
"Well...what am I supposed to do with an unfinished report?" She asked, with an annoyed voice.
"Sarge was rushing me Ma'am."
"That's no excuse Revele. I need finished reports to investigate cases."

"I'm sorry Ma'am."

Clare sighed and examined me up and down. "What am I going to do with you Revele?"

"I could think of a few things..." I said cheekily. I actually made Clare crack a smile.

She stood up and walked over to me. "What did you have in mind officer?" She asked more softly. I smiled and pretended to be standing at attention.

"You could kiss me..." I began, looking into her eyes now. She looked back into mine. She was beautiful. "...detective." I finished.

Then I couldn't keep up the charade anymore. I dropped my report on the desk and leaned in to kiss Clare, caressing the side of her face with my hand.

I hadn't seen her in a few days. I was coming off the night shift and she was on the day shift so we hadn't spent much time together lately.

We unlocked our lips and kept our faces close, resting our foreheads together.

"I've missed you." Clare told me.

"I know. I'm sorry Clare." I said. "I can't wait until we don't have to sneak around like this."

"Mmm. That'll be nice. You'll have to put a transfer in." She said.

"Me?" I laughed. We separated our foreheads and she slid her hand out of mine softly, reaching out her arm as she sat on the edge of her desk, not wanting to let go of my hand.

"Well we'll have to split up after the wedding." She said smiling. "Did you tell Sarge yet?"

"No not yet..." I replied. "Ridley knows."

"Well I hope so John; he's your best man. You guys go in for your tuxes yet?"

"Yah. We have a couple more fittings scheduled." I rubbed my eyes with my thumb and forefinger as I yawned. I went over beside Clare and sat down next to her on the edge of her desk.

I was gravely staring at the ground. Clare placed her hand on my back and began to rub it softly.

"John? You okay?" She asked.

"...Yah baby, I'm alright..." I hesitated.

"What is it?"

"Nothing Clare, I'm just tired. Night shifts are catching up with me." I lied. I was looking into her big green eyes thinking that I was so lucky to have her. In the midst of everything I was feeling lately—the state of the world, the nature of the job we did—it was all so messed up...She made all of that go away when I looked at her. Call it what you will, but I couldn't get enough of her. I got lost in those eyes and forgot about all the things that bothered me, and that was worth *everything* to me.

She was looking at me with such a concern for my wellbeing on her face. *What did I do right to deserve such a perfect woman caring for me?* I always thought. Something *was* bothering me, but I couldn't tell Clare...

We had, had previous discussions about our mutual feelings about the world but I couldn't tell her what I knew about her *father*.

She leaned in this time and we kissed again. Her hand touched my face and her skin was so soft against mine. I was so in love with this girl it was crazy. I closed my eyes and just got lost in the kiss, leaving everything behind for a few brief moments. I think we both forgot where we were and we both had our hands all over each other now. We started to lean towards the desk so that we would have been lying down on it—

—KNOCK! KNOCK! KNOCK!

Overzealous Ridley opened the door, before being called in, and Clare and I jumped up. Thank God it was only him.

"Hi detective Mash." He said, looking back and forth at both of us, trying to hide a grin.

"Simmons." Clare said. "Come in."

"Don't you knock Rid?" I asked, not caring about formalities at this point. Ridley already knew about us so what was the point of hiding it.

"I did." He said, and then he burst out laughing. I sighed and began to smile. Even Clare broke her outer shell and began to giggle.

"Sarge told me you needed this." Ridley said, holding up his end of the report from our arrest.

"Thanks Rid." Clare said. She and Ridley had become friends too. "You can just place it down on the desk." She said.

"Are you sure you guys don't want to use the desk first?" He said, mockingly.

"Haw! Haw!" I said and I punched him in the arm, laughing.

Ridley walked over, slapped the file down on Clare's desk and he smiled at both of us.

"Hey partner." He said, and he presented a closed fist at me. I bumped his fist with my own fist and on impact we both simultaneously opened our fists and stretched our fingers open. Clare giggled.

"What is this thing you guys always do?" She asked.

"What?" I asked, smirking. "The fist thing?"

"Yah the fist thing."

"Potato, fries." I shrugged. "You don't know Potato, fries?"

"Potato, fries?" She asked sarcastically.

"It's a dumb high school thing John and I used to do." Ridley cut in.

"Watch." I said. I made a fist and held it up. "Potato." I said, explaining my closed fist's resemblance to a potato. "And now we're making fries." I continued, and Ridley and I bumped fists again, exploding our fingers apart. "See? Fries." I said, smiling at Clare.

"I still don't get it." Clare said, laughing.

"It's a secret handshake..." Ridley said. "Girls don't have secret handshakes?"

"Apparently not." Clare said.

"It's a sign of trust." I said, looking at Ridley. "I dunno' it's just something we've always done."

"Okay…" Clare said, still laughing at us.

"I guess you guys are getting pretty excited eh?" Ridley asked us, changing the subject.

"We are." I said, looking at Clare, who smiled back at me.

"Five more months?" Ridley asked.

"Four and Half Rid." Clare responded, still smiling at me.

"Sarge is gonna' be pissed John." He said to me. "You know how much he hates transferring people out."

"Yah I know." I responded. "But when isn't he pissed?" We all shared a laugh.

"I don't think it'll be a problem anyways." I continued. "Clare will be out of here pretty soon."

We smiled at each other and Ridley clued in as to why. "You got the call?" He asked excitedly.

Clare nodded with a big grin. "Yep. I'm shipping off to Quantico at the beginning of next year."

"Wow!" Ridley stated. "Clare Mash, F.B.I." He said mockingly.

"She could whip your butt Rid, don't forget that." I said to him.

"I know buddy, I know." He said, laughing. Clare just humbly stood there listening to us. "Well, congratulations Clare!" Ridley said to her, walking over to her and giving her a hug.

"Thanks Rid." She said as they finished their hug.

"Well, we should celebrate guys!" He stated, smiling hopefully at both of us. Clare and I looked at each other thinking it over. We had just been talking about how we missed each other and needed some time together. But Ridley was right and we both knew it. Going out to celebrate was a good idea. We smiled in approval at each other and I turned to Ridley.

"Sure man, sounds great." I said.

"Alright!" Ridley clapped his hands together. "Where we going? John and I are coming into our day shifts…we could go out tonight! Drinks? The Locust?"

"Sounds perfect man." I confirmed.

"Alright guys. Awesome! I'll see you tonight then."

Ridley left and Clare and I were alone again. We looked at each other and sighed.

"I should get back downstairs. Sarge is probably waiting to give us our next assignment." I said. Clare smiled.

"I need to read your reports and get this case to the D.A." She said.

We sighed again. "Okay baby." I said. "I'll see you tonight then okay?"

"Okay."

We came close together and she put her arms around my neck. I loved that. I didn't want to leave. I put my hands on her waste and we kissed.

"I love you." She said.

"I love you too Clare." I responded. "Bye." And I forced myself to walk out of the room, giving her one last smile before I closed the door.

I sighed on the other side of that door and I walked away feeling bittersweet.
As we planned the final details of our wedding the stress of my job grew. I was here now, 25 years old, in love with a suspected criminals daughter. What was I going to do?

I was walking back from the showers at the end of my shift with a towel around my waste. I reached my locker and Ridley was there getting dressed.
"Hey man." He started. "What's up with that?" He asked, pointing towards my locker.
I hadn't noticed it yet but when I looked there was a white square envelope sticking out of the crack of the locker. In pen was written 'Revele'. I walked over and pulled it out to examine it.

'DRUID HILL' is what the note had read when I opened it. I didn't open it in front of Ridley; he had no idea what I was doing. I was at Druid Hill Park now, waiting for the person who sent me this note. I was sitting on a park bench and he sat beside me, not making eye contact and I didn't look directly at him either.
"Did you get me the pictures?" He asked.
I reached into my jacket and produced a big brown envelope. I handed it to the man and he took it. After he looked around the park, he opened it and slid the pictures out.
"These were hard to get?" He asked.
"No." I replied, shaking my head. "He didn't see me."
"And he trusts you John?" The man asked, flipping through the photos carefully.
I looked at him, pondering my response. "No..." I said, and the man looked at me. "He doesn't."
I glanced down at the photos; my work. The man in the pictures was a pretty well-known figure, with many pictures of him circulating in the media. He was no stranger to cameras, that's for sure. But there were no pictures of him like these ones.
The man sitting next to me was Kang. The lead detective in organized crime that had grabbed my attention that day.
"These are good pics Revele." He said, turning back to them. "Jimmy Olive...You son-of-a-bitch. I guess your suspicions were right eh?"
"After I saw him in the mayor's office that day I knew something was up." I replied.
Kang laughed. "How the hell did you recognize him?"
"I could never forget that face." I answered. "I used to work for him. As a teen, Ridley and I got set up doing snow removal for his company when we

were laid off our construction job for the winter. I did the night shift. One night I walked back into the empty warehouse for a piss and I stumbled on Jimmy beating someone on a chair."

"What!?" Kang asked, laughing in amazement. "Did he see you?"

"You think I'd still be here?" I asked him back. "Or if he didn't kill me that I would be working for the cops? No, I got the hell out of there as fast as I could. Collected my paycheck the next day and never went back. But I never forgot his face..."

"Geez!" Kang said, shaking his head. "And here he is..."

"I don't know if I can keep doing this." I said to him, looking down at the ground in embarrassment. I waited for a response from him but there was none, only silence. I glanced up to see him and he was still just staring at the pictures.

"You came to me Revele..." He started, and I knew this would come back to bite me. I hadn't started dating Clare yet when I *did* come to him with what I knew...

"Do you remember that?" He continued, leaving me speechless. "You said you wanted to help us bring this guy down." He said holding up the pictures.

"I—I—it's different now Kang—I—."

"—How is it different? You don't want to anymore?"

"It's not that I don't want to...Believe me...I want the mayor to go down—."

"You told me, three years ago, that the mayor had been drinking all day, performing his duties drunk! And that he orders hookers for himself on a regular basis! Minor infractions compared to the other things you've helped me discover about Sean A. Mash, John! Including this!" He said angrily, throwing the pictures on my lap.

I looked down at the pictures I had taken of Sean. They were pictures of him in his office at home, meeting with some other men. Jimmy Olive was in the pictures as well.

"He wasn't in the mayor's office that day to obtain a business permit!" Kang said. "And these pictures of him at the mayor's home...Jimmy Olive hasn't surfaced in a while, and now over the past couple years he's back?"

I sighed, remembering the truths that I myself had discovered.

"Revele." Kang continued. "these are photographic evidence that our mayor is in direct business with the mob! Our unit has been building a case against him. With your help, we've obtained copies of illegal contracts, business receipts, illegal documents; permits for businesses that shouldn't be allowed to operate. John, you've been a great asset to us. I accepted your help in the beginning...but when you started dating his daughter...that gave us a real edge."

My heart sunk to the pit of my stomach, like a giant anvil crashing into the cesspool of stomach acids, churning my insides and causing a sea storm inside of me when Kang reminded me of that...not that I needed reminding—but it hurt more hearing him say it out loud and I winced a little.

"Oh..." Kang said, taking notice of my reaction. "Don't tell me..." He scoffed. "You actually love this girl now don't you? Is that it?"
I didn't say anything. I just sighed and looked away.
"Aw, man!" Kang said. "That's just perfect. So what? You're gonna' be covering for her daddy now?"
"No!" I shouted, snapping back to him. "No...there's no way I think Sean Mash is going to get away with anything he's done. Clare, she—she doesn't know any of this...doesn't know what I'm doing for you." I hesitated and stared at the ground for a while.
"We need you John..." Kang said. "I need you...you're gonna' break this case for us."
I remained silent. That silence passed for a few moments and then Kang had to leave. "John." He began. "Keep it together man. Just so you know, we've coded this case. This is confidential intel you're providing me. The code name for this project is now going to be 'Olive' ok? From now on, don't use the mayor's name when you're talking to anyone but me! Got it?"
I didn't say anything.
"John? You got it?"
"Olive, yah I got it."
I wanted out. Not that I didn't want to see Sean Mash go down, but because I didn't want to go behind Clare's back anymore...
I didn't want to betray her trust.
"Anything else?" Kang asked.
I thought for a second of hesitation and I reached into my pocket. "Yah." I said slowly. I pulled out the black business card with the clover and I handed it to him. The look on Kang's face was enough for me to know this was a good lead.
"Where did you get this?" He asked.
"I found it at city hall. The mayor dropped it."
Kang just stared at it. "Revele..." He said. "This is Sexrex's card."
"Sexrex? The sex trafficker guy?"
"The kingpin of the sex trade in Baltimore! Revele..." Kang looked at me now. "If Sean Mash has this, then you can be sure he deals with Sexrex himself."
I turned my face towards the ground and leaned on my legs as I put the pieces together. Now realizing that the mayor could potentially have something to do with Maggie, I was reminded why I was trying to bring him down all the more!

* * *

Our beers clinked together, spilling a little bit of foam head out the top of mine. I sipped it all up as Clare, Ridley and I shared a laugh. We were in our favourite hangout spot called 'The Locust' that night to celebrate Clare's news.
"I still can't believe it Clare!" Ridley said with a big grin on his face.

"C'mon Rid..." I cut in. "You're surprised? It's perfect for a girl like her."

"And what's a girl like me?" She asked in a flirtatious tone.

"I'm just saying...you were a security guard when you were eighteen and have been in some sort of law enforcement ever since. It's who you are!" I said, and I took a swig of my *honey* lager beer.

"Didn't I tell you, I used to paint?" She said, making a cute little face that I loved.

"I know...but that's more of a hobby." I replied.

"No way...I honestly used to want to be a painter...it was more than a hobby. I just sort of fell into this work and haven't been able to get out of it." She drank from her bottle as she reminisced.

"That's true." Ridley said. "You've moved up quicker than anyone I've ever seen."

"Well, I hope you're not among the crowd who seem to think I got to where I am because of my father!" Clare said to him.

I stopped and withdrew from the conversation. Anything to do with Clare's dad and I shut right up, so as not to hint at any feelings I might have about it. As Clare and Ridley chuckled I just listened awkwardly.

"There's only so much, somebody in office can do for somebody...I did the rest on my own!" Clare defended herself.

"Well, there's no way your dad got you in with the F.B.I." Ridley commented.

"I'll drink to that." She said, and we all clinked our bottles together again, lightly, before we all took a big sip.

"Ah!" Ridley exhaled in satisfaction as he put his beer down. "Now I guess you're the man Clare." He said.

"Aw, Rid...don't start that." I said.

"Here we go..." Clare said, smiling.

"What? I didn't say anything?" He pleaded.

"C'mon let's hear it man." Clare egged Ridley on. "I'm 'the man' now...because I'll be working on putting the bad guys away and keeping the country safe."

"Are you kidding me? Why would I think that...of all people...We're cops Clare!" He replied. "It's not *that* part of the government that bothers me...just don't start working in politics like your old man alright?"

Clare laughed out loud, almost spilling the beer she had just sipped. "My dad is a great mayor!" She said. "The city loves him...He's really done a lot of good things for Baltimore."

I sat there, listening to my fiancée and my best friend bicker innocently, trying to avoid conversation about Sean Mash, but Clare turned to me.

"C'mon John...you like my dad right?" She said smirking at me.

"Sure I do." I said, making eye contact with Ridley. He stared back into my eyes too with a little smirk. We both knew what the other was thinking, but he didn't acknowledge my awkwardness.

"You guys always seem to get along at dinners and functions." Clare went on.

I just shrugged and took another sip of beer.

"What's the matter with you John?" she asked. "You always get so quiet when my father comes up."

"It's just that..." I was searching for an answer to give her, but I couldn't tell her the truth. Mostly I just didn't think Clare was ready to hear her dad was a crook. Ridley and I exchanged another look, and he looked at me with convicting eyes behind his bottle as he sipped.

"...I—I just get the impression that your Dad doesn't like me Clare."

"What? Nonsense! He's always talking about you...asking about you."

Once again, me and Ridley's eyes met, quickly at this comment, and he froze with the bottle still touching his lips. We both were thinking that Sean was obviously trying to get information on me.

Keep your enemies closer.

"Well...ok. If you say so baby." I said, and I smiled at her. She leaned over and gave me a peck on the cheek.

"Anyways!" Ridley changed the subject. "I think you'll do a fine job with the bureau Clare! I for one, feel much safer knowing that you will be out there protecting our country abroad...while your man and I here take care of things here at home." I reached across the table with my beer.

"Amen." I said, and we clinked bottles. I was secretly thanking him for saving my butt during that last conversation.

"Well..." Clare said, and she paused to take the last swig of her beer. "I feel safe...knowing that my boys are preserving my home town. I'll try not to let you guys down."

"You won't baby." I said to her. "You're gonna save the world."

"I thought *you* were going to." She replied with a grin.

"Geez!" Ridley said. "You're both like this eh?"

"Like what?" Clare asked playfully.

"Apocalyptic! Doom and gloom, the world's gonna end!"

"Something's gonna happen, Rid." I said. "Shit will hit the fan one day, you'll see. And on that day, who do you think is gonna be out there in the middle of it all? The bankers? The convenience store owners? No, man! The cops! Us!" I motioned to the three of us in a circle. "We're gonna be the ones responding to the crisis. Someone has to!"

Ridley stared at me with a smirk because he knew I was right. He chuckled and then leaned forward with his beer in hand. "Well..." He said. "In that case, let's make a toast." And he lifted his bottle into the centre of our table.

Clare lifted her bottle into the middle too, and I so did I.

"What are we toasting?" Clare asked.

"To the three of us!" Ridley stated.

We all looked at each other with a happy grin.

"To our safety...and to us staying friends."

"Here, here!" Clare bellowed in a deep voice.

"Cheers to that buddy." I said, and we all clinked our bottles again and took sips. Clare and I leaned in for a kiss.

"Alright, Alright...get a room." Ridley said. "I hate to run guys...but Holly's waiting for me at home...I should get out of here."

Ridley stood up and pulled his jacket on as he said this. He reached into his pocket and pulled out some bills. After counting them out properly he slapped them down on the table. There was enough there for all of us.

"This one's on me, you guys." He said smiling.

"Oh...Rid, no—." I began.

"Hey...don't do that...I insist...Congratulations Clare."

"Thanks Rid."

Ridley leaned down, and she half stood up so they could share a hug, and then Ridley walked out, winking at me.

"Cya tomorrow buddy." I said.

Clare and I looked at each other and smiled. I looked down at the money on the table. Picking it up, I held it up in front of Clare. She raised an eyebrow at me to ask what I was thinking.

"Extra cash...coffee?" I asked.

It was a perfect spring night. It wasn't too cold—just brisk, Clare and I were wearing our light jackets as we walked down the city sidewalks, coffee in our hands. We had been walking for a few blocks now, sharing laughs and enjoying each other's company as we sipped away.

"So, you never really told me how work was." Clare said to me.

"It was ok..." I said. I always tried to hide my bad-days from Clare, but she could see right through me.

"Oh, I know that tone." She said. "What happened?"

"It's nothing, babe." I gave in. "It's just—did you hear about the guy Ridley and I brought in today?"

"The pedophile guy? I didn't get a chance to read any of the reports before my shift was over. Was it bad?"

"Bad?" I asked. "I don't think that's the right word...Evil, Clare—that's the only way to describe it."

"Oh...I'm sorry hun'. We don't need to bring it up if you don't want. I shouldn't have asked, I—."

"—I can't believe people are so sick Clare!" I continued. We had stopped walking at this point. Now that the can of worms was open, I had to get it off my chest.

Maybe I would feel better.

Maybe...

Probably not.

"John—." Clare started.

"We got a call from this computer repair man. He was on a job call, fixing a customer's computer...The fact that this guy even asked a company to come to his house is beyond me...how could he expect that we wouldn't have found the content on his hard drive?"

"Sounds pretty typical John...wha—?"

"—When we showed up to respond...We heard some noises in the basement. This guy was sweating as soon as we stepped into his place. Rid and I could tell something was up."

I had to stop. My heart began to beat faster as I was saying it out loud. I needed to sit. I could feel my lungs tightening. Reliving the experience was more than awful. We sat down on a nearby bench as we continued to talk.

"There were kids down there Clare. Little kids. Boys and girls, five...some maybe seven."

"How did his home cameras not pick that up?" Clare asked.

"He was bringing them into the basement through the windows at the back of the house. They led right into the cellar." I replied.

"Oh my word..." Clare gasped.

"The looks on these kids' faces, Clare...they didn't even care that we were there. I could see it in their eyes. They were so broken, that it didn't even matter that help was finally here for them. It was too late." I hung my head and buried my face into my palms as Clare rubbed my back.

"John." She started. "It wasn't your fault...people—their just—."

"Evil!" I said, lifting my head. "Their evil Clare. I wanted to kill him today." I looked at Clare with glassy eyes, fighting back the anger, or fear, or sadness, whatever it was I was feeling. I took a breath through quivering lips and looked down at my hands which were shaking. I made fists to control the shaking but they were still moving. "I could have killed him Clare."

"And maybe you should have..." She said, to my surprise. I looked at her with a furrowed brow.

"What?" I asked.

"I said, maybe you should have..." I knew there was another point she was trying to make so I let it play out, staring at her. "Wanting to kill somebody for the horrible things they've done is a natural human response." She continued. "Vengeance, is something we all crave, whether it be in small matters or greater. But John...you didn't." She glared at me and I knew she was trying to say that it was okay. Clare could say a lot with just her face. "Hey..." She continued. "God knows, I agree with you. There are a lot of people out there who probably deserve to die—according to us. I've thought the same things you have baby, believe me. I've been to that place. That dark place, where you think it would be easier to just kill them all. Wipe the slate clean and start over again. But John, isn't that why we do what we do? We're the good guys. Are our thoughts not evil for wanting to murder these people?"

"I don't know baby..." I said, sighing loudly. "But you know the court system Clare. The loop holes this guy is going to be able to jump through. Just to be out and do it again to someone else's poor kids. You're right; it would be easier to just wipe them out." I said darkly.

I was thinking about the pedophile Ridley and I arrested earlier today. I was thinking about the gang losers we had seen Maggie with. Even about Clare's dad.

I had not had a great day. I wondered where our old friend Dave's orphan daughter Maggie was sleeping tonight.

I was thinking what a *horrible* place the world was.

A haunting tune brooded in my mind, as an idea suddenly flashed in my brain.

What if I changed the world? What if I could be the one who crossed the line?

I shut my eyes tightly and sighed, almost in agony, and I lowered my head. I was trying to shake these thoughts out, thinking; *Where did that come from?*

That seed, fully cracked open now and dozens of roots were spidering through my very veins. Black roots. A venom...a poison...this had made me think these thoughts. This blackness was starting to consume me.

"I don't know what to do, babe." I said. I looked up at Clare, who was still rubbing my back. Those beautiful eyes of hers were staring back into mine. I knew she was on my side. I could see understanding in those eyes, and comfort. Most of all I could see her *choice* to be with me here tonight. I wasn't forcing her, she didn't have to be here. She was so amazing, she always sought my feelings out, and dragged them out of me, because she genuinely cared about me. That's all I ever wanted; someone who wanted to be with me as badly as I wanted to be with them, and I had that in her. She was always able to make these feelings go away. Especially now, when I was so conflicted.

...she was always around for me when I needed her.

She was looking at me now with a sympathetic smile. "It's okay hun." she said. "It's okay that you're feeling this way. I'm not judging you."

I sighed in relief. I was tense, but somehow I knew that Clare would never have judged me in the first place. *Why was I so worried?*

"See look." She said. She had glanced away for a second and something caught her eye. I looked towards the store window in front of us that she was pointing to. There was a bunch of television monitors behind the glass displaying a news cast of something.

"The Bears." Clare said, darkly. "Joseph Kovacs. Now there's an evil man John."

The news was showing a clip of an attack made by the Bears, in the middle east. On the screen was an image of Kovacs and Clare was staring at it. "If you want to kill anybody...let it be him." She said. "I don't know what the answer is babe." She continued, looking back at me now. "But the fact is; evil does exist. It's very real." She was looking back at the TV now. "Here I am telling you about right and wrong..." she trailed off. She stared at the TV for a while. "John, I was a little girl when this guy first came on the scene. I grew up watching this guy turn into the horrible *demon* he is now."

I smiled... "Maybe you can help stop him when you're with the F.B.I." I was joking at the time, of course, trying to make light of this topic and move on. She looked at me with a smirk.

"Are you making fun of me?" She asked, squinting her eyes.

"No." I said, grinning now. "Never." And I leaned in for a kiss. She kissed me back and I again forgot all about Kovacs on the TV, about the scumbags of the world, and I was just in the moment now with Clare.

I remember thinking;

How can life be so horrible and yet amazing at the same time?

* * *

That night I lay in bed and I couldn't be sure if I slept or not.

After many sessions of tossing and turning I was lying sprawled out with my limbs all over the place. The sheets were a disaster, half hanging off my body and I stared at the ceiling endlessly. That haunting tune had grown and grown all night.

I don't know what to do...

My own words to Clare echoed in my mind, serving as lyrics to this looming score droning on and on. Never ceasing. Consuming me.

I could actually *feel* the roots of this dark plant inside of me coursing through my skin—as if these feelings had now taken on an actual life and that life was crawling on me and in me.

I couldn't shake this!

Not anymore...

...I entered into that place between dreaming and awake again. Among my other haunting thoughts, that buzzing sound began to grow in my dream. The awake part of me began to think; *not this again!* But the electric noise grew amidst my thoughts of Genocide, torture and murder, stemmed from greed and corruption—

ZZZZZZAAAPP—"*JOHN!!*" My voice called out again. "*PLEASE!!*"

I tossed and turned until I couldn't take it anymore. I forced myself awake and sat up in my bed. My own haunting cries of help echoed in my mind. I threw the sheets off and got up. Shirtless and barefoot, I went into the bathroom and took a leak. I couldn't shake the faces from my mind or those pleas from my ears.

Clare's face,

"*JOHN!!*" My own voice in my head.

Her father's smug face, grinning...

"*PLEASE!!*" What was I pleading about?!

Kang's face, wanting more Intel.

"*DON'T!!*" Don't? Don't what!?

Ridley's face,

The dead woman's face...

"*JOHN!!*"
The faces of those kids...
I shut my eyes tight and sighed, lowering my head to the beat of a defeating blow of dark music that pushed down on my soul!
I shook off the drips and turned to the sink. I splashed some cold water on my face several times trying to wash these images out of my mind. I gave up, leaving the tap running and leaving myself heaped over the sink, resting on my elbows. I moved like a sloth, turning off the tap and I propped myself up, leaning on the counter with my hands. I slowly lifted my gaze to the mirror as the water dripped off my face.
This is the face that they see.
I thought. The people I deal with as a cop. My enemies. It was becoming a hardened face, rather than that fresh pup out of the academy. This dog was growing up. I reached for a towel and smothered my face with it to dry it. Then I ran my hands over my smooth cheeks and gave myself another long stare.
I sighed and started talking to myself.
"Is this the face your enemies will fear?" I asked my reflection. "Are these the eyes that will convict them?" I chuckled to myself at my own ridiculousness and I dropped my own gaze. I looked into the mirror again and shook my head. I still looked so young.

Soon I was slamming back the last drips of a honey lager from my fridge. I jarred the bottle down onto my little apartment counter, right beside the two other empty ones just like it. I wiped my mouth and sighed, leaning on the counter.
The beer hadn't erased the thoughts or faces either. They may as well have all been in the room with me. I itched my skin when I felt the force of these feelings crawling on me again.
There was a pile of wedding invitations Clare had given me sitting on the counter too.
'Please mail these out, Hun' a little note she wrote me said, followed with a couple xo's and a heart she drew. I was able to crack a smile, thinking about her. The good of life and the bad both fought for my attention. I tried imagining my life with Clare. Us with a couple of kids. Me playing with my son.
I felt a sharp stab of the dark side and shut my eyes again, not able to hold on to those good thoughts. My son's face turned into the faces of those kids. Clare's face turned into the dead woman's face.
"*STOP!*" I yelled into the darkness of my apartment.
I grabbed my keys and my smokes and I headed out the door.
Had I have stayed for even 30 more seconds that night I would have seen what happened next. There was an electric arc of blue light in my apartment and a loud—
—*ZZZZAAPP!!*

A piece of mail, in an envelope, landed on my nightstand and tumbled behind the bed, to be remained unseen.

The word; *JOHN* scratched onto the front by hand.

As I walked the city streets I tried thinking about anything else then my current life events. I was able to numb the bad stuff by filling my head with Clare and how good it was going with her. While she was finalizing wedding plans, I was struggling with the weight of the world. The dark music followed me out here and I still couldn't fully shake this stuff. Everywhere I looked I saw hurt and desperation. I ended up in some scummy part of town and all I saw were the places this system, I had so much faith in, failed. Homeless. Criminals. Prostitutes. Sick people. A broken city.

The bass beats in my head copied my slow footsteps and I just walked with my hands in my pockets staring blankly at everything I saw.

I'd love to change the world...

My thoughts began to say.

If only there was someone who could do something...

If only...

*Me?...*I began to have a conversation with myself in my mind.

Yah, you!

I can't.

No one else will.

There has to be another way.

Then what is it!?

I sighed, realizing there was no answer to my own question.

But, *what am I going to do?*...the lyrics in my head echoed again.

I sat on a bench to rest. I landed on it with a thud and I slumped into it. I bumped a smoke out of the pack and lit it up. Taking a big drag, I sat back and closed my eyes. I blew the plume up into the sky and opened my eyes. I stared into the sky, wondering what was up there—contemplating my feelings and considering the fact that there has to be more than this *shit*. *This can't be it!*

I leaned forward and started people watching now. Taking some more drags I looked around and saw a homeless guy trying to keep warm.

I again, thought of my mother,

Back to the day this seed was planted in me.

How can I help? I began wresting with myself again.

I don't know what to do...

I saw all kinds of people slumming around with defeated looks on their faces.

I sat back again and lifted my eyes to the sky once more.

"I need to be involved." I said to the sky. "I can't take this anymore." I had no idea who I was talking to. God...or...whoever the hell was up there...I don't know...

"Please..." I said. "Use me...I'm ready..."

I remained staring up for a while until I started thinking about how silly this was. I shook my head and lowered it and I took the final drags from the stump of a cigarette I had left. I threw it down and looked around one final time, but something caught my eye.

I saw a bunch of girls standing around on the street corner. Prostitutes. A nicer looking car, obviously not anyone who lived in this area, came to a stop in front of one girl and I watched. I watched the young, tall, blonde girl walk over to his window and offer her services. I was appalled when she turned and I realized who it was...

Maggie!

Our friend Dave had knocked his girlfriend up when Ridley and I were still in grade school. Dave was our older buddy; he was held back a few times so he was older than everyone else in our classes. Eventually they let him advance and he made it to high school while we were stuck in grade 7. By the time he was 15 he had had a baby. I babysat this girl for heaven's sake! Now she was selling herself on the streets—*how could this happen?*

The man lost interest and drove away, so Maggie turned and began to prowl the street corner again. I saw her look to her right quickly and become jumpy. A figure emerged from the shadows of the alley and I had to strain my eyes to see him—but there was no mistaking this punk; 'Megga'.

I became filled with rage but I knew I couldn't just run over there and start pounding him like I wanted to—but then again; *why not?*

She was 17! Her situation had gone from bad to worse. I had watched her run away constantly from the orphanage, and brought her back numerous times, but eventually her behaviour escalated there to the point where she began assaulting the staff. The influence those gang losers were putting on her was no good and she accumulated a criminal record, getting her kicked out of the orphanage, sending her to a shelter while she was out on bail. Maggie would run away from the shelters and then get charged with breaching the terms of her bail conditions. She got arrested and even did a bit a time for failing to comply. By the time she got out, the crowd she was rolling with welcomed her back, but at a cost. I guess Maggie's need for acceptance was so desperate that this was the only way she saw fit.

I needed to talk to her. I approached her as if I was a fare, but it looked like her heart stopped when she realized it was me after I pulled my hood off.

She darted in the other direction, but I grabbed her arm to stop her. I couldn't let this scene be out in the open, or else Megga would come out to rough her up or me—well, he could try. I quickly forced us into the dark shadows of the nearest alley way.

"Please don't do this here!" Maggie said, half whispering. She was trembling and on the verge of crying.

"Sshh!" I said. "It's okay Mags. I'm not going to tell anyone."

"I know why you're here." She said, crying now. Tears of embarrassment. "You're gonna' try and talk me out of doing this."

"Well, of course I am Mags! I can't let you stay out here. Why are you doing this?"

She stopped and leaned back against the wall, and she buried her face in her hands. She let out a big sigh. "What else am I gonna' do John?" She said desperately. "I'm an orphan! My parents were murdered by loan sharks; I'm a criminal for god's sake! I can't get a job anywhere else, I don't have an education...nobody wants me John!" She started sobbing now. "These guys that pay me are the only ones who want me..."

"They don't want you Mags. Not the real you...They want to use you up and throw you away when their done with you. This is an illusion! Stop this!"

"And do what?"

"Go back to the shelter...do your time Mags...that's the only way—face the charges, do your time and get this behind you."

"You make it sound so easy John."

"It's not easy...it's never going to be. But you can't do this the rest of your life. I've seen too many girls wash up dead on the coast. You can't become one of those girls...I won't let you."

"You won't let me? Thanks Dad!"

"Somebody has to guide you Mags! What are you staying around here for...that punk Megga? He's not your friend. I'm your friend!"

"You were my Dad's friend!"

I paused and took a deep breath. "Mags...please. Go back to the shelter. Plead out and accept the sentence. Get this part of your life over with and move on. I can help you."

"How are you going to help me? You going to pay for me tonight? Or just give me your money?"

"Maggie! Stop that! Don't be like this! There's programs you can get into, courses...I can help you get back on your feet. But I can't force you...you have to choose not to live like this!"

"I don't see any other choices in front of me John. I have no other options but this. Now if you'll excuse me, you're costing me a lot of money." She tried to sound tougher when she said that but her voice cracked right at the last syllable. She stormed past me and returned to the sidewalk. I was so frustrated that it took me a while to unfreeze and turn around. When I did I saw her getting into the back of a man's car and I just watched the car drive away.

The haunting score in my head beat back up with a vengeance and I let the darkness win. This was my proverbial straw that broke my camel's back. I was so infused with these feelings now and my idea had finally taken root into my heart.

Enough. I said to myself.

Enough now...

No more arguing and trying to convince myself out of what I knew was inevitable.

Something in me snapped and I wasn't going to wait any longer. I ripped off my coat and headed towards the homeless man I had just been watching. I woke him up and gave him the coat. I sat down with him and began talking to him.

I became a police officer to try and change all of this—to make a difference, only to find out that there was a very limited amount of change I could affect from within the law. I could arrest people, but more people would just pop up. I started thinking of ways I could pull this off. I really wanted to help the people I saw suffering on the streets; homeless, victims of crime, young girls caught up in prostitution—those who couldn't help themselves...people like Maggie. Ridley was right when he said it; there wasn't really much I could do for them. If I could become a street person, and fully understand what it meant to be one of them, then I could live amongst them and help them. I could be the one who stands up for their justice when no one else would. I could fight off the predators that stalked them in the darkness, while the rest of the city slept.

I could do what really needed to be done to save Maggie.

I could go and stop that punk Megga.

I could do what really needed to be done to take out the crooks of my city.

Jimmy Olive,

Sean Mash...

I could change things.

But they wouldn't accept me as I was...I would need to show them that I understood what it was like to be them. A hero from within...

CHAPTER TWELVE
The Cowboy and the Bandit

Had I known The Stranger was watching my every move, things up until now would have been different. Had I know anything about Him or had any kind of relationship with Him, this all would have turned out different.

But He didn't choose to get involved until that fateful day in the alley, where we first met.

But He *was* watching me, His chess piece, at every turn.

The day after I had encountered Maggie and learned the truth, I became bolder in what I was doing. I started spending actual nights on the streets; sleeping beside other homeless people, warming my hands on the same trash can fire. Every once and a while I got that feeling that someone was watching me, and I would turn to look into the shadows.

It was always Him...

When Clare was so busy catching Kovacs, I was able to take more time-off and she didn't even notice. I would say I was working, but during my off weeks I was on the streets. I began to strike up conversations with street people and just talk to them. Some of them had some incredible stories; some of which really made me realize how much life is about choices. I talked to homeless men who came from rich families! Men whose greed became so powerful that no one in their families wanted anything to do with them...disowned and swindled...guys used for their money and then thrown to the dogs the next day. The conversations were filled with tragedy. Some of them even explained to me how humbling their whole experience had been. In some really tragic cases my first reaction was to give them some money...but they refused. Put up a fight even...they didn't want *anything* to do with money anymore. And then *I* was very humbled.

The other part of me, however, saw the unfairness of it all, the injustice! I wished I could do one giant swoop and make all the pain disappear for these people. On top of my job and all of my other feelings, I became angrier, and more fueled. Angry at the people who were responsible for putting these people in their situations, angry at the government for their part in all of this.

It was time for change.

2040...Suddenly it was weeks before Clare and I's wedding now. The last few months had all gone by so quick.

I hadn't exactly been focused on wedding plans lately.

Clare and I would walk around cake stores and, as she chatted with the cake decorators, I would just replay conversations I had had with bums and hookers the night before. I would day dream about bringing people the justice they deserved. Men like Megga, Jimmy Olive, and Clare's father. I would try to wrap my head around how I would make my plan work logistically and morally...if that was even an option.

"John?" Clare's voice cut in. "How about this one?" She asked.

I zoned back in and looked at the cake she was trying to show me. I stared blankly at her for a moment or two before she chimed in again. "John? You okay?"

"Hmm?" I asked. "Oh...yah. Is this the one you like?"

"Well, I dunno." She said warmly. "I like the colour and the shape, but I dunno if I like these little swirly designs here, see?"

I looked and watched her carry on.

"I can't decide if I like this one, or this other one." She went on, moving towards another cake on the display. I heard her sweet voice continue to talk but my obsessive look at her muffled the actual words. A smile spread across my lips as I watched her. She was so happy, and I was conflicted within, thinking about her father and all the things I had been up to lately. I could just stay with her and forget all this other garbage. She was my connection back to everything good about life. She was my polar opposite of the spectrum of these profound feelings. But it also made me want to change the world that much more.

"You okay, Hun?" She asked me as we were leaving the store. "You seemed kinda weird in there."

"No, I'm ok, baby." I lied. "Just tired today."

I put my arm around her and brought her in as we walked. I kissed the top of her head and she cuddled on my shoulder. She looked up at me and craned up for a kiss.

"Mmm." She said, rubbing her lips together afterwards. "Are you gonna shave for the wedding?" She asked. "I'm not used to this stubbly face." She went on, rubbing my cheek with the back of her hand. "It's so scratchy."

"Of course I will." I said, running my own hand over my face.

"It's not like you to not shave." Clare said. "I'm surprised Sarge hasn't busted you yet." She joked.

I laughed. It felt good to laugh with her. "I'm just trying something new." I said.

"Well try it after the wedding." Clare smiled and linked arms with me as we walked.

All the preparations were done; reception hall, tux fittings, dress fittings, flowers, catering, photographer...you name it.

In the meantime, we had bought our loft together and were preparing to move in. Clare and I spent many evenings packing up our own apartments and emptying the boxes out. When Clare was helping me with my move, she was standing watch while Ridley and I emptied my bedroom. Bed, dresser, and lastly Ridley lifted up the night stand and walked out. Clare was sweeping behind us gathering any lose items of clothing or other things. On her last look around the room she spotted the white envelope lying by the baseboards where the bed had been. She walked over and picked it up. She flipped it over and read the 'JOHN' written on the face of it. She furrowed her brow and shrugged. Then she gathered any remaining things and tossed them, along with the letter, into a box labelled miscellaneous...

POW!

I was at the Mash family home again for another dinner, and I heard the loud packing sounds accompanied with grunts and screams. Clare sent me out to get some wood from the shed for the old style fire place. She didn't realize, and neither did I; that her dad was conducting some 'business' in that shed. The sounds were growing louder as I approached the doors. I had stopped at first, but my curiosity as an officer was peaked and I had to know what was going on in there.

POW!

I could hear several voices including Sean's and I thought to myself; *this is it. This is my chance to catch him in the act.* I pulled out my cell phone and turned the camera feature on, and then I slid it into my shirt pocket so that the lens was just sticking out of the top of it. I approached the doors with the sounds of the beating going on inside still resounding. I slowly pushed the doors open and they silently revealed the scene inside.

This couldn't have been better—

Sean himself was standing over the man tied to the chair, with his jacket off and sleeves rolled up. He was sweaty and short of breath, and his hands were bloody. His two body guards were with him as well and they stood at either side of him with their sleeves rolled up too. I assumed they were taking turns. I only had a few brief seconds to survey the scene, and I was shocked to realize who the man being beaten was, because he looked right at me through his misery. Jimmy Olive's face was broken and bleeding and he peered at me through swollen eyes.

Suddenly Sean turned around to see me standing there, and we were both frozen for a moment. I knew Sean was crooked, but to see him like this— directly assaulting a man tied to a chair. I assumed later, that Jimmy Olive had screwed up the funds somehow and was now paying the price. With blood dripping off his knuckles, and panting heavily through his fear of being caught by me, he stared at me blankly through wide eyes. The two body guards made a move and I took a step back.

"No!" Sean told them, and they stopped short.

Nobody knew what to do now...we all just stood there looking back and forth at each other. I considered myself tough, but I wasn't stupid. I could put up a good fight with the big oafs but with no back-up and alone out here in the shed, it was three against one. We would need to come back and arrest him later. Before I knew it, the shed doors were both slammed in my face by the guards, and the last thing I saw was Sean's face staring at me.

I stood there for a brief moment and then I came to my senses. I pulled my phone out of my shirt pocket and immediately began to upload the video clip to Kang as I rushed back to the house. Once he got a hold of this footage that was it.

Kang would know what to do...

Like I said before; all the prep was done, and it was coming up to the big day. All I could think about was how beautiful Clare was going to look in that wedding dress. The wedding was on Saturday; only two days away!

I had uploaded the video to Kang right away but I didn't hear back the rest of the day. I went into work on Monday and he wasn't there. Nobody heard from him and Sarge said he hadn't called in sick. They did a home visit and they couldn't find him. On Tuesday they contacted other people in his family—Kang was a single guy, who lived alone in his apartment—they called his known relatives to ask if they had seen him, but none of them had. That afternoon it was handed off to a special investigation team who then began looking into his disappearance, and now on Thursday we still hadn't heard anything.

It was a traditional wedding. Outdoors, in the summer. All the guests were there and Pachelbel Canon was playing now. Ridley smiled at his wife, Holly, as she walked down the aisle as a bridesmaid. He grabbed my shoulders and squeezed a little, massaging out my tension and I breathed out slowly.

I sat on a street corner—Maggie's corner—in the shadows, and I watched her. I watched her pimp, Megga and tried to figure out his routine.

Two days ago, Ridley and I were on the road, cruising around. My cell rang and I answered. Sarge gave me the news; they had found Kang.

The guests all stood and I felt my chest tighten up. I was staring down the long empty aisle and it felt like an eternity until I saw a radiant glare of white round the corner. It looked like she was glowing and I felt the breath leave my lungs, paralyzing me.

I stood at trash can fires and warmed my hands with my new friends. I listened to all their stories.

I raced the cruiser to the scene and came to a skidding stop at the side of the road, at the East Harbour. Forensic teams were standing by, and I flung my door open before the car even stopped. I ran through the yellow caution tape and met up with the lead investigator who had carriage of Kang's disappearance case. He had a very solemn look on his face when he turned to greet me. I turned to look past him right on the shore. There was a group of forensics snapping photos before they covered up the body they had just pulled from the water.

All I could do was stare at her as she walked towards me. I had the goofiest grin spread across my face and I was choking back tears. Clare wasn't doing such a good job holding hers back. She was beaming at me but I could tell she was fighting the happy tears. She was so beautiful; I didn't even remember that the man who led her, with their arms linked, down the aisle was a secret evil mobster; a thug and a murderer.

I approached the gurney with a zipped up body bag on it as they led it towards the ambulance. I stopped the crew who was moving it.

I was on the streets one day and I was hungry. I saw it there...ripe and shiny like glass and a choice presented itself. I stole that apple and killed my innocence. My first crime since life out here.

Flashes, not just from our wedding photographer but from the selected media who were allowed in, were snapping pictures of the city's mayor. His daughter's wedding was a good story and Sean Mash loved the positive spotlight. Clare finally reached the end of the aisle and was standing in front of me in her dress. I had to forget about all of that, and honestly—looking at her now and how perfectly she was presented for me, I did completely forget about it.

The body bag at the harbour was unzipped for me.

"Who presents this woman, to give her hand in matrimony to be wed to this man?" the priest asked.

I already knew who was in body bag, but I still had to see him. The cold and blue face of Kang was revealed, along with the bullet hole right in the centre of his forehead and I sighed when I saw him dead.

"I do." Sean said, and his eyes flicked over to look right at me. I glared back for a moment but tried to keep my eyes on my bride. He still hadn't let go of Clare, who beamed at me under her veil.

Kang was gone. The lead in the fight against the mob and against my new father-in-law. The guy from the coroner's office zipped the bag back up and they wheeled the body away from me.

I approached Clare and extended my hand out to her. While Clare was looking at her dad and smiling I looked at him, and allowed my fury to burn for a few brief seconds. He broke his gaze with me and smiled at Clare as he raised her hand up to kiss it. Clare then turned to me and placed her hand in mine. She stepped away from her father and came to my left side, still grasping my hand. Before we walked up to the pulpit together, I turned to Sean who was still standing there. We were both smirking at each other and I extended my hand out him. His grin grew on his face and he chuckled softly under his breath, and then he connected his hand to mine gripping it tight. I gripped back. I made a decision right then and there, on my wedding day; No more. No more Kang. No more organized crime unit. No more police. Me and Sean Ahab Mash were going to settle this the old fashion way. We didn't say anything to one another, we just stared into the other one's eyes and had a little mind conversation; I was letting him know I was going to get him, and he was saying 'good luck'.

The doors of the ambulance slammed shut and Sarge came up to my side. He didn't say anything, but he patted me on the back and then walked away. I didn't turn my head to look at him once, and I just stared as the ambulance drove away

The rest of the ceremony carried on and I got lost in Clare's beauty, forgetting momentarily about her dad. The end of the ceremony was the best part, when I got to lift Clare's veil for our first kiss. I grabbed hold of both sides of her face and slowly leaned in as we closed our eyes.

* * *

The honeymoon ended.
Summer was just ending and Autumn beginning. I went to the organized crime unit and tried speaking with the cop who took over Kang's investigations.
"Hi." The new guy said.
"Hey." I introduced. "I'm John-uh-Revele, sorry."
"What can I do for you, Revele?"
"I was wondering if I could speak to you about some of officer Kang's old cases."
"Ok...shoot."
"One in particular, um...this one was pretty confidential, I'm not sure what kind of clearance the intelligence department has given you yet. Uh...I was working with Kang on this one, tell you what, I'm not sure how to handle this...can you just do me a favour? If you come across 'project Olive' can you let me know? I have a piece of intel that I obtained before he uh..."
"...We're all still adjusting. It's a huge transition period in this office too man, trying to sort out each detective's work and bringing me in...I'll keep an eye out for sure, ok?"
"Good enough. Thanks."

It ate at me that I couldn't yet trust Kang's replacement the way I trusted him. I stored away my evidence and sat on this one a while.

I didn't want to give myself away to the new detective or raise any kind of suspicion until I knew for sure that I could trust him for one, and that the project Olive case files made it into the right hands.

As Autumn bled into winter, Clare and I's relationship began to deteriorate fast.

She called me one night to tell me she wouldn't come home.

"Baby, I won't be coming home tonight." She said on the other end of the phone.

"Oh?" I said, not surprised. I had lost count of how many times this had been happening the last few months.

"Yah, we have some pretty good leads on Kovacs here...we gotta check em out."

"Mmhmm. Yep. I get it." I said plainly.

"John..." She began. "Mark says he's very pleased with my work! He said I'm becoming a valuable asset to this team! Isn't that cool? This is amazing, it feels so cool!"

"Hhmm." I simply said.

"John? You okay?"

"Yep. I'm okay." I lied. "I'll just see ya later I guess."

"Okay..." Clare said, sounding disappointed.

I didn't even bother saying goodbye and I hung up my cell phone. I lit up a smoke and took a deep drag. I knew I was sabotaging my own relationship and I hated it! But I needed Clare! I needed her so badly right now to connect me back to the world and what was good about it. Without her I roamed the streets of this shithole and regressed further into my feelings.

The nights she was away I slept on the streets but didn't really sleep. I found solace here. I made friends out here. I made plans out here. But something was still holding me back...

The nights she was home, I was kept awake by the sounds of her beating our punching bag in our beautiful new loft we bought together.

My own flesh peeled on the bag as I hammered out my passions. I couldn't tell whose blood on the bag was whose anymore; mine or Clare's.

One night I was so overwhelmed that as I lay my final blows I had to stop. A piercing emotion stabbed me in the heart and I tried to stop it. I gave in and began to sob against the bag. I was a mess.

Spring came and I knocked on the door to Kang's old office.

"Hey..." The detective said. "Revele right?"

"That's me."

"What's up?"

"Uh, well—I was wondering if you ever had the chance to—"

"—Olive!" He blurted out. "Right? Project Olive..."
"Yep...that's it."
"Didn't find anything man."
I sighed. Of course he didn't.
"Oh..." I said, hiding my disappointment.
"Did you have some evidence to file or something?" He asked me, as he pointed to my cell phone that I had been clutching.
"Oh!" I said, when I realized I had been doing this. "Uh...no, no...it's okay. I must be mistaken."
The two of us shared a very awkward stare until I thanked him and walked out.

Just a few weeks later, I was standing in line at a coffee shop with Ridley, avoiding the judgmental stares of the public as they eyed us in our uniforms. I was day dreaming and thinking about most of things I just explained. I was thinking about the last time I had spoken to Clare. I soon remembered that it was that fight we had when I asked her to hurry up and catch Kovacs.
—BANG!
Gun shots snapped me out of my trance.
BANG! BANG
"John?" Ridley's voice...
In a few split seconds I turned to see him beside me in line. He looked worried...
Scared.
The next few minutes went by so fast...
I looked at my hands that were covered in Ridley's blood. I had helped him to the ground and now was putting pressure on his arm wound.
"Rid...it's gonna' be oka—.'"
BANG!
I ducked and laid myself out across Ridley as the glass from the donut display case shattered and rained glass down on top of us. I rolled off of Ridley, at the same time retrieving my gun from its holster. I lay on my back and pointed my gun forward. I scanned the store front rapidly and shouted for everyone to get down. I saw a dark shadowy silhouette move outside the store as everyone hit the floor. I saw him lower his gun and proceed to his left down the sidewalk.
I sat up quickly and propped myself up on one knee. I fired several shots;
BAM! BAM! BAM! BAM!
The store front windows shattered and collapsed and I followed my moving target as he fled along the front of the coffee shop.
BAM! BAM! BAM!
I was only able to squeeze the trigger three more times before he disappeared around the back of the store. The sounds of screams and panic now filled the store.

"I'm fine!" Ridley shouted as I looked at him. "GO!" He was holding his own arm now and sitting against the counter. I hesitated for a second...I couldn't leave Ridley there to bleed, but he held out his fist to me, with blood running over his knuckles.

Potato...

...Fries!

I jumped up with a new determination and ran towards the store front, jumping through the open space that used to be the windows. I turned to my right and began pursuit of the shooter, as I called it in over the radio mic on my shoulder.

I came around the back of the store with my gun raised and I didn't see anything. My heart was pounding and I could hear my breath in my ear drums. I advanced along the line of the building, surveying every inch of space I could see.

BANG! PA-CHIIIIING!!!

The bullet ricocheted off the air conditioning unit and I flinched when I felt the sting on my temple. I hit the ground thinking I was shot, but when more gun fire came I just rolled and rolled to my right. I could see the muzzle flashes, coming from ahead of me and I came to a stop on my belly with my arms stretched out in front of me. I returned fire—

BAM! BAM! BAM! BAM! BAM! BAM!

—until my clip was empty. I watched the same figure that shot at us in the store flee to my right and I quickly got to my feet to chase him. I ejected my magazine to the ground and pushed a fresh one into the handle. I could feel hot blood running down the side of my face along with the sweat. I kept my gun half raised as I ran around the other side of the coffee shop where the shooter had gone. As I cleared the side of the building I saw him dart to his left down the city sidewalk. I quickened my pace, as I called in new information about the direction the shooter was now travelling.

"FREEZE!" I yelled after him, now on the same path just behind him. At the end of the block I saw a black car squeal its brakes to a fierce stop at the corner, mounting the curb. I knew this was his getaway vehicle. "STOP RIGHT THERE!" I screamed. The shooter extended his right arm back and fired off a few shots at me. I dropped to the ground and rolled to my right where I saw a city garbage unit and newspaper box to hide behind. I peeked my head out and saw him turn towards the car. I popped up from behind the box and aimed at the man, but there was too many people scrambling on the sidewalk from the commotion. I couldn't risk hitting them. Frustrated I stood to my feet and screamed at them to move as I advanced from out behind the newspaper box, gun still aimed. Most of them cleared a good enough path for me to take a shot and I didn't miss my opportunity.

BANG!!

A carefully aimed shot hit the shooter where the shoulder turns into the neck, and I saw a red splat shoot out of his trapezoid. He flailed forward to land on his face. I advanced towards him and the car. "GET OUT OF THE

CAR!" I yelled, slowly walking towards it. I saw the shooter trying to crawl towards his gun that fell just a few feet out of his reach. "Stop moving buddy!" I shouted, to which he didn't listen and kept crawling. I fired a shot at the ground beside him and he jumped and covered his head with his hands. The car's tires squealed and smoked as it hopped off the curb in reverse.

BAM! BAM! BAM! BAM!

I was able to land two shots through the windshield and the passenger side window, shattering it. It still drove forward and I ran towards it as it rounded the corner and began to drive down the street towards me. I stopped short of the curb and began to fire again at the tires. Two shots hit the front tires and the vehicle lost control and veered to its left; crashing into the garbage unit and newspaper box I had just used for cover. The car plowed right through those and crashed into the convenience store in front of it. I spun around and kept my gun on the vehicle. I could now hear the distant sound of sirens—my back up wasn't far off. I just had to contain this situation for a few more moments. I glanced back at the shooter behind me who I had forgotten about for a second. Just as I turned to look—*BANG!* I felt the bullet graze my cheek and I dropped backwards onto my back. Immediately I sat up with my gun raised in front of me and fired.

BAM! BAM!

Two shots hit the shooter; one in the arm and the other hit him in the head, forcing him back to the ground.

I just sat there, half seated, half lying down, and I just breathed. In and out. I blinked my eyes as snapped back into reality...the sirens were closer now; almost here.

Just then, I heard a loud crashing behind me and whipped around to see the car door being kicked open. My eyes widened when I saw the man inside the car aim a machine gun at me—

—This just kept getting better and better...

RATTA-TATTA-RATTA-TATTA-RATTA-TATTA!

I was running for my life as the bullets hit the ground at my fleeing heels. I ran past the man who I just killed and ducked behind a corner as bullets riddled his lifeless body on the ground. I called for the back up to get here quicker. I could hear the sirens; so close now. I could just sit here against the alley wall and wait for the cavalry...

"How the hell did you end up in this mess, John?" I asked myself frantically.

RATTA-TATTA!!

The bricks and mortar exploded beside my face on the corner of the wall I had leaned against. I began to run again down the alley away from the second shooter.

BRATTA-TATTA-TATTA!

The echoing sound of machine gun fire resonated down the alley after me.

I had one bullet in the chamber of my gun, and three left in the clip, plus another full clip on my belt, but I couldn't stop to fire or I would be hit. I needed to get cover from somewhere.

I was breathing so hard it hurt. My temple hurt from the bullet that ricocheted into the side of it, and my cheek was on fire from the bullet that grazed it. I was sweaty and tired. There was nowhere to hide...

—"Hey Pig!" A nasty sounding voice shouted from behind me. I froze. I didn't want to turn around but I had to. I had to at least see it coming. I slowly turned with my gun still in hand. The cowboy had himself a stand-off. But if I raised my gun he would fire.

"Drop your gun!" He yelled from the end of the alley.

I thought for a minute and we just stared at each other. The sirens were louder than ever now. *Why wasn't he running?* I thought. To my left there was a dumpster.

"I said drop it!" He screamed.

One more brief hesitation...*No way.*

I snapped my gun up—*BAM-BAM-BAM-BAM!!*—

—*BBRRATTA-TATTA-RATTA!!*

I leaped to the left as I emptied my clip. The slide locked back as I hit the brick wall beside the dumpster and then tumbled behind it. My shots were enough to throw the shooter's aim off as he returned fire my way. I scrambled to a sitting position against the dumpster as I listened to the *PING-PING-PING-PING!* Sounds of bullets hitting the metal dumpster.

"You're a dead man, Pig!" I heard the nasty voice echo down the alley. I ejected my empty mag to the ground and pushed in a new one. I figured he had to be nearing an empty clip as well. I poked my head out from behind the dumpster—

RATTA-TATTA-RAT—KA-CHICK!

Brief firing made me retreat back behind the dumpster but I heard the sound of his gun locking up. This was my chance. As the shooter was taking his mag out I pivoted out and fired.

BAM-BAM-BAM-BAM!

He leapt to the right as my bullets splashed into some puddles on the ground and crashed into the bricks. He slammed into the wall with his back as he shoved a new clip into his machine gun. I couldn't give him the chance to fire again.

BAM-BAM-BAM!

Two bullets missed and shattered the bricks behind him...the third struck him through his right collarbone. I could almost hear the bone shatter as he screamed out and dropped his gun.

I stood quickly and advanced from out behind the dumpster with my gun raised in front of me. He was crouching low to the ground now holding his collarbone and moaning. The gun wasn't too far in front of him.

Suddenly his head snapped up and he shot me a menacing look. I realized he wasn't giving up—I could see it in his eyes. He dove forward towards his gun.

"Don't!" I cried.

He clutched the grip of his rifle.

BAM! I fired a shot in the air to warn him; I didn't want to kill this guy, I wanted to question him. He raised the gun with a grin on his face.

BAM! BAM!

Two shots hit him; one in the upper portion of his left chest and the other his left bicep. He fell back but didn't loosen his grip on the gun. He splashed into a puddle beneath him and lay there with the gun still in his left hand.

I ran up to him now and kept my gun pointed. The first thing I did was kick the gun out of his hand and it slid across the pavement away from us.

I hadn't even noticed the flashing blue and red lights or the blare of sirens coming from cruisers parked on the curbs just outside of the alley. The other units were here and officers were entering the alley with me with their guns drawn.

I was so focused on this guy on the ground. I was breathing fire in my lungs, watching the shooter as he lay on the ground. He wasn't dead and he was breathing blood out of his mouth.

I sighed a deep breath out and I released my tight grip off the handle of my gun. I watched the colour return to my knuckles as I extended my fingers out and then made fists. With trembling hands I put the safety on my gun and placed it back in its holster.

The other officers surrounded me and bombarded me; asking if I was okay, checking me out. Two other officers came in and began to check out the mobster on the ground.

He began to cough and choke causing more blood to spew out of his mouth and we all snapped our attention towards him. I was disturbed to see a smile spread across his bloody lips, baring blood stained teeth.

"Yo—re...de— Re—le." He choked out in broken sounds.

"What did he say?" Another officer asked.

I just froze and stared at him in disbelief at what I heard.

"You're a dead man." He choked out, more clearly this time. "You're—(cough)—dead—(cough)—Revele!"

He could have read my name tag and been making empty threats in the heat of the moment. But I hadn't got close to him, and it started to make sense why he wasn't running when the sirens were nearing. He was on a mission.

To kill *me*.

I glanced around at the other officers who were all staring at me now.

Nobody saw it coming—and we hadn't patted him down yet—someone yelled; "GUN!" and I turned to see the mobster pulling a small pistol out of his jacket—

—*BLAM!!!*

I watched the mobsters face disappear in an explosion of red before I covered my face with my arm. When I looked up, another officer had a smoking shotgun aimed at the now headless body. Old Mac racked the slide of the shotgun and the empty shell flew out. We stared at each other for a long time before anybody moved...

In slow motion, we all began to disperse out of the alley. I exited back onto the sidewalk and breathed some fresh air, placing my hands on my hips. I looked up to the sky and tried to take it all in, as the relief team swarmed the alley now.

I glanced over to my right to where the getaway car had slammed into the store front. The engine was still smoking and the front end was crumpled like an accordion, trunk folded into an A shape, back passenger side door flung open and broken glass everywhere. Cops and EMS personnel were swarming the crash and I noticed that they were dragging a body out of the driver seat. One of my bullets must have hit him because he was bleeding from his chest, red against the white dress shirt he was wearing under his black suit jacket. He was screaming in pain as they pulled him out—he was still alive.

I approached the other side of the car as they were strapping him to a gurney.

"Revele!" A voice came from behind me. I didn't even see Sarge show up. "What happened here!?" He asked, flustered.

"Sarge...I—I don't even know...where's Ridley??" I asked him.

"He's fine John. They rushed him to the hospital already. They say the bullet went clean through his arm...He's gonna' be okay."

I sighed in relief. Knowing he was okay relieved a lot of my tension, and I turned my attention back to the mobster on the gurney.

"John..." Sarge said. I could hear the concern in his voice now. He rarely called me by my first name. "...John! You need to tell me what happened."

"Ridley and I...we were just grabbing a coffee. Honestly Sarge. It happened way too quick...I heard gunshots, I looked back and Rid was hit. Before I knew it, it was a fire fight!"

"Who were these guys John? I gotta' perp over here without a face, and who's this guy?" He asked pointing to the first mobster that I shot. He was lying in a pool of blood seeping out the back of his head and investigators had already begun snapping photos of him. "Was this you?"

"Yah Sarge. That was me."

"Damnit Revele! You didn't leave me any body living! I hope this guy talks." He said pointed to the guy on the gurney. I looked back and they were loading the gurney into the back of an ambulance.

"He knew my name Sarge." I said without looking back to him.

"What? Who?"

"Your headless friend over there. Before he pulled a gun out of his jacket he said 'You're a dead man Revele!' He knew me."

"He probably just read your name tag John!"

"No Sarge. It wasn't like that...why didn't he run away when he heard the sirens coming for him? I almost emptied my clip on the vehicle as it was driving away! After he shot at me I ran...if he wanted to escape that was his chance. He came after me Sarge! He had to make sure I died."

"John...We found their target. In the coffee shop. Do you remember that City Hall employee? The girl? We found her dead a couple years ago, remember?"

"Yah I remember." I was getting frustrated. Sarge thought I was a conspiracy theorist. I touched my head forgetting about the blood running down my face and I wiped the sweat from my brow.

"Do you remember the guy who did it? A young nobody the mob used to get a job done."

"Sarge...are you trying to tell me—?"

"He was found dead at the coffee shop."

"What!?"

"John, that's who they were trying to kill! And they did! They nailed him in the back of the head."

I couldn't believe it. I refused to.

"Sarge...I counted three shots before Ridley was hit. If they got him why did they keep firing?"

"I dunno' Revele! You could have asked them if you didn't blow them all to hell!"

I wasn't going to let this go. There was obviously no convincing Sarge. I left it alone and walked away to sit on the back of a nearby ambulance. An EMS worker rushed up to me and began dressing the wound on my head, wiping the blood away with wet cloths.

"John..." Sarge followed me. "Get yourself fixed up...take the rest of the day. Give me your chip." He extended his hand. I looked at him and then pulled my camera off of my shirt, ejected the chip inside that stored our footage, and handing it over to him. "Go see Simmons." He said. "I'll see you tomorrow John." And he walked away. I held an ice pack to my temple as the EMS washed the blood off my face. I was still coming down off the adrenaline rush and I just rested back on the side of the ambulance.

I wished Kang was still around.

He would have believed me.

* * *

I went to the hospital right away after EMS had stitched me up. I had a bandage wrapped around my head and a small band aid over the bullet graze on my cheek. There was still blood all over my uniform from Ridley and on my collar from my own head wound. I'm sure some of it had sprayed up from the shotgun blast of the mobsters face. I must have looked like a mess when I walked through the hallways to find Ridley's room.

I entered his room and Ridley smiled at me. His wife, Holly was there too. She had been crying but she smiled at me too. We grasped hands and held the grip for several moments.

"You okay?" I asked solemnly.

"Me? Look at you man."

I smirked and chuckled. "You should see the other guys..."
Ridley laughed and then winced in pain. "You didn't leave any for me eh buddy? Had to kill them all yourself?"
I laughed and looked up at Holly. "Don't be an idiot Ridley." She said to him shaking her head.
"She digs my scars now John." Ridley said smiling at me.
"You're delusional." She said laughing.
"How are you holding up Holly?" I asked her.
"I'm okay. Thank you John for having his back today."
"Your welcome. He has my back every other day..."
She smiled and looked back at Ridley. "Do you want anything honey?" She asked. "I'm going to get something to eat from the caf."
"No, I'm okay honey. Thanks."
Holley leaned over and they kissed. "Do you want anything John?"
"No thank you, I'm fine."
She walked around the bed and we hugged.
"Okay, I'll see you guys in a bit."
"Bye sweetie." Rid said as she walked out. As soon as she was gone; "Did you see them John?" He asked. "Who was this, man?"
"I dunno' Rid." I started. "I got a bad feeling today."
"Like what?"
"They found the body of what Sarge says was their intended target. That punk wannabe from a couple years ago who they pinned the murder of the girl from Mash's office on. But...I don't buy it buddy."
"How so?"
"Ridley, they used this guy once already...Who's to say they didn't again?"
"Aw, C'mon man..."
"I think they planted him in there...to make it look like he was the target."
"But you were the real target?"
"You don't know what's been happening Rid!"
Ridley sat up further in his bed, wincing through the pain in his arm. "I do know what's happening John!" He looked at me and I stopped. "You think I'm stupid man?"
"Rid...I—."
"It's okay man...I understand why you didn't tell me what you were doing with Kang...I get it."
"I'm sorry man. But you've seen it. You were there with me in his office. You don't think a guy like Sean Mash is gonna' snap eventually, and get tired of a guy like me trying to get him? Frankly, I'm surprised it's taken him this long to try and kill me."
"John...I dunno' man."
"Well believe it or not Rid, it's pretty obvious if you ask me. I need you to believe me man."
We were looking at each other. He looked skeptical and I looked desperate. My loyal friend was doubting me and that bothered me.

"Thanks for having my back today John." He simply said. "You should go home and be with your wife."

* * *

I rolled my wedding ring around my finger with my thumb and pinky as I walked up the steps of our building. I was thinking about her...and about Kang. Maybe seeing her tonight would make me feel a little better.
But since we got married, well; you know the story...
F.B.I,
Kovacs...
...the end of that phase of life.
I was here now, looking at a picture that hung on the wall of our wedding day. Clare wasn't home. She must have been working still. I looked around at the empty loft and sighed. I took the picture off the wall and took it with me, after I hung my stuff up and put my keys and everything down. I wandered into the kitchen and grabbed a beer out of the fridge. I cracked the cap off and took a giant swig of the bottle and then walked into the living room to collapse on the couch. My body was sore from the intense day I just had. I groaned through the aching and closed my eyes. I opened my eyes and stared up at Clare's big painting on the wall...
...I almost died today! Yet now I was laying here on my own couch, drinking a beer like it was the end of any other hard day's work. I found myself missing Clare, longing for her. We had lost so much and now that I survived this day I just wanted to hold her. I still had our wedding photograph in my hand and I stared at it, taking another sip of beer. The vision of my beautiful bride faded as my focus went fuzzy from the creeping sleep that was coming. My eyelids slammed shut like big iron gates and I couldn't hold them open. Within seconds I was fast asleep, still clutching the photo.

I felt like I was swaying as I slept. I was still half asleep when my eyelids fluttered open. I heard the angelic voice of my wife calling me; "John? John?" Her voice was soft and low, and in this moment I forgot about all of our problems. A blurry version of Clare was in front of me, backlit by our ceiling pot lights. It felt really nice to be woken up by her. As soon as I realized this wasn't a dream, and my eyes focused on Clare, I saw that she was moving my beer to the coffee table and brushing the hair behind her ears. In her other hand I noticed she was holding the wedding picture.
"Clare?" I asked. I could tell she had been crying. "What's wrong?"
She smiled as she looked at the photo. "Do you remember this day?" She asked me, in between sniffs of her nose. I couldn't say anything...I didn't know what to say. Most of the time we just did small talk, but this caught me off guard. *A real conversation? Was this happening?*
"We were so happy." Clare continued. I just stared some more, and I sat myself up on the couch.

"Clare...I—."

"Holly called me John..." There was a long pause. "You almost got shot, and you didn't even call me..."

I thought I was going to get an earful. She was right, I *hadn't* called her. I *did* think of her but a past version of her. I didn't call her, because I knew she would be out of the office or busy...sometimes she was even out of the state, and the odd occasion, out of the country! All of my desire to call her was very real and I wanted to call her to talk about how I could have died. On the other hand; I had been desensitized from being a cop so getting shot at wasn't really a shocker. It's not like Clare called me after every dangerous thing *she* did being a federal agent. I was making excuses now...and I wasn't dumb...I realized that Clare's thought process was probably very similar to mine when it came to this. I knew that in this moment we both were just sitting there feeling guilty about it all. I didn't have any energy to fight, but I thought there was one coming...Clare just stared at our wedding picture and she took a breath. I prepared myself for a lecture, but to my surprise she said; "I'm sorry John!" and her big glassy eyes made contact with mine. They pierced right through me, and she trapped me with them. I couldn't break my gaze with her and I even felt some tears welling up behind my eyes, I didn't even know where she was going with this.

"I'm sorry we're like this." She blurted out behind a choked up voice. "I'm sorry this has happened to us!"

I took a deep breath and sighed it out. I rubbed the sleep out of my eyes, pinching the bridge of my nose with my thumb and forefinger. All I could do was stare at her. I didn't have any words for the life of me. It's not that I didn't have anything to say...I did. I still loved Clare very much, and everything that had happened had taken its toll on me for sure.

But what could I say?

I couldn't exactly tell her about all of the time I had been spending on the street during the first year of our marriage. This had consumed most of my life lately to the point where I couldn't express myself to Clare anymore.

"I was so scared today John." She interrupted my train of thought. "What if I had lost you?" She asked.

After a long pause I replied. "I was scared too." I said solemnly, looking down at the floor now.

"I've been so busy with work, I—I haven't been—oh John...I could never have forgiven myself if I hadn't told you—."

Another long pause. I had perked up at this statement, anticipating the rest of that sentence.

"I love you John." She said through sniffs.

Then she looked right at me and we were both very exposed and vulnerable in this moment. I sat up from my position on the couch to swing my feet to the floor and I was now sitting side by side with her. I leaned forward on my elbows resting on my knees. Clare was facing the back of the couch, the opposite way I was sitting, and we were so close to each other now. Our faces were very close. We both just continued breathing all over the other one's face and I watched Clare's eyes shoot back and forth between my eyes and my mouth. Her mouth went slack and hung half open, her bottom lip pouting out. They looked so soft and wet. My mouth must have been half open too and we both just took a few moments to stare into each other's eyes and examine the other's face. Her nostrils flaring ended whatever chance I had of keeping my heart hardened and at the same time, we both flew in for the kill. We simultaneously took huge breathes of relief through our noses as we passionately kissed. I felt her hand come up my back, then the warmth of her skin on my neck, and then she ran her fingers through my hair. With her other hand she was massaging the back of my arm. I had wrapped my right arm around her back and was clasping where the back of her head met her neck with my fingers, and my left hand was on her side by her midsection.

This had been a long time coming for us! We both eagerly pressed it further as we continued to grope one another, panting heavily. Clare wrapped her hands around my neck and pulled me towards her as she leaned back, still kissing me as we laid down on the couch—

—The rest of the night...

...I can't tell you about.

* * *

—BANG!

Clare was counting the shots at her father's funeral because something happened, forever changing the course of my life.

I could have been saved.

Clare and I made love that night.

Turns out she was shipping off to Mongolia the following week. New intelligence had come in about Kovacs' whereabouts.

It was almost over...She would be done...I would have my link into the goodness of humanity back through my wife. I loved her so much...

I could have been saved...

All I could see was 'red'. My feet tromped the dark pavement of the streets that night, as I marched onwards on my mission.

The week before this night I had discovered something—something awful; I sat in the hospital bed with Clare—she was only getting checked out; a precautionary examination just in case. They say you should always get looked at after a car accident...

It was the first weekend after Clare returned from Mongolia. She had walked in the door with such a huge smile on her face. She broke the news to me that they had caught Kovacs! We were out on a date—our first one in a very long time—celebrating. It was actually going quite well. I was driving Clare's SUV back from the restaurant. We had left Baltimore and driven a little bit out of the city to this little small town restaurant we liked.

But on the way back...

"Hey." I said, blinded by a set of high beams coming the other way on the highway. "Easy buddy." I said quietly. It was late at night and not many people were on the road. In fact this was the first car we'd seen in a while. He was pretty far off, but he still kept his highs on as he approached, so I flashed mine back at him a couple times...he still kept them on.

"What's this guy doing?" I asked Clare. Starting to get a little more annoyed now.

All of a sudden my rearview mirror lit up with a huge white glow as well. My eyes darted up and I saw a second set of high beams right on our tail.

"JOHN LOOK OUT!!" Clare screamed.

I snapped my attention back to the road and realized that the first oncoming car had swerved into our lane—

—SMAAAASSH!!!

The front end of his car slammed into the left driver's side corner of the SUV and forced us sideways. Clare was screaming as the vehicle skidded its back end around—

—CCRRAASSH!!

The car from behind us pinned us with the other car and they drove us off the road.

The front right tire of our SUV hit the shoulder and popped. I swerved all over the road from the flat tire and the two mystery cars disappeared into the night behind us. Clare was screaming and saying my name...this felt like a dream.

Slowly, the SUV began to spin and spin and spin. I couldn't get us back on track or on a straight path. I couldn't even brake to stop us.

During our final spin out, Clare's side hit the gravel shoulder first and I felt the SUV start to lean right, and then begin to tip—Oh no—*this was it*...I thought.

I remember a tiny little pause in time occurring, and a dead silence before—

—SLAM!!

The passenger side of the vehicle hit the ground and I heard the glass shatter in Clare's window—*she'll be scraped along the pavement*—I thought. But we only scraped for a second or two until we started rolling. The sounds were unforgettable;

BA-BOOM—KA-DUM—BOOM—GA-GOOSH!!

Loud, booming, thuds as we rolled and rolled, I don't know how many times! *'Please God, just stop...stop rolling*!!' I remember thinking—I must have blacked out for a second—

Next thing I knew there was one last crashing thud, as the SUV landed on its wheels. It was completely and eerily silent for a moment—Clare!

I snapped my head to the right but I couldn't see her. All I could see was the ceiling of the car, and I realized that the roof had been smashed in—Clare must have been crushed by the collapsed metal. I was sure that on the other side of the sunken roof would be Clare's bloody and crushed body.

But I heard a little noise; a groan. "Clare?" I shouted. And I sighed in relief as a hand stuck itself out from around the roof and waved. I gave myself a once over and I seemed to be fine. Sitting up as far as I could I craned my neck around the sunken roof to see Clare's face. No blood, and she seemed to be fine as well. "You okay?"

"Y—Yah..." She said, and she half laughed, half sighed. "I—uh—I—I think so...you?"

"I think I'm good!" I said, and we smiled at each other. "We have to get out of the car Clare."

"O—Okay. Can you move?" she asked.

I tried my door. Jammed shut. I gave it a few thuds but it wouldn't budge. The frame of the SUV had warped and I couldn't open the door.

"I can't open my door either." Clare shouted. "My windows broken...I'm gonna' climb out this way!"

"Okay."

I could hear the sounds of rumbling and bumping with glass tinkling around as Clare was shimmying out the window. A few moments later she was at my drivers' side window.

"We can both get the door open okay?" She said. I nodded.

"Okay!"

She poised herself at the door, with both hands on the handle. I grasped my side of the door by the handle and readied myself to shove.

"Ready?" I asked.

"One...Two...Three!"

She pulled hard and I body checked the door. It budged but it didn't open.

"Again!" Clare shouted. We readied up again, and made deep eye contact, reassuring one another. "One..." She said.

"Two..." I continued.

"Three!!"

The door popped open. I quickly got out of the car and scrambled to embrace Clare. We both started checking each other over for blood or injuries but that was the miraculous part of it; not a scratch on either of us.

We made a call to 911, and soon ambulances and police cars were there. Clare and I were getting checked out amidst the blue and red glow of emergency lights that flashed in the darkness. I was stuck in a daze, wondering what had just happened to us. Seeing the car being towed away with the roof caved in was a scary sight. Clare should have been split in half by that. I couldn't shake the vision I kept getting of an angel—or some sort of guardian—in the car with us; holding up his arms to stop the roof just at the right spot, like pillars, saving Clare's life. I still couldn't believe that Clare and I had walked away from that with not a single scratch.

I stared down at the black business card with the clover. During the crash I had forgotten all about the two cars that ran us off the road...No doubt the same group who had tried to kill me a week before this—hired by the same person; Sean Mash...

The EMS guys told us we should go to the hospital and get checked out just in case. We were there waiting after our examinations; x-rays, blood work, the whole nine yards...
The nurse approached us solemnly.
"Everything okay?" I asked, hopefully.
"Yes." She replied. "Both of you are perfectly healthy and fine...that part's a miracle!"
Clare and I looked at each other. "That part?" I asked.
"Well...I'm afraid, that due to the great amount of stress, Clare, that you were under...and because of the trauma you endured tonight, that—the baby didn't survive."
There was silence for a while and we just stared in disbelief at the nurse's sympathetic face. I blinked. "What did you say?"
Clare let out a huge sob all of a sudden and she covered her face with both of her hands and turned her body away. I just stood there staring at the nurse in bewilderment.
"I'm so sorry." She said.
And Clare and I were left there to cry as she walked away.
Clare didn't even know she was pregnant to tell me about it. It was so soon after that night, we weren't expecting it at all.
—Sean! *How could he do this to his own daughter?!? Killing me was that important to him, that he would risk killing her?!* I was in disbelief! And this was why I was seeing red.

Seeing red and marching through the city on a dark mission.

Elsewhere in the city; Clare was celebrating with her work friends at a bar about the capture of Kovacs. A couple weeks had gone by and she had processed losing a baby already. I only stewed for those two weeks, fighting a losing battle with myself on how to handle this. As Clare smiled and laughed at the bar, she was actually hopeful. She and I had made a breakthrough in our relationship. She had finally caught Kovacs and felt as if she could move on, and being in a horrific car accident had surprisingly given her a new outlook, despite losing the baby. She, in fact, saw it as a chance to try again and start over. But where Clare had turned terrible life circumstances into hope...I failed. This only served as the last straw in a long history between her father and I. Most nights I would stew in my fury—or cry. I found the business card for Sexrex and thought about Maggie. Sean Mash had some kind of link to him, and supported the sex trade that she was lost in. I crumpled the card in an angry fist and marched forward through the city, searching for him.

At another bar in the city, Sean was exiting while laughing loudly and obnoxiously. He was accompanied by his two big body guards and they chuckled along with him. They turned to their left to walk down the sidewalk but they were stopped by shouting behind them.

I didn't hesitate...

BANG!

The first body guard went down, and then the second. I watched from the shadows as Sean dropped to his knees and covered his head with his hands. I savoured it for a moment and then I emerged from the darkness with my gun drawn.

"Evening Mr. Mayor." I said darkly to him.

He stopped trembling, but he didn't look up. He kept his gaze on the ground and his hands still raised above his head.

"Cowboy?" He finally asked. I could hear the fear in his voice, that he was trying to mask with his typical arrogant tone. "Is that you?"

"Yah, Sean...It's me, you son-of-a-bitch! I finally got you, you bastard." I was breathing heavily and my heart was pounding; adrenaline coursing through my veins.

Then he slowly looked up at me with obvious hate in his eyes. "You don't have me Revele. Even if you kill me now...I'll haunt you. My memory will always be with you." He was panting now too. He was scared.

"The world is a better place, without men like you." I said to him.

"There's always gonna' be somebody like me cowboy. Call me what you want...the 'bad-guy', the 'villain'...whatever. You can't stop it. I can't stop it...We might as well just join in with the world." He was confessing his sins to me, trying to justify his actions to me.

"How do I get to Sexrex?" I asked him angrily.

Sean chuckled arrogantly. "Is that what this is? What, Revele? You wanna have a bit of fun?"

"C'mon Sean...I know you're linked to his sleazy business somehow. You don't think it's obvious that the mob has a hand in that shit? Hell, you guys probably fund half his operation."

"What the hell are ya doing, cowboy? Huh? You think you can take down all the crime in Baltimore? You think you know something about the dark side of life but you don't know anything!"

"I'm prepared to change that." I said, motioning my eyes towards the gun.

"How do you think people like Sexrex are able to avoid the cops like he does?" Sean went on. "They've all been doing it long before me! And they'll be doing it after I'm gone! There's always someone left to fight, Revele!"

"Tell me how to get to him!!" I screamed.

Sean laughed. "You gonna make me!? I got you for double murder here Revele." He said, looking at his dead body guards. "There ain't no way you're walking away from this. You sure you wanna start down this path? I could tell em' I didn't see anything."

"Bullshit." I said. "You won't ever stop coming after me. You almost killed your own daughter in the process!"

Sean lowered his head and sighed. There was a long pause. "The car accident." He said, almost remorseful, but not quite.

I didn't say anything and I allowed him to stew on that thought.

"So I guess we're at a bit of a stale mate here, huh cowboy?" He said. "We both can't leave the other alive...what to do?"

"You can tell me how to get to Sexrex."

"A trade? Life for information?"

I just stared at him hard.

"Megga." He said, to my surprise.

My eyes widened. "Megga?"

"That's his name. Sexrex's contact to me. He sets us up."

"Yah I know Megga." I said.

"Well there ya go. You find him; he can set up a meeting." Sean's face grew angry and bitter upon releasing that information. "Happy?"

"No."

"Good! You little prick. All the grief you've caused me. It would have been worth losing Clare to get rid of you!" He hissed bitterly.

My face dropped in disgust and such a raw and terrible emotion rose up inside of me.

"Congratulations." I said to him. "You were a grandfather."

Sean's eyes widened and his face went white as a ghost before—

—BLAM!

I pulled the trigger and watched his head jerk back and a blast of red spray out the back of his head. I watched his body fall forward and his face hit the ground. I breathed in and out slowly, trying to quell the adrenaline. Hate took over...anger, and revenge oozed out of my pores.

BAM-BAM-BAM-BAM-BAM-BAM-BAM-BAM-BAM-BAM!!!—CLICK!

The slide racked back and locked in that position. I was out of bullets, but I wanted to keep firing. I stood there for a few moments with the barrel of my gun smoking.

Sean Ahab Mash was dead.

CHAPTER THIRTEEN
The Other Side of the Coin

Picture a coin.
An item used forever, down through the ages, as a deciding factor.
Men and women alike have used it to determine the outcome between two things.
Two choices...
Two outcomes...
Two opposing sides.

But it doesn't really matter which side it lands on does it? As long as it lands on *your* side.
What if it *did* matter?
What if somebody flipped that coin long ago? Way back before time began.
I'm not sure what god you believe in, or what 'religion'...but, I think it's safe to say that every religion has a force for good, and a force for evil, right?
What if, after the earth was created. After everything was put into place and all setup, the two opposing sides said: '*Well, now what? Who gets control over it now?*
What if God and the devil flipped a coin for dominion over the earth?
Well, if that was true then I'd say the *devil* won that coin toss!

Games.
Boys and girls have played games down through the ages as well.
Games are a mirror for life. Life on a board.
The earliest games that they discovered were dice and tiles, made from bones!
Roll the dice and see where they land. Let *fate* decide.
It seems our affinity to gamble our lives away was apparent back then too.
But it's always a game. Always was...always will be.
I like to think that it's more specifically about *sides,* and not so much a game though.
I think it's more accurate to say that there are always two sides.
There has to be...
...someone has to win,
and someone has to lose.

* * *

They sat so still, spread across the map. The little coloured pieces being moved and positioned strategically by the master. Small little plastic men, and tiny little artillery pieces.

The two opponents had dug up the old relic game and were meticulously and carefully planning their next moves against each other.

"Ah!" A dark figure said, as he entered the room silently. "Risk!"

Donald Kerst, was staring at the board with his arms crossed. He didn't even notice *Paul Ranston* come in, but he now glanced up at him from underneath his eye glasses.

Ernest Lawrence was leaned over the board almost lying flat on top of it, as he examined all the pieces and what countries they were occupying. He slowly peered upwards when he heard Paul's dark creepy voice.

"I see you two are playing a classic!" Ranston said as he looked down at them.

Donald remained stone cold and immovable as usual, but who knows what was going on inside. Ernest, being the more fidgety of the two, swallowed a lump in his throat. Something about Ranston made him really uncomfortable.

"Uh..." He stammered. "Jay got it out for us." He laughed nervously.

Ranston just smirked back at Ernest eerily.

"It's a very strategic game isn't it?" The old Ranston asked.

Ernest didn't say anything, and Donald just nodded.

"I remember it well." Ranston continued as he feverishly began examining the board. He limped over behind him and grabbed another lab chair. Ernest and Donald looked at each other awkwardly as the old man struggled back with the chair and then sit down at their little game table with them.

"Ah..." He started. "I remember the rush I used to get." Ranston rubbed his hands together and licked his lips. "The excitement of world domination eh?" He said slyly, looking back and forth between them. He examined the board a little more and his expression turned to a false worry, too mock Ernest.

"Oh, Mr. Lawrence...I'm afraid it looks like Mr. Kerst has you beat."

"He thinks he does." Ernest said, looking over at the statue of a man.

Ranston paused for a moment. "Do you mind if I take a roll?" He asked. "For memory's sake?"

"Be my guest Paul." said Ernest.

Ranston greedily reached for the dice and began to shake them as he looked at Donald. "I challenge you for China!" He said excitedly.

"I have over twice the army and artillery than you in that country." Donald said.

"That's okay..." Ranston said. "I'm feeling lucky today!"

Donald sighed and reluctantly reached for the other set of dice. They each continued to shake the dice around in their closed fists for a moment, before releasing them onto the board.

They tumbled and bounced and Ranston looked at them with his dark gaze until they stopped.

"Ha!" He exclaimed in joy. "You see Donald? Today is my day."

He chuckled to himself as Ernest began moving some of his pieces into the space on the board he had just won from Donald.

"Thanks Ranston." Ernest said.

"You're welcome Mr. Lawrence. Now...where is Mr. Richter anyways?"

"Where do you think? He's up working on the ring."

"Of course. And it's break time for you fellas eh?"

"Jay won't take a break...we've been working on this one for months now, and he only stops to eat or sleep."

"Well, I don't blame him..." Ranston stopped. "We're so close."

Donald gave Ernest a look and Ernest only stared back, lost in his own thoughts about Ranston's motives.

"Well, I'll go see him then." Ranston said, wincing as he stood up. The old man wheeled the chair back over to where he got it and went on his way through the lab to find Jason Richter.

Richter was up where his lab partners said he would be, on a lift way up off the floor, tinkering away on the newest project—another giant metal ring.

Ranston limped into the large open chamber and stopped to take it all in. He still loved seeing them, the rings.

It exhilarated him to see his *plan* coming together.

This facility was an open roofed lab and Ranston squinted from the sun as he craned his neck to look up at this ring. It towered over him as he walked closer to its half-moon shaped base that carried the weight and balance of it. It loomed down on him as he reached the base and he just stood there staring up at it.

"Beautiful." He said quietly to himself. He reached out and touched it, wiped some dust off of it and rubbed his fingers together.

His admiration was interrupted by a loud clang and the whirring of a motor. A few moments later the lift reached the ground and Richter was surprised by Ranston. The two of them just stared at each other for a few moments. Ranston smirked back at Richter, who just glared expressionlessly at him.

"Hello Jason." Ranston said, breaking the silence.

"Ranston. I wasn't expecting you."

"Well, I had business next door in Russia...how could I not stop by and see the ring?"

"You've seen one before." Richter said monotoned, as he stepped off the platform and over to a table. He placed his tools down on the table and began rummaging through some various parts. "This is the sixth one, Paul...you'd think the novelty would be worn off by now."

"Not the sixth one, Jason..." Ranston said. "The last one."

Richter stopped with his back to Ranston and paused what he was doing. "Yes." He said. "It's not finished, if that's why you're here."

"Jason." Ranston laughed. "You think so negatively of me. Can't I just stop in and see my crack team?"

"You're just the money Ranston...don't pretend that you care about us."

"I'm more than the money." Ranston lowered his voice to a half whisper so Richter wouldn't hear him. "I have more staked into this than you think." He said, raising his voice back up.

"Yah?" Richter asked. "And what is that Paul? Because you haven't exactly been forthcoming about that."

"I have my dreams, and you have yours, Mr. Richter. Mr. Fienberg found you remember?"

Richter stopped again, and turned to face Ranston, slowly.

"He pulled you out of the science fairs when you were twenty years old. He handed your dream to you." Ranston said.

"Oh, right..." Richter started. "Gerald Fienberg. The mystery man?"

Ranston just smiled awkwardly.

"How come nobody else knows who he is, Paul?"

"What?"

"Nobody else I've talked to from Globe-X knows who I'm talking about when I bring him up."

"Well, you must not be talking to the right people."

"No, no, no..."

"Well, really...who have you talked to besides Kitch? Who, by the way, isn't exactly from Globe-X directly"

"Donald and Ernest don't know him."

"So?"

"So...who the hell is he?"

Ranston looked up at Richter with darkness in his eyes now.

"Gerald Fienberg is not his real name you know..." He said.

Richter's ears perked up. "What?"

"You're not wrong when you say he's a man of mystery Jason." Ranston continued. "He continually changes his name to maintain his anonymity—". He shook his head to himself and scoffed. "He thinks he's so clever..." He said quietly.

"I take it you don't like him?" Richter asked.

Ranston's weathered eyes squinted and he glared back at Richter. He breathed out slowly before he answered. "Let's just say..." He started, with the corner of his upper lip curling. "...He's not my favourite person."

Richter stared at Ranston as he stewed, furrowing his brow in confusion. "You still haven't really answered my question...all you're doing is creating more questions." Jason said.

Ranston turned his attention back to Richter. "I hate that." He finally said. "So I won't leave you hanging...Mr. Fienberg, is a finder, a starter...He plays His role."

"I'm still unclear." Richter said with an annoyed tone.

"Globe-X is a multi-national corporation Jason. They have their hand in every pie and Gerald is very knowledgeable on all the flavours. He...gives people a push in the right direction. He finds the people to do the job that needs to be done."

Richter pondered for a moment and then asked; "Why not just do it Himself?" He asked.

Ranston chuckled. "Because. He has a silly notion that the company would benefit from hiring outside sources. He thinks there's a risk of keeping it all in-house. 'What's the point?' He always asks. He says; 'everyone's talents grow stale after time. We need to keep hiring new help, not only for their sake, but to inspire the old ones.'"

"So," Richter asked. "What does that mean for me? When this is all over, I'll just be obsolete?"

"Gerald was excited about you, Jason. He and I had a long talk about you. Believe it or not, we placed a little wager on this whole project."

Richter raised his eyebrows.

"I was pretty excited myself when you came on board. I mean...time-travel! Jason...I don't think you realize the gravity of what we're doing here."

"Ranston..." Richter began. "I've been working on this project since I was ten! Please don't patronize me. That might work with my partners, or guys like Kitch...but not me. If anyone has the most stake in this project...it's me."

"Of course Jason." Ranston said. "This is your baby."

Richter turned back around to finish looking for the part he needed on the table.

"Damn right it's my baby." He said under his breath, rummaging through the mess.

"This is a second chance Jason." Ranston said passionately.

Richter found the part he wanted and turned to face Ranston again, with conviction written on his face. "For who, Paul?" He asked him.

Ranston only smiled, a dark, sinister smile. Richter's face remained cold as his eyes accused.

He was right though.

He knew this whole time, since he met Ranston, that he was up to something.

Something else, than what the rest of the team had in mind.

"I have to get back to work now." Richter said, holding up the part for the machine.

"I wouldn't want to keep you." Ranston said slyly.

They stared at each other for a moment, before Richter rolled his eyes and turned to walk away. "What were you doing in Russia anyways?" He asked, as he stepped onto the lift platform. "We don't have any projects there."

"Just...visiting some people I'll soon be going into business with."

"Hhmm." Richter scoffed. "Who's got their hand in too many pies now?"

Ranston laughed. "I suppose we both have our hands in different ones. Mr. Fienberg doesn't know about this flavour."

"Don't you think He'll be upset?" Richter asked.

Ranston's sinister smile grew. "I'm counting on it." He said.

Richter rolled his eyes again and started shaking his head. "Sounds like you guys have issues." He said, and he pushed the button on the controls. The motor started whirring again as he started going back up.

"You have no idea..." Ranston said to himself placing his hand in his pocket.

"What was your wager about me anyways!?" Richter shouted over the whirring motor of the lift.

"That it couldn't be done!" Ranston shouted up to him.

"What if it could!?"

"Well...if it could...let's just call it...a rematch!"

"Okay, Paul...I've had enough of your games! I'll cya around!"

Richter turned his attention upward to ignore Ranston as he rose up to the ring.

"It's not a game." Ranston said quietly to himself. He pulled his hand back out of his pocket with an object in it. "It's more of a coin toss."

He rolled the coin around with his fingers, smiling as he watched Richter ascend through the roof.

The last ring of six to be built.

The final piece he needed.

He walked over to a small window at the far side wall of the lab. He smiled to himself and took in a deep satisfying breath. He exhaled out very dramatically and kept on smirking as he took in the magnificence of what they had accomplished.

Just then, his thought process was interrupted by the ringing sound of his cell.

"Ranston." He said as he answered. The voice on the other end chattered away.

"Ah, W!" He said. "I was just thinking about you..."

Richter reached the top of the platform again as the lift clunked to a stop. He sighed and then stepped off, walking down the long mesh platform. He reached the section of the ring he was working on and met Ernest there.

"Ranston giving you a hard time?" Ernest asked him.

"Bah!" Richter replied. "Hardly. He's just eager...as usual."

Ernest shook his head. "Reminds me of someone else I know..." He said slyly, looking at Richter.

Richter opened up a big panel on the side of the ring and pushed a few buttons. He caught Ernest's look and returned the sarcasm.

The two of them worked in silence for a while as Ernest continued to keep an apprehensive eye on Richter.

Richter slid a tray out from inside the panel and there was an empty port available among many other computer parts.

"Is there something you would like to say to me, Ernest?" Richter snapped, after having enough.

Ernest looked away awkwardly. Then he sighed. "I dunno, Jay..." He simply said. "Is there something you want to tell me?" He returned the question. Richter secured the piece and clicked a switch to lock it in place. Then he stopped working and turned to Ernest slowly.

"What do you mean by that?" He asked him.

Ernest stared back like he wanted to spill the beans but he didn't.

Richter turned quickly and pushed the tray back into the ring, closed the panel and took one last long look at Ernest before storming off.

Ernest sighed as he rushed past him.

Back on ground level, Richter went to his desk where papers were strewn about. He lifted stacks of his calculations, rough work and scribblings, and he threw them aside. He moved blueprints aside and dug around but he couldn't find what he was looking for.

"Are you looking for this?" Ernest's voice came from behind him and he stopped. A flush of anger crept up the back of his neck and he turned around to face him.

Ernest was holding Richter's personal journal up in one hand and the other was casually in his pocket.

Richter glared at his lab partner viciously and he breathed in deep.

"Ernest..." He began. "Why do you have that?"

"Because I heard the noises in your room that night." Ernest replied. "And all the other times since then."

Richter had been hiding something...his heart beat in his chest as Ernest began to spell out what he knew.

"You've been different, Jay." He said. "Donald and I have been worried."

Richter just stewed as he listened. "Give me back my journal."
He said angrily.

"This is dangerous." Ernest went on, waving the journal around. "The things you've written in here...if they're true...why didn't you tell us about any of this?"

Richter only lowered his head and silence filled the room.

Ernest brought the journal down and cracked it open to read out of it.

"I saw him again tonight..." He read, quoting Richter's words. "...this strange young man. He appears in the glow of electricity. I know now, that I am not dreaming him. He calls to me in desperation. I only make out some of his words. He tells me not to do it..." Ernest paused and glared at Richter who was still staring shamefully at the ground. Then he went back to reading. "He tells me...again and again and his words haunt me...don't do it, he says...don't do it..." Ernest closed the book and sighed. "Jay..." He began slowly. "...who is this guy?" He flipped the book around to show a rough sketch of *my* face that Richter had drawn.

Richter remained silent for a long while and he shook his head. "I don't know." He said softly and finally looking up at his own drawing.

"Is he from the future?" Ernest asked.

Richter was quiet again but eventually answered; "I don't know..."

Ernest sighed and then chuckled. "Well I'm just a dumb physicist, but...obvious conclusions can be made here can't they?"

"Give me back my book, Ernest." Richter said, having enough.

"We should rethink this."

"Absolutely not!"

"What if this guy is trying to tell us something?"

"This guy...is proof that it will work!"

"Yah? At what cost? We have no idea!"

"How can we not go through with it now? You and Donald knew the risks when you joined me."

"Yes we did, but we were young and excitable. This makes me weary, Jay!" Ernest waved the book around again. "What if this guy has already created those...ramifications, you spoke about? The loops? The alternate timelines?"

Richter suddenly grabbed it but Ernest didn't let go. The two got locked in a stare down for a few tenuous moments until Richter looked away.

"Ernest, please..." He said somberly.

"We could be making a horrible mistake, Jay..." Ernest replied.

Richter sighed deeply and then met Ernest's gaze once again. "Then I'll just fix it." He whispered hoarsely. Then he tugged harder on the journal and Ernest released it.

"Don't touch my stuff again." Richter said. They glared at each other for a moment or two more before Richter stormed off, leaving Ernest to stew.

Then Ernest glanced up and saw a shadowy figure standing across the lab. Ranston was still standing at the window staring out of it.

He had heard the whole conversation and he smiled to himself.

He chuckled to himself and shook his head as he looked out the window at the vast landscape and the great extending stone walls that stretched out on either side of the mountain as far as the eye could see.

The Great Wall of China, with an enormous metal ring stealing its thunder along the horizon.

CHAPTER FOURTEEN
Baptized

I was sitting in church a while back. Clare wanted to try it out. She said it'd be good for 'people like us'—meaning cops. Clare's mother had been a Catholic, and Clare had been raised in that environment. We had been having a lot of talks lately about our line of work and the feelings it brought on. Clare wasn't a goodie-two-shoes in any way, as you already know. When it came to crime fighting, and stopping the bad-guys; she was as gung ho as they come! She fought this fight with brutal justice, and so did I.

Sometimes, the two of us would get lost in conversations about criminality and society as a whole. We both agreed that sometimes leniency was our greatest weakness; *wouldn't it be easier if someone just killed them all?* Is what we sometimes discussed, but...

...what a terrible thought! That couldn't be the answer.

Anyways, Clare thought it would be a good idea to try 'religion' and I went to a church. Well, a chapel actually; the one at our police station...

The Chaplain there took me in and sat down with me. We had a good long talk about the way the world was. About 'evildoers'. I'm pretty sure this was *not* the message he was trying to send to me—but a passage he read me stuck out anyways:

> 'For he is God's servant for your good. But if you do wrong,
> be afraid, for he does not bear the sword in vain. For he
> is the servant of God, an avenger who carries out God's
> wrath on the wrongdoer.'
> -Romans 13:4

'An Avenger'...Now *that* sounded cool! *Finally, the Bible was looking pretty awesome*, I thought. I didn't even bother to pay attention to much else of what the Chaplain wanted to tell me. I just took that passage and applied it to myself. I almost wanted to get it tattooed on to me somewhere, but I never did. It stuck with me though...

* * *

If you've ever seen an episode of those crime shows where two guys in suits, maybe wearing trench coats, are walking around the crime scene together. They both have a nonchalant attitude and they never smile. One's chewing gum; the younger of the two, and the older one is smoking a cigarette and holding a coffee in his hand.

This was our little scene here this morning.

Two detectives, Dex Finley, the older one, around his 50's, and Jake Ryan, in his later 30's. Finley and Ryan had arrived on scene in front of this bar on the street. Forensics was already snapping photos of the dead mayor's body, along with the two big guys dead on either side of him. Officers were holding a line around the perimeter for blocks, holding the media back, who were all craning to get a shot of this story.

"Eech." Finley muttered to his partner. "This coffee is garbage." He said with a scowl. Then he took another sip anyways. They were standing over the mayor's body staring at it.

"Well kid, what'd-ya-think?" Finley asked Ryan.

"Pretty simple Dex." He said, in between smacks of his gum. "The shooter was standing right here when he did it. 'Pop!' close range shot to his head. Then he riddles our beloved mayor with bullets—ten, they counted right?...based on the impact ballistics on our two huge victims here, the shooter musta' been standing further away when he did them."

"Back there seem like a good spot to you?" Finley said, as he motioned behind him. Finley remained facing forward sipping his bad coffee.

"Pretty cut and dry Dex. But who we lookin' for?"

"Mmm." Finley grunted, as he finished a drag of his cigarette. "That's the question." He blew out the smoke from his nose. "Who would want to kill Sean Mash?"

"Well, I'm thinking that the body guards were of no consequence to this guy, because they only got one shot each, plus he shot them from in the shadows...to get them out of the way. Then he comes out of the shadows to personally face Mash."

"You're bang on there Jake." Finley said with the cigarette in his mouth, bouncing around as his lips moved. "One in the head, and ten more in his back—." He blew the smoke out his nose again. "This was definitely a personal kill." Finley took another sip of coffee and when his eyes went upwards he stopped there. "We need to get a hold of that footage." He said, pointing to the CCTV camera mounted to the light post above them.

"I'm on it." Ryan said.

They both were staring down at the bodies now solemnly. "Poor Clare." Finley said. "She was a wreck last night when we told her wasn't she?"

"Yah...poor girl." Ryan replied.

"Wait a second." Finley said, lowering the coffee cup from his mouth. He noticed something: the corner of a white piece of paper sticking out of the mayor's suit jacket pocket. He reached behind his belt and pulled out a pair of latex gloves. He took a final drag of his smoke and tossed it in his coffee. He threw the cup into a nearby garbage can and then pulled the gloves onto his hands.

"You got something partner?" Ryan asked.

Finley bent down over the mayor's body and retrieved the paper out of his pocket. He stood up and held up the folded up paper for Ryan to see. He slowly unfolded the paper and they both examined it. Written by hand was:

'For he is God's servant for your good. But if you do wrong,
be afraid, for he does not bear the sword in vain. For he
is the servant of God, an avenger who carries out God's
wrath on the wrongdoer.'
-Romans 13:4

"What does this mean?" Ryan asked.
"It means we're dealing with some sort of a religious nut." Finley answered.
"Great..." Ryan looked over the bodies again. "What'd he baptize them too before he killed them?"

The guys at the station started calling me that: 'The Baptist'. It was just an easy way to reference the case, but the nickname stuck. Soon the media got wind of the nickname and then I was officially named 'The Baptist', although nobody knew who I was.

That following week was a hard one. Clare and her father had their fair share of issues, but because of the nature of his death, it made her all the more upset. She was more pissed off then anything. It wasn't really a federal case, but the bureau still kept tabs on it, which allowed her to have access to the Baptist case files. I tried to avoid home as much as I could that week, playing it off like I was working. She took the week off of work and stayed home, but she kept saying that she needed to go in on Friday for the big debrief about Kovacs.
Of course, she did...
Richter went on TV and announced his breakthrough in time travel,
And me...I went to the club...
That police scene the next morning...
What did I do!?

And now we're all caught up.
2041. Present day.

The day of Sean's funeral was the start of Ridley and I's days off stretch. Somewhere in that week, we were hanging out at his place. I sat in a backyard lounge chair, scrolling my social media feed, while he was grabbing a couple cold ones.
"How's Clare holding up?" He asked as he returned.
I shrugged. "She's okay." I answered, barely looking up from my phone.
"You alright, buddy?" He asked me. "You look like shit, dude." He pushed the beer at me.
I took it, and I looked at him through ragged eyes. My hair, which was usually neatly cut, was getting longer and less maintained. I wore it under a baseball cap and my scruff was in transition to a beard.

"What's going on?" Ridley pressed. "You get any of my messages? What happened to you Friday?"

"I...I don't know...exactly." I said, returning to my news feed as a distraction.

"What!?"

"I dunno, Rid, I...I got drinking too much and I don't remember."

"You don't remember? Wow...John—"

"I know, man." I sighed. "I know."

"You sure you should be drinking that beer?"

"I'm fine..." I trailed off, still scrolling. I stopped when an article caught my eye:

POLICE RECOVER BODY IN FRONT OF SEXREX NIGHT CLUB.

There was a picture of the police scene in front of the Sexrex that morning and I stopped to stare at the article.

"John?" Ridley asked.

I snapped up to look at his expecting face.

"You hear about this?" I asked him.

"What?"

"Something went down at the Sexrex Friday night."

"Oh. Yah I heard about that."

"What did you hear?"

Ridley shrugged. "Some gangland stuff. I heard them talking about it at the station."

I breathed a sigh of relief. "Oh ok. I thought it might have been this Baptist guy again."

"No, no...there were eye witnesses who ID'd the shooter. Just two local homies from rival gangs. They arrested him already."

I sat back a little more relaxed. It wasn't me then. I chuckled softly and took a swig from the beer.

"Hey, speaking of Sexrex..." Ridley began. "you're not still thinking about Maggie are you?"

I looked at him coldly. "Well, yah...of course I am Rid."

He was quiet and he took a sip of beer.

"What!?" I pressed.

Ridley shook his head. "I'm just worried about you man. Look, I'm worried about Maggie too, but...I know you man."

"Good." I said. "Then you know I'll get her out of there."

Ridley sighed a growling sigh and he shook his head. "Poor Clare." He muttered under his breath.

"What do you mean, poor Clare, Rid!?"

"You're a stubborn son-of-a-bitch, John! You know that?"

I took a sip of beer and looked away.

Ridley sighed again and drank his own beer. "Yah damn Irish bastard." He said softly, not looking at me.

I pretended to be upset but cracked a slight smirk. I dared to glance at Ridley and his eyes met mine too. He smirked back and then we were both chuckling.

We drank our brews, with the mood now lightened, and we sat in silence for a few moments.

"What do you think of this Baptist thing anyway?" I dared asked my friend.

He stared ahead while he shrugged. "I think he's screwed." He answered. "With Dexter Finley and Jake Ryan on the case. Have they come around questioning you and Clare yet?"

My heart sunk at the realization of the impending fact that they would.

"No." I said. "Not yet."

"Well they're friends with the Mash family aren't they?" Ridley asked.

"Yah."

"They'll get him. Eventually they'll follow the trail and knock on The Baptist's door."

I sat there, listening to Ridley's words, sipping slowly on my beer.

After that, I retreated back to the streets again to avoid home. Each night, I took off my hero's costume at the station and slipped on my other disguise. My dirty rags and street clothes. No one noticed me, but then again, no one would on this side of life. No one knew that I had been doing this. Before Sean Mash, I had been scared. Too scared to take this thing far enough. The nights that came after shooting him were spent on the streets, recalling and recalculating my original plans. Evaluating whether or not this thing was over or just beginning...

But now as I wandered the streets, I was only left with my thoughts. Things were almost back to normal with Clare. We almost had it!

Sean was dead.

I killed him in cold blood.

I found myself, over the next few days, huddled in alley ways trying to figure out how I felt about it. The surprising thing was, was that I didn't even feel guilty about it. In fact I discovered that I was spending a lot of time trying to convince myself to feel bad, but I couldn't!

After remembering my process and realizing my true feelings, there was no way I couldn't continue. My fear was gone and the ice was broken now.

My street mission could take on other forms now that I was pushed past the edge.

No turning back...

* * *

Megga was walking alone. I had followed him around in the shadows for a long time one night after Maggie had left with a fare. Several hours had passed, and now it was pretty late at night and nobody was around.

He swaggered down the sidewalk, like he was king of the world, as if nothing was wrong. As if he wasn't a lowlife criminal who profited from selling young girls bodies for sex to a bunch of other degenerates who obviously couldn't perform at home or whatever other issues they had. To Megga, this was just a way of life. To guys like him, this was purely business and he kept his conscience clear by counting his wad of cash at the end of a 'hard nights work'. He was singing some little tune to himself that I guess made him feel better about his life. Really, it was just a cover up to hide his insecurities, and he flipped through a stack of bills.

He didn't realize I was behind him, or he didn't hear my silent footsteps as I closed in…

I grabbed a hold of the back of his coat with both hands and jerked back. Once I successfully flung him, I let go and he went barreling into the grassy hill beside us. He rolled over onto his back and then he had my knee on his chest along with all of my body weight resting on him. He grunted and winced trying to push my knee off of him, before he heard the loud metallic—SSHHIING!!!; of my blade scraping out when I flicked it open. Then he stopped struggling and his eyes went wide when I lowered the tip of the six inch blade to touch the bridge of his nose. He went crossed eyed looking at it, and then he looked at me in the darkness trying to focus.

"You!?" He hissed at me.

"Yah…" I started. "Me."

"Get offa' me man!" He said, wiggling a bit now and looking back and forth between the blade on his nose and me. "You can't do this! You' a cop, B! Get-the-hell-offa' me man!"

I took out my badge and held it up for him to see clearly. Then I slammed it down on his chest.

"Don't move." I said to him, and I reached over to pick up the wad of cash he dropped, still holding the knife to his face. I examined the stack of bills and then held it up.

"Nice little stack of cash you got here Megga. Where'd you get it?"

"Go F—!"

"Ah-ah-ah!" I said, pressing the tip of the blade into his nose. He stopped and let out a grunt of pain. "That's not nice Megga." I said. "Don't worry man…I know where you got it."

I moved the blade so that the edge of it was pressing against his neck now. He was looking at me like he wanted to kill me and he swallowed so that his Adam's apple bobbed up and down, with the blade pressing on it. "Careful man." I said. "This knife is pretty sharp."

"C'mon man…" Megga said more solemnly now. "What'd you want from me?"

"You have a girl who works for you. You remember the one I'm talking about?"

"B, I got lots of girls workin' for me—."

I pressed my knee into his chest harder and sat up a bit so that my body weight increased on him, and I twisted my knee cap around a little bit. He grunted and squirmed.

"Ahh!!" He shouted.

"You remember the girl I'm talking about?" I asked.

"Aah—yah man! Okay, okay, get offa' me!"

"She doesn't work for you anymore, you understand?" I said, not releasing any pressure.

To my surprise I saw a smile break out across Megga's face, and he started to chuckle in between grunts.

"What's so funny?" I asked.

"Man, you have no clue who you're messin' with do you?"

I slid the blade upwards and in a little bit so that he stopped chuckling and choked a little on his own saliva.

"What do you mean?"

"It's not my call, B. I don't decide who hustles and who don't."

"Sexrex?!" I raised my voice. "Of course. Always someone higher up, eh?"

Megga grunted louder and winced through the pain and the choking. He had both hands on my knee and was softly trying to move it or reposition it.

"I heard you were the man to talk to!" I went on. "How do I get to Sexrex!?"

"I ain't tellin' you nothin' man."

I looked at him for a moment.

"You gonna' have to kill me pig!" He shouted.

I breathed in through my nose. "Okay." I quickly raised the blade up and then brought it down hard.

"No!" He screamed, and he let out a loud cry—that continued and then faded, when he realized I didn't stab him. He breathed heavily as he looked at the knife stuck in the grass half an inch next to his face.

I straddled him now, pinning his arms down with my thighs so that I was sitting on him. His head poked out between my crotch and he started to struggle more.

"Hey, what are you doin?" He asked. "You're crazy fool!"

I began to search his pockets of his jacket. I found a pack of smokes. "You smoke Megga?" I asked him. I found a lighter in there and I held up the wad of cash for him to see.

"No!" He shouted, as I put the two together. I flicked the lighter on and began bringing the corner of the stack of his cash closer to the flame. "No man! I gotta' give that to him!"

"I wanna meet him!" I said.

Megga continued to hesitate and looked into my eyes with a vicious hate. I touched the flame ever so slightly to the wad and it singed the corner.

"He'll kill me man!"

"How do I get to him!?"

The corner slowly charred and flaked away more and more.

"Okay!" He finally screamed.
I clicked the lighter off. "You'll set up a meeting!" I demanded.
He remained silent, and he was obviously upset with himself for saying it. He wasn't looking at me anymore and he was biting his lip and breathing faster, looking all around.
"Hey!" I shouted, slapping his face. "Hey! You'll set up a meeting?!" No answer. "Megga!" I grasped the handle of my blade and yanked it out of the grass. I held it up again and then did the same thing beside his face. He was screaming now, as I repeated the motion several more times, stabbing the knife into the grass just inches from his face as he flailed around.
"Okay!!" He screamed. "Okay, okay man! Stop!!"
I jammed the blade deep into the grass one more time, and then I held up the money and the lighter again.
"I'm getting impatient, Megga." I said breathily.
"Yah." He sighed. He raised up his head and slammed the back of it against the grass a bunch of times, closing his eyes tightly and gritting his teeth. "Yah man...I'll do it."
He was shaking his head now and sighing over and over. I smiled at him as politely and sarcastically as I could.
"Thanks buddy." I said pleasantly. I retrieved my badge and clipped it back on to my belt.
"Tell him I'll be coming by the club." I said. "Tell him I'm a new client, wanting to buy some drugs. What's he deal in? Meth? Coke?"
Megga growled. "Everything, b. E is his main game."
"Perfect. Tell him you're bringing a new guy who's looking to buy."
"You think you just gonna walk in there and walk out with your girl?" Megga chuckled now.
I pressed the knife against his neck again and he choked. "You better make sure Maggie's there in the club and not out hooking!" I ordered. "Huh!?" I shouted louder.
Megga nodded.
"Just set it up!" I said.
I closed the knife up and I stood up. I chucked the stack of cash at Megga and it landed on his chest. I took several steps back out onto the sidewalk and waited. Megga remained lying there for a while and he just glared at me. I kept his lighter and lit myself a smoke in front of him. He sat up and clutched his money.
"When?" He asked humbly.
"Next weekend." I said, blowing a drag out. "I'll come to the club."
Then I walked away, leaving Megga to rub his neck and check for blood.

* * *

Clare and I were actually home together for once.
We ate dinner in silence and the metal of our cutlery dinged and clinked off the plates.
"Can you unpack those boxes tonight?" She asked me.
I nodded silently. "Sure." I said softly.
I looked back down to my plate and chewed, but Clare still stared at me. Then she sighed and went back to her food.
Had we had known this was the last night we'd see each other in a long while...

Later on, I sat on the floor removing items from one box and then I slid the next one over. It was a bunch of random stuff; old shoes, a few books, all from a box labelled miscellaneous. Mostly just knick-knacks and a white envelope...
I furrowed my brow and flipped it over. There I read the letters; *JOHN.*
"What is this?" I mumbled to myself.
This was my hand writing!
Clare stirred in the bed behind me and I was startled enough to slip the letter behind me. I looked to the bed and saw she was just turning over under the covers. I folded the letter in half and slid it into the back pocket of my jeans for later.
I was only doing this while I waited for Clare to fall asleep. I tossed most of the other items into a garbage bag I had and then I got up.
I reached up into our closet and pulled down two little revolvers I had stashed up there. I took a few minutes to secure these in holsters around both ankles, looking back and forth to make sure Clare wasn't watching.
Then I walked past the bed and stopped for a brief moment to look at my wife asleep. Then I carried on, down the winding metal steps with the garbage bag still in hand. I went to the door, slid my jacket on, gathered my things, picked up the garbage bag and headed out.

I approached the club, slowly, trying to act as nonchalantly as I could, but on the inside I was nervous. I thought about it long and hard—but the more I thought about the things Maggie was involved in and envisioning her cold, blue and dead face lying in the sand, the more anxious I got. An image of her pale marble eyes blankly staring into mine drove me crazy. Maggie had become the *face* of all of my issues—the feelings I had had all my life. *Everything* I had ever thought about the state of the world, the terrible problems we had, the cruelty, the hate, malice—*all* of it! She was a tangible object that I could place all of these issues on. In retrospect, I thought if I could fix Maggie,
I could fix all of it.

The lights flashed in my face and I could feel each beat of the bass pound in my chest as I walked through the crowds of clubbers dancing all around me. Or was it my *own* heart I felt pounding? I moved stealthily through the groups of people like a cat, weaving my way in and out of the openings they left for me. My eyes lifted up to the balcony, scanning for Sexrex. I didn't see him up there yet. So I scanned the crowd some more, looking for Megga.

When I found him, he was sitting at a table with a bunch of other guys. Probably some of Sexrex's other pimps. He was laughing it up and enjoying the good life, until he saw me and his face dropped. I approached and just stared at him. We both knew it.

Time to go.

Either the bass was getting louder or my heart was really pumping now, as I ascended the steps to the balcony. I passed by a few dancing girls and other people just hanging out on the steps shouting in each other's ears. Sexrex allowed people up here, but only if they were buying. I had to show a stack of bills to a couple body guards and then they started to pat me down, and let me pass.

"He's cool!" Megga shouted, before they reached my ankles. "He's with me!"

Megga and I shared an apprehensive look as the guards let me pass.

Sexrex, the big man himself, was sitting at a long table with a bunch of other cronies standing around him. They were all over the room for that matter. I could feel all eyes on me as I approached that table. There were a few girls lounging around, but no Maggie. I glared Megga down accusingly as he joined Sexrex.

"So this is your friend, eh!?" A gruff sounding voice asked him. "Whatcha' wanna' buy my friend?" It sounded deep and scratchy.

"I'm looking to buy some E" I said right away. I couldn't hesitate or stutter or I would stand out.

Sexrex was staring back at me with one arm as a leaning post on the table and the other tucked into his lap. "How much you want?" He asked.

"I'll take a hundred pills"

A few more moments of silence passed with him just staring at me. I guess he did this to try and create tension, but it didn't matter. "One-thousand" He simply said.

I couldn't help but think; *that's it?* It's almost too easy. Just as I was thinking this he interrupted me;

"Look man." He started. "I don't care who you are...you think you're the only cop to come up here?"

...my heart stopped. No more bass beats keeping it alive. My mouth instantly dried up and I swallowed hard, though, it felt like I was swallowing a mouth full of dust. I didn't know what to say... "I—."

"I can spot you guys a mile away." He said with a grin. "But like I said, do you think I care? Like one little cop is going to come up in here and bring me down? Even if you were wearing a wire...I could make it go away...trust me."

I snapped my eyes to Megga who just shrugged to suggest he didn't tell him. I started to look around at all the other guys standing around. Most of them had their hands near their wastes or even in their coats. They were all looking at me.

"Why are you here officer?" He asked. "I don't judge. If it's just to get a little fun on the side, I understand...I welcome it actually! I won't tell the newspapers. Hey, I wish more of you guys would be willing to expand your minds and admit that you're human like the rest of us."

I just stood there, with nothing to say. What was I going to say anyway? I wasn't expecting it to go quite like this. Somehow, I actually believed he was being genuine and this was not a ruse to trap me. Something in his demeanour told me he really *didn't* care who came up to meet with him.

"I'll sell to anyone." He said with a smile. "I just want to get paid, and get my name out there. This whole country will know my name when I'm done."

"That's a bold statement." I blurted out. I didn't even think and it just was the first thought that popped into my head.

"You're right. It is."

"Look..." I said with a sigh. "I just want to get my merchandise and go."

Sexrex grinned back at me and nodded his head slowly. He chuckled to himself and stared at me for a while.

"If not, then I guess I'll just go." I moved to head towards the stairs.

"NO!" Sexrex shouted. It was the first time he came across as angry or mean this whole time.

Two big brutes stepped in the way of the stairs and I was stopped in my tracks.

"No one who comes up here walks away without something to show for it." He said. I smiled and turned back to face him. "This isn't a drop in boy. You came up here for a reason...and you don't get to change your mind once I let you up here with me. You shoulda' thought about that before you made the decision to climb those steps."

"Okay." I simply said. "Let's do business then."

He laughed, and then tension in the room seemed to fade back down. Again I took my chance to scan the faces of the girls again. Maggie wasn't here, and I shot another menacing glare at Megga. He looked nervous. Sexrex motioned to one of the guys behind him who then placed a silver brief case in front of him. He opened it and spun it around so that I could see the contents; many packages of little blue pills. He held out his hand, open palmed, and he made a gimme' motion with all four of his fingers. Then he pointed downward at the table. I pulled out my stack of cash and held it up for him to see. I had to walk slowly towards the table as everyone in the room stared, and I just as slowly placed the cash down beside the brief case, not breaking eye contact with Sexrex. He smiled at me and then he made a gesture towards the brief case with his hand, giving me an open invitation to remove my own bag for myself. I looked at him funny not believing that he operated under the honour system and he repeated the gesture. I stared at him for a second and then

I took out a bag of ecstasy, held it up for him to see and smiled at him. He smiled back and shut the brief case.

"It was a pleasure doing business with you officer." He said. I was enraged still, about Maggie, about everything—but I hid it with sarcastic smiling. As I was rising, my eyes met Megga's with accusation. He glared back and the two of us had a standoff. Then he smiled at me mischievously. I knew he had screwed me and I grew enraged, but all I could do was stare back.

"Tell your friends." I heard Sexrex say beside me.

With a final smirk from Megga, I had to turn and walk away.

Now, all sound had disappeared. No more bass of the music, just the slow, steady *bump-bump* of my heartbeat.

I looked around at all the men and their positions in the room—
Two guards in front of me, at the top of the stairs,
One to my left,
Two behind me on the far wall,
Sexrex was sitting as his table,
with two guys each, on either side of him,
plus Megga.
10 men. My little pistols had six shots each.
I reached the stairs and stopped.

"Is there a problem officer?" Sexrex asked.

"Yah..." I said, letting a slow breath out through my nose. I smirked at the guards in front of me. "You!"

I had to make it count. I shoved all of my weight, hard and fast, into the chest of one guard. While he was stumbling back, I lifted my left leg up and pulled out one of the guns. I ducked down to dodge the arms of the second guard that were stretching out to grab me. Coming up from the duck I gave the guard an uppercut punch with my finger on the trigger; impacting his chin with the muzzle—BLAM!—the top of his head opened up, releasing a spray of red and his head snapped back as he fell in a heap to the ground. The first guard tumbled down the first few steps of the staircase but had gained his balance by the time I took care of his friend. I had just enough time to raise my gun up and fire a single shot at a third man who had been at my left.

BANG!

I hit him in the head.

I felt a squeezing pressure surround me, before I knew what was happening, and I was forced to my knees by the first guard. He had wrapped his big arms around my torso, pinning my arms in, but I didn't drop my gun. I was resisting hard against his control, struggling to wrestle out of his grip. The other 6 guys were running over now. My right hand, still holding the gun, was dangling near my crotch but I had to take the risk or I was dead. I was able to twist my wrist around the right way, and I felt the hard top of the gun resting against my scrotum but I didn't even hesitate—

—*POP!*

I heard a scream and felt his grip on me loosen that I could breathe again—no time to catch my breath—I straightened out, lifting my gun up.

BAM-BAM-BAM!

My first shot missed, but the second hit a guard in his chest. The third hit another guy in the neck with an eruption of blood. I glanced back to see the guard I had just shot in the nuts and he was still holding them and screaming. I stood up as the remaining 4 men closed in.

One got really close so I smashed his nose with the butt of my gun, and he went down hard.

I had a few split seconds, so I quickly turned to the first guard behind me and slammed the bottom of my foot into his face, sending him barreling down the stairs. I turned back around and whipped my empty gun at the last 3 which distracted them enough to cover their faces with their hands and arms. I dodged to my right and rolled to the ground.

"Don't kill him!" I heard Sexrex yell out. I was reaching down to my left leg to get the second pistol out and I felt a tug on my ankle. The guy dragging me reached down and grabbed my shirt at the chest. I struck out as hard as I could, landing a solid right hook across his jaw and he dropped me. I had my legs free again so I launched one out and kicked the same guy right in the side of the head. I rolled over, off my back, to the right and as I was standing again. I was able to pull out my second gun from my ankle.

"STOP!!" Sexrex screamed in the mayhem. We all stopped, even his loyal bouncers. They pulled their guns and now it was a standoff between me and 2 remaining guys. All the girls were screaming and whimpering. I took a quick look around for Megga.

I watched the man whose nose I had smashed stand up, holding it, with blood trickling all through his fingers and down his face. I couldn't see Sexrex who was behind me and I had two armed men facing me, plus the guy with a broken nose. We all glanced back and forth at one another. Then the guy with the nose reached into his jacket—and it didn't look like he cared about listening to his boss anymore.

BANG!

I took out 1 of the 2 in front of me, aimed past the other one and pulled the trigger—

POP-POP!—both shots hit broken nose and he fell back.

—*BANG!-BANG!-BANG!*

The last guy started shooting and I dropped myself to the floor, shooting wildly upwards at him as I did.

BAM-BAM-BAM!

One in his arm, one in his leg, and the third one missed. I was out of bullets. He fell to the ground and dropped his gun. I had to scramble and I crawled to grab it, before he did. I snatched it up quickly and pressed the barrel into his temple, pinning his head to the ground—*BLAM!!*—His head bounced up as the bullet exited out of the other side of it and then it thudded back down, and a pool of blood began to pour out.

I took a huge deep breath and exhaled out for a long time, still holding my hand and the gun in the same position over his head—then I remembered Sexrex.

I spun around and stood to my feet as fast as I could, aiming the gun at him. He began to clap slowly and I noticed he was smiling.

"Well done, officer." He said softly.

"Where's Maggie!!" I screamed hoarsely, and out of breath.

Sexrex cocked his head and furrowed his brow. "Maggie?" He asked.

I should have pulled the trigger then. But before I knew it, doors were opening at the back of the room—doors on either side, and a whole bunch of other men started to pour out. All of them were holding guns and pointing them at me. I glanced to my right, where the stairs were, and saw a bunch more armed men coming up the steps. Megga was long gone out the back.

I was done for, I thought. But at least I could have taken out Sexrex before I died. My finger went for the trigger, but I hesitated too long. Before I knew it, there were big hands, roughing me up; grabbing me by the collar and shoving me. They took the gun away from me and then—*POW!* –all I saw was blackness...

"I'm not going to kill you." A distant voice said. I was coming to, and everything was still blurry. As soon as I regained consciousness, the only thing I could focus on was the throbbing pain in my head.

"Do you know why?" the same voice asked. I couldn't see him, but I could tell it was Sexrex's voice. All I could make out was the blurry shapes of a bunch of men, backlit by some big lights. In the centre, standing over me, was a bigger green blur.

"Officer..." He said. "Do you know why I'm not going to kill you?"

I was still working on trying to focus, and just as the figures started getting clearer—WHAP!—one of these guys slapped me across the face. I shook it off and then looked forward again at Sexrex, who had his hideous grinning face right close to mine. I tried to move but soon realized I was tied up, with my hands bound above my head to a drain pipe. I looked down and my feet were bound too. I tried to take a deep breath but then choked and gargled my own spit, because my mouth was covered in duct tape.

"You did all this for that piece of trash blonde?" He asked.

At that, I started to squirm in my chains. I lunged at him but got caught by the restraints. I grunted under the duct tape and he leaned back out the way.

He laughed. "I like you man." He said, and then he started to laugh out loud. I looked around and noticed all of his henchmen were chuckling as well. "Nobody has ever gotten that close to taking me out before." He went on. "I'm impressed actually. You've actually got quite a passion to you that I'm diggin' man." And he laughed out loud again. "I really am man, I'm diggin it. And because you're a cop. And I respect the brave men and women of the law, who are out there protecting us every day..." He said sarcastically. "I think I'll let you live man."

I struggled for air and squirmed in my ropes. I wanted to head butt him but my head already hurt so much, it felt like it would explode. I just glared at him and breathed fire through my nose.

"The cops are gonna want to know what happened here...and I think they'll be pretty interested to find out my side of the story." He chuckled and he held up my badge for me to see that he had found it. He touched it to my face and chuckled as he rubbed it all over my skin, seductively and mockingly. He opened up my jacket and placed it in the inside pocket, then he looked at me with a grin.

He peeled his sunglasses off of his face to reveal his creepy glass eye surrounded by scarring. His normal eye was a dark colour—not brown, not even black—just dark. The glass eye was a pale glossed over white, with a bright green clover in place of an iris.

"My boys here are gonna take care of ya now officer." He said softly, almost whispering. He raised a big hand up and caressed the side of my face with his palm. "Don't worry." He continued. "You're in good hands." And he gently slapped my cheek, before turning to walk away. As he was leaving the room I scanned the group of men now surrounding me, and they were all rubbing their knuckles and smirking at me. Just before Sexrex stepped out, he placed the sunglasses back over his eyes and then he turned to me one last time.

"Good luck man." He said, and he laughed out loud as he left.

...what happened after that—I barely remember anything after the first strike.

POW!

They didn't even take the tape off my mouth so I couldn't spit the blood out. It splashed against the back of the tape, spewing out of the borders of it and I choked on the rest as I tried to catch my breath through my nose. I felt a strong pain growing on the left side of my entire head that stemmed from my mouth and spread out to the entire face. At first they gave me a moment or two in between punches. Now my head was hanging limp to the right.

BIFF!

Another fist struck me on the right side of my head, sending it flying back to the left. After that the blows kept on coming in one after the other and I quickly lost track of how many times I was being hit, who was hitting me, or how many fists were making contact with me at any given time. It hurt at first—don't get me wrong—but after a while my body went limp on itself and I felt more numb than anything. My sides throbbed and they felt tight. At some point during the beating, enough blood had poured out of my nose and face to moisten the tape and it lost its stickiness. It opened like a flap—like a flood gate; releasing the flow. I had a momentary relief where I was able to pull in a huge deep breath, but then I was hit in the stomach and I choked on the vomit as it came up. I spewed out chunky red puke all over the place. I heard the muddled sounds of laughter as I struggled to catch the breath in my lungs. Then I was hit again...

And the beating continued...

God knows how long it lasted.
I gathered I was about to die, and I remembered Clare.
The last thought that ran through my head, before I blacked out, was her.

* * *

In a dream-like state, images of my beautiful wife danced through my mind. My great love, that once quelled my feelings of hatred towards the state of the world, was now reduced to memories. I relived our life together in my unconscious state, as my mind played out the various snippets you already know about; our first meeting, our incredible time together while we were engaged, the wedding...

My eyes opened up and I took a deep breath.
I was standing in a public washroom, surrounded by brightness. The light continued to fade and I saw that the bathroom, and everything in it, was white—pure, bright white—no other colours were to be seen, except my all black clothing that I noticed when I looked at my reflection in the mirror in front of me. I also noticed that I wasn't covered in bruises and contusions like I should have been after a beating like that. I examined myself thoroughly and didn't notice anything.
Not a scratch.
I finished examining my arms once more and then I looked up at the mirror again—
"Whoa!" I was startled and had to shout out. Looking back at me now from the glass was no longer my reflection but someone else I knew.
"Whoa!" Ridley mocked me, and then he broke out laughing while I just stared in awe at what should have been me in that mirror. He was also wearing all black clothing like me.
"Ridley..." I said. But when I said 'Ridley'—Ridley also said 'Ridley' along with me, in unison. I stopped, confused. I opened my mouth to talk and was shocked to realize that as I said:
"What's going on?" the reflection of Ridley mimicked me at the same time.
"Ridley!" We both said together. "Where am I? What's happening?" I was perplexed, while his reflection grinned at me. I stopped talking and waved my hands around, and so did he.
"John." He said. By himself this time, without me saying anything. "He's the one John."
"What?" I asked. He wasn't talking at the same time as me anymore.
"He's the one." Ridley said.
"Who?"
"Him."
"Him who Rid?"
I grabbed the mirror frame and so did Ridley's reflection on the other side.

Ridley wasn't saying anything else. He wasn't grinning at me anymore either. He looked very solemn now and it didn't even look like he was making eye contact with me. He had sort of a blank look and he was staring past me, gazing into nothingness. I waved my hand in front of his eyes and he didn't blink or move at all. I stared more carefully at my friend in the mirror and brought my face close to the glass.

I was suddenly horrified to see the whites in his eyes turn blood red. I let out a yelp and stumbled backwards, not able to peel my gaze away from the mirror. Ridley cocked his head slightly as I walked backwards away from the mirror.

I was stopped by a thud behind me when I ran into something. I whipped around to see her standing there—

"Clare?" I asked.

"He's right John." She said, right away. She too was wearing all black.

"Huh?"

"Ridley. He's right."

"Right about what?"

"About Him."

"Who are you guys talking about!?" I was getting angry. Plus I had to shout because of the loud buzzing sound that continued to grow. Clare was moving her mouth but I couldn't hear a word she was saying. All I could hear now was this loud electric buzz or a hum—

—like a magnetic field or something.

Suddenly there was dead silence as the buzzing ceased. A split second later the bathroom exploded! The stalls blew apart, the toilets shattered outwards, even the toilet water erupted—but it wasn't clear like water...it was red. The tiles shattered, the sink did too. I covered myself up with my arms over my head as I crouched down to shield myself from the flying debris, but Clare didn't budge. I peeked out from underneath my arms to see that all the debris had shattered into a billion tiny pieces, but they weren't hurting us. As I looked around I noticed that the bathroom *hadn't* been destroyed but replaced with one just like it. But it wasn't ivory anymore—it was a deep crimson red. No other colours in it now except our clothing which was now a dazzling snow white on both Clare and I.

It was like this bathroom had shed its white shell, exploding it off of itself to now reveal this new red one. I glanced around the bathroom and noticed that all of the pieces of white from the old bathroom were still floating around. I followed a trail of the white debris and saw that the mirror hadn't changed but that now it was like a vortex, sucking all of the white into it. With a final swoosh; the remaining white debris was swallowed up by the mirror.

I spun around to face Clare—or what appeared to be an image of her.

"Clare." I began. "What's going on? Where are we?" I was beginning to think that I had died from the beating of Sexrex's goons, and that this was the afterlife. "Am I dead?"

"No John." She said. "You're not dead. Not yet...You still have so much more to do baby." This apparition of my wife approached me now and laid hold of me. She leaned in and passionately kissed me. When she was done, she looked at me longingly with her hands still grasping my face.

"John." She said sweetly. "He's going to come to you."

"Who's going to come to me Clare?"

"You'll know when you see Him. Trust Him John."

"Who is he?"

"He's a friend—." Clare stopped, and cocked her head a bit. She was staring at me with a confused look now. "John...your eye."

I blinked a couple times. "What?" I asked. I raised my hand up to touch my eye and felt wetness on my fingertips. I looked at my hand and was shocked to see blood. I rubbed my thumb against my two fingers, feeling the blood. I turned to the mirror and ran over to it to see. I gasped at the sight of my eyes bleeding!

"—OFF WITH HIS HEAD!!"

A loud voice boomed out, and I heard that very distinct sound.

"Hwah! Hwah! Hwah!" I slowly turned, reluctant to confirm who I thought it was. But I saw him—In place of Clare was now this man—bleeding everywhere from his body and limping towards me. He had one bullet hole in the centre of his forehead that blood trickled out of.

Sean Ahab Mash stumbled towards me with his arms out. He got within inches and then collapsed on me, pinning me to the sink. He grabbed at my white clothes all over the place, wildly clutching at me.

"They're gonna take your head John!" He boomed, followed by that hideous laughter as he slid down my body and thudded to the floor. I looked at myself, covered now, in Sean's blood—my white clothing stained red. I spun around to the mirror and was horrified at the sight of myself. I wanted to break down and weep.

I quickly turned the taps on and started scrubbing my hands together in a panic. I frantically watched the blood wash off of my hands, but this only lasted a few moments. Soon the clear water was turning red stained again and I noticed that nothing was washing off anymore. In fact it wasn't even water coming out of the tap anymore, but blood. Exasperated I stepped back from the sink, leaving the taps on.

"The wicked flee when no man pursueth: but the righteous are bold as a lion."

"The wicked flee when no man pursueth: but the righteous are bold as a lion."

"The wicked flee when no man pursueth: but the righteous are bold as a lion."

Ridley was back in the bathroom all of a sudden, standing at the wall beside me. He was repeating this phrase over and over.

I glanced in the mirror at my reflection. As I did, the normal image of me flashed, almost subliminally. I saw a brief reflection of what looked like me, but wearing the clothes I had on the night I went to the Sex Rex. I thought I saw myself beaten and bleeding, but it flashed back to a reflection of me in white, covered in blood.

"John." Clare's voice behind me. I spun around to see her standing there in white again. The buzzing sound had started to return softly.

"John...you can change things...time is on your side." She said.

The buzzing grew louder and louder until all I saw was her mouth moving again. Ridley was still chanting at the wall. The last thing I heard when I turned to the mirror again was the obnoxious 'Hwah Hwah Hwah!" of Sean Mash's laughter—but what I saw in the reflection was the worst of it.

I was standing still, holding my own severed head in my hands. The head's eyes opened up but they weren't white—they were red.

"Wake up now John!" My head said.

* * *

I snapped awake and immediately felt a surge of pain rush over my entire body. The pain that was absent the last time I had awoken.

Back in reality, the numbness from the beating had gone away and I had unfortunately regained feeling. The bright passing of lights overhead didn't help as they flashed into my burning eyes. I shut them tight, and reopened them periodically as I tried to gain a sense of where I was. I heard the sound of squeaking wheels and doors being slammed open, along with footsteps running down the linoleum floors beside me. There was somebody over me with one of those air masks, pumping a piston to manually force breath into my searing lungs.

I hurt so bad, it was hard to focus on anything but the pain. Blurry figures is all I saw, but the last thing I surmised, before blacking out again, was that I was now in a hospital being rushed into a room.

I wasn't dead...
...not yet.
Not yet?
Isn't that what Clare told me in the dream?

* * *

The next time my eyes opened, I saw the dripping IV.

It was silent when my mind was able to focus. All I could hear was the steady blips of my heart monitor as I looked around. There was a doctor in the room checking my vitals and looking at my computer screen beside the bed. He was moving his fingers around, swiping in the air to move the projected images around. He didn't realize that I was awake. I couldn't move, or maybe I was just scared to, so my eyes just quickly darted all over the room.

All I could do was cough, or make some sort of a puff noise, and the doctor glanced over. He did a double take when he realized my eyes were open.

"Mr. Revele." He said. "Good to see you awake."

"How long have I been out?" It hurt to talk. My throat hurt, and my jaw ached when it moved.

"Uh...about a week." The doctor replied. "My name is Dr. Lucas. Your injuries were so severe, Mr. Revele, that we put you in a coma to make the healing easier on you. The first stages of X3 take about a week to work their magic. Now, you will still feel a lot of pain, but X3 takes care of the worst of it. You're very lucky Mr. Revele. You were literally beaten within an inch of your life."

Images of grinning goons, and fists flying towards my face flashed through my memory. I could still hear the slamming, packing sounds of their boots hitting my torso. I remember my ribs cracking and cringed. When I did, a sharp pain ran its course through my body and I winced.

"Careful Mr. Revele." The doctor said. "Try not to move around too much."

For the first time I wondered what my face must have looked like...I didn't want to see.

"Mr. Revele..." The doctor began. "Do you remember what happened to you?"

I thought about Sexrex's grinning face and his lucky glass eye staring at me. I couldn't tell this doctor that I had gone to the club to kill him, and that I killed 9 other men in the process of my failed rescue attempt.

I was looking back at the doctor blankly, but something in the way he was looking at me suggested that he already knew all of this. He glanced behind him towards the door out of the room, but I couldn't move my neck to see what he was looking at. He looked back at me with a concerned look and sighed.

"There's a lot of people here who want to talk to you." He said. "I've been able to hold them back for a while. Even now, I was able to convince them that under no circumstances was anyone coming in here to question you, unless I authorized it, as your supervising physician. Now, I need to run a lot of tests still Mr. Revele...but eventually...they're going to come in here and speak to you."

While he was speaking, I started to fumble around with my hand searching for the bed controls. I found it and grasped it tight. I pushed the button to raise the tilt and began to ascend up. The observation window in the room slowly appeared in my sight.

Ridley was the first person I saw and he looked back me with compassion and concern on his face. Two other guys were beside him, and I knew who they were before they even turned around to look at me. Dex Finley was peering at me sipping his coffee with no expression at all. Jake Ryan was next to him, chewing his gum and smirking slightly. Sarge was even there looking gruff and grumpy as usual. He was beside the two detectives with his hands on his hips.

I didn't see Clare.

I looked back to Ridley and he was smiling slightly. He pressed his fist up against the glass which made me smile.

"Make sure, he's the first one in here." I said to the doctor.

When I looked back to the glass I had to double take.

There was a man walking by behind all of them. A familiar looking man, despite His ordinary nature. He was taller than most people so His head floated above all of their heads. His soul piercing eyes met mine as He walked past and again, like the other times I had seen Him, time itself seemed to slow down as we just stared at each other.

The Stranger...

This time, dressed as a doctor, He exited off the right of the glass and I was left blinking stupidly.

"Him..." I whispered to myself.

"What's that?" Dr. Lucas asked.

"He's the one..." I whispered again to myself, repeating the visions in my dream.

A few more days went by where Dr. Lucas performed those tests he mentioned. He wanted to monitor me and make sure my heart was okay, and my lungs were working properly. Even despite all this, my mind remained fixed on everything leading up to this. Every day that I was in here, was one more day Maggie was still out there, under Sexrex's rule. One more man with his greasy hands all over her. One more night. One more trick.

So with the X2 drug now working its' magic; I lay in that hospital bed watching the hours go by...

...Wondering why Clare hadn't come to see me. I stared at that observation window waiting for her figure to appear behind the glass...but she didn't.

They closed the shades once in a while, and I dozed in and out constantly. When I woke up my eyes snapped to the window to see. A few times I thought I saw her shadow behind the shades, or heard her muffled voice from behind the walls...but I couldn't get her attention.

Why wouldn't she come to see me? I thought. Perhaps my appearance was too horrific for her to bear which made me scared! From what Dr. Lucas had told me, I began to think that maybe the truth had come out as to why I was in the night club. I thought Sexrex had been bluffing when he said he would tell everyone about me, but maybe not. Maybe she knew about what I did and what I have been doing...Maybe she was starting to connect the dots and put the pieces together...

The more I lay there, the more anxious I grew—torturing myself with these thoughts. *She's gone*, I thought. I longed for one more chance to talk to her and explain myself.

I had to be done in here. I needed to get out of this bed and go find her.

Before I went too crazy; Dr. Lucas finally allowed Ridley to come in and see me.

The first thing he did was bend over and hug me right there on the bed. That made me smile. It still hurt a little, but I wasn't nearly as sore as I expected. It was nice to feel a warm body's embrace—especially my good friend and partner. Noticing no pain, I closed my eyes and smiled; enjoying the moment. I patted his back and he stood up.

"Don't do this to me again man." He said solemnly.

I cracked a smile, which Ridley didn't return. "Okay man."

"John...I'm serious!"

There was a long pause, and I didn't know what to fill the silence with. I was waiting for him to say something, but he didn't...so I just asked the question that had been on my mind this whole time.

"Rid..." I began. "Where's Clare?"

Only silence from him.

"Rid." I said, reminding him. He looked at me, and now I couldn't find the compassion and relief that was written on his face when he first came in. Now, all I saw was a stress returning to his face.

"John..." he sighed. "Finley and Ryan wanna' get in here and talk to you man."

My heart sank. This is what I'd been dreading; when those two would finally come around asking questions.

"John, Why did you go to the Sexrex?"

"Rid..."

"We got a tip-off! That you were there that night. At least a dozen eye witnesses describe you shooting up the place! Why would you even think about taking on that many men by yourself!?"

"Rid, c'mon man, cut the crap...tell me where Clare is."

"Cut the crap?! Seriously John...what has gotten into you man?" Ridley placed the curve of his hand across his forehead and rubbed, closing his eyes and sighing. "You've lost it man." He continued quietly with his eyes still closed. He lowered his hand and placed it on his hips. "You've lost it." He repeated.

I couldn't think of anything to say. Maybe he was right. I couldn't look at him now, so I just stared at the ground while he berated me. He turned and rested his forearm on the medical equipment beside the bed, and there was silence for a while.

"Damn you for putting me in this spot John." He said. "Look at you. You're a mess man."

"How do you know I didn't slip and fall down a flight of stairs?"

"C'mon man!"

"Rid...He's got Maggie working for him!"

"Aw, J—...!" Ridley threw up his hands and turned his back to me.

"C'mon! What was I supposed to do?"

"So, what? You went there to tell him...To back off? To stay away? You made yourself man, he knew you were a cop! You undertook an unsanctioned undercover op! What's wrong with you!? You wanna die, John?"

"Maybe I do Rid!" I screamed, creating a dead silence in the room. I held back my tears and continued with my bottom lip quivering. "Maybe, rather than sit and watch this screwed up planet tear itself apart, it'd be better to die!" My voice cracked. "I am so sick and tired of this place Rid." I went on, with tears rolling down my cheeks now. I can't live knowing what really happens beneath the surface of every street corner. There's too much guilt! How can we hide in the light and pretend that everything's okay?"

Ridley only stared at me and when I did bring my eyes to meet his, I could see that compassion on his face. I remembered again, that he was my friend.

"John..." He said. "I can't stop them from coming in here. I wanted to talk to you first. We can get you help when all this is over man."

"What? When all what is over?"

"The courts have a lot of good programs..."

"Courts? Rid, what are talking about man?"

"Plead guilty John."

My sorrow turned to rage in an instant. "Plead guilty?!"

"John...c'mon man."

"Rid...what are you telling me? Sexrex is out there! Go and get him! Look what they did to me, go and tear that club to the ground!"

"Yah, that's what we're gonna do man! Right..." He yelled sarcastically. "And then explain to the media that one of Baltimore's finest was there buying drugs!"

"What? ...I'm not a user man!"

"He told us you came there to buy drugs!"

"Buy, yes...but I'm not doing E, man! C'mon!"

"No, you just went undercover...on your own, without backup...you weren't even on duty! John...I'm sorry." Ridley sighed out and looked at the ceiling, then back at me. "They're ready to convict you man. I'm sorry buddy, I really am...but this one's on you." Ridley shook his head. "You messed up." He said grimly.

There was a long pause, and I didn't know what to say. In the midst of my racing thoughts and burning emotions, I began to put the pieces together.

"Where is she Rid?" I asked, not looking up at him.

"John..." He began.

"Where!?"

"Finley and Ryan came sniffing around man..." He finally said, and my heart started pumping even faster. "They caught wind at the station of what happened, I dunno...I guess they just heard the office chatter. They came asking Sarge, out of concern at first." I could read the distress in Ridley's voice as he told the story. "But Sarge told them...John, he had to."

"Had to what?" I asked.

"He told them that he thought something had been...'off' with you, in the past little while. That you weren't yourself. He was worried. I can't say that I haven't noticed it either."

"You didn't...?"

"I didn't have to tell them anything. They knew right away. They're detectives."

"Aw, man! Rid..."

"I've been warning you for a while! I've tried to help you, I've left it alone. You killed nine guys!!"

"Does Clare know about this?"

"I told Finley that you guys were going through a rough patch. That things had been going south in your marriage for a while..." He paused, and sighed. I wondered what he was going to say next, but I had my suspicions. "I told them about the baby..." He said quietly.

My eyes widened. "Rid, did you tell them anything else?"

"No. I didn't mention your relationship with Clare's dad."

I released the breath I was holding in my lungs in relief.

"But, like I said." Ridley continued. That word; 'but' scared me. "They're not stupid man. And I don't think I have to say this—when nine guys are killed, and you're the one alleged doing it, well...they have to investigate. Even if they're friends of Clare's family. Hell, John. That may be even more of a reason to investigate. Out of concern for her!" Ridley shut his eyes tight and exhaled out. He began to shake his head, saying "Geez John! What the hell were you thinking man!?" and he pinched the bridge of his nose with his thumb and forefinger.

I couldn't help realizing that despite everything going on, what a good friend I had in Ridley. This guy didn't have to be here talking to me, but he obviously gave me the benefit of the doubt and wanted a chance to speak with me first. I guess I couldn't blame him. The facts did look pretty bad. But I was too stubborn, at the time, to realize how loyal he was actually being by standing in the room with me now. I was too clouded with rage and self-pity to see it.

"The information about the baby would have led them to Clare." I said. "And Clare would have told them, in innocence, about her dad and me. How much I didn't like him, how we didn't get along..." I stopped talking mid-sentence, as a revelation popped into my head. I don't know why I didn't think of it before. Maybe she has known all along, or maybe the grief of losing her father hadn't wore off yet—

Now that it had...

Maybe, now that she had had some time to think about things she had started to put the pieces together too. Or maybe she hadn't realized it until she had to recount her story to Finley and Ryan.

Either way,

I realized that she must have put it together in her head by now.

Suddenly I was overcome by a crushing weight and if the pain in my body was paralyzing, this was ten times worse. I couldn't move, I couldn't look up...all I could do was stare at the ground.

"Rid." I started.

"Tell me you didn't kill Sean Mash, John." Ridley asked grimly. I still couldn't say anything, in the wake of realizing that everyone had figured it out. I was out in the open now, exposed like a festering wound. My heart was beating so fast and it felt like someone had boiled a pot of water in my stomach. All the bubbles popping and water churning. My thoughts were racing and my emotions burning.

My best friend now condemning me with his eyes...and my wife didn't even want to see me in the hospital, despite our recent marriage revival.

"Oh man..." I heard Ridley say, through my screaming, tormenting thoughts. "John, tell me you're not this 'Baptist'!" He said.

I finally made eye contact, reluctantly, with him, but once I did, I couldn't snap my gaze away from his. I was trapped in his stare, but it wasn't conviction I saw behind his eyes...

Not even pity,

It was pleading that I saw.

I could see that he so badly wished that it wasn't true.

But he knew. As well as I did. When I peeled my eyes away and shamefully lowered my head down, I guess that was enough to confirm his suspicions. I wasn't looking at him but I heard him make a weird scoffing noise mixed with a grunt. I heard the sounds of his rapid footsteps headed towards the door. When I looked up I caught the last glimpse of his back before the door slammed shut.

That slam seemed to echo through the small room, ending the tense conversation with a bang. Now I was alone again; with my thoughts and my guilt. I kept replaying the vision of how Sean Mash looked as I shot him. I thought to myself that, that might have been the last time I'll see my friend.

Sitting there in that hospital bed, bruised and broken, I thought about my life. I still hadn't saved Maggie, or fixed the streets, though I now had the scars which proved or showed nothing! My best friend gone, who even now couldn't be as loyal as he once was. My wife...absent and angry.

Did she even care that I was okay?

Two of the city's best detectives waiting outside to talk to me. Ridley being in here with me had stalled them, but now there was nothing stopping them and it was just a matter of moments before they got in here.

What to do?

I had lived on the streets on and off for the past little while and seen a fair share of desolation. I set out to correct the mistakes of humanity and work my way out from the centre of poverty and desperation. Thinking I had crossed the line back then when really I didn't. It took getting beaten to a pulp and losing my entire life in an instant to really get to a low spot. I realized that maybe that's what drives everyone who crosses the line, to cross it in the first

place. Maybe having your sins exposed and put on display is what makes a man go to that place.
 Now...
  I knew about the dark side of life.
  I had hit my rock bottom in this moment.
   Only, when most people hit rock bottom, they want to go back up.
   I didn't.
   I wasn't done.
    I wanted to go further down...

CHAPTER FIFTEEN
Escape

What to do?
Yes, that was the question.
I had forgotten about the pain in my body, and I sat there with my heart pounding.
Everyone knew now. I was going to be arrested for my killing spree in the club and I would be charged for killing Sean Mash after Finley and Ryan got to the bottom of their investigation.
I couldn't just give up now. I didn't take the risk of throwing everything away, adopting life on the streets, and becoming a criminal and violator of the laws I worked to uphold, for nothing. If I let Finley and Ryan walk through those doors it would all be over...
...what to do?

In that moment I made my decision and I lifted my arm up, rolling my wrist and clenching and unclenching my fist to test mobility. I rubbed my forearm muscles with my other hand and tested mobility in that hand. I cautiously placed all my weight on the palms of my hands which I stretched behind me. I lifted my butt in the air to shift my weight and sit up completely straight. I winced through that pain, which was bearable and I held my ribs and massaged my legs. I rolled my neck a few times, hearing the cracks and feeling the tension there. I arched my back and a burning sensation spread.
By the end of all my stretching I was winded. I rested, placing my forearms on my legs. I ran my fingers through my hair and ended up with my face in my hands. I was still in rough shape, no doubt....but I think I was well enough.
I could make it out of this place.
In a pile on a chair, there were my clothes I had worn that night at the club.
I peered at the door that Ridley had slammed, allowing myself one last opportunity to give a thought to my old life.
Things would never be the same after this.
Sighing, I went into 'go' mode. I looked out the big observation window and caught a glimpse of the back of the officer they had posted on me. I knew this guy. His name was Jimenez. I had shared a drink or two with him on some of our morale nights. He was a newer officer—one that I trained actually. One thing I knew about him, something that I critiqued him on during his training, his security awareness sucked. I was constantly reminding him to check his blind spots and cover all the possible threat points, but he always forgot.
He looked over his shoulder into the room and I looked away. He saw me sitting up in my bed and glanced around the rest of the room. I swung my legs

over the side of the bed in agony and stood slowly to my feet, testing my balance which was surprisingly good.

One more glance to the window, and Jimenez still wasn't paying attention. I scurried over to my clothes and began rummaging through. I lifted my badge up and took a brief moment to consider my old life again. I chuckled and then stuffed the badge into my pants pocket before putting them on. My shirt was gone, probably thrown out because of all the blood on it. I started going through the pockets to see what was there. I could feel something in the back pocket and I pulled it out.

The letter...

I ripped it open hastily and dropped the torn envelope on the ground as I pulled out the actual letter. Taking glances up and down at the door and the letter I began to read.

JOHN,

It started.

CANT BREAK THROUGH. CANT REACH YOU. DON'T KILL MASH.

My heart fluttered and my belly suddenly groaned with tension. My eyes went wide and I looked around the room. At the door, Jimenez was still being Jimenez.

I turned back to the letter eagerly.

DON'T KILL SEXREX. YOU CAN STOP IT. YOU CAN CHANGE IT.

My heart was pounding now and I turned down to the bottom of the page and read the final words.

FIND JASON RICHTER...

I looked up slowly from the note, awestruck, and for a brief few moments I forgot about everything in the wake of this new development.

"Hey!" I heard Jimenez's muffled voice shout from the other side of the door. I stuffed the paper back into my pocket quickly, then the click of the door handle sounded and it was swinging towards me. Jimenez entered the room and lived up to his reputation—not checking his threat points—he didn't see me.

"Revele?" He asked.

There he was, with his back to me. Right there on his hip was his gun. Mine for the taking. I really didn't want to hurt young Jimenez...but...

It was almost providence. I needed to escape and the man guarding my door ended up being a cop who I knew had a poor security awareness. It had to be Jimenez.

I would need a gun to get out of here and I had to make it count. I rushed up behind Jimenez and grabbed the grip of his gun. I shoved him forward, but my grip remained on the gun and it popped out of the holster as he stumbled. When he spun around he went for his gun but quickly realized it wasn't there. He looked up at me wide-eyed and scared, and I was pointing the gun at him now.

"You should have listened to my advice when I was training you Jimenez." I said grimly. All he did was swallow a lump in his throat and he stared at the gun.

"I'm not going to shoot you buddy." I began. "I'm not the bad guy man. But I gotta go."

He still didn't say anything. His resolve was surprisingly good. He wasn't trembling or anything. He just stood there staring at the gun and he couldn't look at me.

"Jimenez..." I started slowly. "I'm walking out of here now. I'm gonna borrow your gun."

"They're right down the hallway." He said.

"Ridley?" I asked.

"I'm not sure where Simmons went." Jimenez said.

I took a deep breath and exhaled slowly. Thinking.

"Which way Jimenez?"

He hesitantly pointed to his left, my right to tell me which way out of the door everyone was.

"You're a good kid Jimenez. I'm sorry; I don't remember your first name."

"It's uh...*ahem*...it's Jim." He actually smiled nervously and shrugged.

I laughed. "Jim?" I asked. We both shared a bit of a laugh together.

"Jimmy Jimenez?" I asked, half laughing. "I guess that's why I would get your first name mixed up."

Surprisingly, he was laughing now, even with his own gun still pointed at his face. It was just as if we were sharing a laugh at a bar again after work. His smile quickly faded as he remembered the situation he was in.

"Can I ask you a question?" He asked.

"Sure man."

"What do you plan on doing next?"

The question shocked me.

"I mean...you're a cop." He continued. "You know how we work. You know we always get our man eventually. How far do you plan to take this thing? This...whatever it is you're doing..."

"Why?" Was all I could think to ask. "You wanna join me?"

I was reminded now of something I had commented on in his written evaluation. How his intuitiveness and quick thinking made up for his lack of other qualities. And how he was able to stay calm in high stress situations and look for a solution.

"I might." He stated. "God knows, I agree with everything you've done. This city...the world...it's far gone. I may know your thoughts a little more than you think."

"But?"

"But...there's gotta be a better way than this to fix things."

"Well Jimmy Jimenez..." I started. "When you find that better way...you come and find me"

"The Baptist..." He said.

For the first time, I acknowledged the name. "Yah. That's me."
Just then, I began to hear commotion in the halls. Footsteps and shouting. Keeping a suspicious eye on Jimenez, I backed up with the gun still pointed at him to peer down the hallway. I saw the commotion at the reception desk. Finley and Ryan were speaking with the nurses saying: "You need to close off this entire wing!" A number of other uniformed officers were with him. Finley was directing them to spread out and cover the exits. I guess they had assumed I was already on the lose...but I had stayed here and blabbed with Jimenez. He had been stalling me. I shot him a glance with both a bit of anger and a bit of pride. He shrugged back with a cheeky little grin. I looked down and noticed his radio flashing its emergency signal that he must have triggered when I pushed him.
"Nice work kid." I said with a smile.
"Must have been my training." He replied, still grinning.
I gave him a wink before I turned and ran to the right out of the doorway.
"Hey! John, stop!"
I heard their voices behind me as I ran down the hallway. My body ached from the pain of my injuries but the adrenaline overpowered that and I charged down the halls, through a few nurses and orderlies.
Now the chase was on.
I wasn't awake when they brought me in here so I had no idea where in the hospital I was. But I had been here enough times with people in custody, and with Clare and with Ridley to get my bearings. Every step I took, the crowd chasing me got closer and I could hear their steps and voices growing louder.
I came to a meal cart—those really tall ones—and I grabbed hold of it and pulled hard to knock it over. Then metal crashed and echoed through the halls, and jello and tuna sandwiches flew everywhere. That slowed them down for a bit as I rounded the corner and went right again. I just needed to find something familiar, something to gain some orientation and help me work my way out of here. I was looking, searching all around, but it was difficult to focus on one thing while I was running as fast as I could through the hospital.
A nurse tried to stop me...
stupid nurse. Don't do it. Don't. Damnit.
I tried to dodge left, then right but she was a persistent girl. Brave girl. But stupid. I ducked down and dived forward trying to avoid her as best as I could, but when I rolled, my legs smacked into her torso knocking her right over. I scrambled to my feet, stumbling and tripping as I tried to gain some momentum again. I looked back and saw the crowd catching up. I finally finished stumbling and started running again. I came to a T in the halls and made a quick left. I finally noticed something after running for another twenty yards or so. I stopped briefly and examined the waiting area to my left. This was where the nurse had come out and told Clare and I that our baby had died in her womb.

I kept running, knowing now, that if I kept on going down this long hallway I could make a right towards the ER. If I could make it through the ER there was a set of automatic double doors to freedom. But the team of officers was closing in.

At the end of the long hallway I saw two security guards appear. These guys didn't have guns, but I did. Not that I was going to shoot them, but I raised mine up as I ran towards them.

"Get outta my way!!" I screamed at them.

I heard them both shout a few profanities as they dove in opposite directions. I was now forced to make a right down a sooner hallway. All the staff down this hallway screamed, ducked and hid at the sight of me; a mad man with a gun. I maneuvered my way through the crowd and nurses stations making sure to hold my gun in the air. When I broke through that group I looked up and began to follow the ER plaques to get there. I came to a spot where I could go left towards the ER but when I came out into that hallway opening I was tackled by a lone security guard who slammed me into the wall.

I kneed him in the side and shoved him off of me. I tried to run left but he grabbed my leg and tripped me so I fell onto my face. I spun around to be on my back and kicked this guy right in the face. I think I broke his nose, but it stopped him and I spun back onto my front so that I could push myself up and keep running.

As I was getting up I saw the crowd of officers round the far corner and shout at me. As I began to run towards the very close ER I heard Ryan shout "block off the ER doors, all officers close in on the ER!!"

I was almost there. Almost out.

I was chased right into the centre of the ER and I had the same reaction that I previously had. Everyone started shouting and screaming as they ducked for cover and hid where they could at the sight of an escaped patient with a gun in his hand. I approached the double doors but came to a skidding stop when I saw the flashing purple haze of mixing blue and red cruiser lights and heard the winding sirens as a bunch of them skidded to a stop right in front of the entrance, some even hopping the curbs and stopping directly in front of them.

I spun to see the crowd chasing me about seven yards away now. I darted left out of the waiting area and crashed through the doors leading into the actual ER floor.

More panic. More screaming.

I was headed through here to the real emergency doors where the ambulances brought in patients. I guess the officers had taken another route because now they were emerging from a hallway just ahead of me and coming at me from the front. I turned to run but was faced with several hospital security guards with their batons opened up ready for a fight.

Everyone stopped for a moment. Finley and Ryan, and several of the officers with them had their guns drawn, but I don't think any of us, including myself, were dumb enough to start discharging our weapons in the middle of an ER room.

"John!" Finley shouted. "Don't be an idiot now! Drop the gun!"

Both sides slowly moved in on my position as I remained planted in the middle. I stood bladed to both sides; the guards now on my left and the cops to my right. Just ahead of me was a nurse's station with a second hallway on the other side of it. To my fortune there was a pathway through the nurse's station to that hallway. Finley saw my eyes go there and started motioning some of his group to go around and cut me off.

Before they could move I lunged forward and ran through to the other side of the nurse's station.

"Move! Go around, cut him off!!" I heard, along with the scurrying of many footsteps. I turned right and charged towards the ambulance intake area which was just ahead of me, about thirty yards.

I could make it.

What happened next, happened so fast. But I'll have to explain it to you in slow motion almost.

The officers who had run around to cut me off we're rounding the corner just as I was approaching it. For a split second my pounding heart sank to the pits of my stomach thinking that this was it. I'm finished...

I'm sure their hearts were pounding just as bad as mine was. I almost stopped and gave up in that instant, but—

—WHAM!!!!

Out of nowhere, a hospital bed came barreling down the opposite end of that hallway and slammed into the group of officers--smashing them back down the hallway they were emerging from. There was a porter pushing the bed and he was running with the bed it seemed.

At first I didn't give a second thought to it. When I realized that they were now immobilized I just ran, seeing my opportunity and taking it. It wasn't until I happened to glance to the right as I passed that I saw the porter's face.

I originally glanced at Him and then just turned to run, but a few split seconds after, when the connections were made in my mind, I spun back around in a double take to get a second glance at my saviour.

I could only allow myself a brief look but I was certain it was Him.

He had that same gentle grin on his face that I had seen all along. The one that said; *don't worry I took care of it.* For a seemingly very simple and average looking man, I could never forget His face. Here at the hospital He would have blended in and looked like any other hospital porter, but I definitely recognized Him.

I wanted to stop and ask Him all kinds of questions but I had to run now. I turned and charged the doors, fifteen yards ahead of me now. Amidst the yelling voices and thundering feet of everyone chasing me, my thoughts were only about Him now.

The Stranger!
What was he doing here?

Why was he helping me again?
I burst through the doors and into the garage where the ambulances parked. Nobody was in my way and I was free and out in the open.
But all I wanted to do was go back in and talk to Him.
For a second I was frozen but my drive kicked back in and I ran.
Why? I thought...a few seconds after and I would have been the one He was slamming with a bed--stopping me and allowing me to get caught. But I was allowed to escape one more time.
I thought about nothing else as I limped away from the hospital.

CHAPTER SIXTEEN
Time is of the Essence

The desert sands of Israel were teeming with life.
Scientists and workers—the usual Globe-X worksite.
Jason Richter stormed, as fast as his old legs would carry him, through all of the busy workers.
"Mr. Richter!" Kitch's whiney voice called out after him.
Richter cringed and kept walking to ignore Kitch.
"Mr. Richter, my employer has not app—"
"—shut the hell up Kitch!" Richter snapped. "Your employer isn't in charge of this project, I am!" He went on, still storming through the worksite.
Kitch struggled to keep up, dodging workers and falling just short of Richter's strides.
"You better be careful about what you say Jason! We could pull funding at any time if we don't like what y—"
Richter whipped around quickly and put his face right into Kitch's. Kitch stumbled back to not collide with him.
"If I don't conduct these trials now, then we have to wait another three months for all the rings to synchronize again. Everything's ready to go now Kitch!"
Kitch just stared at Richter, leaning slightly back. He had to look away, adjusting his glasses in discomfort.
"Mr. Richter..." He began. "You're on very thin ice—"
"—bah! Your threats are useless as usual." Richter turned and began heading towards the site again.
"We don't even know if it'll be operational!" Kitch shouted after him, not following this time.
"We've already made it work you idiot!" Richter responded, glancing over his shoulder, and Kitch was left there, adjusting his glasses and sighing.
"I hate scientists." He said out loud.
"And they hate you Kitch!" Ernest laughed and patted him hard on the back as he hurried from behind him, to catch up with Richter.
Kitch rolled his eyes and sighed again.
Ernest caught up to Richter.
"So what happened?" He asked him as they walked.
"I don't know Ernest. Things were too rushed somewhere. The rings all got turned on too early."
"We weren't scheduled to go for another few weeks."
"You don't think I know that? All I know is that we received reports while I was overseeing the one in India. Someone turned the China one on..."
"Who did that?"

"I don't know. But it threw everything off. Now all the magnetic fields are aligning and we can't stop it now."

Ernest breathed out slowly and they reached the centre of the worksite.

"Uncover it Mr. Kerst." He said, as the two of them met up with Donald, who was waiting for them. Donald gave a signal to other workers and they started pulling a giant cover off the project. It slid off to reveal a different type of machine.

This one was a ring also, but a smaller version. At the base of it there was a big iron canister, about the size of a man. Its lid was opened revealing the inside of the egg like compartment—an indented or contoured shape of a person on the back of it, with some heavy duty straps where the legs, arms and head would go.

"Can't we just turn them all off?" Ernest asked.

"And wait another three months to run any kind of tests?" Richter retorted. He gazed upon his life's work.

His baby all grown up.

His creation complete!

"No..." He said. "we're too close to do that..."

"People could get hurt, Jay!" Ernest said.

"I don't care!" Richter snapped angrily.

Ernest stopped and was taken aback. Even Richter was taken aback by his own comments. He looked away.

"What about your machine?" Ernest asked. "What if something goes wrong and it all falls apart...are you willing to lose your life's work?"

Richter sighed and took a long look at his machine as Ernest lectured him.

"We don't know what's going to happen!" Ernest went on. "What if we break the space time continuum? What if we can't get the subject back?"

Richter stared at the ring long and hard before turning back to Ernest.

"There's always risks, Ernest." He said. "That's science...it's now or never."

* * *

Everything was a blur. Hazy.

I kept seeing fuzzy, out of focus images in between my blacking out.

I don't really remember what happened. One minute I was limping away from the hospital I just escaped, the next I was seeing stars and blurry images. My head was spinning.

Was I caught? Did they catch up to me?

The last time I woke up like this, was in a hospital.

When my eyes opened this time, a fuzzy figure appeared standing over me. I think I was in an alley...

An alley...again. I spent more and more time in the alleys of the city. Now I was waking up, yet again, in another alley.

"Here." His muffled voice said. He sounded like he was talking into a pillow. "Drink this." I thought I heard him say and he crouched down to my level.

I felt the warm ceramic touch my lips and then knock against my teeth as he pressed the mug further into my mouth. The hot liquid poured into it forcing it closed and I spit it out as I lurched forward from my seated position. I began coughing and I rested my head again against the wall behind me. I kept my eyes shut and tried to bring the world into focus. Blinking a lot and shaking my head back and forth, the figure with me became a little clearer. He seemed like a young guy. He offered me the mug again.

I shook my head. "My throat hurts." I forced out.

"This will help." He said, his voice a little clearer now.

I groaned in protest as he forced it to my lips again. He dumped the liquid into my mouth and most of it spilled over my lips and dribbled off my chin. My mouth filled up and I was forced to swallow. As I came to my senses I caught the faint flavour of lemon, mixed with...

that old familiar favourite. Honey.

"Mmm." I hummed with my lips still on the mug, and I guzzled up more of the hot beverage until I went too far and began coughing. I swallowed my mouthful and smacked my lips. "Mmm. Mmm, that's good."

I sat up a little and put my head in my hands. I had a headache as well, but now my throat felt soothed. I looked up and was able to see my helper now. A young guy, I was right, but gruff looking. Well built, but with grubby looking clothes. He had a short beard and shaggy hair. He was wearing a jean jacket with a brown vest, lined with sheep's fleece.

He smiled at me and that felt nice. I had become accustom to all the condemning eyes and faces I got at the hospital. It was good to see his gentle face. But then again...he probably didn't know what I had done.

I grabbed the mug out of his hand greedily and drank up the hot concoction, slurping and spilling it out of the corners of my mouth. He just chuckled to himself and looked at the ground.

I drank up the last of it, raising the mug up away from my mouth and throwing my head all the way back, allowing the last drop to fall onto my tongue. I lowered my arm in disappointment and looked at the young man.

"What happened?" I asked groggily.

"What happened!?" He repeated my question. "You tell me. You come stumbling in here, to my alley, you look like you've been hit by a truck. I have no idea brother, what happened to you."

A vague memory of limping around the city with no energy came back to me.

"I remember walking around for a while after leaving the hospital." I said.

"Well that would explain your hospital gown." The guy laughed sarcastically.

"I...I don't...I can't remember." I staggered. I held my head, trying to stop the headache. "I must have tried to hide here."

"You collapsed against the dumpster and passed out." He told me.

I looked over to the dumpster a few feet away and groaned. "Ugh...I...I can't f—...I don't remember a thing."

"So, what? You escaped?" The guy asked me.

"You wouldn't understand, man." I replied.

"I might understand more than you think, brother."

I sighed and shook my head as I closed my eyes. I sat there with my knees bent and my elbows resting on them. I was still holding the mug and I handed it back to the guy.

"Where did you get honey out here?" Was all I could think to fill the silence with.

"Where anybody on the streets gets anything." He simply said. "I stole it."

I looked up at him for a moment, puzzled. Then I shrugged. "Makes sense."

He started to wrap the mug in an old t-shirt, and I rested my forehead on my knees, sighing.

"My name is John." He said, as he stuffed the wrapped up mug into his old pack.

I didn't look up but I paused in my thoughts. There was silence for a moment, and then I chuckled.

"What's so funny?" He asked.

I slowly looked up at him with a grin. "My name is John too."

He chuckled. "Well how about that?" He asked.

I suddenly realized how much pain I was in. The refreshing moment of meeting John—a man who didn't know anything about me—had distracted me entirely. We could have been sitting in a coffee shop enjoying a friendly conversation over hot beverages.

But we weren't.

We were on the concrete of a city alley with the rest of the garbage, and it all started to come back to me.

Clare's face flashed in my mind's eye.

I remembered Ridley slamming the door.

I could hear the sounds of the street pouring in through the end of the alley. The rushing water sound of cars. The honking horns and distant sirens. A symphony of sounds that used to fill me with joy. Now it only snapped me back into my reality.

The pain in my body reminded me of what I had done.

That reminded me of Maggie, and all of my other problems with the world.

I remembered escaping the hospital.

I remembered *Him*...

Most of all I suddenly remembered that letter! I reached behind me quickly and felt the crumple of paper. The letter was still stuffed in my back pocket and I pulled it out. I unfolded it again and read a second time.

FIND JASON RICHTER!

Those words stuck out to me the most.

I flashed back, in my head, to those nights where I had seen those weird images of myself, giving a vague and unclear warning message, now specified in this letter;

DON'T DO IT...DON'T KILL MASH. YOU CAN CHANGE IT. YOU CAN STOP IT!

"Well, brother." John 2 said, as he finished packing his pack back up. "We better get going."

"Going?" I asked. "Where are we going?"

"I'm going shopping." He grinned, as he stood to his feet, flinging his pack onto his back and tightening the straps.

"Okay..." I said slowly. "Have fun then man, cya around. Thanks for the drink and making sure I was okay."

"What are you talking about?" He asked. "Let's go."

He stood there grinning and I remained seated against the dumpster looking up at him. "What? You want me to come with you?" I was confused.

"Would you rather stay here by yourself bro?"

I looked down with a frustrated sigh. He was right...I knew that much. What was I going to do?

"I've seen you before you know..." John 2 said.

"What?"

"Out here...I've seen you."

"When?" I asked with a little disgust in my voice.

"What? You think you're the only person on the street?"

"No, I—"

"—I've seen you...in corners, huddled around the trash can fires. You were quite talkative with some of the other guys."

I realized that he must have been among some of the groups I had hung around when I was first trying this street life thing.

"Yah..." I started. "...and?"

"You're new on these streets aren't you?"

"Why do you ask that?"

"Nobody who's been out here long enough is as curious as I've seen you be with some of my other friends."

"Yah...okay. So what?"

"So...why don't you hang around with me for a while bro? I'll show you how to get your own honey." John 2 smiled a pleasant smile at me.

I couldn't reveal my other agenda to this guy. I needed to get out of this alley. I needed to regroup. Strategize. Plan better if I was going to go up against Sexrex again. I needed to find The Stranger and ask Him questions. I needed to now, apparently, find Jason Richter, but how the hell was I going to do that!?

I laughed and returned the smile.

"Well alright then." I said. "I've got my own agenda, but I'll go with you...for now." I reached my hand up and winced through the pain as John 2 pulled me up by clasping it. I brushed myself off as he stood there patiently with his hands clutching the straps of his back pack.

228

"You hungry?" He asked politely.

"Starving." I replied shyly. I waited as he shuffled through his pack. And then he produced a shiny red apple in front of my nose.

I chuckled to myself.

There it was.

Glistening from the beam of sunlight shooting into the alley.

Just like the first time I had begun life out here.

I glanced to my right out of the alley and I had to do a double take because a familiar sight caught my eye.

The big billboard at the other side of the street read; *'THIS IS NOT YOUR LIFE'*

I looked around and it didn't take long to realize that this was the same alley in which I first encountered The Stranger. I couldn't help but chuckle.

John 2 was waiting for me when I looked at him again. He was still holding out the ripe looking apple in his hand. Was this some kind of providence? I couldn't not go with him now. I took the apple into my hands, smiling. I felt it out, rolling it around with my fingers.

My second chance.

I tossed it up while I laughed out loud and caught it. Then I took a big juicy bite.

* * *

"So how does it all work Mr. Richter?" The interviewer asked him on TV.

"Well. It's all very complicated of course." Richter answered. "I could just tell you it's a very complex process that you wouldn't understand anyways. A clock strapped to some electric wires and a microwave or something."

The interviewer laughed along with Richter.

"I actually discovered the whole thing when I was ten years old, do you believe that?"

"Really?"

"Yes, I was tinkering with an old television set, and I had the tube out on the table, with a magnet on the other end of the table. All it needed was an electric charge. Long story short, I broke the tube open creating a vacuum. I spilled my juice box, short circuiting my stereo, creating the perfect blend of elements, save one...radiation. Combined with the electro-magnetism and the vacuum of electrons, the radioactive portion of my equations provided the amplification of this whole process to perform on a massive scale that is needed."

"You're right, that doesn't make any sense."

Both of them laughed.

"I think I like the clock hooked up to a microwave idea better."

They laughed again.

"So, why the multiple sites around the globe?" The interviewer pressed.

"Well. Each site is a giant field of electromagnetic energy. The rings all create a buildup that gets projected to the next. They have to be turned on weeks before they're used, in order to create a large enough charge between all of them."

"And then what? The Israel site? What is that for?"

"Israel is the receiver. The tower picks up all their energy and synchronizes all of it. It makes a sort of zigzagged tunnel across the globe."

"And that's what the subject will pass through?"

"Exactly right. If my calculations are correct...and they always are...the subject is attracted, via magnetism, amplified by microwaves, in between each ring. Once the power is turned up to it's full potential, the subject will be moving so fast around the planet, that they will surpass the confines of space and time!"

The interviewer's face was dumbfounded.

"Well..." The interviewer started. "I'm sure we all can't wait to see if it will work!" He said, sort of half sarcastically.

* * *

I stared down at this letter in my own hand writing, analyzing it to death. There was no mistaking my own writing. I couldn't figure this out.

I was waiting outside a department store. John 2 was inside. I was actually behind the store, staring at this letter again.

"Here." I heard his voice behind me. Sneaky guy. Before I got the chance to fully turn around, I was startled by the heap of clothes he threw at me. I quickly caught them as John 2 came back.

"Put them on, quick." He said.

I ripped off the hospital gown and stood there in just my pants, while John 2 kept watch.

"What's that piece of paper you keep reading?" He asked me brazenly.

I took off my old bloody jeans as I spoke.

"I don't even know myself to be honest." I pulled on the new jeans he had gotten for me as I kept talking. "Some sort of letter. I don't really know who wrote it." I rifled through the other items looking for socks. I stuffed my feet into those. They were a nice thick wooly pair, high quality.

"Nice." I said, wiggling my toes.

"You'll need a good pair of socks out here." John 2 replied.

"Huh...I guess I could learn a thing or two from you. I would've just taken a cheap-o pair."

"Why?"

I paused to think. "I dunno...I guess I would feel better knowing I didn't rip the store off for too much money." I laughed. Looking at John 2, I saw the funny look he was giving me.

"Really?" He asked sarcastically. "You're already stealing...you might as well grab something good!"

I picked up a t-shirt out of the pile and shrugged.

"How bout that?" He said to himself. "The man has a conscience."

I smirked and shook my head at his sarcasm as I pulled the t-shirt over my head. He continued to keep watch while I found the remaining items he grabbed for me. A good quality leather belt for my pants, a thicker long sleeve t-shirt and a black zip-up hoodie. I continued to get dressed behind the store and didn't notice that John 2 was staring at me. As I finally pulled on the hoodie and zipped it up I looked at him.

"Did you get the smokes?" I asked eagerly.

John 2 rolled his eyes and reached into his pocket. He tossed me the pack of cigarettes and I caught it and put it in my hoodie.

"I got you a lighter too." John 2 said, and he tossed it to me.

"Is it a zippo?" I asked as I caught it and inspected it.

"Why did it have to be a zippo?" John 2 asked.

"Cuz they're cooler." I simply said.

John 2 just chuckled and shook his head.

I kicked my discarded jeans and hospital gown into a heap and then I flicked the lighter on as I crouched down. I touched the flame to the hospital gown and held it there until it caught fire. Then I stood back up and both John 2 and I stared at the clothing as it went up in flame.

I glanced over at him and saw the look on his face. He looked like he was about to ask me something.

"What?" I asked.

He hesitated again. He opened his mouth and I anticipated a question.

"Nothing." He simply said. "We better get going."

I crumpled up the plastic from the cigarette pack and tossed it in a trash can that we passed. I felt refreshed with the new clothes. They were really comfortable. John 2 knew how to pick out good quality stuff. I felt normal walking around with him. I even would momentarily forget about my bruised and scarred face. I admired my new threads as we continued to walk the streets. Although, I wished I had grabbed my leather jacket from the hospital...not to mention the rest of my clothes!

"So, listen." I asked him as I lagged behind. "I've got a whole bunch of stuff that I need to figure out. Where are we going, if you don't mind me asking, John?" I flipped open the cigarette pack and pulled one out as I talked. He had been leading me around town and I had just been following him without asking any questions until this point.

"We...are going home...John."

I laughed to myself. "I guess were gonna need to come up with a better system for this." I said, placing the smoke in my mouth.

"Better system for what?"

"Our names...the Johns." I replied bouncing the smoke all over.

John 2 laughed as he looked back at me. "Okay, so what?"

I clinked the zippo open and hovered it with one hand as I stopped. "What if I call you...well, wait...what's your last name?"

"Gramhain."

"Hmm...well, that doesn't really help." I flicked the wheel to light the zippo, and used my other hand to shield the flame from the wind as I pushed the tip of the smoke into it.

John 2 laughed out loud. "It's Irish...it means 'loved one' or, 'one who is loved'."

I snapped the lighter closed and inhaled the first drag I had had in a while. I took out the smoke and exhaled dramatically. "A fellow Irishman." I said. "Still not helping me out here. I can't even pronounce that."

"Gram...Hain. It's easy."

"I don't think you're getting my point here."

"All of our names mean something, John. Even yours...Re..." He trailed off suddenly, after barely pronouncing the R.

I furrowed my brow, in the middle of a drag.

"...I don't know your last name." He said instead.

I blew out. I hesitated to tell him, but he had helped me out so much, just in the past few hours, that I felt I owed him at least my name.

"Revele." I said carefully. "I don't know what it means..."

John 2...or Gramhain...maybe I'll start calling him...stopped walking and turned to smile at me. "You will." He said. "One day."

I shrugged nervously. "That's a nice thought I guess." I quickly took another drag.

"You guess?" He asked. He turned to keep walking and we were moving again. "I dunno, I just think no man should die before figuring out his name."

"Yah, like a legacy."

"Legacy...good word."

I inhaled a big drag and closed my eyes. "Mmm." I said to myself. It had a been a while. This felt normal again. I slowly let the drag out and began to admire my city streets as we walked in silence for a while.

We walked for quite a long time. Through the city streets, weaving our way in and out of back alleys and shortcuts. My new friend John G was really impressive actually. We eventually wandered out of the main downtown area—the nicer area—and we passed by so many things I knew from my old life. The old dominos sugar sign, the clock tower, Edgar Allen Poe house, even the giant Barnes and Noble store. Oriole park, where I had gone to many ballgames as a kid. Happy memories, mixed in with the darker ones. City hall...reminding me of Clare's dad--the man I killed. Seeing city hall brung a flood of bad feelings with it. I remembered Kang and the girl from Sean's office that washed up on shore.

All of it.

Maggie...Sexrex...

The state of world all together. The wars, the desolation, and all of the garbage left over—oozing that nasty orange-brown garbage juice everywhere.

All of this brought on by the sight of one building.

We passed by one street and as we exited out of the alley I got a view of the open harbour. Baltimore's harbour was beautiful this time of day. The sun was just setting and the bright orange danced on the waves of the water. The glass in the skyscrapers trapped the colour and reflected it radiantly back out towards the people walking on the boardwalk. I saw the old relic, the tall-ship anchored in the bay and the suns beams were stuck behind the masts, trying to break through where they could.

A beautiful scene. Clare and I had taken many walks down here—shared laughs and held hands as we walked—where others were walking now. All those people going about their daily lives. Here in the city, aside from all the major problems of war and genocide.

Terrible as they are.

Never mind those here. These people struggled with more common everyday problems. Not the proverbial 'first world problems' that I joked about before, but real issues and struggles of the common man.

Here in these streets—where *life* happened.

As we wandered the avenues and boulevards I was afforded an opportunity to reflect. These were all buildings and streets that I'd attended as a cop. In the last several years I had seen firsthand the problems that burden us as a race.

Business men wanting to jump off the roofs of their buildings, because they were too ashamed. Homeless people who felt that same shame. Men who had worked so hard their entire lives to gain a position over other men because they were told that's what you had to do. Who sacrificed relationships until they could prove that they 'had it all together', not realizing they had missed out on other great opportunities. Yet similar minded people, who also worked hard to get somewhere. Individuals who did everything right and then had no luck finding work after college. Forced to work a job they hate to pay the bills. Making sacrifices of their own to make ends meet. Too bad nobody ever told them that their self-worth had nothing to do with their titles. To the point where these people felt like failures and losers, when in fact they had so many other strengths.

Sick people...dying people.

Married people who were once so in love, but now struggled because of the pressures life puts them under. Whose failing love has nothing to do with a lack of feelings but rather an enormous and unnecessary insecurity.

Drug addicts. Prostitutes. Gangs. The real obvious stuff.

Fathers and sons. Mothers and daughters. Brothers and sisters...ripped apart by the never ending cycle of family dysfunction.

And yes, even the 'first world' stuff contributes to the weird and bizarre degenerative state of the human race.

Life is hard.

* * *

At the same time, in real time.

The deserts of Israel were heating up, in more than just temperature.

"It's going to be mayhem here, Donald." Ernest said to him, as he stood near the smaller Israel ring, looking around the now empty perimeter. "If this test goes smoothly and the press gets ahold of it."

"Let's hope it goes smoothly." Donald replied. "He's got about a week left till the six rings align up. Let's just hope he doesn't disappoint."

The two men looked at each other blankly. "You don't think it'll work?" Ernest asked.

"I don't know Ernest. I mean...tachyons? I was on board with the other science. The electromagnetism, the radioactive aspect..."

"Tachyons exist Donald."

They turned and began to walk towards the centre of the site where the machine was. "Do they?"

"*Tachyons...*" A talk show host began. "*...scientists are baffled by them, physicists are skeptical of them. Hypothetical 4D particles that, if real, move faster than the speed of light! That's what we'll be discussing today. I'm here with renowned scientist Jason Richter, who you all know as the man behind the recent time experiments. An advocate for time travel, the man who's going to change the world, here he is everyone; Jason Richter!*"

The live audience applauded during this old broadcast, which aired before the Israel site.

A slightly younger Jason Richter smiled and waved at the audience as their applause subsided.

"*So, Jason, tell us about these tachyons.*"

"*Well, Bill, as you said; they are hypothetical. What do exist, are particles that move at the speed of light called luxon, and particles that move slower than the speed of light called bradyon. Consequently, people have theorized for ages, that there must exist particles that move faster than the speed of light!*"

"*Tachyons.*" The host confirmed.

"*Correct, Bill.*"

"*So, what can be done with these particles, Jason?*"

"*Well, in terms of my experiments, I require things to move extremely quickly. So quickly in fact to break the barriers presented by known physics.*"

"*The speed of light you mean?*"

"*Right.*"

"*Your theory that if the subject travels through the six rings at a an enormous rate—*"

"*—an impossible rate.*"

"*...excuse me, an impossible rate of speed, he will break these barriers?*"

"Exactly right, Bill!"
"But it's like you said, impossible..."
"I said it was impossible according to known physics."
"Known physics..."
"Known physics...it's in the unknown that I'll find my answers."
"But how will you hone in on them?"
"Oh, they're everywhere."
"Really?"
"Yah, just like dust...they're floating around us everywhere. They would just require a...boost, if you will."
"So, a particle accelerator then."
"You stole the words right out of my mouth, Bill. Yes, a particle accelerator. That's what the capsule is."
"The capsule?"
"The canister, where the subject sits."
"Oh, right. Okay."
It's a miniaturized particle accelerator. It creates a field around it that speeds up the particles around it. Working together with all the other aspects of the machine; the electro-magnet, the micro waves..."
"And this will work?"
Richter paused. Taking a breath; he smirked cheekily at the host. "We'll see..."

CHAPTER SEVENTEEN
Nothing Is The New Everything

John G and I walked and walked—right out of the downtown core of Baltimore, until we crossed over the tracks, onto the wrong side of them. Into the slums on the east side of the city. The skyscrapers turned into old dilapidated apartment buildings and rows of broken down townhouses that weren't even safe for a dog to live in. Slumlords had taken these places over and taken advantage of the people who were desperate to live in them. Boarded up shops and smashed windows. The streets seemed eerily empty, though they weren't. The garbage was littered all over the ground and newspapers blew around. Even the colour seemed faded here. It could have been the fact that by the time we reached the slums the orange glow of the sun had disappeared past the horizon, but it was as if someone had photo shopped this area of town and turned the saturation down. There were broken down cars all over the place, with flat tires. Long abandoned by the owners.

A haven of crime.

Of desperation and loss.

Everyone who lived here was either the victim of a crime or the criminal.

I guess I would fit right in here.

I flicked the butt of my second cigarette down to the ground.

These people definitely knew about the dark side of life, and here is where I would hide from the people hunting me. There was an aspect of this stuff that I did like a little bit. The grittiness and rawness of it all was intriguing. An escape from the rules of higher society and upper living. No more pretending out here...even if you were...nobody cared.

"So this is home..." John G said. He raised his arms up in presentation and spun around to face me. He had a little smile on his face. He didn't seem ashamed of anything.

"Why are you helping me man?" I had to finally ask.

He shrugged, and looked away nervously. "Why not?"

"Because..." I started. "Even though I'm somewhat of a rookie out here...I know it as well as you do. People out here don't help anybody but themselves."

I stumped him, and he didn't have anything to say. Until he glared at me. "It was always obvious to me. Watching you."

"What was?" I asked.

"That you came from privilege. That you were out here by choice."

He and I stared at each other for a few moments.

"That intrigued me." He piped up.

"Okay..." I replied. "But that still doesn't really—"

"I realized that you must have been trying to run...I thought maybe you were planning something...reconnaissance mission." John G hesitated and looked at the ground. "I used to get angry with you."

"I never even saw you in the circles when I was talking." I cut in.

"I know who you are." He said. "You don't remember me, because you never saw my face in that diner."

My heart sank a little. "W...what?"

"You and your partner Simmons would always come in and chat with my group."

I started to breathe a little heavier, realizing that this was the weirdo who always sat at the back of that diner.

"Bart...Ken..." John G went on.

"Oh, shit!" Is all I could think to say. My hand slid, involuntarily to the pocket my badge was in. I was sideswiped here! "I can't believe I didn't...wow..." I stammered.

"I knew you were a cop even when I first started seeing you on the streets." He said. "I thought that how could somebody who came from where you came from...how could you want to leave what you had, in the lap of luxury, and put yourself into this life." He looked up at me, and for the first time I saw a glimpse of negative emotion behind his eyes. "I thought...how arrogant of you!"

I could see an anger on his face as he glared at me. I should have been alerted to something, and turned my thoughts to the fact that maybe he wasn't helping me but, for some reason, I still trusted him. I wanted to hear what he would say next.

"But..." He finally said through the silence. "I realized something as I thought about it, and I always remembered your speeches about life you would give to Bart and Ken. The times when you weren't around...all I did was think about you. I realized that...whatever it is you were running from, must have been the exact thing—the same issue we all face. You're problems, even though I might not have agreed with their merit, were still bad enough to push you out here. I guess humans will always find things to complain about. Something I used to get pissed about. But I figured out that it's not because of boredom or about being whiney. There is a sense...that we all feel."

I couldn't believe what I was hearing. I stared at him intently as he monologued away. I knew what he was going to say next.

"A void." He said. "Something is just not right with the world."

There it was.

My thoughts,

  my words,

    coming out of John G's mouth.

"It's the human condition." He continued. His emotion turned to a softer understanding. "Privileged or not...we all feel it. Like it's built into us. It's what connects all of us."

I stared at him for a while, not knowing if he was done or not.

"So..." I slowly cut back in. "What about me? Why are you helping me?"
"You made me realize all of this. Something I was very bitter about. I've changed the way I look at things now. It's almost liberating to just accept this simple truth about life."

"So, you're trying to repay the favour or something?"

"Well...I told myself, that next time I saw you that I would treat you different. I would accept you. I didn't think I would find you in an alley in a hospital gown, freshly bruised and beaten. And then when I heard you—"

He cut himself off, and his voice trailed away. He caught his own words and I could tell he was restraining himself. He calmed himself down and cleared his throat. There it was again. That weird sense I got from him before, that he was hiding something.

"Heard me, what?" I demanded.

John G looked at me. "Let's go." Was all he said, before turning and walking forward. I remained standing there for a moment staring after him, until I let out a sigh and started following him again.

We walked a little further through these slums in silence. John G led me into a really crummy little street of townhouses. Old townhouses that were falling apart and nobody had bothered to fix. Some of them did look a little normal, and even had cars in the driveways, but they still looked very old and the cars were lemons. It looked like people did live here. As we walked down the middle of the street the light of dusk was disappearing quickly, making these streets even more threatening. As I looked around the neighbourhood I saw groups of shady looking characters everywhere.

When I was a cop, I had been on this side of town a few times, but not often—only to help out another district in a few drug busts or arrests. I guess I just figured that the criminals ventured out of these slums and hit the main part of the city. But I was wrong. This was a place where a crime was happening on every street corner. A place where the victims of crimes hid from their predators. A place the people knew the cops and ordinary citizens were afraid of and wouldn't dare come in, unless they had to. Not a lot of people here had a phone to even call the police if they wanted to. Which, no one did want to. More cops makes more trouble. I was now in a place that I used to pretend didn't even exist.

I saw a group of thugs hanging out on one of the porches, surrounded by weed smoke. I was shocked to see them actually showing off their guns to each other and laughing. The beats of their music were so loud, but who would dare tell them to turn it down. Other people were just sitting on their steps drinking casually, like this was normal for them. They didn't even bat an eye at the gun flashing gang punks across the street. I saw a couple of guys exchange money for a bag of drugs right out in the open. Another group of gang guys in a parked car at the curb, talking out of the window with some other guys.

I was looking around so much that I almost walked by our stop. I hadn't seen John G make a right turn towards his place until I glanced to the right and saw him heading up the steps to it. I quickly followed John G, who never looked back to make sure I was following him, up the steps to the front door as he opened it.

When the door was closed it was dark. I heard John G rummaging through his pack until a light came on from a flashlight.

"C'mon." He said, and we walked slowly through the front hall. "Wait here." He said at the top of a stairway, and I heard his footsteps descend an old creaky staircase to the basement. Shortly after, I heard some clunking switches and loud snaps. I heard one last buzz and a zap, followed by some profane words from John G. The lights flickered and then came on. As I was looking around at the now dully lit and empty house, I heard John G's footsteps coming back up. He was sucking his fingers and shaking off his hand.

"You okay?" I asked.

"Works every time." He simply said, as he was putting his flashlight back in his pack.

"You live here?" I asked.

"Sometimes." He replied. "When I'm in this end of town."

"Hhmm."

The place was empty. The paint was faded, and old wallpaper was peeling. Cobwebs in every corner and it was very dusty. A lot of areas had water damage and everything seemed brown. It was echoey in here, and you could hear water dripping somewhere, if not multiple places. The kitchen had a small old table and two chairs, and the living room had a very worn out cloth fabric couch. To my surprise, there was a little stand with a TV on it. While John G dropped his pack in a corner and headed into the kitchen I explored around the house a little bit. I found the bathroom. Just a small powder room with a sink and a toilet. The lights were off and I searched the wall for the switch. I switched it on and the light flooded in.

I glanced up and froze in fear for a second, until I realized it was me staring back at myself. The dirty mirror reflected an image I didn't recognize. This was the first time I had seen myself since the whole incident at the Sexrex.

I slowly approached the mirror and placed my hands to rest on either edge of the sink. I had forgotten that I was even beaten until seeing myself this way. The pain felt like it was returning as I stared at my face. My left eye was still swollen and blue with bruising and I hadn't realized that the bridge of my nose had broken. There was an open wound running across it and there was still some medical tape over it from the hospital. I examined my eye closer and a blood vessel had exploded, turning the white to red. My other eye looked okay, except for the big shiner underneath it. I reluctantly touched my face where they had stitched up gashes on my right cheek and forehead. My whole face appeared slightly swollen and red. My jaw was yellow with bruising and my lips were cracked. There was one huge split on the right half of my bottom lip. There was a huge brownish-blue bruise on the right side of my face, despite the pale blue tinge my entire face had. I was horrified at the sight of myself.

What am I going to do? I thought. I sighed and just stared at the new me. *If Clare could see me now.*

Where was she? What was she doing right now? Is she wondering where I am? Is she worried about me?

I was worried about her. A rush of feelings came on and I got a sense of panic when I imagined Clare realizing the truth about me.

I mean, right now, while I was standing in the dingy bathroom of a rundown old townhouse with my new homeless friend John Gramhain, a team of investigators was reviewing evidence on a case called 'the Baptist'...me! I'm sure the search teams were still looking for me...at least the rest of the night anyways. They would have uniforms posted at the hospital and at my loft with Clare. I'm sure Finley and Ryan were with her too.

I thought about Ridley for the first time in a while. Last time I saw him he was pissed off at me, when he discovered I was the Baptist too.

I had lost—or rather—given up, so much to be standing here. *Was this worth it?*

I looked like the bloody vision of myself I had seen in that elaborate dream I had before I woke up in the hospital...

...the dream.

Where everyone had been telling me about 'Him' and how important He was...

I had to pee. The water was clear, but the bowl was stained with rust and urine. While I was in there I took a leak and then hesitantly flushed.

"Watch the water use!!" I heard John G call from the kitchen, and I flinched.

"Sorry!!" I shouted.

One last look at myself in the mirror and I smirked a bit. *The new me.*

I reached into my pocket, retrieved the pack of smokes and got one out. I placed it in my lips and stared at my reflection in the glass as I dug for the lighter. I chuckled at my appearance. A happy chuckle. I had crossed a line now and seeing my face drove that fact home. I lit the smoke and my new face was illuminated with fire glow for a moment. I snapped the zippo shut and inhaled the drag with my eyes squinted. Then I blew the smoke at the mirror.

I sauntered out to the kitchen where John G was sitting against the counter eating some beans out of a bowl.

"You hungry bro?" He asked, motioning to the table. There was a bowl on it with beans he had scooped in for me, and a fork sticking out of them.

I shrugged and walked over to the table. "You have food here?" I asked, taking a drag.

"Sure." He answered. "Just cans and dried goods mostly. Non-perishables..." He laughed at his own joke with a mouthful of beans. I chuckled and placed the smoke in my mouth so I could pick up my bowl. I placed the cigarette down on the table, with the ashes end hanging over the edge. I raised a bite to my mouth and shoved the beans in. I didn't realize how hungry I really was, and I kept on shoveling it in greedily. It was amazing what I would eat when I was so starved. To me, these beans could very well have been a fillet mignon.

"Oh...just a sec." John G said as he remembered something. He stood up and turned to a large pantry to open the doors. It was fuller than I thought it would be, with cans and cans of beans, soups, lentils and even diced fruits and veggies. There were even a few big tubs of protein powders. John G was proving to be extremely resourceful and smart, despite it all being stolen.

"It's not all stolen." He said, taking me by surprise. Like he read my thoughts. "A lot of it I pick up from shelters and food bins." He crouched down to the bottom shelf and I saw that it was stocked with a few cases of bottled water. He squirmed one out of the plastic wrap and turned to me.

"Here." He said, and he tossed me the bottle. I did know I was thirsty, and I couldn't have twisted that cap off fast enough. I chugged the water, spilling a lot of it down my face and chin. When I was done, I opened my eyes to see John G smiling at me with another bottle of water in his hand, which he tossed at me. I caught it quickly. "Thanks." I said, cracking the seal of my second drink. I had to control my urge to chug this one too, and I paced myself, taking a small sip. John G was now cracking his own water open and taking a controlled sip. I let out a small sigh and took another sip of my water. John G was still staring at me and he took another sip of his.

I picked up my cigarette again and sucked on the end to light the embers back up. We stood in the kitchen for a long while...in silence. I could hear every sound as I smoked. The drip of water somewhere, the hum of the lights, John G's feet shuffling and clothing rustling. I could still hear the beats of the rap music coming from that gang house across the street.

"So..." I finally said. "G...can I call you G? How did you end up out here?"

"Brother...I wandered in here after years on the streets." He started. "I was actually told about this house by another dude from a shelter I was at. He said that this street had a bunch of unoccupied houses. The cops never check, hell...they never even come in here. There's no landlord, the government doesn't even care about this part of town. Honestly bro...no one has set foot in here for decades. This place doesn't exist!"

"I meant more like...how you ended up on the street to begin with."

"Oh."

I smiled as I took another drag.

"That's a whole other story, man...and I gotta go to bed. You can hold up here with me for a while. Until you can figure out what your letter says." He finished with a chuckle.

I sighed, feeling a little embarrassed. I reached behind me and pulled the crumpled letter from my back pocket. Leaving the cigarette stump hanging from my mouth, I unfolded the letter and flattened it with my hands onto the table. I took a long apprehensive look at G as I could tell he was curious.

He just stared back as I blew another drag out.

"Have you heard of this Dr. Richter guy everyone's talking about?" I asked.

G nodded slowly. "The whole world has heard of Jason Richter." He said, still staring at me eagerly.

"Time travel..." I went on. "...do you think it's possible?"

G shrugged. "Sure." He said. "But I don't think it'll work."

I furrowed my brow. "You think it's possible...but won't work? I'm confused."

"Meaning I don't think that going back or forward will actually change anything about this life. Whatever happens, happens. Or...it'll get so screwed up in the process that we won't be able to fix it. It won't work."

I stared at him as he spoke. "Hhm." I said. And then I just went for it. I spun the letter around and slid it across the table to him.

He looked at it and then up at me. Then he took the letter and his eyes feasted on the words, his mouth moved along silently as he read. I just waited, puffing away on the last little stump of my smoke.

When he was done, G looked up at me slowly.

"That's my own hand writing." I said to him, pointing with the cigarette butt in my fingers.

"So, what are you saying?" He asked. "That your future self wrote this to you?"

I shrugged dramatically. "I don't want to think that...but I do..."

"How could—?"

"—I've seen myself too." I cut him off.

He just stared at me funny.

"I know it sounds crazy..." I went on, "...I used to chalk it up to dreams, but they weren't dreams. I saw visions of myself. Telling me the same thing written in that letter."

G stared at me for a long time and I didn't have anything I could say that would make me seem less insane to him.

"So..." He said, looking down at the letter. "You want to find Jason Richter? And...what?"

I didn't have an answer and I got frustrated. I reached over and snatched the letter away from him angrily. "I don't know..." I said, feeling stupid now. "I shouldn't have even told you about any of this. Look, I'll sleep here tonight and I'll be on my way in the morning, ok?"

I slipped the cigarette but into the empty water bottle and I got up from the table.

"So you killed the mayor?" He asked me harshly.

I froze in my tracks.

"You're this 'Baptist' that was all over the papers?" He asked.

"Well, while I didn't make up the title...yah! That'd be me."

"You killed the mayor!"

"He was my father-in-law."

He stopped and just stared at me with his mouth gaping open and stunned. He threw his hands up and made an exasperated noise.

"And he was a crook G." I retorted.
"Your father-in-law!?"
"Sean Mash was an evil son-of-a-bitch! He was a mobster."
"And you know this, how?"
"When I was a cop, I was involved in a special team who investigated mob activity. He dealt in prostitution...on top of being a womanizing drunk; he was helping big mob players run their businesses, and laundering their dirty money man!"
"So you killed him!?" G asked, cutting me off, and not letting me finish. "What happened to the cops just arresting people?"
"He tried to kill me G!" I shouted. "Twice!"
G was quiet now, and he wiped his mouth off and stared at the ground.
"He sent the mob after me in a shooting spree down town...almost killing my best friend in the process! Then again, they tried to run my car off the road...with his own pregnant daughter inside of it!" G looked up at me with sincere remorse in his eyes. I could see that he felt bad for me now, and maybe regretted coming at me so angrily. "Not to mention the numerous other things the team caught him doing; beatings, other murders...G trust me...he was a bad guy!" I let out an exhausted sigh. I knew I would eventually be telling all of this to G at some point. But reliving it all was filling me with all the old emotions.
"John, I'm sorry..." G said solemnly. "I had no idea."
"Of course you didn't...how could you?"
"Is that why you were running away bro?"
I nodded quietly.
G looked at me long and hard. I didn't know what else to say at this point.
"I'll just go now." I finally said. "I'm sorry I even came with you, man. Thanks for everything...really."
"Where are you gonna go, John?" He called after me.
I didn't reply and I just stood there staring at his door.
"So that was you who shot up Sexrex's club." He went on.
I closed my eyes at being discovered.
"Bart did say you used to always ask him about Sexrex." G continued. "Is this a new venture you're gonna pursue, John? The Baptist? Hero in the streets?"
I sighed. "I have to finish what I started." I said to him.
"What's that exactly?"
"He's got a friend of mine working for him, G." I said, turning towards him now. "A girl..." I pleaded. "...a girl too young to be involved in his seedy garbage."
G didn't have anything to say and he looked as if I had struck some kind of a chord within him.
"I don't care what you or anybody thinks, I can't leave her there."
"So you're just gonna take on the kingpin of Baltimore by yourself?" G asked harshly. "Look where that got you!"

"Well, I gotta try." I said. "I gotta find people out here who'll help me. I can't be the only one."

I walked off and my footsteps on the creaky old floor echoed into the silence.

G sat there and listened to the slam of his front door. He didn't even look up. He just sat there staring at his floor, and he thought long and hard into the night without ever getting up.

I walked down the slummy street G's house was on, with my hands in my pockets. I was angry with myself for daring to bring the time-travel nonsense up to G. I should have just kept my mouth shut until later. He might have helped me but I lost his interest.

I don't even know how long I walked for, or where I was even going. All I knew was that I was going to get back into the city and find a way to get back on track. The city's downtown skyline was visible from here in the slums, so I followed the thousands of little yellow lights that were the windows of the skyscrapers.

Eventually I stopped because I was too tired to go on. I found a spot to hide for the night, under a bridge. I groaned as I sat down and I leaned back against the concrete with a very dramatic sigh. I bumped a smoke out of the pack and lit up again. I blew my first drag out as I looked up at the city skyline again, which was beautifully back lit by the moon. I sighed. A deep, regretful sigh.

"This isn't what I meant." I said to the sky. "You hear me up there? Huh? You son-of-a-bitch...this isn't what I meant..."

No response and I puffed on my smoke some more, just sitting there. I pulled the note out again and fixated on the part that told me to *'FIND JASON RICHTER'*. G's mocking words rang out in my head and I suddenly felt so foolish. I scoffed at myself for being such an idiot and shook my head. Then I placed the cigarette in my mouth and left it pursed in between my lips. I clinked open my zippo and scratched the wheel to produce flame. Then I slowly pushed the flame and the corner of the letter together and I watched Richter's name get swallowed up by fire and disappear. Then the entire thing was aflame and I tossed the burning paper aside to forget about that for now.

It was a distraction to me—

To my mission.

I needed to focus.

I sucked a big drag and removed the smoke from my lips to exhale a big plume.

I reached into my pocket and pulled out my silver badge. I palmed it and stared at it for a minute and then I tossed it into the river that ran beside the bridge and watched it float away. I thought about G again and his house.

No possessions there...

No car in the driveway that he paid for.

No insurance plan on the house, or no mortgage.

Nothing owned...

...and nothing owned him.

I used to put handcuffs on people for a living. For the first time I realized that I didn't need to. Everyone is already living life in shackles.

I was now entering into this new life of *nothing*. I thought about that as I laid my head down onto my rolled up hoodie.

I was so tired...

I began an attempt to replay the past several hours of my life in order to try and make sense of it all. It was as if I had died after I escaped the hospital and when my eyes opened, the new me had awoken.

There was a weird sense of eeriness ever since I woke up in that alley.

I had been dreaming before I woke up in the hospital. Perhaps this was a dream too. I wanted to believe that this dark and dank hole John G brought me too was a part in the nightmare...but I knew deep into my soul that I was not dreaming and it was as real as the scars on my face. It would be nice if this side of life didn't exist—but it did,

And this was my life now...

I was soon asleep, to the lullaby the dark hours of the city sang to me.

* * *

A purple haze of mixing blue and red flashes lit the scene, as the roof lights spun on the several police cruisers parked there. They were parked out on the curb and the officers were in the alley leading off that street.

"We found it!" One of the officers shouted out. It was that same night as they had been searching for me. Now this piece of evidence added to their clues. The officer scooped the item up carefully and placed it in a bag.

Sarge walked over and examined it. He sighed when he saw it.

"Where's Jimenez?" He asked. "Jimenez!" He then shouted. Young Jimmy Jimenez rushed over.

"Yah Sarge?" He said timidly.

Sarge glared at him and then without saying anything he held up the evidence bag that contained a gun. "Missing something Jimenez?" He asked sarcastically.

"Yessir...that's my gun."

"It's evidence now son!" Sarge snapped. "Don't lose your weapon again." He ended sternly and Jimenez hung his head.

"Yessir." He simply said quietly.

Sarge turned back to the other officer and handed the bag back to him. "Get that looked after." He barked, and then he pushed past Jimenez giving him a final glare as he breathed out.

Sarge headed out of the same alley where I had met John G earlier that afternoon, and he walked up to the cruiser parked on the curb. He waited as the person sitting in the back of it rolled the window down.

"He was here." Sarge said to them.

There was a long silence.
She didn't say anything.
She stared straight towards the front of the cruiser.
"Clare?" Another voice from the front asked. Ridley, who was sitting in the passenger seat of the cruiser, twisted backwards with his arm stretched across the back of the driver's seat. "Clare did you hear what Sarge said?"

Clare finally turned to look at Sarge. If I had been there to see her face, I would've expected anger written on it. But Sarge saw the sorrow and despair that lay behind her eyes.

"Please find him, Wade." She said desperately. (Wade was Sarge's first name.) Her big glassy green eyes, wet with tears, pleaded with Sarge.

"We will hon'." Sarge told her softly. "We'll find him."

Sarge patted the open window frame and walked off. Clare's gaze remained fixed down the alley, wondering what had happened to me.

"He's alright Clare." Ridley said from the front. Clare turned her attention to him. "He's not here." He continued. "That's a good sign. He got up and walked out of there." Clare was silent and only gave a halfhearted little smile pathetically at Ridley. "C'mon Clare." He went on. "We both know John." At this, Clare's bottom lip quiver couldn't be contained anymore and her face screwed up as she fought hard against the coming sobs.

"He's alive Clare." Ridley waited on Clare's response, as she swallowed her tears.

"I know, Rid." She finally choked out. "I know he's okay."

Clare kept playing with her wedding band and engagement ring nervously.

"We'll find him."

CHAPTER EIGHTEEN
A Tale of Two Johns

Sunday.

When they were ready, my eyes opened slowly to the blue light of dawn. It was eerily quiet and I was staring at the charred crumbs of paper leftover from the letter. They were swaying in the soft breeze and haunting me. Taunting me in disapproval of my decision not to pursue its instructions. I sat up and rubbed the sleep out of my eyes. I looked around my new home and sighed. I slowly brought myself to a stand and lit myself my first smoke of the day. I blew out and looked around, breathing in the muggy air. It felt like rain. In a part of Baltimore that had dropped out of existence long ago, while the life I had left behind was out there...

Somewhere...

Looking for me.

My old life that I was so disappointed in. A planet that humans had destroyed in their laziness and arrogance, both physically and relationally. Our little 'pale blue dot' was placed in the sky at just the right distance from the sun in order to allow life to be sustainable. Any closer or any further away and we wouldn't be able to survive. Spinning at just the right axis, and covered with a series of gases to protect us from the harmful, yet beautiful rays of the sun...now ripped apart by our disgusting ways. Deteriorating more everyday...

Driving me to my obsession.

I couldn't accept this,

I *wouldn't* accept it!

Ultimately, I would end up here in the slums by myself.

But, I did miss my friend Ridley. I missed my job, I really did. I was happy cleaning up the streets and protecting people from the evil within them.

But it wasn't enough...not enough to fix the world. Something else had to be done.

I missed my loft. I always loved that place and the gritty, bohemian style of that entire building we lived in. I missed my bed...my warm bed, lying beside Clare and feeling her warmth.

Losing her was losing my last grip of goodness. I had been holding onto her and how good she was...how good we once were. I could have made it with her!...I missed my wife the most.

I made my way back into the downtown corridor with my mind switched back on. It was kind of helpless, thinking of how I was going to attack Sexrex again. Maybe I needed more guns, maybe more people, or maybe I could simply find Maggie working her corner and grab her out of there. But, that wouldn't be enough. Sexrex would come after her. All I knew was that I wasn't going to leave her in there.

I scrounged myself some breakfast where I could, and I stole a backpack. I was able to grab a sleeping bag and a change of clothes too.

I was walking down the street, with my backpack slung over one shoulder and a smoke hanging from my mouth. I passed by a newspaper stand and just barely glanced down at today's front page, and then I kept walking until...

...wait...*Did I read that right?*

I flung my butt away and I rushed back over to the stand to snatch up the paper. I had thought I had seen the face of Jason Richter, and I was right!

'*THE DOCTOR IS IN*'

Is what the clever headline read, printed above his picture. Then I kept reading the subtext.

'*THIS IS IT. DR.JASON RICHTER IN WASHINGTON TO CONFIRM FIRST LAUNCH OF HIS TIME MACHINE.*'

I stared at the paper in awe. "It's happening." I whispered to myself.

"Hey!" The voice of the paper stand owner shouted. "Either buy it or get out of here, pal!"

I looked at him and then held the paper up.

"When is this?" I asked him.

"When is what? Buy the paper..."

I made a face at him and then went back to the paper to read the actual article for more information. The grumpy stand owner began to walk over as I frantically skimmed the page for the date.

"Wednesday." I whispered out loud when I found it.

The stand owner was right on me now, and I quickly folded the paper in half and thudded it into his chest as he stopped right beside me.

"Thanks pal." I said to him, smiling.

He glared at me as I trotted off, and he flipped me off.

* * *

In Israel.

Richter, the man himself, was rushing around the work site, tweaking this and fixing that. Jotting down calculations and triple checking everything. A large computer panel, like a space control switch board was to the far left of the smaller ring. It lit up like a Christmas tree with little buttons and screens. A team of scientists and operators sat at several stations across this outdoor control centre. The console itself was protected by a large, overhanging, metal canopy—not that it ever rained much in the dessert.

Richter stopped when he reached the end of the console. He stood now, at the foot of the tall stretching radio tower that collected all the signals of the other rings around the globe and helped to synchronize the magnetic fields. He looked up at it into the sky beyond its pinnacle, and he got that old sense he always used to get as a boy.

"It's gonna be my turn soon." He said to God. "You'll see."

He stared into the open sky which reminded him deeply of the possibilities he was about to open, and he smiled.

"Jay!" Ernest's voice called to him from the side.

Richter looked down from his dreaming at his approaching lab partner.

"Are we all set?" Ernest asked.

"I was all set yesterday, Ernest." Richter replied.

"Ah...but we must wait." Ernest added. "Kitch's orders."

"Kitch...pah!"

"I hear ya, old friend. But we have to listen to legal...they want to make this a PR thing."

"Well I'd rather just get it over with. Why do we have to wait till Wednesday?"

Ernest shrugged. "That's the only day D.C. could accommodate I guess."

"And why D.C. anyways?" Richter snapped. "The press just couldn't come here?"

Ernest again shrugged and put his hands up. "This is legal's thing, Jay, I dunno...they want to make this a big patriotic thing, announcing it in the Capitol, you standing beside the president, big American flag behind you...you know..."

Richter puffed and shook his head. "It's like the moon race all over again." He said to himself.

Ernest chuckled. "Except the Russians are not even close to this technology."

"No, Ernest." Richter said, looking to his left where about 100 feet away was the smaller ring with the man sized capsule locked into the centre of it. "I'm the only one."

Ernest looked at the ring with him. "They're gonna turn the tower on when we leave, Jay."

"I know, Ernest. Everything will be radioactive when we come back."

And he sighed long and despairingly.

"Wednesday couldn't come sooner." Richter said.

* * *

Sunday night.

It was darker than it should have been at this time of day, with the overcast sky. I had wandered around most of that day, thinking about Wednesday too. Richter would be next door in D.C. The closest I would ever have been to him.

I panhandled until I had enough money for a bus to the other side of town where Maggie's usual corner was. I was waiting at the bus stop as the sun went down. I was sitting in the glass enclosure with my hood pulled over my head and face, and I was staring down.

The bus brakes squealed to a stop in front of the curb and everyone else who was gathered around began to file on. I got up and merged in with them, keeping the hood on my head. A rumble of thunder rolled in the clouds above.

As the bus drove through the city, I leaned my head on the back window. Little droplets started to appear on the glass from the light drizzle. I stared out at Baltimore, much like I used to do when I cruised around with Ridley. I watched the urban art spray painted on the walls as they passed my eyesight.
"Hey!" A woman's voice in distress broke my train of thought. I raised my head up off the window and peaked over the back of the seat in front of me. There was a man about halfway up the bus. He was seated and there something going on, though I couldn't quite tell at this point. An obvious commotion involving a man and a woman.
The driver brought the bus to a stop as a precaution.
"Get off of me!" The woman's voice cried. I sat up in my seat to get a better look.
Then the unmistakable sound of a—*SLAP!*—rang out throughout the bus, and I rose to my feet. By the time I got out into the aisle I heard another voice get involved.
"Hey dude, that is so not cool!" It said. I stopped at the back of the bus while the small figure of who this voice belonged to, approached the situation. The little wiry guy reached into the seats and grabbed the guy by the shirt forcefully. He pulled the man out and slammed him onto the ground.
"You're gonna regret that, you little prick!" The angry voice of the assaulter said, as he rose up and towered over the little guy.
WHAP!
To my surprise, again, the little guy socked the man right across the face!
SLAM!!
But the assaulter quickly retaliated with a strong blow across the little guy's face, and he crumbled to the right.
"Anyone else have a problem!?" The assaulter asked loudly. "Huh!? Anyone else feel brave!?"
"You're such an asshole!" The girl he assaulted originally cried.
Then he reached into the seat again and grabbed her by the hair! He yanked her out of the seats into the aisle and she screamed.
No one moved.
No one.
"Bunch of pussys!" The vulgar man erupted.
Then the driver suddenly got up and confronted him.
"Oh you want some too?!" He asked him. He threw the girl down, smirking and chuckling. Then he produced a blade and glared at the driver.
"This is gonna be fun!" He said sinisterly, and he began to approach the front of the bus.
I began slowly from the back of the bus, and built up speed, like a charging rhino.
SLAM!!

"*OOF!!*" He huffed, when I smashed into him and launched him off of me towards the windshield.

CRACK!!

His big dumb head slammed against the glass and split it. Big crack lines spidered out from the impact point, and a small little splotch of blood stained the middle. The assaulter dropped like a rock!

I was standing there, with my shoulders heaving, over the lump of flesh. I reached down and hoisted his body up to an appropriate level for a straight kick—

—*WHAM!!*

I sent him tumbling down the steps and he crashed against the bus doors, forcing them open. The big heap flopped onto the sidewalk.

My adrenaline was screaming through my veins and I stood at the top of the stairs with my back to the rest of passengers. I could now hear the sounds of them chattering and even clapping. I slowly turned towards them and was met with the frenzy of cell phone cameras all pointed at me! Then my heart sank the second I realized that my hood had come down. My face was exposed.

"Revele?" A voice said out of the crowd.

I furrowed my brow and began searching the faces.

The little wiry guy was standing up and looking at me, smiling.

"Bart..." I said softly to myself.

The two of us just stared at each other, gawking, until he rushed towards me and soon he hurried me off the bus.

"C'mon, man, let's get the hell outta here!"

I reached down and picked up the blade that the assaulter had produced, and we stepped over the heap of his body and ran off into the night.

We ran from the sounds of the responding police sirens and ducked into an alley. The light drizzle misted us.

"Officer Revele!" Bart said, slapping my arm. "What the hell happened to you, man!?"

I huffed for air and just shook my head. "What do you mean?"

"What do I mean?" Bart asked. "One minute, we're talking in the diner...me you and Ken...and the next I see your face all over the news! Dude, you shot up the Sexrex!? Is that why you were asking?"

I shrugged and began to pace, looking back and forth to where we ran from.

"I'm not a cop anymore, Bart." I said.

"Well obviously not!" He laughed.

I shot him a look and he kept laughing.

"The damn goon squad!" He laughed harder. "What are you some sort of vigilante now man? That was awesome back there!"

"I'm not anything." I said, wiping some built up moisture off my face from the rain. "I gotta keep moving. I can't stay here—"

"—hold on there cowboy!" Another voice rang out from the shadows of where we were.

I stopped moving and faced the direction the voice came from. I hadn't seen him standing there before, but now that I was looking I could make out the outline of a man's shape. I looked at Bart and he looked back kind of sheepishly, as if he knew this person was there all along. When I looked back to the shape, it moved and came forward into the light.

"G?" I asked, more out of exasperation.

"I thought I saw the last of you when you left my door." G said.

I stared back in silence for a long while, then back at Bart. Bart shrugged playfully. "We're you watching me?" I asked him.

Bart laughed and shook his head no.

"He wasn't watching you, John." G said for him. "But I don't believe in coincidence."

Again I was just staring. "So, what?..." I asked sarcastically. "This meeting is...fate?"

G chuckled. "I don't know if I believe in that either. But maybe someone wants us together."

I passed my hand at him and scoffed. "Bah..." I said. "I gotta get to Sexrex"

"Oh yah." G began. "To go take him out? To go fix the world!" He was making fun of me.

Bart perked up excitedly, and he wiped some rain off his nose. "What? You're going back?"

"Yah, Bart." G said as I turned and glared at him. "John here is gonna go and get himself killed, is what he's gonna do." He glared back at me while he spoke to Bart.

Bart looked at me like a giddy kid and I just sighed and looked at the ground.

"What happened, Bart?" G asked, changing the subject to current events.

Bart gave me an apprehensive look and then bashfully at G. "This guy on the bus..." He started. "...he was an animal, man. He was hurting this girl. I stepped in." Bart turned his face to show his bleeding lip to G. "He was gonna stab the bus driver, or cut him or something."

G looked at me now. "So you kill him?" He asked me harshly.

I furrowed my brow defensively. "What!? No...he'll live, G."

"But he'll have one hell of a headache for a while!" Bart laughed.

G didn't respond. He just stood there with his arms crossed staring at me. "You've got heart, John." He said plainly. "I'll give you that."

"G!..." Bart whispered. "He could help us man." He said, stepping closer towards him.

"No." G said quickly.

"C'mon, man—"

"—No, Bart."

Bart opened his mouth to retort again, but he just sighed instead.

"Listen guys." I said, shaking off some rain. "I'd love to stay and catch up, but I have things I gotta do, so if you'll excuse me..."

"John!" G called to me as I turned to go. I stopped with my back to them and closed my eyes in frustration as I sighed through my nose.

"What?"

"Maybe I was a little rough on you before."

"You weren't rough on me, G. I dropped a lot on you all at once, which wasn't fair. I get it man. My mission is more of a solo thing anyways, so..."

"You're mission?" Bart asked.

"John..." G continued. "...I think I have an idea what you're planning, brother. Taking on the criminals of Baltimore is not a solo mission, trust me."

"G!" Bart whispered again. "C'mon man!" He urged.

G looked at Bart with a smirk and I looked back and forth between them both.

"My face is all over the Internet by now, man." I said.

"All the more reason to lay low for a while." G replied. "C'mon, John." He went on. "Come meet the family."

"The family?..."

I gave in and several minutes later, the 3 of us were stepping behind a building and into a back alley. We were shielded a little bit from the rain back here. G and Bart led the way and I sauntered up behind the0m. All I could see was their backs but as they both parted it was like a curtain and I saw a rabble of people huddled around and warming their hands on a trash can fire.

"Everyone..." G began.

They all looked up at him and I already began to see a few familiar faces. People that I had seen and met already during my trial run on the streets. The most recognizable was big Ken. The other bruiser from the diner. Bart's friend. He noticed me and grinned subtly at me.

"This is John." G introduced me. I wandered into the alley and met the eyes of each of them as G introduced them.

"John, this is Hank, Linda, Tom, Jeannine, and...I think you already know Ken."

Ken stepped forward and nodded. I just stared at him. "Good to see ya big guy." I said. "Stayin' outta trouble?"

Ken chuckled softly. "Tryin." He said gruffly.

I looked around at the faces I had already spent time with out here. This woman Linda, and another guy Hank; they were ones I often had conversations with when I was first starting out. They both smiled warmly back at me. I didn't know Tom, or Jeannine.

"So what..." I started, panning the faces and looking at G and Bart who brought me here. "...this is like a merry band of men or something?"

Bart laughed.

"Something like that." G said.

"And you want me to join you guys, is that it?"

"We watch out for each other, John." G said. "That's all. These streets are rough. Rougher then you know. We need each other. We're all down and out in some way or another and we're here for each other."
I nodded along as I planned across the faces of all of these new people. G's words got me thinking of something I'm surprised I hadn't already thought of.
"You're new out here." He continued. "You're gonna need some support. I'm just offering you a chance to be a part of it. Nothing more. Nothing less."
Maybe these guys *could* help me...
I stared at the ground for a while, not answering. Then I nodded slowly. I looked back up to G and he was just staring at me awaiting a response.
A very loud peel of thunder echoed and startled us all. The sky lit up and everyone looked around. I looked again at the faces of all these people.
"One night." I agreed.
G and I just stared at each other for a few moments.
"I'll stay for the night."

The rain was picking up now and falling harder. These guys all had make shift shelters and I shared a space with Bart. The sounds of snores echoed in the alley and I watched the breath rise out of their mouths. More lighting crashed above. I couldn't sleep, but I sat against the wall watching them all as they slept. The sounds of crashing suddenly rose up into the silence. A distant crashing of metal and other junk. It sounded close enough that it could be a few blocks over maybe. I saw Bart sit up, and Ken woke up too.
"*Aaaaaaiiiiieee!!!*" The sound of a woman's screaming echoed into the darkness and then, the rest stirred in their sleeping bags and began to get up.
The sounds of crashing and screaming continued and it was obvious this victim was in trouble. My new friends were all up now and they listened for a bit. I could tell by the expressions on some of their faces that for a split second they were showing concern. Then they stuffed it back down and shrouded the uncomfortable burden of knowing with lowered eyes and ignorance. The crashing sounds continued and I could tell now that they were close by. Everyone was quiet and listening. In between the screams there was only the steady sound of the rain pour. As I scanned the group's faces, I stopped at G's whose eyes were locked on mine. He was staring at me with conviction, wondering what I was thinking—trying so hard to pierce my skull with his gaze and see my mind. I stared back at him for a moment, and I think he knew.
Lighting crashed and I slowly stood to my feet, gaining the attention of all the eyes of the group. The screams echoed more and more in the next alley over and I couldn't bare it anymore. One last look from G, as he faintly shook his head *no*.
I couldn't heed his advice. I wouldn't.
Without further hesitation I quickly turned to head towards the commotion. G sunk his head down and sighed amongst the chatter of *what is he doing* talk that erupted within the group.

Once again I was headed into danger. Pouring rain cascaded off my face now and every few moments the darkness was lit up with bright lighting. The closer I got I could hear the screams getting louder with the sound of rustling clothes and bodies hitting into dumpsters and trash cans mingled into it. As I rounded the corner I could begin to make out what the girl was saying.

"Stop! Please don't do this! Please, no! Don't! Please, please, please! No! Stop!" Were interchangeable phrases repeated over and over by the girl, in between grunts and slapping sounds. I arrived on scene, just at the end of the alley. Just in time to witness, and hear one last scream beginning to emerge from her lips and grow into the dark night. In the middle of her scream, her breath was cut off—

—WHAM!

The perpetrator's fist slammed into the girls nose and, even from where I was standing, I could hear the snap of it breaking and the gurgled gasp for breath she made as she choked on a mouth full of blood. The perp had her by the neck and he dropped her after he struck her. She fell to the ground with a thud onto the cold hard pavement. This few second scene filled me with rage and horror. I watched as the girl struggled to look around and sob pathetically in a heap on the ground. There were other marks all over her face from several other times the beast had hit her.

He was a large guy. Probably about 6'5" and 250lbs. I looked around on the ground for something to use as a weapon. A trashcan? No that would probably just bend the aluminum on his back. A two-by-four...possibly...

The large beast wiped the saliva from the corners of his mouth as he towered over the girl. His knuckles dripped of her blood as lighting continued to light up the sky. He ran his bloody, sweaty hands through his nasty, long, greasy hair and chuckled a dark twisted sound under his breath. Then he loosened his belt buckle and released the belt from the loops...and he undid his fly...slowly...

—CRACK!!

The two-by-four slammed into the back of his head, on the right side, when I swung it. The beast lurched to his left and stumbled to the ground.

I was filled with adrenaline and white hot rage! I allowed myself a glimpse of the girl on the ground and almost let out a sob. She looked at me through half closed eyes and tried to moan something.

"You okay?" was all I could think of saying. *Of course she's not okay you idiot!*—She was very badly beaten. I heard some hurried footsteps and looked up to see G standing at the end of the alley.

"John?" He called to me. "You alright?"

"Yah!" I replied, rain pouring down my face. "Come and help me!" I cried, still staring at her bashed in face with tears in my eyes.

I snapped myself out of it and dropped the two-by-four, to crouch down beside the girl and help her up. As I was trying to get my hands under her back—

—WHAM!

I was hit hard from behind and I fell forward to scrape my face on the pavement. A sudden tug on my ankle and soon I was weightless, as the beast lifted me off the ground and swung me like a pendulum by my ankle. He hurled me across the alley right into a pile of trash. I knew I had to get up fast or I'd be f—
—*WHAP!*
A fist struck me across the face and I was back into the pile of garbage.
Yep...I was f—
—*BIFF!*
Another blow to the head while I was still on my back, then the crushing weight of 250lbs squeezed the air from my lungs as he straddled me. I couldn't let this pummeling start or I'd be *dead*.
It was him or me now.
In a spilt second I glanced over and found a broken beer bottle. Good enough. I grasped the neck of the bottle and let out a battle cry as I launched my assault through the air.
SMASH!
The shards made contact with the side of his fist and the beast let out a roar with the broken bottle jammed into the side of his hand. As he was screaming and distracted with that I found something else useful among the trash. An old fire extinguisher. I swung it at his head and it clanged right into his temple, causing him to fall off of me. I quickly got up and ran for the two-by-four.

I glanced over and saw that G was with the girl. He had her arm around his neck and was propping her up as they were headed out of the alley.
"John?" He asked in a worried tone.
"Just get her out of here!" I growled. Blood was pouring out of my brow, above the right eye and he had opened up a wound on the other side of my face. Even the rain pouring down on us couldn't wash the blood away fast enough. I was gasping for breath as I stumbled past them. I gave G a menacing look and he knew I was serious. He didn't try talking to me anymore and he proceeded away with the girl.

I bent over and retrieved my wooden weapon, and I turned to go back to the screaming beast. More lighting crashed above.

He was in the process of yanking the bottle out of his hand, trembling and shaking from the pain and nerve damage. I wasn't going to give him any more chances. I swung that lumber like Bautista—right into the side of his head. He went barreling over and fell back into the trash pile. He rolled onto his back with a moan and saw the butt end of the piece of wood rushing towards his face.

That might have been the last thing he ever saw.

I slammed that two-by-four again and again into his face, as if I was using a plunger. The wet, hard packing sounds resonated and my grunts turned into yells. I pounded him until he was limp and dead.

I was out of breath and my lungs were screaming. I had been so scared, that this huge man was going to beat me to death...it was him or me...and that was the only way to kill him.

I stood there, heaving to catch my breath with the wood still in my grasp. I looked up to the sky and screamed! The rain poured down on me and lighting crashed. I finally threw the wood aside and dropped to my knees.

A long time passed before I finally looked up. I was startled to see G again, standing at the end of the alley alone.

We stared at each other for a long time and then I got up and walked over to him.

"Where's the girl?" I asked.

"She's safe...the others are watching her."

I started to walk away from him.

"What about him?" He asked.

I glanced back at the lifeless body of the beast.

"What about him?" I returned the question. "He can rot with the rest of the trash!" I spit out some blood onto the ground, and started to walk away again.

"John!" He cried. "Someone's gonna find him!"

I had to stop in my tracks. Up until now, I knew this fact...but I didn't care. It gave me an idea though...

Monday Morning.

As the dawn was just rising and the storm had ended, we were all sitting around still. While everyone in the group was chattering about what to do; I was writing on a piece of paper. I was having a cigarette to calm my nerves. I blew the smoke out as I reread what I had written. Satisfied, I began to draw a little symbol on the corner of the paper. A make shift little doodle more than anything.

I drew a circle, with two intersecting lines inside of it, one vertical, one horizontal, so that they touched the edges of the circle.

As I was rubbing the palm of my hand into my eye socket, footsteps approached.

"What are we doing John?" It was Tom.

"Hey Tom." I said, with the cigarette butt, smoked down to the filter, still pursed between my lips. "How is she?"

"Linda says she's got a broken nose...maybe a broken orbital bone too." Tom said, looking back and forth between me and the others gathered around the girl. I had drawn away from the group to rest. "She needs a doctor John."

I folded up my piece of paper and put the pencil in my pocket along with it. I looked at Tom.

Tom was a short little guy, but he was stalky. He had short curly hair that was matted from living out here, and a beard like the rest of us men. He was probably around 40 years old. I liked Tom. He was a good guy, a caring guy, loyal as any good friend would be. He didn't get involved too much and he just stayed to himself. He wouldn't ever *doubt* you...as long as you could back up what you were saying.

I sighed, and flicked my cigarette away. "I know Tom...I know." I thought about it for a moment, before sighing again. "So let's take her."

Tom looked around, nervous and unsure. "What? Now?" He asked.

I sprung to my feet. "Yah man." I walked past him to the group. Linda was kneeling beside the girl, tending to her wounds with a wet cloth. Linda was a very nice old lady. She had been a nurse before her husband got sick and then even she couldn't afford the medical bills anymore. Her husband eventually died because he wasn't getting the meds he needed, but not after Linda had to quit her job in order to take care of him. When he died, Linda was left with too much debt and was eventually forced out by the government. They didn't care...How do you like that?

Here she was now, washing the wounds of this poor girl, looking up at me with her old, wise, compassionate eyes.

"How is she, Linda?" I asked.

She just shook her head with a sad look on her face. "Hank," she looked up at Hank who was standing nearby. "We need some more ice please." She stated.

"Sure Linda." Hank said as he rushed off.

"It's like Tom told you, John." Linda said to me. "She's gotta get to the hospital soon."

"Thanks for taking care of her Linda." I said. She smiled softly and went back to work wiping away blood from the girl's cuts.

The girl...she was sleeping on her back on top of a bunch of our sleeping bags. The group had all pitched in their stuff to help her out. We also lent her some of our blankets to keep her warm.

Last night had been a rough one. When G and I got back to our camp, Linda had already started to do some first aid and the others were scrounging up their things to try and make a bed for her. There were lots of questions. I explained what had happened with the big brute that was responsible for the state she was in now. The group was horrified when they realized that I had *killed* him. That was why I had retreated from the group. After that, they had all begun to look at me in a different light. The questions all stopped and it was a very quiet night. Most of the others went to sleep and Linda did what she could to bandage up the girls wounds. Linda cleaned me up and washed my wounds. I personally handed my pack to her and told her she could pull out the clothes to use for bandages or rags. I could just get more, it wasn't a big deal and the girl needed it. G made up some of his honey-lemon concoction for her when she eventually came to. But, even he was acting differently around me now. I spent the rest of the night alone, thinking again, about what I had just done—although...I came to a disturbing conclusion that I wasn't at all bothered by it. I did what I had to do to save that girl and prevent myself from being killed by him! To prevent him from doing this kind of thing to anyone else ever again! I thought about it long and hard into the night. I don't think I got any sleep, but who knows? I could have dozed off once or twice or just gone into a half awake, half asleep daze. But whatever it was, I just stared into the blackness of the night realizing that my mission had just begun. I thought about the body of the beast I left lying lifeless and bloodied back in the alley. That's when I quickly needed a paper and pencil...

Now...this morning; as dawn was just starting to break, it seemed everyone was looking to me. Waiting for me to give the okay to take her to the hospital. But why was it my decision? If anyone was considered the leader of this little band of misfits, I would have said it was G.

He hadn't said anything to me since we got back last night. As I stood there, slightly apart from the others with my hands on my hips, thinking about getting this girl to the hospital, I caught a glimpse of him standing there in my peripheral. Our eyes locked and we just stared at each other for a moment. I thought he was trying to size me up or figure me out or something...I couldn't quite tell and I just stared back.

"We gotta get her to the hospital G." I said.

He just nodded slowly, still staring. I stared back for a few more brief seconds, and then this tingling feeling of annoyance began to stir itself in me. I shook my head and shrugged my shoulders. I glanced around at everyone else in the group. Everyone was just standing around either staring at me or staring at Linda work on the girl. I was starting to get really sick of this. I gave the okay to take this girl to the hospital and I had to start rounding everyone up who would help. I felt like I was giving orders and I didn't like that. But it seemed it had to be done.

We were on the move shortly. Only a handful of the group decided to come, as there wasn't really anything binding us together. We were all roamers, wanderers, or whatever you wanted to call us. Home was where we laid our heads.

Linda didn't come. She cleaned and bandaged the wounds as best she could and sent the girl with us. She was too old to make the hike anyways. Tom came. He was quite adamant to help out actually. Ken and Bart came along too. And of course myself and G.

While the group moved along, we planned our route through all the back streets and alleys, like a secret maze through the city. G led the way, since he knew all the best ways through, to stay undetected. Ken and Bart took the first shift, helping the girl walk and making sure she was alright throughout the trip.

I lagged behind at first, because I didn't want G up front to see me make my little detour. It was when we first set out, I was able to sneak away quickly to go and find my heaping bloody mess I made last night. When I entered the alley, his big body was still lying there lifeless. I approached slowly and took a moment to stare at his face. I briefly replayed last night's action in my head and I reached into my pocket to retrieve the paper. By now the sun was just peaking over the horizon...it was probably around 7:00am. No one had found his body yet, but they would soon. I glanced around for on lookers and then I bent down and stuffed the piece of paper into his shirt pocket.

Since we were in the down town core, the hospital wasn't far. We walked for about 45 minutes, and nobody had noticed my little sneak away.
We all switched off, helping the girl out and monitoring her condition. It was Tom and Ken's turn when Bart came up beside me.
"Hey John." He said.
"Hey Bart, what's up man?"
He kept looking up ahead at G, still leading the way.
"This is pretty nuts eh?" He asked me.
"Yah." I said with a sigh. "It's pretty wild."
"You seem like you're used to this stuff though man."
His comment threw me off guard and my words got stuck in my throat. I had to stop and regain my thoughts. "I don't know if 'used to it' is a phrase I would pick." I said.
"Yah but John, we've all been out here together for a while. We've seen this before...this stuff happens all the time. I mean, you saw us last night...everybody froze and didn't know what to do!"
"Anybody would man, you can't—."
"—you didn't man!" Bart realized how loud he had gotten and he glanced up ahead to see if G was listening. The he lowered his voice again to a half whisper. "I'm sick of it out here man...a lot of us are."
Bart kept looking around nervously, especially at G. I was unsure of what he was trying to tell me, but I think I had a pretty good idea.
"What's G's story anyways?" I reluctantly asked, looking at G myself now.
"John's great, man."
"But...?"
Bart hesitated and, again, looked around nervously. "He was different bef—"
"—Bart!" G's voice boomed into our conversation, cutting him off.
"I think it's your turn to walk with her." G continued, motioning to the guys trailing behind Bart and I. We both looked back.
"You guys alright?" Bart asked.
"I'm pretty tired Bart." Tom piped up.
"Alright, man." Bart said. "I guess I could take a shift, old boy." He gave Tom a wink and then glanced at me. We locked eyes in an awkward gaze. I wanted to know the rest of that story...
Bart raised his eyebrows at me and slapped my shoulder as he walked back to relieve Tom.

I glanced in front of me again to lock eyes with G. He had a concerned look on his face and I gave him an awkward smirk. Then he turned and continued to lead us forward.

By now the sun had begun its rise in the morning sky. It was a beautiful morning in good ol' Baltimore. The glass buildings were reflecting the bright orange rays of the sky. It was a big orange sky this morning.

Shortly after Bart had taken over for Tom, G was announcing that the hospital was just at the end of the next alley. This was the alley I had woken up in after I passed out, where G found me. My heart jumped in my chest as we walked down it and my eyes locked on a sight that made me nervous. There, blowing in the morning breeze, stuck in some garbage, left over from the investigation scene, was the bright yellow police tape...

...they had been here!

I looked up to see G noticing the tape too. He looked at me and motioned to the tape. I didn't have anything to say, and I just imagined the police being here. I thought about Ridley for the first time in a while.

Had he been here looking for me? Had everyone been here searching? Had Clare?

We rounded the corner and the hospital was now in sight. I swallowed a lump in my throat because the last time I was here, I was fleeing the police and the events of that whole day came flooding back. The events leading up to that day all came flooding back to me...Sexrex, Maggie, Clare's dad, all of it...

"Let's do this." I said. We were all standing there staring at the entrance. We remained at the edge of the alley, hidden from everyone else. G walked up beside me and gave me a nervous smirk.

"You can't go back in there, bro." He said with a hand on my shoulder. I looked over at him and gave him an awkward smile back. It was nice to have him talking to me, and show concern. I nodded silently and then returned my gaze to the hospital entrance in the distance.

"I know." I thought for a moment and then I saw a few police officers walking through the sliding doors. I definitely couldn't go in there. I looked at G again and squeezed his shoulder as I walked a few yards back into the alley where the girl was seated against the wall and the three other guys were standing.

"Ken." I said looking at him. "You gotta take her in."

Ken sighed with his hands on his hips. "Alright." He said.

"How we gonna do this John?" Tom asked.

"Well, Tom...I'm pretty sure none of us want to be found after last night's events."

All of them, including G, looked down at the ground nervously, as if they were just reminded about it.

"Well *you* certainly don't want to be." Tom said with a hint of annoyance in his voice. I snapped him a look and he couldn't maintain the gaze and looked away.

"Tom!" G snapped. "That's enough."

G was sticking up for me. I was starting to get worried about what he thought about my actions, but now I was just confused. But hopeful that maybe he *was* on my side.

I looked over at Bart who gave me a nod of reassurance to let me know he was with me.

"It's fine." Ken said, looking at Tom. "I'll do it, it's fine."

Tom looked a bit flustered, realizing that the rest of the group hadn't shared in his small little outburst of stress. I tried to think that that's all it was. As Ken walked over to the girl, Bart helped him get her on her feet. She winced in pain and I walked over to her too.

"Thank you." She whispered. It looked like it hurt her to speak. But she made eye contact with me and smiled.

"You're welcome." I replied, returning a soft smile. "Take care of yourself."

"I'll help Ken, John." Bart said, nodding at me.

I smiled at him. "Thanks Bart."

They set off from the alley and the three of us watched.

It was a long five minutes.

A quiet five minutes.

Then, Ken and Bart came walking out of the doors at a fast pace, constantly looking over their shoulders. I could feel the tension lessen from all three of us.

Ken and Bart made it back to the alley.

"So?" Tom was asking.

"It's fine man...no problem." Bart said.

"Ken?" I stopped him. "She okay?"

"Yah...they rushed her in right away."

"No one stopped you guys?"

"Well, they said don't go anywhere." Bart said. "But during the commotion, they wouldn't let us go with her into the room, so...we got outta dodge."

"Nice work guys." G said.

"Let's get outta here then." Tom piped up.

We were all starting to leave when I caught a glimpse of something and stopped.

At the hospital doors,

A woman I thought I knew was walking out onto the sidewalk.

Clare!

"John!" G shouted. I looked at him, then back at my wife...

...only, it wasn't my wife.

I looked closer this time, realizing that it was just a girl who did look very similar.

Was I hallucinating?

262

"John, let's go!" G cried.
I gave my head a shake and then snapped out of it, turning to leave with the other guys.

Later on, we were walking silently back to our camp. Every one of us had something different on our minds.
Tom, I'm sure, was thinking about last night and what we had just done.
Bart, I could guess, was thinking about how things might change now. He seemed excited about the change. From our earlier conversation, he was eager to start something else. I felt I would be able to count on him when the time came.
And G...G must have been thinking about his past. The one Bart was about to tell me about. Bart bringing it up must have sparked it up for him again. He seemed plagued by it as we walked. Guilty almost. But it was definitely eating at him.
Me, I was thinking about *everything!*—All at once. The complexity of everything I had been through in the past few years that had led me to here.
My mission.
I stopped, when I looked up. I had been staring at the ground, trailing behind the other four guys. But when I looked up I noticed that they had all stopped walking and were looking to their left. We were taking the sidewalk down a small street that was filled with little shops on either side. I looked to my left when I caught up and saw that they were looking into a bar window.
"What are you guys looking at?"
I looked all around and finally noticed the TV on the wall.
We couldn't hear the news broadcast, but we could clearly see the police trying to push back cameras and news crews away from an alley. The caption on the bottom of the screen read; 'BODY FOUND DEAD IN ALLEY'. We all watched anxiously until the screen showed us a shot that some camera man was able to zoom in and get. We saw the body of the big brute who had beat and tried to rape our girl, and who would've killed me if I hadn't killed him.
G and I looked at each other. Then back to the TV.
Now there was a police detective on screen giving a live statement to the cameras. He was holding a piece of paper, unfolded, in his hands. I could feel G looking at me in my peripheral and I sort of side glanced at him a bit nervously.
But I smiled on the inside, realizing they had found my little note.
We continued to watch and I read the *new* caption on the bottom of the screen; 'MYSTERIOUS RELIGIOUS MESSAGE FOUND ON BODY...THE BAPTIST STRIKES AGAIN?'.
The detective held the note up and the camera highlighted the little doodle of the circle and cross.
Then I couldn't contain my grin anymore.
It worked.

CHAPTER NINETEEN
Back On Our Feet

Monday Afternoon.
The Baltimore city morgue.
The big man himself, dressed in his usual lucky green, was walked into the cold storage room by the staff.
Sexrex.
He arrived with a few of his entourage and he was playing with his gold rings while he waited, glancing over at the handful of cops who were posted there, watching him. His charm bracelet rattled as he moved his hands around. Dex Finley and Jake Ryan were there, watching the seedy Kingpin.
The mortician slid the drawer open and it slammed to a stop. Cold steam rose up off the body, covered in a sheet.
The mortician looked at Sexrex. "You won't be able to facially identify him." He said. "The blunt force trauma has rendered him unrecognizable."
"Let me see his hand." Sexrex said. "He has some tats I might recognize."
The mortician cocked his head and winced as he went to the body and peeled the sheet back, revealing the hand, which was also mangled. "I'm afraid his hand was severely damaged as well." He said. "We removed as much glass as we could but..." He trailed off.
Sexrex sighed and rolled his rings around. "Let me see his chest." He said next.
The mortician sighed and complied with his request. He lifted the sheet up slowly and then Sexrex had enough. He shoved the little mortician out of the way and yanked the entire sheet off himself, to reveal the grotesque face which was mangled by my two-by-four plunging. Sexrex just fixated on the face and stared in plain horror, yet with no expression on his face. He finally reached out to caress the face and then he slid his hand down, running it along the body until he stopped at his chest. There, tattooed on his left pectoral, was a small Irish clover.
Just like the one imprinted on Sexrex's own glass eye.
With confirmation now, Sexrex lowered his head and sighed.
"Boss?" One of his cronies asked.
"Find me this...'Baptist'!" Sexrex whispered harshly, and not looking up.

As they left the morgue, Sexrex was furious now. He didn't say much as the cops followed him and his entourage out the door.
Once the door to his escort vehicle closed he began to rant.
"Rip this city apart! I want him alive! I want his head! My *brother* will have vengeance!"
"Uh...boss?" One of the cronies said. "You might wanna see this."

The crony passed him his phone and Sexrex flipped it around, ripping off his sunglasses to get a better look.

On the screen was news coverage of 'The Baptist' he was seeking. The cell phone footage taken on the bus of 'The Baptist' taking out that monster, the footage of the police recovering his brother's body out of the alley and finding the note, and coverage of Sean Mash; the late mayor of the city's death. The news story ended with the usual broadcast; *"anyone with information regarding the whereabouts of former police officer John Revele, is to contact authorities immediately, he is to be considered armed and dangerous..."* And so on and so forth.

As the reporter finished, the screen showed the end of the cell phone footage from the bus where my face was revealed to the world.

A slow grin appeared on Sexrex's face. "Well, well, well..." He said darkly. "This just got interesting."

* * *

"What are you thinking brother!?" G was angry!

We had made the long hike back to our house in the slums that day, to spend a few days there and regroup our supplies and ourselves. It was a quiet walk back after we parted ways with the rest of the group and headed out. I had kept pleading with G to talk to me but he wouldn't. I finally got him talking by the time we got inside.

"You're leaving little notes on the body?" He asked. "Implementing yourself?" He went on. "I'll ask again, what are you thinking? You're going to go on some sort of killing spree now?"

"If that's what it takes!" I shouted.

G was shocked. I was frustrated. The weight of the world's problems. Again explaining how sick of it all I was, and how drastic a change I was willing and ready to affect. "Aah..." I made a desperate sigh. "...G..." I threw my hands up. "I dunno man. You don't get it..."

"What don't I get, John!?" G asked, getting angry now. "What, you think I ended up out here cuz life was good to me!?"

I sighed, and stopped short, realizing the stupidity of my comment. I thought about what Bart had said—or—what he was about to say...

'He was different before...' Before what?

"Are you ever gonna tell me your story G?" I simply asked, breaking the silence.

"What are you talking about?" He asked back.

"I'm talking about you."

"What about me John?"

"How'd you end up out here?"

"Why does that matter to you?"

"It matters, because I can tell you agree with me...on some level."

G looked embarrassed. Discovered. Found out.

"I'm nothing like you John." He said darkly.
"I don't think that's true man. Not at all."
"What do you think you know about me?"
"I know this; on that first night, when you brought me here, you and I shared a connection. I know you felt it too. You made a big speech about voids in all of us, and holes in the moral fabrics of the universe. You knew it at as well I did...and you still know it."
"What do I know John?"
"That there's just something not right with the world. Isn't that what you said?"

Silence again filled the room.

"And then, the other night, you were spouting off about fate and how someone wants us to be together'"
"That's not why I took you in." He finally said.
"It's not..." I replied sarcastically.
"When you came into the alley that day you were delusional."

He was saying stuff now that I didn't remember about that day. After I left the hospital I couldn't remember much. I remembered leaving the hospital and I then I was waking up in the alley staring back at G.

"You were all wide eyed and frantic." He continued. "You looked right at me man! You don't remember any of this?"
"No...I don't."
"John...I grabbed hold of you. I shook you."

G had me riveted now. I was staring at him as he told me the story.

"You looked right at me." He went on. "You grabbed me back. And you asked me; 'where is He?'"

My heart sank.

'He'?
'Him'.
"What?" Was all I could think to say in my bewilderment.
"You kept asking me..." G said. "Over and over. 'Where is He, where is He'?"

I couldn't believe that I didn't remember this.

"I helped you to the ground. You went on and on about *Him*. You kept telling me 'He was there, I saw Him, He saved me, where is He'?"
"I—I don't—" I stammered and shuddered for a moment trying so hard to remember any of this.

"You were all doped up on X, John. You were in the hospital for a reason man. I'm gonna assume that the trauma of escaping was too much on your system. You were all messed up, bro."
"I don't remember any of this." I blurted out.
"Hence...the drugs, John."

I suddenly remembered G's original point.

"So...what's your point then man? Why did you take me in? Pity? You thought I was crazy? What?"

"Because John...Because of Him."

I stopped and my lungs trapped the breath in.

"H—Him?" I hadn't given The Stranger much thought over the last few days.

"Yah man. Him."

"You—you know who He is or something?" I said, half laughing out of nervousness.

"I think I do...if it's who I think it is..."

I looked at G now, desperately, not knowing what to say.

Was he talking about The Stranger?

"That's why I took you in man." He said. "Because I knew...that you'd seen Him too."

"There's no way you could have any clue who I was talking about."

"A very average looking man..." G began. "But with a friendly look to Him." He was right so far. "Sort of a half scruff on his face. Plain clothes. Ordinary features."

G was right.

He was accurately describing *my Stranger*...

But He could have been describing anybody.

"But that's not it." He continued. "Is it John?" Asking *me* questions now. He caught me off guard though, and he drew me in. He engaged me into this. "When you look at Him...you can tell He's on your side. He's got a humble look about Him, yet, you probably wouldn't challenge Him."

I had never thought about G's last point, but hearing him say it described The Stranger pretty well. A point I could never put words to.

"An indescribable quality about Him," he went on. "That you can't quite put your finger on."

Everything G was saying about The Stranger was true. These were all feelings I experienced when I saw Him.

"But..." G went on. "Somehow...you know He's good..."

Perfect description of the man I had encountered.

The man who had saved my skin twice when He could have stopped me. I was clearly doing things outside the law on both the pivotal points in my life where I had encountered Him, yet, He made it obvious that He allowed me to continue on.

"In my head." I started. "I just call Him The Stranger." I accepted the fact that G and I had both shared in meeting this man.

"That's what this about, John. That's why I'm so intrigued by you. I've been doing everything just to keep my group safe. But then you come along. I want to be rid of you but I can't!"

I left a long silence before speaking again. "So...you've met Him too then?" I asked.

"A few times." G replied.

"When? How?"

"The first time...is a bit of a long story."

"Because...we're in such a short supply of time here." I said sarcastically, and looking around mockingly at the old empty walls and floors of this house.

"I know, I know...jackass." G pretended to be mad still, but grinned at me. I think the tension between us was finally gone. I guess G had been holding on to that little nugget of information since the day we met! I could tell he felt better getting it off his chest.

We took a break in our conversation, to go into the kitchen and grab a bite. G brought out some cans of tuna and bottles of water for us and we were soon sharing a meal together...sitting at the little round table across from each other.

"When I was a little boy..." G began. "My dad was a cop." I laughed a funny laugh, thinking; *what a coincidence.* "I loved trying on his police hat. I was always examining the stuff he had on his belt; the cuffs, the extra bullets, pepper spray, the 'stick' I called it, and of course his gun. He was a good man. I was proud of him."

I started to get a bad sense, that this wasn't going to be a happy story.

"I wanted to be just like him." G continued. "But...he got in trouble at work. During a big arrest, he and some of the other old boys were tasked to, this punk kid—gang bangin' loser—tried to run from them. My dad chased him and followed him into a warehouse. The kid pulled a gun on him and my dad reacted. The courts and internal affairs convicted him of manslaughter...said he drew too quickly and reacted too harshly. That he should've given the kid the chance to surrender first. You think that kid would've given my dad the chance if he hadn't fired first? You think the courts would've asked the kid; 'why didn't you do your part to avoid this and just cooperate with the arresting officers?' 'Why did you run?'...anyways...my dad did some time for that. He lost his job. Being fired from the police force doesn't afford you many chances to other employers. He got odd jobs where he could, and he and my mom struggled for a long time. I could tell when I looked at him that he wasn't the same man I knew as my hero."

G paused for a good long while, and silence filled the house. I certainly didn't know what to say.

"I wished I could've told him..." He started again. "...that it didn't matter. That he was still my hero..." Another long pause. "I wished I would've told him I loved him one more time, before—".

My suspicions were apparently true and this wasn't a happy story.

"Things went from bad to worse." He continued. "We eventually ended up on social assistance, living off of food banks and soup kitchens, clothing donation boxes, church charities...all of the above. We were in one of these fine establishments...minding our own business...when this guy—no—this vermin, started hitting on my mom. My dad still had his values despite losing everything else. He still had his code and did his best to keep his honour. Especially when it came to us. He tried warning the guy several times before he had to get a little physical. I guess these scumbags like to travel in packs...when we were leaving the shelter that night him and his crew followed us out. We got caught in an alley and next thing I knew my dad was swarmed with a bunch of other guys. It all happened so fast. Some guys grabbed me and my mom and held us down while they beat my dad. They made us watch. Then...th—then...th—then they held him down. And they held me down too...while the guy my dad punched at the soup kitchen *raped* my mom. They made us watch that too. All I could do was lay there and weep, while my dad screamed at the top of his lungs. His screams still haunt me in my sleep..."

More silence now. I was just staring at G's face as he relived this horrific part of his life. I could see the anguish, still fresh in his eyes, as if it had just happened.

"They hit me so hard I blacked out. When I came too...my parents were dead."

I was dumbfounded and heartbroken for him. G had every reason to hate the world just as much as I did.

He had a thousand times the reasons to want to do the exact same thing I was planning out here on these horrible, evil streets.

"That's when I met Him for the first time." He said darkly. I snapped my attention back to him as he continued his story. "I was sitting in a corner shaking and rocking. Staring at my parents dead bodies a few feet away from me. I had been crying for hours now. I was so scared. What was I gonna do? I would have stayed there and rotted, or worse. God knows who could have come and picked me up, or taken me...I heard footsteps on the pavement. When I looked up I saw a pair of ratty running shoes and legs covered with a worn pair of jeans, standing right in front of me. I was in so much shock, though, that I didn't even care. I didn't care enough to look up and see who it was. But He cared enough to come down to me. He crouched down and I saw that gentle, sympathetic face of His. He was a young man probably I'd say, late 20's."

I was a bit puzzled at that point, because that's about how old I would have said He was when *I* met Him a few years ago...

But G was telling a story from when he was a boy.

How could that be?

"I wished so bad that it was my dad coming to comfort me after I had skinned my knee or something." G went on. "But He reached out His hand and touched my head with it. He smiled at me and rubbed the back of my head with His palm...the same way my dad used to. That's when I knew. Because how would He have known that? He was a stranger to me too. But I knew something...like you probably did the first time you saw Him. I wanted to lash out at Him too...I wanted to tell Him to screw off and leave me alone! That I didn't need His help! But for some reason, looking at Him, I had to be honest with myself and realize that I did need help. His eyes convicted me in that moment, without Him even saying anything. I knew that He was there to help me."

Listening to G's account of his meeting of The Stranger was amazing. It filled me with sense of hope, and I didn't even know why.

So we both met the same guy, big deal right?
Well...
Right!
Taking the circumstances into account; that we had both met The Stranger at pivotal points in our lives, and that we had met up after all of my recent drama *was* a big deal!
The whole idea of Him and the mystery surrounding Him; a man, who is walking around out here,
silently working in the lives of people like me...
and like G...
Clare too!
And who knows who else?
(At this point in my life, I had no idea that He had also appeared to Richter).
Surely G and I weren't the only two people down on our luck, or facing hard times. In fact, I'd even say that a guy like this was helping people with normal problems too.
And that...was cool!
It was now that I first realized that G was right. So I shared my mind with him.
"G," I started. "What if this guy is something else altogether?" I asked. G was still in an emotional daze, I could tell. He was staring at the ground and trying to compose himself after telling his awful story.
"You mean...like, supernatural or something?" He asked me.
Supernatural...
Supernatural...
I had never been a 'religious' guy, expect for my little church lesson from the police station Chaplin. I wouldn't have chosen that word; *supernatural*. To me it always sounded like a stupid cliché and cheesy word...but hearing G say it, it was very fitting.
This entire time, since He helped me out in the beginning of my street career, and when He helped me get out of the hospital. Now knowing that He apparently didn't age and I *for sure* wasn't hallucinating Him...
How else could I describe it?
There was a certain element that just didn't seem to follow the *natural* rules of things.
Un-natural...
I would have to admit that it was *super-natural*.
"Yah." I simply said. "Like supernatural."
"Well." G said. "After our first meeting that night, He helped me to my feet. I was too paralyzed with fear and grief to move. All I could do was stare down the alley to the opening at the end of it that led back onto the street. I might not have ever moved if it wasn't for what happened next. I looked around and He was gone, making me even more scared. But then...as if it was perfectly timed, a man and a woman were walking by and 'something' caused a stray cat to let out an awful piercing meow as it jumped from a ledge and

ran towards me. The cat caught the woman's eye and her gaze traveled into the alley where she saw my silhouette standing frozen in the middle of the alley. I guess it's because I was a small boy that she had pity on me. I watched as she tugged on her partners arm and began frantically pointing down the alley at me. In a few seconds they were rushing towards me. If I had been curled up into a ball still, hiding in the shadows, no one would have found me and I wouldn't have moved for days. Who knows what riffraff might have found me. All because He picked me up and set me back on my feet. I happened to look past my two rescuers and saw Him standing there at the end of the alley, just emerging from around the corner. I saw that forgiving look on His face as He smiled a subtle grin at me...as if He was telling me; 'you're welcome...I got you'."

As G explained his story I was mesmerized by it. I sort of got lost in the moment and forgot where I was. It was so much like *my* story with The Stranger when I first met Him. I transported myself there with him as a small boy. I time-traveled. G was a good story teller.

"So then what?" I asked eagerly.

"Brother..." G began again. "I couldn't tell ya. The next few hours were all blurry and very fast! I was wrapped up in a swarm of ambulances, police, flashing emergency lights, statements, doctors, statements, social workers, statements, doctors, more social workers, and child therapists. I was well taken care of in the following days...spent a few nights in an orphanage and undergoing grief counselling..."

G proceeded to tell me most of his life story.

Basically; he was bounced around in between foster homes for several years. The grief counselling didn't help much as it was all he thought about to get revenge on the guys who had killed his parents. Bad behaviour got him booted out his foster care and thrown out of most of the shelters he went to. This was all over a few years until he was 14. Then he came out here to the streets. He didn't hide out here though, he got involved. G picked fights with guys he didn't like...anyone who reminded him of the guys who killed his parents. He got into trouble all over the place, even accumulated a bit of a criminal record. I was surprised that I didn't remember his face at all, or if I ever saw him at the station. He told me that he used to be as gung-hoe as I was. The connection that we had when we first met started to make sense.

He got it, like I did...the way of the world...and all the reasons to want to change it.

But...

G's saga on the street ended with his exile and he went into extreme hiding at a young age. While he used to roll with some bad dudes, he changed his tune and started accumulating new friends; Tom, Bart, Ken, Linda, Hank, and eventually he and the gang I met up with was established.

"So what happened then?" I had asked him.

"What do you mean?" G replied.

"I mean...in the middle. The transition. How did you go from street bad ass to exile with Tom and Linda?"

G chuckled. "That's another story..." He said.

He looked at me sheepishly, knowing that I didn't care. I returned a convicting look letting him know the obvious.

"Well..." He started. "You know Jeannine."

"Yah of course."

She was a young teenage girl. She always reminded me of Maggie.

"I never really rolled with any particular crowd." G went on. "But, I was trying to find the guys who killed my folks right?"

"Right."

"So, I ended up hooking up with these guys who were real pieces of shit you know? They had all been in and out of shelters...they all had criminal records. I assumed that they knew a lot of other people like them—in fact they bragged about how 'notorious' they were around the city. I played along hoping that I would eventually meet up with my enemies but..."

He had been looking down at the ground as he spoke, but now he looked up at me seriously. "I got in too deep." He said. "I forgot what I was fighting towards and became one of them." G couldn't hold my gaze anymore and he looked down again in shame. "I didn't even realize it." He continued. "Not until..."

There was a long pause in the conversation. I was giving him time to collect his thoughts but I soon realized that he wasn't doing that. He was trying to hold back a lump in his throat. I saw the look on his face of despair, and I suddenly remembered how we got on this topic in the first place.

"Jeannine." I reluctantly said, almost in a half whisper.

More silence. Just a simple, slow head nod. Which then turned into him shaking his head no to himself followed by a long winded sigh.

"We had been robbing people." He started. "Not just petty theft where no one gets hurt...these guys had guns! W—we..." He couldn't get the words out. He was trembling. "John...we stuck guns in these people's faces man! I—I...I can't believe we did this bro." G took a minute to relax. All of the old guilt and shame, and...whatever else attached to it was stirring up in him, I could tell.

"The looks of sheer terror in their eyes staring down the barrel of the gun. These people had wives and husbands, kids...hell...some of them even were kids."

I was at a loss for words. These types of people; the ones who victimized others and intimidated everyone they encountered were exactly the types of people I *hated*. Hearing my new good friend G say that he was one of these...I'm not sure if I was angry or embarrassed at thinking that somebody I was so close too was capable of this at some point. But then I came to my senses as I saw G's demeanour as he was telling me this. This was not the appearance of somebody who was proud of what they had done.

"You're nothing like those guys man." I said. "Look at you...you're in distress just talking about it. You've got a strong moral fibre that holds you together obviously. While others don't think twice about it...it bothers you. You're different G."

"Maybe...but I still did it John. Jeannine...she was a young preppy kid. Mad at her parents for...who knows what? I used to hate girls like her, who had everything they ever wanted. Spoiled little brats. She was in the wrong place at the wrong time. She was hanging with the bad kids, doing it all. I couldn't have known." He paused. "I couldn't have known...we knew this group of guys who sold pot out of their place. A lot of the local kids would buy from them, business was good. My group wanted some money and we knew these guys had a lot of it, so...we're there, masked faces, guns-a-blazing, shouting orders, pushing and shoving people all over the room. I notice this one girl huddled in the corner but she was on the wrong side of the apartment. The plan was to herd everyone into one group and two of us would be on crowd control detail. Our lead guy is yelling at me; 'get that bitch over with the rest of them!' 'Cmon man!' Everyone's freakin'...and all I can think about is how much she looked like me after I lost my parents. Huddled in a corner with no one around. Too scared to move. Our leader is still yelling so I go over there, aggressively, trying to prove myself to the rest of the group. I'm yelling at her now 'get up, get up, let's go!' I'm waving a gun all over the place. I grabbed her by the arm and yanked her to her feet. That's when her face and mine came next to each other's and our eyes met. I looked into her eyes and it was like looking at a picture of myself if I could have seen myself as a boy...after my parents were killed. I saw on her face the same emotions I felt and I knew. I could see into her eyes. I knew that she too was scared. She too was desperate. She was alone, misunderstood and forgotten. I saw that even a 'little preppy brat' could feel the deep hurt that the blade of this world can cause. I didn't know any of her problems but I could see...it was the first time I had actually stopped and looked at one of my victims. I saw that her soul was empty like mine. But on top of everything...I saw that she was full of fear. Fear of me. I suddenly felt disgusted and in an attempt to compensate for my oncoming insecurities I let go of her arm and she stared back at me. I asked her later and she told me that she saw all the same stuff in my eyes. She walked voluntarily over and sat with the rest of group. Our eyes kept meeting during all the ongoing commotion—until...we should have expected it, robbing drug dealers. One of the dudes pulled a gun...do I have to explain the rest? Now...don't ask me why I did what I did next...maybe it was because I realized that I had become the fear that paralyzed me as a boy, and I didn't want that. During all the shooting, the whizzing bullets and splintering wood, the thundering sound of all the guns blasting and the screams, I had a thought. This girl. She shouldn't be a part of all this. She shouldn't be killed in the crossfire of a bunch of losers like me. Through the dust I could see her cowering and screaming. I crawled on the floor underneath the gunshots until I got to her. The two of us escaped the apartment and fled down the stairs, and out onto the street."

"And that's where you and Jeannine have been ever since?" I asked.

"No...I convinced her to go back to her home and work things out with her parents..."

Oh-no! I thought. I sensed there was a *but* to go after that.

"She hadn't been home in months..." G started. "I guess the grief of having their daughter run away ate them from the inside out." He paused and bit his lip, closing his eyes. "The police deduced that they had been arguing, probably about their daughter running away, and that her dad had gone mad and killed her mother...and then turned the gun on himself. They blamed each other."

"Oh man..." I said.

"That's when I took Jeannine in." G went on. "It was the two of us in the beginning until we met the others."

"And Bart?" I asked. "What was he talking about when he referred to 'before?"

"Well, when we first started rolling together I was still prone to most of my old ways. People don't just change overnight. I kind of protected the group—the ones who couldn't protect themselves, like Linda and Hank and Jeannine. Bart was always so gung-hoe. He wanted to fight too. Ken was always a big help, but Bart was just too young and I wouldn't let him help. Eventually...the more I gained the responsibility of protecting them, the more we went into hiding. The more we would avoid situations like the one you ran into last night!" He stopped and sighed.

"But it didn't change the fact that it was all still out there did it?" I asked with conviction. I had been listening intently to his story and pieced together the rest in my mind: the reluctant leader who never wanted the responsibility, yet couldn't help but doing the right thing for his group, though they never fully understood his decisions.

"So I'm assuming Bart didn't agree with your decision to go into hiding." I said.

G looked up at me, kind of shocked that I figured it out.

"Bart's under the impression that unless we go out and exterminate the vermin that they will continue to spread." Said G.

"Well..." I began. "He's kind of right G!"

"John...c'mon. You think I should lead my group out there to fight crime or something. We're not the Justice League man. This is real life!" G was getting a bit worked up now.

"What kind of a life is it that they have G?" I asked.

He stared at me, as if he knew I was right. "At least it's a life, and not a death." He said.

"For how long?"

"They're safe!"

"The streets will get them eventually."

"I keep them safe!"
"We've got to get the streets."
"Get the streets? Do you hear yourself?"
"Damn right I hear myself! Loud and clear!"
"Oh, right...I forgot...you're a super hero! The Baptist!"
"At least I've chosen."
"So what, a hostile takeover then?"
"Nobody was ever meant to live like this man! Time to stop hiding! Open your eyes!"

G stopped. We had been eye locked during our little heated exchange, but I could see his breath get caught in his throat when I said that. It shut him right up and he only held my gaze for a second longer until his eyes dropped to the floor. I wondered what I had said to make him do so. I gave him a second until my curiosity got the better of me.

"What?" I demanded.

G was looking at me again with bewilderment. Another few moments passed until he answered. "That's what He said."

My ears perked and I gave my head a little tilt.

He? The, He?

"You mean...?"
"I told you I had met Him more than once." G said.
"So, he told you to smarten up too?" I asked.
"Open your eyes John!"
"Mine are open—it's you that needs to—"
"No, man! That's what He said to me..."
"What?"

"It was shortly after Jeannine and I had escaped the gun fight. Her and I ended up at a shelter. A very crowded one. That's where we met Bart actually. Linda too...anyways...I was so on edge, so wired. Jeannine was sleeping beside me safely , there was very limited space. I was scanning the crowd, waiting for someone from my old gang to find me and kill me. I hadn't been able to sleep for days since we got away. And I saw Him."

I was so intrigued again, and my annoyance with G disappeared the deeper he got into his story about The Stranger.

"What did He look like this time?" I asked, curiously.

"The same as He did the first time I saw Him as a boy. He was moving through the crowd. It looked like He was looking right at me...only me. I had never forgotten that face. He was wearing clothes just like the rest of us in here, there really wasn't anything special about His appearance...only there was. I know that doesn't make sense but—"

"—no, no...I get ya'. I know what you mean." I said in validation.

"So...He came towards me...He came right up to me. Sat down. He talked to me."

"Really?" I asked. "He's never actually said much to me...just; 'you're welcome'..."

"He said His name was Joshua."
"Joshua?"
"Joshua Christopher."
"Hhmm."
"We talked for a while...He asked me how I ended up in the shelter, though something told me He already knew. I told Him anyways...but, I left a few details out. All I told Him was that I was recently going through a life change. He said He could tell...I told Him that I didn't want the responsibility that was surely to come with taking on Jeannine. I couldn't believe how much I was willing to give up to this stranger. Only, in the back of my mind I knew that I had met Him before. It was one of those weird déjà vu moments where I knew that I knew Him, the vision of Him picking me up off the ground as a boy was so clear in my brain...but I couldn't ask Him. So I just talked. In fact, it was me doing most of the talking while He just listened. My heart beat faster at the thought of bringing up the obvious, and I don't know why."

"Because." I cut in. "Then you'd be admitting to the obvious."

"What? What do you mean?"

"I mean, we all have thoughts...little revelations on life. We like to answer the world's questions for ourselves in our heads. I do it all the time. Ideas that seem viable to us in our thoughts but absurd when we say them out loud. Stuff that gives us hope, but also uncertainty...that's why we keep it in."

"You're not making sense John."

"Sure I am...you know what I'm talking about. It's scary when the stuff we think as..." I paused for effect. "...'supernatural'...materializes."

"Still not following you bro."

"Bringing up the fact that you recognize The Stranger from your childhood, and that He worked through a set of circumstances to change the direction of your life...and that He looked exactly the same, when you had aged. That would force you to talk about the obvious when you were unsure of it."

"Which is?..."

"That there was something special about this guy. Something you couldn't explain."

There was a long pause until G started nodding slowly.

"I think I get you." He finally said.

I laughed to myself. "I'm just piecing this together as I say it man...I'm trying to figure it out the same as you are."

"Open your eyes John." G said. "That's what He said to me. After my long winded outpouring, He just smiled at me gently, and said...'open your eyes John.'..."

I stared back at G, anticipating more to the story.

"And that was it." He only said.

"That was it?" I asked.

"Yep. Then He left."

"What did He mean?"

"For the longest time...I didn't know. Until now."

I snapped my eyes to meet G's with a furrowed brow. "Now? Now what?" I asked.

"You, John. I had to wait to meet you."

I let out my breath and dropped my shoulders, kind of relieved. After all of this talking, it seemed G and I were finally getting on the same page.

"I can't believe I didn't get it until now. Being out on the streets I saw Him a couple more times...just walking around, among the crowds. I was starting to think I was crazy. Until I saw a deranged man wearing a hospital gown come stumbling into my alley and tell me that he had been seeing a stranger too."

I hung my head while I thought about all of this. I tried to just focus on big breaths in and big breaths out. "So that's why you seemed so interested in me." I stated.

"Yah." Replied G. "The fact that I had seen you out in the streets before had intrigued me, like I told you. But when you said that you had seen Him too...I had to stick around until you woke up. I actually didn't realize it was you at first, when I saw you in the alley. I was staring at you while you were passed out and then I recognized you."

"Hhmm." Is all I said. "Well how about that."

What a huge load of information all at once.

But there it all was now.

"You keep drilling me." Said G. "What's your story John?" He asked.

After a long sigh, I proceeded to tell G my story, which I don't need to repeat for you.

You've just read it.

I went through my life as a cop and my life with Clare. I told him more about the Sean A. Mash saga.

I don't need to tell you again...

But as this part of my story comes to a close I need to add in the dramatics.

The world.

The world and all its problems.

I went way back...time travelling again,

I told him about my childhood days and my adolescent years in which I had discovered the truth of the world.

The evil behind every door.

I explained my descent into despair the more I lived,

and my strong desire to change it.

I pieced together the tale of my policing career, fitting in everything to do with Clare...

My sweet wife.

I explained how I had lost her, losing my last grip on the goodness of humanity. Even that I had found a sketch she had drawn and discovered she sees this Stranger too!

We talked for hours...I told him about Ridley, my loyal friend

who I also had lost in my stubbornness.

That punk kid Megga.

Maggie.
Sexrex...
"Well..." G said. "That explains your face."
I laughed pathetically, and there was a long silence.
"So, I think I know where you're going with this bro." G said.
I didn't say anything and I just looked back at him sheepishly. It felt like one of those moments I explained to G, where my own solutions seemed viable in my head, but made me nervous now that someone else knew.
"Why?" He asked.
I furrowed my brow again. "Why what?"
"Your plan...what you've done to yourself, man. I get what you're saying. I do. You know, now, that I have just as much reason to hate the world like you do, but..."
"But what G?" I cut in. "It's gotta stop! All of it! It has to stop!"
"I understand you hating it, but why?"
"Because nobody should have to live this way!" I cried in desperation. "We were not meant to live like this, man!"
"How do you know what we were supposed to live like?" He asked, a little angrily.
"Because it can't be this G!...it can't be this...who would be that cruel? C'mon, man...you said yourself that you felt the void. How can you be defending anything?"
"I'm not defending anybody! But what are you gonna do about it? You think you can go up against the system and change everything?"
"Not as a typical law abiding citizen, no! That's my point! There is nothing we can do and live inside the law to stop it. We can do our best, and that's all. The legal system is a system of values. Well what good is that when the fundamental sickness of humans is to disobey and nothing gets done about it?"
"So we kill everyone John? Is that it?"
I opened my mouth to retort but I stopped myself, and sighed out exasperatingly. I realized by G saying it back to me how bad it sounded.
"No, man! That's not what I'm saying..."
"So just the people you think are evil." G said.
I looked at him through frustrated eyes thinking *how can he, of all people, not see what I was trying to do?* But I also respected him and trusted him, so I wasn't angry with him. I valued his opinion.
"I became a cop," I started. "to make a difference...to put myself between the weak and the ones who would stalk them. To protect those who couldn't protect themselves." I paused and stared at G, waiting for a response that didn't come, frustrating me. "The bad-guys, G— c'mon man! Don't you see what I'm saying here?"
I stared again, as I could tell he was thinking now. A while went by before he spoke.

"I get it man." G said. "Look," He went on. "Bart and Ken and I...we've been talking about this. Trying to figure out some way we could do what you're talking about without crossing the line."

"It can't be done." I said. "Not without crossing the line."

"Then what do we do then, John?"

"Isn't it obvious?" I asked. "We cross the damn line!"

"We can't just go around killing people man!" G retorted.

"That's not what I wanna do, G! But it's like you said..."

"What did I say?"

"You told me that you and your group watch out for each other. That you protect each other. Does not everyone out here deserve that same protection?"

G stared at me and then sighed. "Of course they do." He answered, looking at the ground now.

"Look, man..." I began. "I'm just talking about a trial run. We catch a few robbers, bust a few punks, turn the victims on the prey, empower the people a little. We do that...we could start to see a turnaround in the whole city."

G thought for another few moments. "We can't ask my whole group to be a part of this, John." He finally said. "Hank and Linda, they can't be involved in this..."

"I know Hank and Linda...I agree completely. Tom...I dunno about him."

"Tom might surprise you, bro." G said a little cheekily. "He's reluctant, but...we could try."

"We could try?" I asked happily. "Are you saying you're considering this?"

"I'm saying I'm thinking about it. John, you gotta realize it's been a while for me. I told you about my start out here. God knows I agree with everything you've been saying. But I've suppressed this stuff, man. I buried it."

"G," I started. "I think it's time to resurrect that stuff. Open your eyes remember?"

G sighed and shook his head over and over. "Aah!" He said. "I can't bring myself to do it again, John...I...I can't put my group in that kind of danger again."

I lowered my head and bit my lip.

"I'm sorry." G said. "I really am bro."

I chuckled softly, still staring at the floor. I shook my head too. "Me too, I guess." I said, looking up at him.

G stared back and we just looked at each other.

"I know there's some purpose to us meeting, John." He finally said. "Maybe I can offer you support, shelter...something...I...I dunno...maybe that's all he meant, was to be ready for when you walked in...you'll always have a place here with us, but..."

I looked up to the sky beyond the roof of this house in frustration. G didn't hear me relay the frustration back to the higher power. There was no follow up to that 'but' from G and I looked at him.

"It's okay, man." I said.

We spent the next few minutes in silence, just barely looking at each other in glances back and forth from the ground. Neither of us knew what to say really. I reached into my pocket and got out my smokes. I slipped one out and lit it.

"I guess I'll go." I said, after blowing out my first drag.

G's face got a look of anguish on it, and he bent his head. "John..." He pleaded. "You don't have to go. You can still stay here while you figure this out."

I nodded quickly and stupidly. I again felt dumb after all this. "I know." I simply said. "I'll see ya' around, G".

I turned to go and G said nothing. Behind me he was sighing in regret. I took another drag as I left the house.

Outside I closed the door and looked around the slummy neighbourhood G's house was in. Then I descended the steps and walked down the sidewalk to clear my head.

Across the street...

The eyes of the city watched me. Hired eyes. One of the gang bangers from the drug dealing house across from G's was hanging out on his front porch. He watched me go and he pulled out his phone to dial. Then he waited for the other end to pick up.

"Yo, boss." He said, when they did. "Yah, it's me...I'm at home in the slums...me and my boys have been lookin' for that APB you put out on that cop...yah...well, I'm lookin' at him right now..."

CHAPTER TWENTY
The Justice League

Tuesday.
Richter and his lab partners marched down the jet way, rolling their suitcases behind them. Richter was still miserable about the whole thing and it was written all over his face. Ernest walked up behind him and slapped him on the back.
"Cheer up, Jay!" He offered. "Kitch is taking a different flight if that makes any difference."
Richter chuckled very softly. "A little." He said, smiling at Ernest.
"There you go." Ernest said, patting his back some more.
They were seated and Richter stared out his window as the plane took off, on its way to America...

* * *

"Hi, Mike." Clare said during her usual morning routine I.D. check.
She arrived at work at the field office and entered the mission room. All eyes were on her, including her partner Ray. Because of everything that had just happened she wasn't able to shake the concern everyone unintentionally showed her. She walked liked a victim of a crime down the steps into the mission room.
She was carrying her brief case and a coffee and she placed them down on her desk.
"Morning." Ray greeted her from his desk.
"Morning, Ray." She said back, as she sat down. She turned her work station on and propped her head in her hand for a moment. She then ran her hand through her hair and flipped it up out of her face as she glanced left. She stopped when her gaze met the cardboard box that was still sitting there. The words weren't facing her, but she knew that on the other side was written: 'The Baptist'. She stared at the box for a long time, imagining the whole scene of her father being killed again. Hearing the shots.
From his desk, Ray could see her staring at it and sighed. Then he went to his workstation and used his fingers to grab the corner of the floating projected image in front of him. Like he was peeling the backing of a sticker off, he peeled the image off the main screen and now a double image was floating, hanging like a piece of paper from Ray's fingers.
"Hey Partner!" He said to Clare.
Clare turned from the box and looked at him.
"Incoming." Ray said, as he crumpled his hands like he was crumpling a page. The digital image crumpled into a ball as a result. Ray tossed the image and the projector moved it across the air from his station to Clare's.

She caught it and then unfolded her hands to open it back up. Then she snapped it like a doctor examining X-rays, to make the saggy image stiffen up in her hands. Then she inspected it.

"What's this?" She asked.

"New assignment." Ray said.

Clare placed the image on top of her screen and it sank in to gel with her work. The file Ray sent her was an image. A Chinese symbol. Red.

"They're called 'The Lung'." Ray announced.

Clare made a face. "The Lung?" She asked.

"It's a Chinese word."

"This is just a Chinese letter character." She said, pointing to their symbol.

"Not a letter. A word." Ray replied.

"What word?"

"Lung!" Ray confirmed. "It means 'Dragon'."

Clare stared at the symbol looming in front of her. "So, what's up?" She asked.

"Not too sure yet, Partner." Ray answered. "Mark just wants us to keep an eye out for this group."

"And? What do we know about, 'The Lung'?"

"Not a whole lot yet. Small terrorist cell out of the East. Homegrown stuff. Only local attacks so far, but intelligence seems to suggest they have a hate on for us here in the West."

"Hhm. Okay, let's keep tabs on it."

"Ooo-rah." Ray finished quietly to himself.

Clare sighed and took a sip of her coffee. Then she started to scroll through her dailies.

Ray sat back in his chair and stared ahead for a minute. Then he took a glance back towards Clare at her desk. He was keeping tabs on her behaviour after everything.

"Don't you dare ask me if I'm okay, Ray." Clare said, before he could ask.

Ray laughed. "What are partners for?" He asked.

"I'm fine!"

"Clare..."

"Just let me focus on work. Please."

* * *

"Simmons!" A voice called at the station.

Ridley looked up from his desk.

"Sarge wants ya!" The other officer barked.

Ridley walked through the halls of our division, with eyes on him as well. Everyone knew we were best friends and after everything the other cops all looked at him too. Only not as a victim. Accusing eyes followed him around everywhere he went. Somehow they thought we were in cahoots or something.

He knocked on Sarge's door when he got there.
"Come in!" His voice yelled from behind it.
Ridley opened the door and walked in to be met not only by Sarge. Dex Finley and Jake Ryan were there too. They had been sitting in chairs, facing Sarge but they both looked back at him when he entered. Dex glared with his stone cold, and Jake smacked his usual gum while smirking.
"Simmons." Sarge greeted him. "Come in. Sit down."
"No, I think I'll stand." He said gruffly, eyeing the two detectives.
Dex and Jake both rolled their eyes and faced forward again.
"Sarge..." Ridley started, looking at him. "What is this?" He looked at the two detectives now. "I already told you guys, I had no idea what John was planning!"
"Calm down, Simmons." Sarge said.
"And how about where he's hiding?" Another voice said from the side. It belonged to a fourth person Ridley hadn't seen when he came in.
Another man, dressed in a detective suit was in the office with them, and Ridley shot him a look.
"Simmons, this is detective Shannon," Sarge said. "From internal affairs."
"Internal affairs?" Ridley asked with a hint of disgust. "Sarge...am I under investigation?"
"You were the last one to speak with him before his exile to the streets." Detective Shannon said. "Did he say anything about where he was going?"
Ridley sighed angrily and had to control his words. "No. I have no clue where he is! Look, John was more than just my partner he was my best friend, do you think I'm okay with him being alone out there? If I knew where he was I'd go and kick his ass and bring him home! I don't need this..."
Ridley turned to storm out.
"Simmons!" Sarge called.
Ridley stopped and closed his eyes in frustration.
"If he is your friend Officer Simmons..." Shannon went on. "...then it's in your best interest to cooperate with this ongoing investigation."
Ridley spun back around to face Shannon again.
"What are his motives, officer?" Shannon pushed.
Ridley sighed and looked down. They all hung on his response. "Look..." He began. "John was a passionate guy. Always was. I can't tell you what he's thinking, what he's doing out there...but...the way he sees the world...it's..."
"It's what?" Shannon pushed more.
Ridley glared at him. "Let's just say, it's not suited for a cop."
Shannon scoffed. "What's that supposed to mean?" He asked.
"It means he's not willing to deal with all the red tape crap to get the job done. He's not one to observe the rules. Not willing to tolerate all the bullshit!"

"Simmons! That's enough!" Sarge hollered.

Ridley stopped and Shannon just stared smugly at him. Then he got up and walked over to him. He produced a card at Ridley and stared at him.

"Well..." He started. "If you think of anything you want to add...you let me know."

Ridley took the card and glared back at Shannon. They stared each other down for a minute until Shannon cracked and scoffed. Then he walked past him.

"I'll be in touch, officer." He said.

The door closed and then Ridley immediately tore the business card in half and threw the pieces on the floor.

Then he turned to Sarge and the other detectives.

"What the hell was that, Simmons!?" Sarge asked angrily.

"Sarge, c'mon. That guy's an asshole!"

"It's his job to be an asshole. How else is another cop supposed to investigate other cops? We're all assholes! Get yourself together!"

Ridley sighed. "I'm sorry, sir. I'm coming off my last night shift. I just wanna get home."

"Simmons." Dex Finley began. "We're friends with the Mash family. Clare's our girl, and John was our friend too. We just wanna see him come in and be safe. That's all."

"It's like I said to numb nuts guys..." Ridley began. "If I knew where he was I'd be going after him myself, believe me."

Ridley got home just as his kids and wife were off to work and school. He chugged some juice from the fridge and slowly made his way up the stairs. In the process, he passed by their home office and den when he had the sudden urge to do something. Something he thought might ease his pain a little bit. He sauntered into the den and went to the bookshelf to recover something.

Once he was in bed with the yearbook of our graduating class he began to skim through. He found the section where I had signed and he read it.

'Rid,
One goal. One mission.
The academy won't know what hit 'em!
Can't wait to be there with you man!
Here's to changing the world!
Potato. Fries!
Brother for life,
John.'

Ridley chuckled at the irony of my statement to him back then.

"Damn you, John..." He said softly to himself. "I hope you know what the hell you're doing, man." He shook his head, and he flipped through more pages.

He found a picture of me and him and smiled. He stopped when he found the image he had been thinking about since detective Shannon had asked him where he thought I was.

It was a picture of me, him and our older buddy Dave. The three of us were laughing and looking at the camera.

Dave held his little blonde baby daughter in the picture. She was leaning over, away from Dave and trying to reach for me and she had a huge smile on her face.

She was sweet as pie.

Little blue eyed Maggie!

* * *

G left his house in the slums early that day, and got into the downtown core by mid-morning. He was walking towards the usual spot where his group congregated and he entered through the alley that led behind the building.

He had had been walking along with his head down, thinking long and hard about our conversation last night. He glanced up and over, nonchalantly, at the bricks and he had to double take when it caught his eye.

A white symbol, scratched into the bricks.

G couldn't believe it.

He reached up and touched the bricks gently and he could tell it was carved in by a rock or knife or something.

A simple little circle with two intersecting lines crossed inside of it. One that matched the one I drew on the note I placed on Sexrex's brother. He stared wide-eyed at it with his mouth open. Then he marched off behind the building.

He came out into the opening and the group was sparse. Hank and Linda were there, and Tom.

"Where's everyone else?" G asked.

"Ken's working..." Tom said. "He got another side job."

"Bart?" G asked.

Tom shrugged. "He's off doing his own thing."

G nodded and looked at the other two. "Hey guys." He said to them.

"Morning." They both said.

"Was John here?" He asked, pointing towards where he saw the symbol.

Tom shook his head. "Nope. Was he supposed to be?"

G sighed and looked back behind him at the alley again. Then back to Tom and he shook his head. "No." He said. And he stopped to think about who might have drawn that symbol.

"G?" Tom asked. "You ok?"

G snapped out of it, not realizing how long he had drawn away to think. He just stared at Tom blankly—

—"G!!" A frantic voice cut in. It was distant and echoing down from somewhere.

"G!!" It called again, a little louder this time.

G's face turned to concern and he and Tom shared a worried glance.

"That's Bart." G said.

Then they both turned to start looking for the source of the panicked voice.

"G!!" Louder and closer, the voice echoed again down the alley ways. They could hear hard slaps on concrete from running feet.

"Bart!?" G called back.

"G!!" Bart answered, and his voice was no longer echoing, but clear and present within the square of where they were.

G and Tom spun around to see him running in from the side, and their eyes went wide at the sight of him.

"Bart!" G cried, rushing to his aid. "What the hell happened to you!?"

Bart was bleeding from his head and he looked roughed up. He collapsed into G's arms as he got there and G eased him down.

"Whoa, whoa, buddy...take it easy." G said, lowering him. "What happened!?"

"Se..." Bart wheezed. He was out of breath from running, and taking heaving breaths. "John!..." He wheezed barely. "Sexrex!" He panted.

G's eyes widened again and he grabbed Bart by the collar. "What did John do, Bart!?"

Bart shook his head to disagree with G and his mouth made the word 'no' without him actually saying it. "Sexrex...he...he took them!"

"He took them!? Took who!?"

"I got away! *(cough)* But John, and...*(cough)...*"

"John and who!?"

Bart grabbed G's collar now and looked straight at him intensely. "Jeannine!"

G's heart stopped and he felt a flush of fear turn over in his stomach.

"He's got Jeannine, man!" Bart cried, and then went into a coughing fit.

Tom, Hank and Linda all panicked and G just stared back at Bart in horror.

"Why, Bart!?" He asked. "What happened!? What were you doing!?" He shook him as he asked.

Bart sighed heavily and lowered his head. "You're not gonna like it, man." He said. "John and I were talking—"

G snapped and shook him harder. "That son-of-a-bitch got to you!?" He asked.

"No!" Bart snapped back. "He didn't recruit me...I volunteered."

"Bart, you stupid bastard!"

"I've had enough, G!" Bart hollered back. He shook off G's grip and scooted up into a more stable sitting position. "We used to stand for something didn't we!?" He went on, glaring at G. "In the beginning? I'm done out here! Enough is enough!"

G glared back and sighed, looking away to the ground. "So what happened then!?" He asked harshly.

"The three of us were walking along. That's it—"

"Going after his friend Maggie?!" G cut in angrily.

"We were talking about it!" Bart replied. "Just talking...Sexrex's goons pulled up and grabbed us.

More clamour rose up from Tom, Hank and Linda. G steadied them with his hand, still looking eagerly at Bart.

"How'd you get away?" He asked Bart.

"We fought back. John smashed a couple of the goons down but they knocked him out. I fought too, but they cracked my skull as you can see. I ran! I ran to come get you guys! We gotta go help them!"

G paused, only for a moment, staring intensely back at Bart. He breathed in slowly trying to calm his nerves and heartbeat.

Then he looked to Tom, who only returned the same expression. Then G looked over to Hank and Linda. Finally he looked back to Bart who was standing to his feet now. Then he slowly nodded.

"Ok..." He said. "We go. But we need to go and get Ken. Tom, where is he?"

"I know where he is." Bart said. "It's on the way."

G looked to Tom who began to look worried at what they were about to do. "Let's go, Tom." He said.

"G...we can't..." Tom said.

"Jeannine is like my little sister, Tom! She's my responsibility." Then he looked towards Hank and Linda with concern. They nodded back to signal that it was ok. Then G looked at Bart.

"Let's go."

* * *

Once again,

I was in trouble.

Once more, in the lion's den.

My ears rang and all I could hear was an echoey sound like emptiness. My head was spinning when I came to

My eyes snapped open and I jerked my head up with a gasp. There was a bright light in my face and I squinted immediately from the shooting pain stabbing my eyes. I breathed in and out trying to focus until I slowly adjusted to the room. I could feel the sweat pouring out of me and my clothes were soaked with sweat. I couldn't move my hands as they were tied up behind the chair I was sitting in. My feet too, when I looked down. I looked all around the room and it was some sort of warehouse. Then I started to piece together the events that led me here, just as Bart described to G. We had only been

talking, but Sexrex came to us! His goons pulled up and grabbed Jeannine and I. I hadn't seen that Bart had got away.
"Bart!!??" I called into the emptiness. "Jeannine!!??"
Nothing. Only the echo back of my voice. I sighed out a massive breath and threw my head back in frustration. "Ahh!!!" I breathed out. I lowered my head back down and began looking around again. "Bart!!??" I called into the darkness again. "Jeannine!!??" I panted. Then I looked around when I got an idea. "Maggie!!??" I called. "Maggie!! Are you here!!??" I panted again. Then I grew angrier. "Sexrex!!" I screamed.
But my voice just echoed back to me—
—and the despairing thought sunk in, that Sexrex wouldn't be as generous to me this time...

* * *

G rushed through the city with Bart and Tom.
"It's just up here!" Bart announced.
They came up on a big fenced in area where they were digging foundations for a new building. G passed Bart and began smashing the chain link.
"Ken!!" He started to call.
"Ken!!" Bart repeated.
They both started banging on the chain link now. They both scanned the area rapidly until they spotted his big six foot frame towering over the other guys.
"There he is!" Bart called, pointing.
"Ken!!" G started calling again.
"Ken!!" Bart repeated.
They both repeated it over until Ken finally turned to face the noise with a confused expression. His brow furrowed even more when he saw his friends all banging on the chain link and calling his name. He looked around the worksite and sighed, before shuffling over towards them.
"What the hell guys!?" He asked, looking around for his boss. "You're gonna get me fired!"
"Jeannine's gone man!" Bart pleaded with him.
"What?"
"Sexrex took her."
"What!?" Ken's eyes went wider and he gripped the fence tighter.
"John too."
Ken sighed and hung his head. "Why?" He asked, looking back up at them.
"Probably in retaliation to John's attack on his club." G said. "C'mon man..." He went on, pleading with Ken. "We can't just leave Jeannine there, bro...we need your help."
Ken looked deeply and conflicted into G's face while leaning on the fence. He sighed hoarsely before answering.
"Give me a minute." He said in a gruff voice.

Bart slammed his hand against the chain link in excitement and G nodded sharply.
Then Ken pushed off the fence and trotted away.

A few moments later Ken was dropping a nylon work bag of tools at their feet. It clanged and gonged as it flopped onto the ground.
"What's this?" Tom asked.
"What'd you think you're gonna go up against Sexrex with?" Ken asked.
"Your hands?"
G bent down and opened the bag. He pawed through a hammer, a cut off piece of pipe, some chains, screwdrivers, crowbars, and other various things. G looked back up to Ken.
"This'll do." He said.
Ken nodded back and then bent over to pick up the bag again.
"K, guys..." G said looking at the other 3. "Let's go get 'em."

* * *

Israel.
 The Globe-X worksite,
  abandoned by its founder and his lab partners.
A black SUV pulled up to the security gates that surrounded the site. Men on guard remained posted, and heavily armed, while the technicians inside maintained the stability of the equipment.
Inside the car, a faceless man sat behind the wheel. Who knew shadows could drive? The dark shadowy face that looked like plumes of smoke turned to look behind him at the old man in the back seat.
"S?" He asked, anticipating his orders.
"Go ahead 'W'." Ranston, the old devil acknowledged.
Immediately the driver pulled the SUV up towards the gates and opened the back passenger side window where Ranston was.
"Mr. Ranston?" The security guard asked. "To what do we owe the pleasure sir?"
"Mr. Richter has asked me to come down and inspect the machine while he's away."
"By all means." The guard said. Then he stepped back and motioned for his colleagues to open the gates. There was a buzz and a metallic rattling sound as the gate began to slide open on a track.
Ranston smiled at the guard, who returned a nod, and W drove the car forward as Ranston disappeared behind the tinted glass window as it closed.
The SUV rolled through and came to the edge of the giant bowl of earth where down in the centre was the smaller ring. The receiver tower was on the far left corner of the bowl and the control module was next to that. A small team of scientists was down there monitoring the machine.

After they had suited up in radiation suits the lift carried them down there and Ranston and W approached the team of techs.

"Good afternoon gentlemen." Ranston greeted with a muffled voice behind his mask.

"Ah, Mr. Ranston." One of them said from behind his own mask. "What brings you here?"

"Just here to oversee the project while Richter is away." Ranston answered. "I'm still in awe of his work." He continued. "I like to see the magic behind the scenes.

"Well you came at a good time." The technician said, turning back to the console. "We're having a hell of a time keeping the energy at bay." He started clicking buttons and adjusting a few faders. "Richter's actually pissed. I dunno if you heard, but someone turned the ring on in China."

"Yah..." Ranston said. "I heard about it..."

"That wasn't set to be turned on for a while. But now that it has, all the energies are aligning. We're trying to keep it at bay to control the radiation levels but...it's too strong. That's why we're forced to go this weekend!"

"And the device." Ranston started. "The stabilizer they took with them. The one that controls everything?"

"No, we control everything from here. It's a dead stick over there. *This* console controls it. It's linked, but only if we push the right buttons. As long as the link is turned off on this end it's just for display."

"Hmm. Interesting."

"Yah, I dunno who turned everything on. Maybe it was just an accident. I mean, who would do that?" The tech turned to ask his question.

"Someone with their own agenda, I suppose." Ranston replied coyly. Then he looked to W who was beside him and gave a sharp nod.

Immediately the radiation suit crumbled to the ground in a heap as the material form inside transformed into a shadowy formless mass. The dark shape whipped over to the other end of the console and then sliced through all of the other technicians like a long blade. They all let out screams as they fell dead onto the surface of the console. The lead tech they had been talking to started to panic and he stumbled back onto the console in paralyzing fear. He stared wide eyed in horror at the floating black cloud hovering behind Ranston now.

The tech huffed and panted heavily and just stared in shock. "You!" Was all he could stutter out.

"Yes, me." Ranston answered.

W formed into a sharp pointed shape again and gusted suddenly towards the tech.

SLITCH!!

The tech couldn't even scream, but he let out a gurgled grunt as the bladed shape gutted him through. W hoisted him up off the ground and brought him closer to Ranston, who took his radiation mask off now, dropping the facade.

"Show me which button to push." He whispered hoarsely to the man.

W flipped him around with the spike still through him and the tech groaned and cried in pain until he was facing the control panel now. W hovered his body in the air above it. The tech pointed to the button desperately, hoping they would spare him. Ranston simply smiled.

"Thank you." He said. "W. We're done with him."

W's spear like shape thrust outwards now, like an explosion and the man's body shredded into nothing. Then W returned to a regular formless mass beside Ranston.

"Good work, W." Ranston said. "Now it's time to clean up."

W whisked away again, in a swirl, and he swooped past the bodies of the technicians who lay dead on the console. As he passed through their bodies again, their forms rose up and had life in them—but not their own. A new dark life force controlled by W himself. Lastly, his shapeless form now morphed into a new man. The likeness of the lead technician now stood before Ranston and he smiled.

"Perfect, my dear W...perfect." Ranston said sinisterly.

Then he stepped past W and went to the button the old tech had showed him. He chuckled and paused.

"Queen, to Bishop 3..." He said in a dark voice.

Then he pushed the button to activate the uplink to Richter's stabilizing device in D.C. He smiled again and turned to face his subordinate.

"You stay here." He ordered.

"Yes, Master." The new W said.

Ranston walked away, digging into his pocket. He pulled out his precious coin and flipped it around in his fingers.

CHAPTER TWENTY ONE
Luck of the Irish

Richter's flight soared majestically through the sky. Even *he* couldn't help stare out into the clouds. The sky wasn't just blue. It was a deep and royal blue. So deep that it was almost dark. It drew him in like he was being hypnotized. It was such an enormous sky! The sun was dazzling up here, more so than seeing it from land. It lit up the tops of the clouds as their flight soared above them. It created such drastic shades and shadows. The clouds looked fake. They looked like cotton candy that he could reach out and pluck a chunk off, almost good enough to eat.

The cabin dinged, breaking Richter's pleasant thoughts, as the pilot came on to announce their descent into Washington.

Several moments later the plane sunk into those fluffy clouds and Richter's little window filled up with the colour grey. Several more moments later they dropped out of the bottom of the clouds and Richter could see land.

The roar of the airplanes engine screamed across the approaching runway and the landing gear squealed as they hit the tarmac.

Richter hugged himself awkwardly, holding his carryon bag tight to his chest, as passengers all clamoured around him trying to be the first ones off. He cringed as they bumped him and got to close for comfort. They reached for their carryons, and rubbed their butts on his arm and shoved their junk in his face. He grew to the point of claustrophobia until Ernest slapped him on the shoulder.

"C'mon, Jay!" He invited. "We're the last ones."

Richter sighed and loosened his grip on his bag as he looked around the empty fuselage. Then he slowly stood up and went with Ernest and Donald who had waited for him.

Richter sighed and rolled his eyes when he saw the little twerp, Kitch, waiting for them at the bottom of the escalator. Kitch was stewing with annoyance and looking at his watch.

"There's a little thing called customs, Kitch!" Richter said as they reached the bottom.

Kitch sighed in annoyance and dropped his arm. "Will there be customs with your machine, I wonder?" He asked sarcastically.

"Is that supposed to be funny?" Richter asked back.

"Where's the payload?" Kitch asked.

"What, you think I carry something like that on me?" Richter asked. "It's a little big for the overhead compartment there, Kitch. It's in check you dumbass!"

Ernest and Donald both chuckled, and Kitch shot them a look of disapproval. They just shrugged and kept laughing.
Then Richter pushed passed him, shaking his head.
"Jet lag." Donald offered, as he too passed Kitch.
And all three men walked past him towards the checked luggage area.
Kitch turned and watched them. "Indeed." He whined to himself.

Sure enough, the four of them were soon sitting in a crowded waiting area. The airline had misplaced their luggage.
"How could this happen!?" Kitch complained. He was on the phone pacing back and forth. "This piece of tech is the most important piece of the whole machine!"
Richter sat, leaning forward onto his lap, holding his face in his hand. He just stewed. Donald sat beside him, ignoring Kitch.
"No the attendant said it probably ended up on the next flight!" Kitch went on with the person on the other end of his phone. "I know this is bad PR!" He went on some more. "Now do you see what I'm dealing with!?"
Richter just shook his head and kept looking forward.
Then something distracted him. He had just been staring out at people, not really paying attention, but this little boy stepped on his toes as he ran by.
"Ouch!" He yelped as he startled back. Angrily he got himself ready to give a good tongue lashing. He hadn't realized it was a little boy, and he stopped short when he did. He still didn't care, in his grumpy way, and he glared at the boy as he frolicked away giggling. The little boy had his coat tied around his neck like a cape and he was wearing a homemade mask. He was striking super poses and making all the mouth sound effects to go along with his game. Richter was just about to go over and teach the kid a lesson but someone else beat him to it. A frumpy, miserable old lady who probably never had kids came trotting over and got in the kids face. He stopped and began to stare at the ground. She waved her ugly finger in the kids face and continued to berate him about proper little boy behaviour that she was obviously an expert about, until the father came over and scooped up the boy.
"What's going on here!?" He demanded of the woman.
Richter watched as the woman lectured the man on his parenting skills and all the social injustices she was a defender of.
Then a funny thing happened. A very unusual thing for Richter. He felt disgusted at the woman. After all, the child wasn't being overly bad or defiant. He was just having fun. Now all of a sudden he was defending the child in his brain. He wasn't breaking anything, or climbing the walls or being disruptive. He was just being a super hero.
The father told the woman off and Richter found himself celebrating on the inside.
Then a slightly disturbing thought crossed his mind. *I was about to be the one who told off the boy.*

He looked back and saw the man carrying the little boy in his arms who was asking what he did wrong and saying sorry to his daddy. The father shook his head and assured him of the opposite. Then he tickled his side and the boy release the most joyous burst of laughter. Even hardhearted Richter cracked a smile on his face.

"Richter." Donald's voice broke the moment.

Richter snapped out of his people watching and turned to look at Donald.

"What's on your mind Dr?" Donald joked.

Richter chuckled. "Oh nothing..." He replied. "Just that...this may be the first time I've actually been forced to stop."

"What do you mean?"

"I mean, I've been so busy. Ever since I was ten. I've had this drive to finish this damn machine. I haven't taken a break!"

Donald chuckled now too. "Now that can't be true." He said.

"No I'm serious, Don."

"You haven't stopped once in like 60 something years? I find that hard to believe."

"Well, I've gone to the bathroom, eaten my meals, had a coffee, shut down for the night and gone to bed, but...even those times my mind was racing about what was next." Richter stopped and took another look back out to the people he was watching. "Now that the machine is done...I...This is actually nice just sitting here."

Donald gave Richter an inquisitive look now. "You hit your head on the flight or something?" He asked.

Richter just chuckled.

"Here comes Ernest." Donald said.

Richter looked to see Ernest approaching.

"Okay." Ernest said. "They've verified that the package is on the next flight."

"How do they misplace something like that?" Kitch asked. "It's not like it could be confused with a regular piece of luggage."

"I dunno, Kitch, ok? But it's on its way. That flight left a few hours after ours, so it should be right behind us."

Richter sat back and flopped into a slouched position now and he let out a huge sigh, vibrating his lips.

After that few hours passed, they were clamouring at the baggage carousel. Richter shoved his way through the crowd to get to the front. His old grumpy self had come back.

"There it is!" Ernest called from behind him.

A big metal case slid down the conveyor belt and thudded onto the big round track that brought the luggage around.

"Geez!" Richter yelled when he saw it crash down, and he cringed.

Donald wheeled up a luggage dolly and was ready at the side of the belt. When their package came around, both Donald and Ernest grabbed either side and hoisted it on the dolly with loud grunts.
It was a large silver case with Globe-X's logo printed on the top face of it. Richter ran his hand across the top and sighed in relief upon seeing his equipment safe and sound.
"Let's get it out of here." He said to his lab partners. "I need to see if they damaged it."

They got to the car Kitch arranged for them and Donald and Ernest placed the case down with a thud and a grunt.
Richter eagerly unfastened all the clamps.
"Should we really be opening this out in the open like this?" Kitch asked.
Donald and Ernest shrugged, while Richter continued open the lid.
"He knows what he's doing." Ernest said.
Richter flung the lid open fully. There, all encased in pre-shaped foam was his equipment. Richter was happy to see it didn't look at all harmed on first inspection. It was a large piece of tech with a big red radiation symbol on it. He pushed a button that said 'TEST' and a light began blinking.
"I just need to see if the core has been damaged in flight." Richter announced.
Then they all waited while the scanners did their job.
Finally the light remained green and it beeped. A message on the screen read; 'CORE INTACT. LEVELS OK.'
Richter sighed in relief and smiled. "Ok." He said, reaching for the lid and closing it. "We're all set. Let's get it in the car." And he began to fasten all the clamps back up. Then Donald and Ernest stepped up and hoisted the heavy piece of tech up into the open trunk.

* * *

The loud clunking of a door, somewhere in the room I was in, broke my racing thoughts of doom. The second sound of the door hitting the wall after its swing sounded. I couldn't see extra light anywhere and realized the door was behind me. A single pair of feet began echoing their footsteps closer and closer. My heart was pounding with each slow step and I stiffened up in my chair.
The big man himself...
Sexrex rounded my left side and appeared before me once again. He held himself at a distance. Smart man. He stood out of reach and just stared at me. No smirk on his face this time. No smirking goons either. He just stood and cracked his big knuckles. I glared into his eyes and he glared back.
"Where's Maggie you piece of sh—"
"Sssssshhh!!!!" Sexrex put up his hand while loudly shushing me.

I seethed. I panted heavily and angrily, and I burned holes in the back of his head.

"Where's Maggie? Where's Maggie?" He whispered, mocking me. "That's all you want isn't it?" He asked with a hoarse voice. "What about what I want?" He went on.

I panted more, just staring at him.

"Do you know what I want, John Revele?" Sexrex asked harshly.

I didn't respond. I simply stared back and breathed fire at him.

He left a long pause before he took a deep and vengeful look into my eyes. Then he slipped a knife out from his waist line and brandished it at me. It gleamed in the light of the warehouse and shone into my eyes.

"I want my brother back you son-of-a-bitch!" He hissed.

My brow furrowed as I had to give some thought to that statement. When it sunk in, my heart did somersaults and I felt the grave feeling of doom consume me.

Sexrex tightened the grip on his knife.

I knew I was dead.

Staring into Sexrex's vengeful eyes, I was done for. He gripped that knife firmly in his hand and seethed as he glared holes back at me.

"You know..." Sexrex began slowly, lifting the knife up to inspect it as he spoke. "There's this whole stupid legend..." He went on. "...about the luck the Irish are supposed to have." He took one slow step forward. The sound of his foot clomping with a dooming hollow note filled my ears. "I never really bought in to that garbage." He went on, taking another deathly foot clomp. "Seeing as how the Irish are the most unlucky poor souls there are!"

Clomp.

"But, you..."

Clomp.

"You proved me wrong."

Clomp.

"Cuz here you are."

Clomp.

"I found you."

Clomp.

"I'm the luckiest man alive right now!"

Sexrex brought his big ugly mug right up to my face and I saw his hideously scarred eye with the glassy clover iris. Then he brought the knife right in front of my eyes and held it there.

I swallowed a lump in my throat. "I didn't know that guy in the alley was your brother." I said to him.

"Well, how unlucky for you." Sexrex grinned behind the knife.

I swallowed another fearful lump and I was sweating profusely.

"But you're not off this easy, officer." He said, lowering the knife. To my surprise he slit the duct tape that bound my feet. "You bashed my brother's face in."

"I had to!" I quivered. "He was gonna kill me! You guys are huge, how else was I supposed to stop him?"
"You could have just run off like a good little piggy."
This comment snapped me back into my right mind set. I chuckled. "That's not my style man." I said. "Your brother was raping and killing that girl."
"The girl?" He laughed. "That ain't nothin'. Just another bitch. She ain't worth dying for, man. You wasted your time."
My eyes burned against his. I seethed and panted as I stared at him now.
"You and I are gonna settle this." He said.
"Untie me from this chair and we'll see what happens." I hissed.
"That's fully my intention." He replied.
We stared each other down for a long while, seeing who would break first. Then I suddenly thought of something. A smirk came to my lips.
Sexrex returned the grin.
"Something on your mind, cowboy?" He asked.
My smile grew and I started to chuckle. "I just thought of something." I said.
"Please share." Sexrex invited sarcastically.
"Hahahaha!" I laughed in his face. "I'm Irish too! Ahahahaha!"
Sexrex chuckled. "Revele?" He asked. "That doesn't sound Irish, my doomed friend."
I laughed louder. "Hahaha! It's French! On my father's side! Hahaha!"
Sexrex laughed out loud. "French-Irish?" He asked. "Huh...interesting"
I laughed some more. "Maybe I'll get some of that luck today, eh!?"
"Hey I just thought of something too." He said. He laughed. "What if that night...the girl you had to save was your girl, Maggie?" Then he let out a huge bellowing laugh right in my face. I could smell his stinking breath and saliva on my skin.
SMASH!!
I jolted my head forward and smashed his nose with all I had. He stumbled back and I very quickly stood up with my hands still tied behind the chair and I swung the chair as a weapon, cracking him on the side with the legs of the chair. He fell to his right and crashed to the ground. I saw the knife still in his hand so I acted quickly, spinning into an attack position with the legs over his hand and I sat down in the chair to crush it underneath the corner leg.
"*AAAAAHHH!!!*" He screamed out and his hand splayed outwards.
I gave the chair a vicious twist to crunch his bones a little more and then I stood up fast and kicked the knife away that it slid far away across the warehouse floor. Sexrex rolled over and held his hand screaming. I kicked him in the face and then started to run, knowing I couldn't fight while I was tied to chair. I ran in the direction of the knife and could hear other footsteps rushing towards the scene from the other side of the door. Most likely his goons. I slid on my knees to get to the knife faster and I flipped around to grab the knife with my hands. I fumbled with it to get the sharp edge facing the tape, but the door burst open!

Here we go again...I thought.

A half dozen guys poured in and rushed towards me. The only thing I could do was charge at them full force crying a war cry as I did.

SLAM!!

I twisted sideways at the last second to cover more territory and slammed into two guys at the same time. I landed on top of them and another one of the four tripped against the protruding chair legs and tumbled over behind me. One of them raised his leg to stomp me but I got up and moved so that his foot landed on one of the chair legs and snapped it off. I body checked one of the other two men and we went towards the wall together. I thudded him against the wall and pressed into him to hold him there. The other 5 guys all got up now and headed towards me. One of them picked up the chair leg that had broken off and came at me with it. I still had the knife but couldn't do much with it behind my back. I wasn't letting go of it though.

CRACK!

"Ahh!!" I cried out when the goon hammered the side of my arm with the chair leg.

POW!

A fist landed a solid strike across the opposite side of my face and my head jerked the other way. I ripped myself off the guy I was holding against the wall and rolled away from everything, just ducking the bear hug of one of them. Because I stumbled, I fell backwards hard on the back two legs of the chair, snapping them off too. This also caused me to drop the knife. I rolled away into a stand and missed the kick of a goon. His kick missed and snapped off the last leg of the chair.

CA-CLICK!

The unmistakable sound of a cocking hammer stopped me dead in my tracks. I looked up to see the muzzles of 3 guns facing me. The other two goons cocked their hammers too.

"STOP!!" Sexrex's voice called out.

He came clomping over, holding his broken hand and grimacing. The other 3 goons all rounded the front of me holding the chair legs as weapons. One of them handed the knife to Sexrex. I panted heavily, lowering my head.

I couldn't help but laugh to myself.

"Here we are again, Sexy!" I hollered looking back up at him.

"I'm gonna make your face look like my brother's face!" He steamed—

—*CLANG!!*

A loud metallic gong echoed and Sexrex crumbled to the floor!

Bart appeared behind him and smashed one of the guys pointing a gun at me down with the long piece of pipe he had as a weapon. Rattling chains echoed and then whipped across the arms of the two other gun brandishing goons, coiling around their hands and binding them.

I looked to the right.

Ken yanked the chains hard and pulled the two guys by their arms so they stumbled and fell.

"John, get up!!" A voice called.

I looked to the left and saw G charging in behind, sporting a claw hammer as a weapon.

A fight broke out between the other 3 goons and G, and Bart who joined him by his side.

Ken kicked one of the armed goons across the face and yanked his chain off their arms. Then he whipped the third guy in the face with it.

"C'mon, John, let's go!!" He called to me.

I struggled up to my feet and moved towards the door. G and Bart turned the fight around so that their backs were facing the door too and they were in escape position. I looked and saw Tom at the door, holding it open.

"C'mon, cmon!!" He shouted.

I ran towards him.

Ken joined G and Bart and they were able to fight back the other 3 goons together.

They each were able to push their opponents away to create enough distance and make a break for it.

As they ran for the door, the 3 armed goons raised their guns up and fired.

BLAM, BLAM, BLAM, BLAM, BLAM, BLAM, BLAM!!!

Shots rang out and splintered into the wood, and pinged off the metal walls.

PING, PING, PING!!!

The last three shots ricocheted off the steel door as Tom pulled it closed. A final bullet dented through and a small bump where the bullet almost broke through, popped out right by Tom's face. He looked at it wide eyed and gasped.

"Guys!!" I cried out. "How did you find me!?"

Bart cut the tape around my hands and what was left of the chair fell to the ground. I brought my hands up and began rubbing my wrists. I looked at all the guys who came to save me.

Before I could say anything, Ken was grabbing me by the arm and rushing me away.

"Let's get out of here!" G ordered.

And we rushed away from the door.

Moments later Ken was thudding against an exit door and it slammed open. Daylight poured in and it hurt my eyes so that I had to shield my vision with my hand. The rest of the guys went through and I stepped slowly through looking up to the sky. As my eyes adjusted I lowered my arm and saw a familiar sight. To my surprise I saw the big neon sign to Sexrex's night club. The sun was low as evening approached and it was a bright ball cresting the tops of most of the high rises.

Bart slammed the door behind us and then rushed over to the dumpster lining the wall beside the door.

"C'mon help me with this!" He shouted.

Ken ran over with me and we all shoved hard against the side of it. It skidded and scraped the pavement as we struggled to slide it in front of the door, but we got it there and puffed and panted when we were done.

"Let's put the other one there too!" I suggested.

With a sigh the three of us ran to the second dumpster.

"C'mon, c'mon!" I shouted.

We had to pull this one away from the wall in order to slide it in front of the first one and then we heaved on the side of it to slide it in place up against the other one.

Just as we finished, there was a strong slam against the back of the door that made us all jump. The door did open a crack but stopped against the dumpsters.

The five of us then bolted around to the other side of the building.

Before I could do anything else, I felt a strong tug on my clothes and then I was slammed up against the wall by G.

"Where's the girls, John!?" He yelled.

"G! I don't know!" I answered. "They separated us! How did you find me!?"

"We came here!" G said, pointing to the sign with his hammer still in his hand.

"Are you okay?" Bart asked me.

"I'm alright, man. We gotta get Jeannine."

"Yah, no shit!" G asked, pushing into me a little.

I shoved him off of me forcefully. "Back off, G!"

He stumbled back a few steps but returned in my face. We stared each other down. "G..." I stared. "I got a friend in there too, man. Don't make this about only you. C'mon, man! Make this about everything! Make this about your city! Make this about your world!"

G and I stared at each other for a long moment.

"We have to stop him." I added.

G sighed and dropped the stare, taking a step back. I sighed too.

"Guys..." Tom piped in. "I hate to break this up but Sexrex's guys are gonna be out here soon and after us."

"He's right." Ken said. "We better get out of here. We got you back, John. We have to regroup somewhere."

A few moments later we were hiding across the street behind another building and peeking out. Sure enough we saw Sexrex's guys eventually shove hard enough to move the dumpsters to a spot where they could open the door and get out. The six guys rushed out and began to run towards the club next door. Sexrex stomped out holding his hand still, and he looked menacingly around the area.

"Go back to the club and get those bitches on a truck to D.C.!" He yelled at his goons. "Now!! They'll be coming for them!"

I gasped. "D.C..." I said, looking back towards G. "We gotta hurry up, man."

"We need an army to get in there." Tom said.

We ducked back in behind the building to talk. I sighed deeply and tried to focus.

"How did you know I was in here?" I asked Bart, looking at him now.

"Sexrex always conducts his other business in that warehouse." He said. "It's a known fact on the streets. Hides in plain sight."

I realized this was probably the place I was beaten in the first time and I turned to look at the building. A faded sign above it said it was an old sporting goods warehouse.

"We just took a shot in the dark." Bart said. "We got lucky."

"Lucky!?" I asked, with a sudden smirk. I had to laugh at that!

"We gotta get in the club and find Maggie." I said. "And find Jeannine." I added, looking strongly at G.

"They've got guns, John!" Tom piped in.

"John..." G stared with a desperate tone in his voice. "This is helpless, bro." His breathing was quickening.

"Maybe we should just call the police." Tom added.

"And tell them what, Tom?" I snapped. "That Sexrex runs an escort service? You think they don't already know that? You forget I was one?"

Tom sighed in frustration.

"G!" I said turning to him desperately. "If he gets Jeannine out there, he'll pump her so full of drugs she'll barely remember you!"

G couldn't hold my penetrating gaze and he lowered his head.

"He'll put her to work!" I continued. "He'll force her to do things against her will! Unspeakable things! Slimy men, will use her up and spit her back out!"

G's breathing quickened even more and he was getting upset.

"They'll beat her! Sexrex will beat her!"

G looked up with a new conviction in his eyes. He was taking all this information and letting it fuel him. I didn't need to go on, but I did.

"If we let her get out of Baltimore..." I went on. "...she'll be sold to another guy, just like Sexrex! Or worse! And this isn't a Liam Neeson movie! She'll be so lost into the sex trade that you'll never find her again!"

G seethed. He breathed through his gritted teeth and burned his eyes at mine. "We can't let that happen, John!" He said.

I glared back and nodded. "That's right." I said. "Now...do you see how I feel about Maggie?"

G closed his lips and clenched his jaw tightly. He kept on panting; heaving, angry breaths. "What do we do?" He asked.

"We go in there." I said staring right back at him.

Then I looked away from him and at the other 3 men, panning across their faces. "Please, guys..." I asked them. "I need your help."

"Me too, guys." G added.

Tom's face grew worried and he looked down.

Bart nodded slowly.

"They'll kill us!" Tom said, looking back up. "I still say we should let the cops handle this one. I'm sorry John, but...maybe you need to sit this one out. Either that or it's time for this mission of yours to come to an end."

I was staring at the ground and I could feel all their eyes on me now—All expecting an answer. Then I nodded in agreement somberly.

"I dunno, John..." Ken began. "There's gonna be more of them. How are five guys gonna take down his whole gang? And you heard what he said. We're not gonna be able to catch a truck!"

I sighed and looked up to the big neon sign of the club. That sun was dropping fast behind the building.

"Well then..." I began. "Maybe you guys are right. Maybe this is a job for the cops." But I smirked cheekily to myself and then looked at Bart. "And I know just the one." I said.

Bart paused but then smiled when he realized who I was talking about.

"The goon squad." He said.

I smiled back. "The night shift is coming." I said.

"As for the truck..." G chimed in. He looked to Ken dramatically. The rest of us all followed his gaze and we're looking at Ken now too. He shrugged.

"Why is everyone looking at me?" He asked.

CHAPTER TWENTY TWO
A Night on the Town

Sexrex tore through the crowds of dancing club goers and partiers, surrounded by his cronies. All of them had a hand on their waste lines or in their jackets on guns they were ready to use. The strobe lights all flashed and the base pumped in their ears as they urgently made their way up to Sexrex's loft by the big stair case. Sexrex couldn't help but remember the last time he had encountered me up here.

They made their way into their back private room and closed the door.

"Radio the boys downstairs!" Sexrex ordered. "Tell 'em to be on lookout for that little asshole!"

One of them immediately got on the radio, and Sexrex turned to the other guys.

"Let's round up the merchandise and get 'em on a truck out of here! Call ahead to the crew in D.C. Let 'em know we're coming!"

The goons all left his side and scrambled away. Sexrex was left panting and his mind racing.

"You think you're tough with your little friends now, huh?" He asked me out loud, and rhetorically.

The goons tore through the door of another room behind the private room.

"Alright ladies!!" One of them shouted. "Time to go!"

In this room, were all the girls Sexrex pimped out of this club. They were all in beds and they were all lethargic and drugged. The goons grabbed, pushed, and yanked most of them out of bed.

"Get your asses up!" They shouted. "C'mon!"

One little blue eyed, blonde hair girl was on the last bed, so drugged up that she had no idea what was happening, even though she was awake.

Maggie!

Her eyes glossed over and she just stared at the wall amidst the commotion.

Then a strong tug on her arm, and she was being lifted out of the bed and tossed like a rag doll towards the door with the rest of them.

Sexrex watched his guys herd the 'merchandise' as the pig he was called them, out the back door and down some stairs behind the club. Then he turned and marched out of the private room, to a blast of base and strobe lights, across the loft and to the edge of the railing to look out into his club.

He watched the crowds and the front door.

"C'mon..." He murmured to himself. "Come on through that door you bastard..."

303

"Boss!" One of his guys yelled behind him, without getting his attention. Sexrex had begun to stare, wild eyed and obsessively.

"Boss!!" His guy yelled louder.

"What!?" Sexrex snarled around like a rabid animal.

"We're all set!!" His guy yelled.

Sexrex remained there panting, looking back and forth to down into the club and back at his goon. Then he slowly walked away backwards from the banister, until the front door was out of sight, and then he turned to leave with his guy.

I counted 4 bouncers standing outside the front doors of the club. One for each of us. The commotion slowly built in the lineup of clubbers trying to get in for the night. The confused chatter rose into more panicked voices and then screams and shouts as people saw the sight of four guys charging at the club, armed with various items.

I charged in first and swung my baseball bat at the side of the first bouncer I came to.

WHACK!

A hard thud into the side of his chubby love handles. He let out a groan and the crowd screamed and scattered. The bouncer fell to his knees and I held the bat like a rolling pin now and gave him a quick jab to the throat.

"*Oohcck!!*" He choked and grabbed his neck as he fell back.

A bouncer reached at Bart as he came in but Bart quickly slashed at his arm like a hockey stick—

—*CLANG!!*

With his long piece of metal pipe. Then—

—*CLANG!!*

Again the metal gonged as Bart quickly whisked the pipe upwards to strike the bouncer down.

G ran up behind the third bouncer and put him in a chokehold. As he squeezed, the bouncer tried punching frantically without being able to hit him. He began to pound on G's arms but G wouldn't let go. He just winced and grimaced from the hits, but slowly guided the bouncer down to the ground.

Tom came running in, brandishing a crowbar out of Ken's tool bag. He shook it nervously and hesitated too long. Long enough for the final bouncer to pull his gun out and point it at him.

I swung my bat as fast and hard as I could as his finger went for the trigger—

SLAM—BAM!!

I cut down his hand with the bat just as he squeezed. Tom jumped back as the bullet hit the ground at his feet. The bouncer dropped the gun and then I used the heavy end of the bat and jammed it into his stomach.

"OOF!!" He spat and heaved, and he keeled over to a bent over position, then—

—*POW!*

I shot out a knee and struck him in the side of the head to send him to the ground.

G had the bouncer to sleep now and he twisted him away from his grip and dropped him on the ground.

Panting, I turned to face Tom. He was frozen and just gripping the crowbar still, staring wide eyed at the bodies.

The crowd of people were all still panicking and shouting. I turned to see the glow of a hundred cell phones aimed at us.

"Get the guns." I said, spinning the bat, that I picked up from that sporting goods warehouse, in my hand. "I like this thing." I said to myself.

I turned and Bart and G were slipping the pistols out of the waist bands of their bouncers. I bent down slipped one off the first guy I knocked over and then I scooped the one that fell out of the other one's hand. I turned to Tom and looked at him as I tucked one of them behind my pants. I flipped the second gun around, faced the hilt towards him and he just stared at it.

I gestured the whole gun towards him urgently and he hesitantly took it with a sigh.

"C'mon, we gotta move!" I said to everyone else.

Behind the club, the rear exit door burst open. An idling truck waited as the goons all walked their 'product' line of girls towards it. Another goon waited at the back of the truck with the cargo door open. He ushered the girls in as the other goons shoved them up onto the truck.

Sexrex marched through the club door too and looked all around, paranoid. He had his gun out and he gripped it tightly as he walked towards the truck.

An escalade was parked behind the truck and he headed towards it. He looked around once more before climbing in and closing the door.

SMASH!!

We kicked the doors of the club open and rushed in with our guns ready. G and Bart both knocked out the two extra bouncers who were posted inside the doors. They didn't hear the commotion outside over the loud bass beats.

The strobe lights flashed in our eyes and we swept forward. Our heads were all on a swivel, looking all around for Sexrex's thugs. It was hard to see anything else but the dancing club goers. The crowds parted as individual groups of people noticed us coming through aggressively.

"*MOVE!!*" We each shouted. "*GET OUT OF THE WAY!! CLUB'S CLOSED!!*"

Our guns were drawn but we weren't pointing them at anyone. Their presence was enough though, and people got out of our way and ran for the doors.

"*EYES UP BOYS!!*" I shouted.

The four of us looked all around, constantly pressing forwards towards the back of the club. We looked up to the upper deck loft. A handful of goons were posted to stay behind while Sexrex made off with the girls. One of them hoisted a big machine gun up and over the railing and took aim.

"*HEADS UP!!*" I yelled, ducking down. Diving, I reached for a girl who was in front of me and I drove us both towards the ground.
RATTATATTARATTATATTA!!!
Machine gun fire erupted and everyone in the club stared freaking. G grabbed another kid and ripped him to the ground to protect him.
I lay on top of the girl I took down and aimed my gun upwards at the loft.
BAM, BAM, BAM, BAM, BAM!!
Bart shoved someone out of the way and then took aim himself.
BLAM, BLAM, BLAM!!
The goon retreated and dove behind the railing as our bullets pinged off the metal.
I took the chance to hop up to my feet. "*EVERYONE GET OUT OF HERE!!*" I screamed.
The DJ stopped spinning music and all that could be heard was screaming and clamouring. Crowds rushed the opposite way we were going, some bumping into us as they passed. G and Bart joined my side with their guns pointed up at the loft.
"*C'MON TOM!*" G shouted.
Tom rushed up behind us clumsily with his gun drawn.
"*Stay tight boys!*" I told them. "*Keep your eyes peeled!*"
The four of us stood there with our guns up, waiting for the crowd to dissipate past us.
"*SUCK THIS PIG!!*" A nasty voice shot down from over the loft.
The goon with the machine gun surfaced again and opened fire.
BRRATTATATTARATTATTATATATA!!!
We all dove in different directions. As the bullets pinged at our heels I was diving towards the loft to hide underneath it. I crashed desperately and frantically under it and I rolled until I thudded on the wall behind it. G scrambled under it with me and Bart and Tom were stuck out in the club. Bart scrambled behind a bar on the left side and the gunner turned his focus on him. Glasses and bottles smashed apart and rained down on him as he panted to resting position against the bar.
"*TOM! TOM!*" I screamed. He was behind a table, and the gunner was focusing on Bart.
"*CMON TOM! GET IN HERE! CMON!*"
Tom was frozen. He just cowered behind the table and shook his head no to me.
"*TOM!!*" I cried again.
He still wouldn't dare to move.
Up above us, two more gun men surfaced over the railing with hand guns.
RAATTTAATATTTATTAAATTAAARATTATTA!!!!
The machine gun thug concentrated more fire at the bar where Bart was. He fired it at the wall of glasses and bottles on purpose, and liquor and shards of glass rained down towards Bart who just covered his head with his arms.

"Look down there!!" One of the other thugs commented upon seeing Tom behind the table.

"Oh no." I whispered to myself when I heard them.

They took aim down at Tom—

POP, POP, POP, POP, POP!!--PING, PING, PING, PING, PING!!

They opened fire and their bullets pinged off the metal table and chairs around him.

Immediately I stepped out, grabbed one of the metal chairs by the leg and chucked it into the air, as hard as I could towards the banister. When it crashed against the railing, the three gunmen were startled backwards and the firing ceased.

"*BART!!*" I called over to him, while I had the chance. "*MOVE!!*"

I walked backwards towards where Tom was, a few tables deep, and I raised my gun up.

Bart peeked out from behind the bar with his gun raised. The three men were quickly returning back over the railing.

But I squeezed the trigger first.

BAM, BAM, BAM, BAM!!

I sent up some cover fire as I reached Tom.

BLAM, BLAM, BLAM, BLAM!!

Bart began to fire too, standing and walking towards the cover of the lofted area.

I grabbed Tom by the shirt and hoisted him up. As we ran for the loft too, I fired a couple of cover rounds up at the thugs. I threw Tom under the loft before I made it there myself—

"*BART!!*" I yelled over to him.

BLAM, BLAM!!

He fired a couple more shots up and then made a sprinting dash for the loft.

I kept my gun up and fired while he ran.

BAM, BAM!!

Bart slid safely under the loft and then I dove under too. Bart raised his arm up to point his gun up at the floor under their feet.

"No!" I stopped him. "Don't waste your bullets!"

"What!?" Bart asked. "Why!? We could take him out right now!"

"It's not a Bruce Willis movie, Bart! It doesn't work like that. Trust me, save your bullets."

The four of us panted and took a moment to just collect ourselves. My mouth was dry from breathing so heavily and I licked my lips and swallowed, looking all around.

"I didn't fire any shots, bro." G said. "I still got a full clip."

"Good." I said.

"*You can't hide down there forever little piggy!!*" The nasty voice of the thug above us growled. "*We're gonna getcha!!*"

"Tom." I started. "You okay?" I asked him.

Tom just panted and nodded.
"Good." I said. "So are you gonna start helping us out here?"
Tom sighed and looked down. "I'm sorry, man..." He said. He motioned around with his hands to signify the overwhelming situation. "All this..."
I grabbed him by the collar and glared into his eyes. "Use it!" I said. Then I slapped him in the chest and turned back to the other two.
"I've only got a couple rounds left by my count." I said. "Bart, you've gotta be half empty."
"John..." G said, now reaching over and clutching my arm.
I stopped and looked down at him to see concern.
"We gotta get to Sexrex, bro." He said. "He's gotta have 'em loaded up by now. We gotta get to that truck!"
I sighed. "I know, man." I said. "Let's hope Ken comes through." I said, looking at Bart.

Back behind the club, one of Sexrex's thugs secured the latch on the cargo door of the truck. Sexrex, secure in his Escalade behind the truck, watched as the thug jogged around to the cab section and climbed in.
"Okay, let's go!" Sexrex said loudly. He was looking all over the scene and back to the exit door to see if we were coming.
The trucks engine roared to life as they pulled away slowly. Sexrex fixed his gaze on the exit door as the Escalade began to follow the truck.
They made it down the back lane way a little ways until a dooming sound for them blared.
BLAAMMPP, BLAAAAAAAAAMMP!!
A low toned but loud truck horn blasted from off scene and Sexrex spun his head to the front in time to see it.
"No..." He whispered.
The goons in the cab of the truck looked to their right suddenly and their hearts stopped when they saw it too. A giant cement truck sped in from the intersecting lane way, barreling straight for them!
KERAAAAAASSSHH!!
Metal crunched on metal as the cement truck thundered into the passenger side of the cab like a battering ram! The whole truck was forced to the left by the punch of the cement truck and the front passenger tires even lifted off the ground. The cement truck steered away and drove ahead of the truck as the tires hit the ground again.
"Where do you think you're goin!?" Ken yelled at the drivers from behind the wheel of the cement truck. He sped up and took a big loop around until he parked the truck sideways to block the exit path they would have taken.
Their engine block was smashed in and steaming now. The driver tried to turn it over but was just met with the chugging and choking sounds of the damaged engine.

* * *

Elsewhere...

At the police precinct, my old partner, my loyal friend, Ridley, walked to his desk at shift change and said his greetings and goodbyes to the afternoon crew when they passed him. He sat down and began going through his unfinished paper work from last night's shift.

While he was barely into his work the precinct started buzzing. He looked up from his paper work and saw other officers clamouring. He stood up from the desk to get a better look.

"What's going on!?" Ridley asked another cop as they crossed the front of his desk.

"There's something going on downtown." The cop said. "Shooting at a night club."

"Shooting? Where?" Ridley pressed.

"The Sexrex club."

Ridley paused and looked down in thought. The cop he was talking to rushed away, leaving him to those thoughts.

Ridley had an inkling.

A sudden suspicion based on the location.

He stared at the ground, mulling the idea over...

Could it be? He thought. *Could it be John?*

Who else would go after Sexrex?

Ridley snapped his head back up to watch the other cops. He threw his pen down, forgetting the paper work and he rounded the desk to join his colleagues.

"Simmons!" Sarge's voice called. "No, no, no! Not you!"

Ridley scoffed. "What!? Why!?"

Sarge walked up closer to him now. "We both know why." He whispered.

"It's him, Sarge." Ridley whispered back. "It's gotta be."

"Sshh! I know."

"C'mon, Sarge! Let me have this one!" Ridley pressed urgently. "Please!"

Sarge and Ridley stared at each other intensely. Ridley pleaded with his eyes. Behind Ridley, the internal affairs detective, Shannon, saw the two interacting and stopped what he was doing to lean against the doorframe and cross his arms. Sarge noticed him glaring and sighed. He looked back to Ridley.

"Ok, fine." He said.

Ridley clapped his hand on Sarge's arm and trotted away.

"Hey take the rookie with you!" Sarge hollered after him.

Ridley looked over at the young rookie officer, Jimmy Jimenez and motioned with his hand. "C'mon kid!" He called. "Let's go, hurry up!"

Jimenez scrambled after Ridley.

"You better keep up, Jimenez!" Ridley said to him as he lagged behind his quick steps. "You go get the shotgun out of the gun locker and meet me at the car."

"You got it." Jimenez said, and he scooted off.

Ridley didn't take 5 steps before he slowed down upon seeing him. Detective Shannon was still in the doorframe with his arms crossed. He was staring at Ridley with an arrogant smirk from a short distance away. Ridley glared back and their eyes followed each other's gaze as Ridley crossed the precinct floor towards the garage. Ridley shook his head and turned his back on Shannon to exit into the garage.

He looked around to make sure Jimenez was gone and then he pulled out his phone. As he descended the steps towards the garage, he began typing a text. He stopped at the bottom of the steps to focus and finish.

'We found him.'

Is what he typed in and then he sighed in hesitation briefly before hitting send. A confirmation on his screen read;

'Message sent to: CLARE'

* * *

On the other end of that text, Clare's phone buzzed on her desk. She picked it up and read the message from Ridley.

Clare stopped what she was doing and sat back slowly. All she could do was stare at the words. Then her phone buzzed again in her hands and a second message popped up from Ridley:

'Sexrex. Now!'

Clare gasped and immediately snapped her head up to the newsfeed they had constantly running, which she wasn't paying attention to before. There on the screen was news footage of a reporter in front of the club with the breaking news logo flashed all over.

"Tell us what happened inside?" The reporter asked an escaping club goer.

"I dunno! These guys, they came out of nowhere. One minute I'm dancing, the next I look back with my other girlfriends and the bouncers are fighting with these guys! Gunshots started going off so we got out of there!"

Clare began to look around the room and saw that her team was all busy, including Ray. She could slip out unnoticed.

* * *

"We gotta get back there!" I told the other three I was with. G, Bart and Tom all readied their weapons. "There's an exit back there." I said, pointing to the back corner of the club. "We can make it."

"What are we waiting for?" G asked.

"When I say go," I started. "All of you run as fast as you can for the exit. I'll draw their fire."

Outside.
Sexrex grew impatient.
"Go get that guy!" He ordered his goons, still inside the Escalade.
His goons scrambled and got out of the SUV, all drawing their guns. They readied the guns and marched in a line towards Ken in the cement truck. The other two goons who were in the smashed truck hopped out and marched with them.
"Uh..." Ken said to himself when he saw the dozen armed men walking towards him. "...this is not good."
They opened fire all together and Ken ducked into the passenger seat. As bullets clanged and hit the sides of the truck, Ken crawled desperately towards the passenger side door to open it. He flung it open and dove out of the truck. When he hit the ground, he frantically scrambled to a position against the truck and took cover there.

"Now!!" I yelled to my guys, inside.
The three bolted, out from under the lofted area and straight at the back corner exit. I ran up behind their heels and grabbed another chair leg as I passed. Just as the three goons up top had noticed us making a break for it, I spun around and hurled that chair at the steps leading up to the loft. One of the handgun shooters stumbled back as the chair crashed at his legs.
BANG!
I planted myself and fired with a more careful aim, clipping him in the shoulder. I snapped my aim to the next handgun guy and fired.
POP!
He fell from the centre shot I landed on him, but the machine gun guy now took aim at me.
BAM, BAM, BAM, BAM!!
Shots started sounding from behind me and I watched the thug fall after being hit. I looked back and G was walking up beside me and firing.
BAM, BAM, BAM, BAM, BAM!!
Machine gun guy was forced back and he fell over the handrail of the stairs to flip over and over as he crashed to the ground with a thud.
G looked at me and nodded. I lowered my gun and sighed.
"John, look out!!" Tom's voice cried behind us.
I snapped my attention back and the first guy, who only got clipped in the arm, was raising his gun up again—
—BLAM, BLAM, BLAM!!
Three shots whizzed from behind G and I and the guy was definitely dead now.
We both looked to see Tom, holding the smoking gun. He looked shocked at what he just did, and he lowered his gun and looked at me.

"Thanks, Tom." I said to him.
"Yah..." He said chillingly. "...no problem."
"C'mon!" I ordered and the four of us made for the exit door.

Outside, Ken was pinned down behind the cement truck.
The goons fired short bursts of rounds at the truck just to keep him there.
Sexrex watched nervously from the back seat of the Escalade, gripping his hand gun.

We only pushed the door open a crack, large enough to see what was going on out there. I saw the smashed in truck and smiled.
"Atta boy, Ken!" I whispered loudly.
Then I spied the dozen armed guys and saw they were firing at Ken behind the cement truck. I turned to the three guys.
"We need some more fire power." I said to them. "Sexrex has to keep an arsenal here in his club. Probably up there." I motioned towards the upper deck of the loft.

Several moments later we were shoving the doors open to the room behind the loft. Sexrex's private VIP. There were two big closet doors on the far right side of the room and I immediately rushed over to them. I flung them both open and chuckled.
"Jackpot." I said, upon seeing the impressive arsenal Sexrex kept. Several machine guns with extra magazines, multiple hand guns, and knives.
I grabbed the first machine gun and handed it to Bart. I gave a second to G, and a third to Tom. Then I threw them each a mag.
"This is how you load 'em." I said.
I pushed the clip into the rifle so they could see and then I racked the slide and looked at them.
"Did you see how many guys are out there?" Tom asked. "We can't win this on our own."
"That's why the cops are coming." I said. "We just had to create the action here. That's been done. They'll take 'em out for us! And we'll pick up our girls and get the hell outta here. C'mon let's go!"

Outside in his SUV, Sexrex wasn't going to wait any longer. He flung his door open and got out of the vehicle. He marched over to the smashed up truck and banged on the cargo door.
"C'mon, open up!!" He yelled. "C'mon! C'mon!"
The cargo door rolled open and he was met by one of his thugs.
"Boss?"
"Gimme the girl!" He ordered.
"What? Which one?"
"Who do you think!? The little blondie!! The one he's here for!"

The thug turned to go retrieve Maggie. He grabbed her by the arm and started dragging her out.

"Hurry up!!" Sexrex ordered.

Two thugs jumped down out of the truck and kept guard as the other guy brought Maggie over and tossed her to Sexrex.

"Come on, cutie!" He yelled at her. "Let's go for a ride! Bring me the other one too! The one we kidnapped!"

Sexrex grabbed Maggie by her hair and yanked on it, causing her to scream.

"You know, you're little cowboy friend is giving me a *DAMN HEADACHE!!*" He screamed in her face. Then he moved her by the hair towards the SUV.

He shoved her in the back seat. "Get in there!" He yelled, and then he slammed the door.

He looked and saw the thugs dragging Jeannine out now too.

They brought her over to the Escalade.

"Throw her in there with blondie!" He ordered.

They opened the other door and shoved Jeannine in too.

In the back seat, the two girls gave each other a haunting stare upon meeting.

* * *

The scene in front of the club now was chaotic. All the people who were in the club for a good time were scattering. News crews and police were everywhere.

Sirens wailed continuously as more and more police cruisers pulled up to the scene. Ridley brought their car to a stop and he and Jimenez bolted out of the car, just as S.W.A.T. was pulling in.

Ridley and Jimenez drew their guns and approached the front lines.

"What do we got!?" Ridley asked the Sargent on duty.

"We don't know yet exactly!" The Sargent answered. "We don't know how many shooters or who's who. Witnesses say there were three, maybe four, maybe five guys who came in, and that the bouncers started shooting at these dudes. No one has made any demands yet, but...sounds like some kind of gang war to me."

Ridley stopped to think for a second. "John..." He whispered to himself.

He didn't realize that beside him, Jimenez had heard him say that.

"So what's the play?" Ridley asked the Sargent. "Are we making a move?"

"Soon." He answered. "Now that SWAT's here. We think the fighting has made its way behind the club."

* * *

Behind the club, Ken remained trapped behind the cement truck, but his job of blocking their escape had been carried out.

"Kill that guy, and get that truck out of the way!" Sexrex ordered his guys.

The crew of his thugs began to sweep forward with guns raised. They approached the truck with caution and they carefully began to flank the sides--
RATTATATTARATTATATTA!!!
One or two of the goons fell as our gun fire burst in!
Me and the other three came rushing in from the right with our weapons drawn.
The rest of the goons whipped around and returned fire.
BRATTATATTATATTA, BRATTATATTATATTA!!
We dove behind some dumpsters for cover and their bullets whizzed over our heads and pinged off the metal dumpsters as we fell behind them.
"Where's the Cavalry, John!?" G asked me.
I panted and rested my head against the dumpster. "They'll be here." I said. I stood up and shot some return fire at the goons and quickly ducked back down. It went back and forth like this as each of us popped up and ducked back down, back and forth as we returned fire.
I was able to peek around the edge of the dumpster I was covering behind and I saw Sexrex's Escalade. I could see the two girls in the back seat and I cringed. I looked over quickly and saw Sexrex standing behind his SUV, with a gun drawn right at me.
"Hi, Officer!!" He boomed.
BANG!
He shot at my head and I dodged back behind the dumpster. The metal sparked as the bullet grazed it beside my face.
"You're not getting her back!" Sexrex continued. "She's mine now!"
I began to stew in anger.
"Oh, and your other friend?!" He still went on. "This other bitch..."
I looked over to G who I could see was growing furious now. He looked at me too with burning eyes. He began to clench his jaw and narrow his eyes.
"She's mine too!" Sexrex yelled.
G was fuming. He breathed out through pursed lips.
"C'mon, pretty boy." Sexrex said to himself. "Show me that pretty face."
G was staring at me and I looked back.
"I'm gonna make these two girls my best sellers!" Sexrex continued. "Men from all over will come far and wide for a piece of these...sweet...tail!"
"That's it!" G said.
"G, no!!" I cried after him.
G didn't heed that advice at all, and he was up and pointing over the dumpsters with his rifle—
—"*Police, freeze!*"
"*BPD, hands in the air, now!*"
"*Drop your weapons!*"
BPD, drop it! Do it now!"
The shouts and commands of officers all broke in to stop the fire fight momentarily. The Cavalry had arrived!

They swarmed in from all directions, aiming their rifles at Sexrex and his goons. G ducked back down and remained unseen by the cops.

The goons and Sexrex did not comply with the police's orders and they pointed their weapons right back at them for a standoff.

"Drop it!" A cop shouted to Sexrex.

"You first." He replied calmly back.

"Not gonna happen pal! Drop it now!"

The other cops all shouted similar commands to the other goons and had no success either.

Behind the dumpsters the other three guys all looked to me on what to do. I just looked at them and told them to hold on, and hold position.

Ridley crept in behind the tact team with his gun drawn. Slowly he approached the back of them and craned his neck over to try and see if I was around and his suspicions were true. Jimenez trailed behind him.

"Last chance!" The cop squaring off with Sexrex warned. "Drop you weapon or I will shoot you!"

"Well..." Sexrex started slowly. "...not if I shoot you first!"

BANG!

Sexrex pulled the trigger, with no warning, shooting the cop in the upper chest.

Both the goons and the cops immediately erupted into shooting. Sexrex ducked behind his Escalade for cover as bullets whizzed by and struck the side of his vehicle. The rest of his goons scattered, most, which hadn't been shot, dodged behind stairwells, stacked skids and piles of shipment boxes for cover. Ridley grabbed Jimenez and they dove behind one of the cargo bay walls that jutted out.

The four of us remained hidden and waited the fire fight out. I looked back out, around the dumpster at the SUV. Sexrex was pulling the handle in-between gunshots over the hood, and he got into the car.

"Shit! He's leaving!" I cried!

I rose up and aimed at the SUV as he sped off. I couldn't risk hitting the girls in the back. Sexrex's SUV revved loudly as he peeled through the fire fight, right down the middle, ducking low to the steering wheel as he weaved through.

I stamped my foot and then looked at the cement truck Ken had brought.

"You guys need to get out of here!" I told the others. Then I made a break for it.

"John!" G called after me.

I ran, crouched low to the ground and I headed for the smashed up truck.

Ridley peered over the edge of his wall and saw me running. He squinted his eyes for a better look.

"John?" He asked himself.

I made it to the truck, with the rest of the girls still inside. Mid stride I hopped up onto the back of the truck and then jumped up to grab the nylon strap of the cargo door. I grasped it tight and then leapt off the truck to get to the other side for cover. As I jumped down, I pulled the cargo door down with me to slam it closed. I quickly latched it shut to protect the girls inside, then rushed behind the truck.

Ridley watched the whole stunt and confirmed now that it was me.

I ran down the length of this truck towards the cement truck. I made it to the end and looked around for Sexrex. He was speeding towards a fence that separated his club from the sporting goods warehouse next to him. I climbed up the truck and whipped the door open to hop in.

"Ken!" I shouted down to him through the open window. "Get outta here man! Go!" I said to him. The truck had been left idling, and I threw it into gear quickly.

CRASH!!

Sexrex crashed right through the fence and ran over what he knocked down. Then he sped over the grassy section, hopped the curb and started making his way through the service path behind the sports warehouse.

Suddenly, the passenger door of the cement truck was ripped open and I snapped my head over to see G climbing into the passenger side. He was looking at me with enough determination that I had to let him tag along.

I pulled the truck forward, revving that engine and hammering on that clutch. The truck jolted all over the place and the tires screeched. I steered hard right to loop the truck around.

The gun battle raged on between the cops and the goons Sexrex left behind.

Ridley still watched, carefully from behind the wall. He saw the truck begin to make its hard turn for the fence.

"He's going after him..." Ridley deduced in a whisper.

"What?" Jimenez asked from behind him. "Who?"

Suddenly Ridley raced out, and ran! Behind the line of tact guys who were advancing towards Sexrex's thugs.

I arced right towards that same fence Sexrex plowed through and shifted up a gear to gun it through.

As I was turning, Ridley jolted out from around the corner of the battle and stopped, looking right at the truck. I didn't notice him at first. He was just a guy in a cop uniform. Until I noticed he was running straight at us! He stopped when he got close enough for me to see his face and then I just stared. It felt like slow motion for a moment as the two of us caught each other's glares. Our eyes followed one another's until—

—"John!" G shouted nervously. "Whoa, John!"

KERAAACCK!!

I plowed through the fence, splintering the wood and smashing a huge hole in it. I thundered over the grass and over the curb. I shifted gears as I jerked the wheel left to peel after Sexrex's SUV down the service lane way.

Ridley now bolted away, back towards the street where they pulled the cruisers in.

The SUV and the cement truck tires crashed over the speed bumps as we both sped down. I glared ahead at the back of the Escalade as we chased it through this windy lane way. I couldn't shake Ridley's face in my mind.

"Ridley..." I whispered his name to myself.

The corners were tight and I had to jerk the wheel, constantly shifting gears to control the truck. The girls shrieked as they were tossed around in the back of Sexrex's Escalade. Sexrex hammered the gas, and hit the brakes, constantly back and forth as he maneuvered his vehicle through to the end of the lane.

He reached the end where it exited out onto the road and as he was turning left onto it, we caught up—

—*CRUNCH!!*

Our front bumper smacked into the rear corner of the Escalade and it lurched to the right.

"Damn!" I cried out, as I turned hard to the left. "Sorry girls!"

"Careful, John!" G warned. "That's my friend in the back too!"

"I'm trying, I'm trying!" I replied, coming out of the turn.

The Escalade started to pull away from us as we drove on a straight away now.

Ridley hopped in his cruiser and jammed it into gear quickly. He reversed out and actually bumped into another cruiser as they were all jammed up in front of the club. Then he rammed the cruiser into drive and screeched his tires to peel after our chase.

Sexrex ducked his SUV in between cars where he could, weaving all around traffic. It wasn't as easy for me to do that in the big truck, but as I tried to weave, I smashed into bumpers and pushed cars that were in my way, out the way. During all this, we were able to keep up with Sexrex but on clear straightaways he was able to pull away from us.

"He's getting away man!" G screamed.

"Thanks, G, I can see that!!" I replied back harshly.

Another black SUV pulled into the commotion in front of Sexrex's club. A standard issue, FBI vehicle. Clare pulled it to a stop and opened the door. She stood up out of the driver's seat and looked all around the busyness. The news crews were all still out front but she saw that all the cops who were left were making their way towards the back of the club, with guns drawn.

"What's going on?" She asked herself.

SSKKKRREEEEEEEE!!!

Ridley's tires peeled as he dodged the police cruiser around our path of carnage the truck left behind.

"John, you son-of-a-bitch..." He grunted.

He flicked his lights and sirens on to clear his path and he sped through traffic.

317

CRASH!!
The front of our truck shoved another small car out of the way and I sped after Sexrex in the Escalade up ahead.
"He's goin' for the highway!" G said.
"I know he is!" I shouted back. "He's goin' to Washington!"
"This thing ain't fast enough!" G said, slamming the dash. "John, he's gonna get the girls out of Baltimore! What are we gonna do?!"
I sighed angrily, still shifting gears and forcing the truck past its capabilities.
WHOOP-WHOOP!!
The sound of police sirens flashed behind us suddenly. I looked into the mirrors to see the flash of a single cruiser's lights.
"Cops, John!" G shouted.
I stared back and forth into the mirror at the lone cruiser and thought...
"Rid..." I whispered. "...G, there's only one car!" I told him. "If they were after us, it'd be a whole squad!"
"What!?"
I smiled to myself. "It's my friend." I said.
Then I turned to G. "G!" I started. "We're not gonna be able to catch Sexrex! And we can't keep this up! I can't keep smashing up all these cars and endangering all these lives!"
G just looked at me desperately. Then he looked into the mirror and saw Ridley rapidly catching up to us in his car.
"G, look around for a pencil or sharpie or something!" I told him.
G looked at me funny.
"C'mon, man! Do it!" I yelled.
G started scrambling all around the truck. In the visor, in the glove box, in the centre console, until finally he found one of those thick contractor pencils in the side door compartment.
"Got it!"
"K, and paper!" I added.
G scrambled up an old work order receipt and un-crumpled it.
"Ok, start writing..." I began.

In his cruiser, Ridley slammed on his gas and dodged one last car as he caught up with us. He jerked the wheel right to come up on our back passenger corner and then he pushed the gas further to begin speeding down the side of the truck.

"Okay, here he comes!" I said to G. "Get ready!"
Ridley approached the side of the cab and saw G. He craned his neck to see me driving and I looked at him. Our eyes locked for another few moments.
"K, G, show it to him!" I said.
G slapped the paper up against the window and broke Ridley's stare with me. Ridley, looking back and forth at the road squinted to read the message...

'*D.C.*' It read in 2 thickly scribbled pencil markings.

Ridley's brow furrowed.

G moved the page and I looked down at Ridley. He shrugged at me and had a confused look, until I pointed dramatically at the SUV we were chasing. Ridley looked ahead to Sexrex's Escalade and then back at us. His brow unfurrowed as he figured out what I was telling him. Then he looked at me angrily. I nodded at him, pleading with him to help us. For a long tenuous moment he just stared at me, until he realized this was not the time or place to be angry at me for recent events.

Then he nodded back at me and allowed himself to fall back in the cruiser.

"What the hell, John!?" G asked me.

"You asked for the Cavalry, G? Rid will call it in."

"What!?"

Ridley fell, just behind our truck now and maintained speed to follow. Then he grabbed his phone and scrolled through to the number he wanted.

Back at the club, Clare's phone rang in her pocket. She quickly got it out and answered.

"Agent, Mash?" She said.

"Clare!" Ridley shouted.

"Rid? Where are you? I'm at the Sexrex, where—"

"—I'm with John, Clare!"

"What!?"

"Listen...he's trying to leave the city! You need to call in your friends!"

"Rid! What are you talking about? What's going on?"

"Did John ever tell you about our friend Dave from high school?"

"What? The one with the daughter? What does that have to do with—"

"Sexrex has her, Clare! That's what this is all about! John's going after him!"

Clare paused and sighed. "Damnit." She said, a little softer to herself. "And what am I supposed to do, Rid?"

"Tell your office!" Rid answered.

"Tell my office what?"

"Clare, don't you want John back? We can use this! This city has been trying to nail Sexrex forever! Now we've got proof that he's in on some serious human trafficking! We got him! Tell them to setup at all the edges of the city! Block Sexrex in!"

Clare didn't answer, and she just put her hand on her head and sighed.

"And Clare..." Ridley added. "We'll get John too!"

Clare lowered her hand and stood up. "Alright, Rid." She said.

"Hurry, Clare!" Ridley finished, and he threw the phone down and kept on the tail of our truck.

Up ahead of him, in the cab of the cement truck.

"G, listen to me!" I started. "They're gonna set up roadblocks! Sexrex is getting away; he's too fast for us! I'm gonna follow him until the roadblocks stop him and I'll grab the girls there!"

"You'll be caught too!" G said.

"I'll be fine, G. But I need you to stay back in this truck."

"Wait, what!?"

"Follow us in this thing." I said, patting the wheel. "Stay behind and meet us there."

"John what the hell are you talking about!?" G asked. "Where are you going!?"

I had my eyes on a nice shiny convertible on the road beside us and now I looked over at him with a smirk. "I'm gonna go get us a getaway vehicle." I said. "Take the wheel."

"Take the wheel!? Are you crazy!?"

"Apparently...take the wheel!"

G reached over, shaking his head. "I can't believe this!"

I let go and the two of us shifted and shimmied past each other awkwardly. Finally G sighed into position behind the wheel and assumed control, while I flopped into the passenger seat. I looked out the window quickly and found the car I had been eyeing. I looked up ahead and saw Sexrex's SUV quickly getting away from us.

"Step on it G!" I told him. "Stay on him, just until I get after him!"

As G sped up I returned my focus to the convertible car. "G, this'll have to go quick! Keep it steady!"

The convertible was just cruising and not going at a high speed at all. We were quickly gaining on it and it was coming up on the right. I opened the door of the truck and the rushing wind forced me back a little.

"John!" G shouted. "Be careful!"

I grabbed the door frame tightly and onto the side handle with my other hand. I braced to jump, planting my feet firmly on the steps. "Steady, G!" I shouted back to him. "Here it comes!"

We closed in on the car and came up right beside it. The driver did a double take when he saw me hanging out of the truck. He slowed down intentionally to fall behind us and avoid the danger.

"Damn!" I shouted. "Slow down a bit, G!"

G brought the truck down a little slower and we began to match the speed of the car again.

"I got a bad feeling about this!" I shouted, more to myself then anything. As the car was still coming up beside us and not quite in line beside the truck yet, I jumped!

"*aaaaaAAAAAAAAAAHHHHHH!!!!*"

I timed it right and I crashed into the open back seat with a thud!

"Whoo!!" G shouted in relief.

I grunted in pain as I lay in the back seat of this guy's car.

"Hey!" He shouted. "What are you doing!!? Are you insane!?"

"Uuuggghhh!!" I groaned, forcing myself up onto all fours. "I just might be pal." I groaned. I flopped back onto the seat and sighed, checking myself over for injuries.

"I'm getting off!" The driver said, beginning to slow down.

"No!" I cried, lurching forward. "No, don't!" I climbed over the seats, into the passenger chair. "Move over, bud! I need your car!"

"I don't think so!"

"Well, I do!" I replied, pulling my gun out and pointing it at him.

"Oh my God!" The driver said in fear. "Okay, okay..."

I reached over with the other hand and took control of the wheel.

G watched from up in the cab as we switched control. The car swerved a few times but once we had switched I regained control.

"Look, pal." I said to the guy. "I'm not gonna hurt ya alright!?"

The driver just quivered in the passenger seat now.

"I'll drop you off somewhere." I told him. "But I gotta catch this guy!"

I looked up at G in the truck beside us and gave him a thumbs up. He nodded and then I jammed the gas pedal and sped off after Sexrex.

I could see him, far up ahead now, and he was pulling off the road onto the on ramp to the highway. I quickly gunned into the next lane to follow.

CHAPTER TWENTY THREE
End of the Line

In D.C., next door to all this chaos.

While Sexrex was speeding down the highway with our girls in the back, the press was getting ready for the arrival of the guest speakers.

While Clare was calling in the closure of all major exit points from Baltimore,
 a limo was arriving at the hotel that Globe-X was putting Richter and his associates up in.

While I was following Sexrex down the highway,
 there was a knock at Richter's door.
Ernest answered and a representative from Globe-X was standing in the frame.
"It's time." They said.
Ernest turned and looked at Richter who was lying in the hotel bed.
"Ready Jay?" Ernest asked him.
Richter just sighed.

Moments later they were all in the limo and headed down the road. Richter was staring out the window, trying to remember what he was supposed to say at this thing.
Richter turned to his binder of notes. He was pawing over the calculations and scribblings once again, and he got lost inside of his work.
Ernest spied him carefully from the opposite bench and kept a suspicious eye on him.
Richter didn't see him and thought he was clever by hiding what he was *really* looking at. He placed his smaller, more personal, and more private journal inside the binder to hide it from everyone else. He flipped through the pages, reading his nervous scribblings. The ones that kept him up so many nights. The ones that Ernest had challenged him on. He spied them, secretly now, across from his lab partner. He read the warning words that the version of me had spoken to him.
"*DON'T!...DON'T!...*"
Ernest noticed his brow furrow and watched closer.
Richter turned the page and saw the rough sketch he had made. The one of my face. Seeing it caused him to flash back to those times in his lab, where an electrically charged image of me appeared to him. Richter forgot where he was and looked up from his journal and out the window. His eyes went blank as he thought and his face grew an expression of anguish and confusion that

Ernest couldn't help but notice. Richter shut his eyes tight and shook his head to rid the thoughts, and he blinked a lot as he forced himself back into the moment. Slowly he turned his head back towards the inside of the limo. His eyes involuntarily locked into Ernest's across from him, who he now noticed was looking at him in apprehension.

"What?" Richter asked him.

Ernest said nothing and just kept on glaring.

Richter cleared his throat awkwardly and closed his binder with the journal inside.

It seemed like a long drive from the hotel to the convention centre. The limo pulled into the media frenzy that was waiting there and Richter sighed. He hated this attention and public storm.

The guys in suits opened the doors and it was like a gate opening into a lightning storm. The flashes bombarded his eyes as Richter climbed out of the car, hugging his binder to his chest. He couldn't distinguish between any of the questions being asked from the flood of voices. The guys in suits escorted him, Ernest and Donald through the crowd to the front doors of the convention centre, until the doors were closed to shut out the screaming questions and flurry of camera flashes. Richter sighed in relief on the other side.

"Right this way, Mr. Richter." One of the suits said as he gestured down a long hallway.

Richter looked at Ernest questionably. "Where's the tech?" He asked.

"The stabilizer is already here, Jay." Ernest answered.

"Who's had access to it?" Richter pressed, as they started to walk.

"It's under strict lock and key." Ernest went on. "And only we have the keys."

Richter sighed. "And no one's touched it since we dropped it off?"

Ernest chuckled. "You're so paranoid, Jay!"

"Ernest!" Richter started. "This thing is the key to everything. It stabilizes and synchronizes all of the radiation through all the rings! Yes...I'm paranoid, okay?"

"Yah, but it doesn't do anything if the link is turned off at the other end, right?" Ernest asked back.

"That's not what I'm worried about." Richter said. "I'm worried about these Globe-X morons mishandling it and breaking it! I didn't even want to bring it with us to begin with."

"Yah, but we gotta show the public something, Jay. Just telling them about it isn't enough anymore."

"Pah!" Richter scoffed. "That's just Kitch talking. If someone messes with this thing, I swear..."

"Relax..." Ernest urged. "Let's just get this press conference over with and go back home, okay?"

Richter sighed heavily, and he shook his head. "I'll feel better when I see the stabilizer."

"Right this way." The guy in the suit said.
They had reached the end of the hall and made a left into another storage room. Richter stopped when he saw the large metal case in the middle of the room. The same case they had hauled off the plane. He rushed over to it, pulling out his keys and he carefully unlocked all the locks they had secured it with. He fumbled with all the latches until they were all unfastened and then he flung the lid open.

He sighed in relief, seeing the piece of tech safe and sound.

"Jay." Ernest said behind him. "Satisfied? We have to be on stage in twenty minutes."

Richter looked back to his machine and ran his fingers along it.

"Yah." He said, reaching up to grab the lid. "Let's get this over with." And he closed the lid.

* * *

VVVVVVVRRRRROOOOOOOOMMMMMM!!!
The engine of the Escalade still revved loudly into the night and Sexrex raced down the highway. He looked frantically into his rear view mirrors to see if I was still following him. He had thought he lost us when he pulled away from the truck and got on the highway, but he was still filled with paranoia and continued to check his mirrors.

Maggie and Jeannine still slumped in the back seat. They were both still lethargic from the drugs they were forced to take and they just lay in the back glossy eyed. Maggie's mouth hung open and she just stared out the window. The headlights of all the cars glared in her eyes and she heard the muffled voice of her captor coming from the front seat.

"Yah, I'm on my way." Sexrex said. He was on the phone now. "I've got two pieces of fine merchandise I want you to distribute...yah they're good...some of my best stock...I've got a problem here in Baltimore that I need to take care of first...yah...yah...I'll be there within the hour...alright, man...sounds good...cool...yah...the usual drop point...k, bro...cya soon."

Sexrex hung up the phone and looked back into the mirror again. He smirked this time, thinking he had won...

But behind him, just far enough back to not be noticed, I was on him. I *was* able to stay on his tail for the past forty minutes or so while we traveled down this highway. It was easy enough. I just had to look for the smashed up left taillight on his Escalade. When he changed lanes, I changed lanes and when he passed cars that were going to slow, so did I. I looked up above me as we came up on a road sign: '*WASHINGTON D.C. 20 MILES*'.

I looked beside me at the guys whose car I was driving now. "Almost there buddy." I said to him. "Then you can go."

He just sighed and kept staring out the window.

I looked in my rear view mirror now too, only not as paranoid as Sexrex. I was merely checking to see if G was still bringing up the rear.

Behind me, more of a ways back, he lagged behind us, still driving the big cement truck.

The night passed as we travelled those next 20 miles.

Richter waited nervously behind the stage Globe-X had set up. That crowd of reporters had now migrated inside the convention centre and were eagerly waiting the presentation.
"Ooohh," a voice said beside one of the young reporters. The reporter looked up from his notes to see who said that.
"Isn't this exciting?" The voice went on.
The young reporter looked beside him at the old man the voice belonged to. Who else, but the old devil; *Ranston* stood grinning beside him.
"This is what we've all been waiting for!" Ranston said excitedly.
"Uh...yah." The reporter said. "It's pretty exciting."
"Exciting isn't the word." Ranston said. "The suspense is killing me..."

'WASHINGTON D.C. EXIT'
The big green highway sign displayed.
Sexrex immediately began to drift quickly to the right lanes, and I followed closely behind. I made sure to stay far enough back to not raise alarms.
"Okay, here we go." I was growing excited as we approached the lights off of the off ramp, but I didn't see any barricades. No roadblocks. "C'mon, Rid..." I whispered to myself. "Please tell me you understood my message."
Sexrex turned off the ramp and headed down the road towards the outskirts of D.C. I soon turned as well and followed him.
"Where 'ya goin' Sexy..." I whispered. "Where 'ya goin'..."

"...please welcome, the man of the hour, Dr. Jason Richter!" The Globe-X PR guy announced him.
Reporters clapped as Richter came on stage to yet another flurry of camera flashes. He dragged his feet, and walked sloth-like up to the podium. He did not want to be here. He reached the podium and raised his hand up to subside the applause and the chatter. His face had a sense of *'yah, yah...'* written all over it.

We weren't met with the blockade I was hoping for. We must have traveled maybe 5 minutes down this dark road until finally—
—The bright light of dozens of high beams flooded our eyes!
Sexrex slammed on his breaks and jerked forward in his seat.
"What the f—"
"FBI!" A loud echoing voice said out of a megaphone.
The sound of Sexrex's demise!
"There we go!" I exclaimed, punching the wheel excitedly.

Sexrex's eyes were wide now and he frantically looked across the long stretching line of black FBI vehicles and cop cars. All of their high beams were blasting him in the face and making silhouettes of all the countless agents and officers who were there to stop him.

In the back seat, the girls knew something was going on but weren't quite coherent enough to know what. Maggie raised herself up groggily and squinted out at the sea of white lights.

"Turn the engine off, and step out of the vehicle!" The commanding voice said over the megaphone.

Sexrex's heart beat so hard in his chest as he faced the end of his road. He looked to both ends of the roadblock and knew he couldn't make it around at either end. He began to quicken his breathing.

A little ways behind him, I shut my headlights off and pulled off to the right side of the road. I looked over at the guy in the passenger seat.

"You might wanna get out of here now." I said.

He panted in fear and nodded nervously. Then he fumbled for the door handle and fell out of the car when he pulled it. He scrambled to his feet and took off running the opposite direction of this scene. I chuckled to myself and then turned eagerly to watch the show.

"I repeat! Turn off the engine and step out of the vehicle!" The megaphone voice repeated.

Sexrex was so stunned, and he just stared wide eyed out at the line of lights and officers. They all had their guns pointed at the SUV. Sexrex, the mighty, was actually scared now in this moment. He swallowed a lump in his throat and caught his breath.

"Step out of the car!" The voice ordered. "There's nowhere for you to go!"

From within the group of officers, the person who had organized all of this stepped out into the front lines. Clare stood defiantly in Sexrex's way across the intersection they had stopped him at.

At the press conference, Richter rambled on about his device as it was wheeled in. It all had become a haze of the same questions he was always asked and he entered into a zombie like state, not really paying attention to the questions. They were mere muffled voices in his ears. Even his own answers had become muffled and distant as he gave them.

Grunts from Globe-X handled the piece of tech and that was the only thing Richter paid any attention to. He watched them like a hawk as they took the thing out of its protective casing, flinching at every questionable move they made with it.

The crowd chatter grew when the entire thing was revealed to them. Richter proceeded to explain to them what you already know about it.

All this time, he failed to recognize the old Ranston, who blended cleverly into the crowd of media. He was the only one not clamouring to get a better look at the stabilizer or asking any questions. He just stood in the crowd with a sinister grin spread on his face...

On the road to D.C.,
Behind the commotion, I sat in the car.
We were stopped at an empty four way intersection in the country outskirts of the city. The roadblock was on the opposite side of the lights, and Sexrex was stopped on the other side across from them. I was simply waiting for my opportunity to drive in and grab the girls away from him.
 —*CA-CLICK!*
The metallic sound of a gun broke my concentration and I stopped. I could feel the presence of someone there and I turned my head slowly to see the muzzle of a police issued pistol pointed at me. Then I focused on the blurry figure standing behind the gun.
"Hey old friend."
"Rid." I said. "You gonna shoot me?"
Ridley smirked. "Oh, I sure would like too John." He said. All of his emotions were bubbling to the surface and showing on his face.
I just stared back calmly, knowing my friend wouldn't pull the trigger.
"There's bigger things going on right now, man!" I said, raising my voice a little, and gesturing towards the scene ahead of us.
"You arrogant prick." Ridley said, seething. "You know how worried we are...you leave your best friend and your wife for what? To pursue this crazy ass mission of yours to fix the world? You're gonna save everyone is that it? Damn you, John!"
I sighed slowly, and turned my attention towards the roadblock.

"Get out of the car now!!" The voice over the megaphone commanded.
But Sexrex just breathed and gripped the steering wheel tightly.

"Ok, everyone!" Kitch said, at the press conference. He had taken over answering questions for a few minutes. "Now for what you all came here to see."
A hush fell over the crowd and Kitch turned slowly, along with every other eye in the place, back to Richter on the stage.

"Rid..." I started. "Look, I know you're pissed buddy."
"Pissed?" He repeated. "Pissed, isn't the word! I should take you in right now!"
"Then why don't you?"
Ridley didn't say anything and just glared down at me.
"Because you said so yourself..." I went on, distracting him, as I reached slowly for the door handle. "...you wanna save the world too."
"Ah, this again!"
"Yah, Rid! This again! Always this! Until it stops! You agree with me!"

"But we were doing it legitimately, John!" Ridley shouted.
"Sshh!" I warned, looking back and forth between him and the roadblock.
"We were cops, man!" He went on. "We were the good guys! We were stopping people! What was the problem!?"
"Because it's never enough, Rid!"—
—*SLAM!!*
"Ooff!!" Ridley groaned as I smashed the car door into his legs. He lurched forward and pointed his gun away from me. I stood out of seat and shoved up on Ridley's chest to send him backwards. He fell onto his back and I marched quickly towards him.
"You're gonna shoot your best friend, Rid!?" I yelled. "Huh!?"
I kicked the gun out of his hand and grabbed him by the shirt to hoist him up. He reached up and grabbed my shirt too. The two of us were now both on our knees and clutching each other by the clothes around our necks. We burned holes into one another's skulls with our vicious stares.
"It's not enough anymore, Rid!" I shouted.

Richter swallowed the nervous lump in his throat and looked around at all the people. They were waiting anxiously for his display.
"You're up, old buddy." Ernest whispered beside him.
Richter looked over to his lab partner who was grinning like an idiot at him. "Easy for you to say, Ernest." Richter whispered back. "You don't have to talk to them."
"That's why you get paid the big bucks, Jay."
Richter sighed and shook his head, turning back to the crowd.

"I'm taking you in, John!" Ridley shouted at me, as we clutched at each other still. "You need to come home!"
When I heard these words I grew sad, because I knew what I had to do next.
"Then I'm sorry old friend." I said, looking regretfully at him.
I swept his arms off of my neck with my right arm and then I spun him around so he was resting on me now. Then I locked up his arms against his own neck and began to squeeze him to sleep. He struggled and kicked his feet wildly.
"Ssh, Rid, don't struggled man!" I said as I squeezed. It hurt me to do this and I just stared ahead blankly.
He pounded my arms and tried to look at me.
"When is it gonna be enough!?" He managed to choke out.
I just squeezed harder and he stopped hitting me to try and pry my arms off. I closed my eyes and waited for him to fall asleep.
"I'm sorry, Rid." I said into his ear. "I'm sorry, man." I slowly felt him go in my arms until finally he went limp and then I sighed in anguish. I loosened my grip and looked to my right at the roadblock scene ahead of us. I fought back

tears and then turned back to my friend. I found his pulse and sighed in relief. Then I slid him to the ground and sat there in a heap for a moment.

"Last chance!" The agent's voice ordered to Sexrex. "Get out of the car now!!"

Sexrex sighed and squinted his eyes in preparation. His heart was beating so fast, but he didn't care anymore.

He was done.

One last stand.

He smirked...and then—

VVVVRRRR...SSCCREEEE!!

The tires peeled when he hammered the gas! Maggie flew back and crashed into the back seat with Jeannine. The SUV jerked forward.

"Look out!!"

"He's not gonna surrender!!"

Voices all began to erupt from the ranks of officers.

I snapped my head up when I heard the engine revving and the commotion of voices. I saw the SUV start to speed through the empty intersection that separated them.

"Oh no!"

I scrambled clumsily to my feet.

Sexrex kept his foot on the pedal and pushed it right through the floor!

Clare's eyes went wide as the headlights of his Escalade burned into her eyes. They grabbed her, like a tractor beam, freezing her in place.

I ran as fast as I could towards the convertible and crashed into the driver's seat.

Clare couldn't move. The Escalade barreled right towards her but she couldn't move.

Sexrex's eyes raged and he growled as he charged the line.

I had barely even put the car in drive. I was completely and utterly helpless back here.

Useless.

But then I heard the sound—

—*BLAAAAAMMPP, BLAAAAAMP!!!*

Sexrex snapped his head to the right suddenly when a separate flash of light caught his eye.

After the horn blasts, he didn't even have time to be scared. The only thing he did feel was his heart drop out of his feet—

CRAAAAAASSSHH!!!

The cement truck flew in, as if out of nowhere! Everyone had been so focused on the charging SUV they didn't see it.

I was even startled and I jumped back in my seat.

G *thundered* into the side of the SUV, right into the sweet spot!

A carefully timed, carefully aimed shot by G. He smashed into the passenger side engine and drove the Escalade sideways. The truck stopped the SUV in its tracks and forced it off the rails. It slid left and spun 90 degrees to be parallel to the cement truck. G locked up the brakes and skidded the truck to a stop.

"Oh-ho-ho!!!" I bellowed as a grin spread across my face. "Yeah!! G!!"

The line of cops all unshielded their faces and turned their attention back to the centre of the intersection.

The broken pattern of the skipping truck brakes squealed and the whole scene became eerily silent.

I jammed my car into drive and drove towards the scene, not wanting to miss my chance. I left Ridley behind, asleep on the pavement.

At the press conference, Richter descended the podium steps towards his piece of tech.

Ranston squirmed nervously in the crowd, awaiting the fruition of his plan.

Richter took the keys off his neck and approached the stabilizer.

"Hold your fire!" Clare ordered to the confused troops at her call.

Everyone froze and waited on edge.

G threw the truck into reverse and backed it up as a wall between the Escalade and the roadblock.

"Hold!!" Clare reordered.

Then her attention was taken by the red convertible speeding in from her left. She turned her head and watched me race in, taking a big arc to loop in behind the truck. Her heart leapt in her chest when she realized it was me.

"John?" She asked out loud.

"Agent Mash!" Another officer asked impatiently. "We can't just stand here!" He went on. "We have to move on this!"

Clare just watched, wide eyed, as I drove in out of sight behind the truck.

"Agent Mash!!" The other cop screamed.

"Our priority!..." Clare snapped, turning to him. "...is to stop the subject from entering D.C. Hold your positions!" She ordered, glaring back into the defiant eyes of the eager cop.

Behind the truck, I screeched the convertible to stop and I couldn't get the door open fast enough.

Sexrex pushed his door open and he slumped out of the seat. He had smashed his head against the glass and was bleeding. He staggered out of the vehicle in a daze and then fell back against it. As he was sliding down to the ground I ran in.

POW!

I flew in with a fist and smashed him hard across the face, screaming as I did.

G opened up his door and jumped down.

"Nice shot, G!" I said to him. "C'mon, come here! Get the girls!"

He rushed around the other side of the SUV as I grabbed Sexrex by the collar.

"Get up!" I said. "C'mere big guy!" I hoisted him up and brought him to my face. He stared at me in bewilderment and even cracked a smile. I stared into his one good eye with anger and seethed through clenched teeth.

Richter pushed the key into the port on the stabilizer and sighed out slowly. After a brief hesitation he turned the key in the ignition and the machine lit up, humming to life. The crowd all took an instinctive step backwards.

G opened the back door of the Escalade and started to haul the girls out.

On the other side of the big truck, the line of cops still waited.

"This is ridiculous!" The impatient officer said again. "Why did we come here, if not to apprehend this suspect!?"

Clare didn't answer and just watched eagerly for any kind of movement behind the truck.

Sexrex chuckled as blood ran down his face. "Congratulations Cowboy." He whispered. "You got me."

"I should kill you right now!" I told him.

He laughed. "You're right. You should..."

Richter began to switch things on, on the stabilizer. One by one he pushed buttons and flicked switches.

"But it wouldn't matter." Sexrex went on, to me. "You think it'll stop with me?" He asked. "There's more like me."

"I know!" I said. "and I'll have to stop them too!"

"There's always gonna be someone left to fight, cowboy." Was his answer.

It stopped me. Those words. I had heard them before. Sean Mash had said that to me when I killed him. I looked away from Sexrex, still holding onto him and I panted as I looked around. I thought back to that day, and suddenly the haunting words of my time travelling self filled my ears.

"*DON'T!!...*" They cried. "*DON'T DO IT!!...DON'T KILL SEXREX!!..*"

I gave my head a vicious shake, trying to expel these thoughts.

"What I'm doing here..." Richter began to explain. "...is activating the radioactive core within this stabilizer." He finished, placing a hand on it. "Since the link on the other end is turned off, I can turn it on just to show you how it works..."

"What the matter officer?" Sexrex asked. "C'mon, man...I know I'm done. Jail ain't my style!"
I looked back at him now with new determination.
"Do it, man." He said. "Do it..."

"This device," Richter continued to the crowd. "Synchronizes with the control console in Israel. Once the tower there has collected all the rings radioactive signals, this device aligns them all. Connects them in a stream. Forces all the waves to form into one giant rope between all the different rings around the globe. All by pushing this button here." Richter popped open a protective cover to reveal the execute button, and Ranston stiffened up in anticipation.

"Do it, cowboy!" Sexrex screamed in my face.
I panted heavily, and looked to the side as G pulled Maggie out of the back of the SUV. She was limp and he had to carry her. She could barely even hold herself up and her face had lost most of its colour. Her hair was matted down and sweaty. The look on her face reminded me of the looks on those kids faces, who me and Ridley had saved from the creep. Hopeless...
I slowly looked back to Sexrex with burning rage.
"C'mon do it!" He screamed.
"Aaaaahhhh!!!" I screamed, raising my fist.
I was going to kill him with my bare hands!

"C'mon..." Ranston whispered to himself, anxiously watching Richter's demonstration.
"And..." Richter said casually. "Voila!"
Click.
He pushed the button!
Ranston smiled to himself.
"Just like that folks." Richter ended, thinking that was it. "Thanks for coming out tod—"
—BZZZZZZZZZZZZ...
Richter's brow furrowed at the rise of a sound he wasn't expecting. He looked around the room and then down at the machine where the sound was coming from.
ZZZZZZZZZZZZZZZZ...
"*Jay!?*" Ernest rose to his feet. "What's going on!?"
"I dunno, Ernest. I—"
ZZZZZZZZAAAAAAAAAPP!!!
The machine flashed and a bright blast of light emanated from the inside of it. Richter was thrown back as a blue electric energy was sent out, like a shock wave, knocking him and everyone else in the room over as if they were dominos.

The shockwave shattered the windows of the convention centre and spread out into the city.

It didn't stop there, and it kept on spreading. A giant, blue, electrically charged circle of energy grew bigger from the centre outwards, like a ripple in the water after dropping a rock, it expanded—

out

and out

and out!

It shattered car windows and knocked over anyone who was standing in its path. Any electric device it passed went crazy until exploding in a blast of sparks.

This thing grew so large that it expanded over all of D.C.

The White House windows were shattered, the Capitol building windows were shattered. Everyone in congress was knocked down, all the tourists were knocked down.

Military personnel looked out of their windows in the Pentagon and saw this giant blue shockwave heading right for them! Before they could let out a scream, it swept over the stronghold and wiped them out.

From up above, Washington was like a round maze of dominos that this anomaly was blowing over.

It spread all the way to the outskirts of the city, approaching the roadblock Clare had set up...

"Aaaaaaahhhh!!!" I was midway through my first strike towards Sexrex's face as the shockwave approached. I didn't even see it coming and as it swept our chaotic scene I suddenly felt a sharp jolt of energy running through my veins. It tensed up my muscles like a taser, stopping my blow. My jaw bit down hard and I arched my back, spewing spit through the cracks in my teeth. My eyes shut tight and I felt so strange. That's all I remember before I blacked out.

CHAPTER TWENTY FOUR
Anomaly

My eyes stayed shut, and a strange sound filled my ears. It was both loud and quiet at the same time. No other noise except this soft and steady rushing. A buzzing or a hum. So loud that it just drown out all other noise to create a white noise illusion of silence.

I opened my eyes and I was on my back.

I wasn't staring up into a night sky anymore.

It was blue.

But not a daylight blue.

It was a glowing, electric blue. Almost purple. And it wasn't holding still. It was like a running current. A flow of energy.

I sat straight up with a gasp and everything was lit by this electric glow. The sky was a spotlight and it made everything blue.

Every once in a while there was a loud electric snap. A loud crack and sparks of lighting danced around the entire scene. Lighting whips snapped across the electric sky.

Sexrex was still there, but he was frozen the way I left him. He was on his knees anticipating my fist. Only he was deadly still, as if someone had pushed the pause button. I looked to my left and saw that G was the same way. Maggie too. They were a paused image of him helping her into the back of the convertible. Jeannine was also frozen in the back seat. The cement truck was still there, and the SUV. The whole scene was still here, all stuck on pause but me.

I couldn't believe what I was seeing here.

Richter groaned in a daze. His old bones hurt from the shockwave blasting through him. He rolled over onto his elbows and reached around for his glasses. He could only see a blurry blue haze until he found them.

"Everyone alright!?" He yelled into the silence. He sat up and rubbed his head. He fumbled to get his glasses open and he lifted them to his face. Everything came into focus and he stopped. The blue he had seen was caused by some sort of light coming through the shattered windows. The whole room was lit up with a blue glow as he looked around.

But that wasn't the odd part.

Everyone was frozen. All the reporters were paused in that frightened moment as the shockwave exploded out. Richter stood up and stared in awe at all of their frozen faces.

Then he turned to see his associates. Ernest, Donald and Kitch were all paused too, with frightened and urgent expressions. Everyone looked like cardboard cutouts.

I staggered to my feet and looked around the whole intersection in bewilderment. More lighting whips continued to crack all around everything. I breathed in and out heavily, trying to fathom what I was seeing. I craned my head up into the sky to look at this magnificent electric current running through the sky. Electric arcs raced across it.

Then I started to walk around. I passed through where G was helping the girls and put my face right up to his. He was definitely paused somehow, dead still. I looked over to Maggie and her face was frozen with that utter hopelessness. I looked into her lost eyes and I was filled with sadness. Then I turned from this scene and began to walk around the cement truck.

Cautiously, I peeked around the truck, unsure of what I would be met with on the other side. I showed my full figure slowly and walked towards the roadblock.

No one shouted for me to get down or put my hands up. I approached as slow as I could until I was sure they were stuck on pause too.

No one batted an eye at my approach, or turned an eye my way. They all still faced the truck, fixated on it with their arms stuck forward, pointing their guns. I walked towards the line until...

...I gasped.

Clare!

I didn't realize Ridley had called her in on this. I froze now, staring at her. Those big green eyes that I missed were right there, staring ahead.

Richter waved his hand in front of Ernest's face. He didn't flinch or seem to notice anything was there. Richter snapped a few times and even grabbed his face—

—*BBBBBZZZZAAP!!*

"Ouch!" Richter cried out as a shock of electricity coursed through his veins. He put his finger in his mouth to sooth the pain. He shook his hand to get the blood flowing again and grew such a look of confusion on his face at what was happening. He slowly turned to face the crowd of cardboard reporters. He walked down the podium steps very carefully and entered into the crowd. He took a glance at each frightened face as he passed them. Some cameras were frozen with their flashes blaring. He weaved through them all as carefully as he could to avoid more electric shocks.

When he finally passed them all he made it to the doors and stepped outside.

The blasting sound of that rushing electric current in the sky hit him and he squinted and shielded his face. Those lighting whips cracked all around him and he flinched and curled into himself thinking they would hit him.

After a moment or two he realized he was fine and he uncurled. He unshielded his face and began to look around in awe at this phenomenon he was standing in. He marveled at the electric sky and all the sparks and lightning. He walked down the front steps of the convention centre into the empty and frozen streets of D.C. Even the American flags were frozen mid wave.

I stepped in front of my wife.
She was so beautiful standing here. Her hair was tossed around by the shockwave as it crashed into our scene, and it was frozen in place, all a mess and flowing behind her head. Some strands crossed her eyes and her face was frozen with a stern expression. Her action face.
I raised my hand up apprehensively, to brush the strands away from her eyes, but stopped. Had it been too long? Had too much happened for me to be deserving of touching her again? Hesitantly, I reached slowly to caress her face. But as my hand got closer to her flesh it grew hot and felt tingly. I retracted and started opening and closing my hand into a fist and I shook off that sensation. Then I went for it again, pressing my palm to her cheek—
—*ZZZZAAAPP!!*
"Aaah!!" I pulled my hand away from the shock and clenched it into a tight fist. "What the hell?" I whispered in fear.
—"You can't touch her!" A voice called out.
My heart jumped as I was startled and I gasped. I spun quickly around to see who it was, but there was no one. I panted and looked all over for the source of the voice but couldn't see anyone.
"You can't touch any of them!" It said again.
"Who's there!?" I yelled.
No answer.

Richter wandered out into the streets of Washington. He looked in through the broken windows of cars and saw the frozen people inside. He stepped on the broken shards of glass that the shockwave left behind and it all crunched under his feet. People who were startled by the wave that were walking down the sidewalks were frozen in startled positions. Even the coffee was frozen in the air as it had splashed out of their cups.
Richter wandered into the middle of the busy street and looked down the long stretch. He could see the dome roof and steeple of the Capitol building at the end of the road. He just stood and circled around not believing what he saw as electric whips snapped all around.
CRUNCH!!
Then the sound of broken glass being crushed under foot cracked in Richter's ears. He gasped and spun around to where he thought it had come from.
He wasn't alone...

"Who said that!?" I asked loudly into the street.
I looked frantically around the whole scene, becoming frightened and frustrated. "What is all this!?" I screamed.
Then I stopped when I looked down the left side of the line of cops. Something was moving. Behind the officer's heads there was something moving. I couldn't make it out but it was a person. It was hard to make out any kind of form or features, but someone was definitely walking behind the line of cops.

I stopped and stared, straining to see who it was. He stared back as he marched in a straight line behind all of the heads. We both caught faint glimpses of each other in between all the heads and shoulders as they passed. I was frozen now too except for my head as I followed the figure across the line.

A pair of black dress shoes crushed the glass as it walked over top of it all towards Richter. Richter stared in horror as a person he knew well approached, dressed in his usual black suit.
"Ranston?" He asked with a shaky voice.
Ranston approached with a grin on his face.
"Wha..." Richter stuttered. "...what is this, Paul? What's happening?" He was too perplexed to carry on his dislike of Ranston. He was too frightened.
Ranston stared back, still grinning.

As the mystery person got closer to the middle of the line I could make out a head of brown hair and some white clothing. Then He stopped right behind Clare and turned to face me. I gasped when I saw His simple yet unforgettable face.
"You?" I asked in a whisper.
The Stranger simply smiled back at me with a gentle smirk.

"Paul..." Richter asked again.
Ranston was just standing there eerily.
"Say something!" Richter urged him. "How...what is this? What's wrong with everyone!?"
"Mr. Richter." Ranston said slowly. "Don't be alarmed."
"Don't be alarmed!? Don't be alarmed!? This was supposed to be just a demonstration! What the hell happened!?"
"Time has stopped, Mr. Richter."
Richter stopped. "What!?"

At the roadblock scene, me and The Stranger just stared at each other.
"Hello, John." He finally said to me.
I gasped softly. "You..." I started. "Y...you know my name?" I asked with a whisper.
"Of course I do." The Stranger replied. "Did you think I was just watching you for fun?"
I actually chuckled in bewilderment. "Why?" I asked. "Why *are* you watching me?"
"Because, John." He said, moving forwards now. "Because you're important to me."
I scoffed.
The Stranger slipped in between Clare and the officer beside her and walked towards me.

I took a step back as He approached. I was starting to grow fearful of this whole situation.

The two of us just stood across from each other and stared at one another for a few moments.

"What is going on here?" I asked with a shaky voice. "Am I dead? Is this...heaven, the afterlife...whatever..."

The Stranger smiled. "No, John." He said. "You're not dead."

"Then what am I?"

"You're stuck."

"Stuck?"

"In time."

"Time-Travel." Ranston said. "Mr. Richter, Time Travel!"

Richter stared back blankly.

"Don't you remember what it is you're trying to accomplish?" Ranston asked, laughing.

"Ranston." Richter asked. "What are you talking about? What is this?"

"You know what this is!" Ranston gave Richter a discerning look now to suggest he should know what this was.

Richter stopped for the first time since waking up in this environment and he began to think.

"Time travel." The Stranger said. "Jason Richter. You know that name don't you?"

I nodded slowly. "Yes, of course, but what does this have to do with...wait..." I stopped, remembering the newspaper I had read. "He was supposed to be in D.C. this week. Is that what this is!?"

"Yes, John. It is."

I took a moment to process what he was telling me and tried to figure it out.

"Okay...so...what the hell is this then!" I asked, pointing into the sky. "Why is everyone frozen?"

"Well," The Stranger said. "That's the right question, John."

There was a silence as He left a dramatic pause. Electricity popped loudly and startled me.

"It's broken." He said.

Richter looked around at all the frozen images of people everywhere, as he figured things out.

"Things are stopped." He whispered to himself. "Why is time stopped?..."

"C'mon, Mr. Richter." Ranston said. "You know the answer already." Ranston just watched, grinning, while Richter racked his big brain.

Electric snaps and lighting whips cracked all around them.

"Time..." Richter whispered again. He spun around and around to look at everything. "I've come across this..." He said. "In my calculations,"

"Yes..." Ranston said.
"I've seen this outcome." Richter said. "..only..."
"What?" Ranston asked, taking a small step towards him.
Richter's own conclusions terrified him. He gasped and put a hand to his mouth. "No..." He whispered. "This isn't possible."

"It's like a film strip." The Stranger said to me. "Right now, you are in a single frame of time." He started to walk across the line of cops. "You're inside one square of the film strip."
I shook my head again and held my skull. "Wait a minute..." I started. "Why aren't I frozen too?"
"You are!" He admitted to me.
My eyes went wide. I felt my stomach sink. With my mouth hanging open I just stared.
"Turn around." The Stranger said.
Reluctantly I followed direction and slowly turned.
"You're still here." He said. "Look."
I took a few steps forward away from The Stranger so I could see around the cement truck. My eyes went wide when I saw it. There I was! Sure enough, kneeling in front of Sexrex. I was frozen on pause like everyone else. My face was stuck in a rage and my fist was raised into the air, waiting to strike Sexrex.
"I don't..." I panted. "I don't understand."

"We..." Richter panted, while staring at the electric event all around him. "...we broke it!"
"Just like Kitch was worried about." Ranston said. "And Donald. And Ernest."
Richter swallowed in his throat and it was hard to make eye contact with Ranston now. He nervously looked at the ground and stumbled around.
"The funny thing is..." Ranston pressed. "That it was your own calculations that foretold this."
Richter's breath quickened and he took big heaving pants while staring at the ground.
"But you were so bent on finishing your project." Ranston added. "So obsessed. Your own ambitions caused this."

"You've heard of this thing called; 'the space time continuum', haven't you John?" The Stranger went on to me.
I couldn't find the words to say. I just stammered my mouth open up and down but only air came out.
The Stranger started to walk as he spoke. He crossed my right side and began to walk in a circle around me. "A cosmic balance," He continued. "of the physical passing of time, the matter of our being, and the invisible fabric that holds it all together."

I only stared ahead as he spoke, still trying to figure this out.
"What?"
"This is a rip. A tear. One hole of many in the space-time continuum."
I gave my head a shake and scrunched my face up in confusion. "Holes?" I asked. "How did that happen?"
The Stranger rounded the front of me again and now raised his hands up to put the electric atmosphere around us in display. "Man wasn't meant to travel through time." He said. "It's completely unnatural, and it breaks every law of physics. If it's forced, it isn't without consequences."

Richter looked at the smug Ranston across from him. "This kind of damage to the continuum would only be possible if the machine was abused. But...we haven't even used it once yet!"
"Hey, you're the scientist." Ranston said. "I'm just the money remember?"
"How can you be laughing!?" Richter yelled. "Look at this!" He motioned all around. "It's broken! Time is broken!"

"What you're in right now," The Stranger said. "is the result of your own ambitions.
I shot my head up with a look of sheer frustration. "Me!?" I asked angrily, upon hearing the explanation. "How does this have anything to do with me? Because of that letter? I didn't even go and see Richter!"
"No," The Stranger said. "But you will."
"What!?"

"The machine's been used before!" Richter concluded. "That's the only explanation." He started to pace the scene, rubbing his head and running his hands through his hair. Then he stopped pacing suddenly as a thought came to his mind. "That guy." He said.
Ranston furrowed his brow and cocked his head in curiosity.
"Of course." Richter went on. "The guy, my sketch, my ghost..."
"Who are you talking about?" Ranston asked nervously.
"I have no idea who he is. Some guy who kept appearing to me all the time. I used to think it was dreams but...it wasn't."
Ranston looked away to hide his anger. He clenched his fist to squeeze out some frustration. "Sneaky bastard." He whispered, cursing The Stranger's interference.

"I told you something bigger is going on." The Stranger said to me. "This is because you did go and see him at some point. You used the machine and tried to fix things. But you used it too much, John."
I looked up to the sky as he spoke and I focused on the whips of lighting that sparked across the sky and all around us. As they flashed it reminded me of the visions I had in my apartment on those long dark nights. These lighting

arcs were the same type of flashes that happened during those visions, when I had appeared to myself.

"That's what that was." I concluded. "When I showed up to myself those nights."

"Yes." He confirmed. "You stepped into snapshots just like this one. Tears. Holes."

I sighed at the magnitude of all this information.

The Stranger sighed too. "This...anomaly in D.C." He said, shaking his head. "Something happened with Richter's demonstration. It was the nail in the coffin, so to speak. The radioactive surge. It made the rip bigger. Bigger than any before ...I don't know how it happened."

"Look!" I shouted. "I'm not the scientist here...guy...whoever you are...ok? I honestly have no clue what you're talking about!"

The Stranger patiently chuckled and looked down at His feet.

"You're right." He said. "The best way I could think to describe it is like this...every time Richter's machine was used—"

"—by me..." I cut in. "Apparently...I'm still having a hard time with that."

The Stranger laughed. "Really?" He asked. "That's what you're having a hard time with believing? Not the fact that you're trapped inside a living moment in time with the very fabric of time zapping all around you?"

I opened my mouth to retort His point but my words fell short. "Hmm. Good point." I said.

"Anyways. Every time that machine was used, it created another path of time. The original timeline didn't go anywhere. The first time it was used, a second set of events was made, running parallel to the first."

"Like an alternate reality?" I asked.

"Exactly. It's impossible to change time, John. Richter knew that. He calculated that, but...didn't care. He wanted to eventually find the alternate reality where everything was perfect, but..."

"But, what?"

"But you, John...you've already been to the future. And you've been back and forth so many times...You've created enough alternates to stretch the fabric of existence too thin."

"Too thin?"

"If the fabric of existence was like a piece of paper, it's been sliced extremely thin. Peeled apart, and separated. Like plies of toilet paper or sticker backings. Over and over again as each new timeline was created. Before this blast, it was a row of alternate timelines all parallel to each other. Set up like a paper set of dominos. Thinner then tissue paper. Eventually it got too fragile and...the radiation shockwave, well...it was enough to shred the slices."

"Shred the slices..." I whispered. I really didn't have anything to say, other than just stupidly repeat back what The Stranger was explaining....

"This shockwave destroyed the space time continuum." Richter said to Ranston, in D.C.

Richter was pacing the scene now, mostly monologuing to himself as he pieced it all together. He had nearly forgotten that Ranston was even there.

He sneered behind Richter's back, secretly knowing he had been the instigator of all this. But he was ready for the next step of his plan...

"Isn't there some way to set it right?" He asked, impatiently.

Richter stopped pacing, while his back was facing Ranston. His voice reminded him of his presence there. He slowly turned.

"How are you here, Paul?" He asked.

Ranston's face froze and his sneaky smile began to fade. "What?"

Richter glared suspiciously at him. "Me being here, can only mean one thing." He started slowly. "That I'm still connected to the continuum somehow." He dropped Ranston's gaze and looked at the ground as he figured out this next piece. "I...I must have ripped myself into a slice along with it. Like those shadows you see on the wall. The ones that get burned onto the surface after a bright radioactive blast."

Ranston, thinking he could distract Richter's line of thought and get himself off the hook, spoke up. "Which means you must have time travelled, and already used the machine. Connecting yourself with the fabric of time."

"Imprinting myself into it, yes..." Richter agreed. "But...that explains me." He turned his expression back to Ranston again. "It doesn't explain you, Paul!"

Ranston's face faded again.

Richter took a step towards him now. "How are you imprinted, unless you used the machine too!"

Richter allowed a silence for the answer but none came. The silence was long and awkward as Richter stared at him, remembering his disdain for this guy and how shifty he was.

"Well!?" Richter demanded.

Ranston looked sheepishly away. "I...I guess I must have travelled too." He lied.

Richter continued to glower at him suspiciously.

"I don't know if those details are important right now." Ranston suggested.

"Oh you don't huh?"

"We need to focus on fixing this."

"Now there's a we?"

"Mr. Richter, please! Focus! Is there any way to set this back?"

Richter glowered at Ranston, stewing in his old hatred for him. He was right though. Now was not the time for this battle.

"So...all this." I started slowly with The Stranger. "This has already happened? My life? Everything that's happened? And you're what? You're from the future or something? You've been trying to warn me is that it?"

He chuckled again. "No, *you've* been trying to warn you." He said. "I'm something else entirely."

342

I sighed in frustration and threw my hands up. "Whatever." I said, passing my hand in the air at Him. "I've heard enough. How do I get out of this? Let me out of whatever this is!"

"I'm afraid you're stuck here."

Now I snapped my eyes at him angrily. "Excuse me!?"

"You've been stuck inside this paradox for a long time now, John." The Stranger said walking up behind me. "Unless the fabric of time is fixed, this imprinted version of yourself is attached to it. What happens to time, happens to you now."

I dropped to my knees and held my head. "Has it been so long??" I asked in agony.

"Your mind is fuzzy." He went on. "I know. "Travelling through time has that effect."

I felt like I wanted to weep. This was too much.

Richter stormed past Ranston, glaring at him.

"Where are you going?" Ranston asked.

"I need to see the uplink!" Richter replied, walking back towards the convention centre. "On the stabilizer!"

Ranston watched him leave, but stood in place. He knew Richter was growing more and more suspicious so he took his chance here while he could.

"When I powered on the stabilizer, the machine turned on!" Richter continued explaining, not looking back. "Which means the link to Israel was turned on when it shouldn't have been! Someone..." He turned, but his voice trailed off when he was met with no one. He looked all around but,

Ranston was gone...

"Look, John." The Stranger said. "Here's the facts. Richter was giving a demonstration today in D.C. It was supposed to be just a display for the press. Something to prove that he wasn't full of it. But...someone...sabotaged the whole thing." The Stranger placed an angry emphasis on 'someone' as He ironically referred to His opponent, Ranston. "And that's why I need you." He added.

I stopped rocking and paused. I slowly raised my head up to look at Him.

"I said, you're important to me." The Stranger said.

"What about my old life?" I asked.

"Oh, that'll still go on. It has to. That timeline has to proceed in order to create this, right?"

I shut my eyes and gave my head a shake. "That's..."

"A paradox, John. It's called a paradox."

I sighed heavily and dropped my shoulders. In my slump I looked over to the frozen scene of my confrontation with Sexrex. I looked around the whole scene. At G. At Maggie. At Clare.

"This all seems kind of silly now, doesn't it?" I asked. "In the grand scheme of all *this*."

"Try not to focus on that, John." He said. "*That* world has enough problems of its own. *This* world..." He said, looking up and putting the electrically charged atmosphere on display with his hands. "This reality is something a little different."

"How?" I asked.

"Remember what I said about this being like a single frame on a film strip?"

I nodded.

"Well...this world is kind of like the whole film strip."

"What?"

"It's filled with all the holes. The rips and tears. Other frames like this one. You can literally move up and down the 'film strip' and jump into any moment in time you'd like."

I chuckled. I shook my head. "This is crazy." I said, scoffing. I placed a foot on the ground for leverage and I began to stand up, grunting through my words as I pushed up. "So..." I grunted. "what do you need me for?" I asked, standing to face The Stranger.

"John," He started. He placed a hand on my shoulder. "I need you to find Jason Richter." He said. "I need you to help him."

I furrowed my brow. "Me?" I asked. "Why me? I'm just a loser cop from Baltimore. Look at the mess I've already made trying to help. How am I gonna help a man like Jason Richter? I'm not a scientist. I don't know anything about any of this stuff, outside of what I've seen him say on T.V. and what you're telling me now. I'm not the guy to send."

The Stranger smiled at me warmly. "Trust me, John." He said. "You're just what he needs."

I stared back at Him humbly.

"What else are you going to do anyways?" He joked. "Seriously, it's the only way out of here for you. On a personal level, you're only hope is to find him and figure out how to put it back."

"But..." I stared. "I need to get back in *there*!" I pointed towards the frozen scene of Sexrex and me. "I need to help Maggie. There's so many other things I have to set straight."

"You will, John." He said in retort. "I told you, that timeline will go on."

"Yah but, knowing what I know. Knowing the universe is gonna explode and everything..." I said sarcastically. "that kind of changes things a little!"

The Stranger chuckled. "John, you have the chance to change things from this side! More so than ever!"

I looked at Him for a long time before answering. Finally I let out a long breath and lowered my head. "How am I supposed to find Richter?" I asked, finally accepting my task.

"Easy. He's in D.C." The Stranger answered. "Just head into town and you'll find him near the convention centre."

I raised an eyebrow inquisitively at Him. I looked past Him to the long stretch of road that spanned behind the line of frozen still cops. Then back to The Stranger.

"That's a long walk." I said.
"Well, good thing you've got time on your side." The Stranger joked some more.
I even broke a small grin at that one. Then I looked around once more at the frozen scene. "If this reality continues to go on..." I started. "If all the different realities continue to go on despite all this." I gestured my hands around all the electricity around us. "Then why does it matter? I mean, won't it be only this realm of reality that'll be effected?"
"John, were you not listening?" He asked back. "Yes the other timelines go on, but...If the fabric of time suffers one more blow then that's it."
"That's it?"
"It'll be obliterated...the end of all time as we know it!"
I suddenly felt very foolish for asking and I swallowed a lump in my throat. "That's what I thought." I said.
"I joked that time is on your side," The Stranger added. "But you'll need to be quick, John. If you and Richter can't find a way before the *you* from *that* realm uses the machine—"
"—hold on." I interrupted. "How will that matter if it's the first time in history the machine will be used?"
"The first time in *that* physical history, yes. But you have to understand something about time, John. It's a circle. A never ending loop. If there's any kind of forced time movement again, on any spectrum during all this..." He motioned to the electric blue sky once more. "...then say goodbye."
I nodded along. "Oh..." I said stupidly. "Well, ok then. No pressure right?"
The Stranger didn't chose to add anything further, and His joking mood seemed to be faded now. He just stood there staring at me.
"Or...you could just go on killing everything in your path, and hope that changes something." He added quite sternly.
Humbly, I looked at my feet. I suddenly felt quite embarrassed about my original intentions.
"John..." He started again, but I could read a sense of compassion in His voice this time. "...I know you want to change the world. I get it, ok? I mean, no one understands more." He said, placing a hand on His own chest. "Where I'm from...the world will one day be judged. And judged right."
He caught my interest again and I started to raise my head up at His words.
"Believe me." He said. "Your intentions are righteous. Evil does indeed need to be dealt with."
I felt my old sense of crime fighting swell up and through squinted eyes I raised my head to look at Him again.
"But please trust me." He said. "There *is* another way."
"Who are you?" I asked. "You're from the other side of all this?"
He just smiled. "Something like that."
I sighed through my nose and controlled my raging emotions down.
"John." He finally did say. "You'll have to hurry."
I stared back at Him for a moment and then nodded. "Ok." I said. "Ok..."

There was more long silence between us. We just stood there and listened to the snaps and cracks of the lighting whips slashing around us and in the sky. Then before I set off, I looked over to the frozen version of me from this realm of the frame we were in.

"Can I ask you something?" I said to break the silence.

"Of course." The Stranger replied.

"Can they hear us?" I asked. "These people?"

The Stranger shrugged. "I suppose so." He said. "But it may only pass through as a fleeting thought for them."

"That's ok." I said. Then I looked at Him again. "Can I just have one second?" I asked.

"Be my guest." He answered.

One more apprehensive glance at Him I took, before turning and walking slowly over to my paused self.

The Stranger waited patiently for me.

I approached around the corner of the cement truck and walked in between where G was helping Maggie into the convertible. I paused a moment to look upon their faces. Then I stepped through and was faced with the two poster cutouts of Sexrex and myself. I came to a stop right beside them, and I looked back and forth at the faces. I saw the hate and the anger written on them both. I sighed. Then I took a long glance backwards to see if The Stranger was still watching. He was. Turning back to face them again, I lowered myself down on one knee beside the frozen image of me. I took a long hard glance at my own face. It was definitely a hardened face now! Not the fresh faced young cop out of the academy anymore. It was scarred and bruised and dirty. It had wilder hair and more intensity. I stopped on the eyes. These eyes had become like a burning fire. I had once asked my reflection in the mirror if this was the face that would strike fear into my enemies. This was certainly that face now. I followed my own gaze over to Sexrex's face. I took a moment to stare into his face now too and I sighed. I turned back to myself now and took a final look at my face. Then I leaned in close to the ear. I could feel my face grow hotter and begin to tingle from the electricity. But I whispered:

"Let him live. You can do it. You can still fight for what's right. Enough violence. There's a better way. I think I've found it. Go see Jason Richter. Don't do this."

A very subtle, very tiny thing happened. Even within this frozen still shot of time...upon those words seeping in, a thought was planted. Barely even noticeable, my brow twitched, almost like a pondering furrow.

I rested back, pulling away from my face. I took a look back at The Stranger and then I rose to my feet. I began to hesitantly walk away from the scene, walking backwards as I went. It was hard to leave this behind, hoping that my words did anything. At last, I turned my back and marched away from the whole scene.

I didn't look back.

"God speed, John" The Stranger said as I returned.
I nodded to Him silently and continued past Him towards the line of police. I stopped at Clare to fill my eyes with one last glimpse of her beauty.
"For you." I said to her frozen image.
Then without looking back I started to squeeze through her and the other cops to be on my way.
"Oh, John?" I heard The Stranger's voice call behind me.
I stopped and looked back at Him. He was approaching the other side of the line and digging into His pocket.
"When you see Jason." He said, bringing His hand out with something in it. "Give him these."
He reached His hand through the line, over the shoulders of the officers and I reached out my palm to accept what He had. The sound of little wooden beads clacking against other ones rang out as He gave me the stringed object. I closed my fist around it and met The Stranger's gaze.
"Tell him he's not alone." He said.
I nodded. "Ok. I will."
"See you in the future, John." He said to me kindly. "I look forward to speaking with you again soon."
I looked back at Him apprehensively and pocketed the object He gave me.
"Right." I said.
And with that, I turned and saw the long road ahead of me. There was a sign that read; *TO DOWNTOWN D.C.*
I sighed and took my first step of my new mission. Then my second, third, and I was off on this insane journey.
Behind me, The Stranger watched me go.

CHAPTER TWENTY FIVE
Beginning's End

ZZZZZZZZZZSSSSSSSSHHHHHHOOOOOOOOOMMMMMMM!!!!
A radioactive blast spread across all of D.C.
A shockwave.
Back inside the frame.
"This timeline will still continue..." The Stranger's words foretold. *"...it has too..."*
Reset.
Unpause...

"Aaaaaaaaahhhhhhh!!!!" I screamed out a cry of war with my fist raised into the air.
SMASH!
I carried out my first strike and thundered my fist across Sexrex's face.
He fell to the ground and I fell with him following the force of my blow. I stopped myself with my hands and fell onto my side.

The blast swept through the FBI barricade and it pushed them all off balance like a strong wind. All the glass in their cruisers and SUV's shattered. They all stopped pointing their guns and shielded themselves. Clare ducked for cover.

The glass in the cement truck windows exploded out, as well as the windows and mirrors of the convertible. The blast shoved G, like a wind, and he tumbled forward onto Maggie shoving them both into the car. He landed on top of her in the back seat.
Both me and Sexrex shielded our heads as the glass from the Escalade rained down on top of us.

Then the outside rings of the shockwave weakened and dissipated into the sky. It had reached the extent of its spread and now died off on the outskirts where we were.

Amidst the chaos, I lay on the ground and my thoughts grabbed me tight. It had felt like a voice just started talking to me. It was a confusing feeling as, from the ground, I watched Sexrex squirm across from me. I couldn't shake this strange conflicting thought that was so contradictory to what I had been feeling a mere second ago. I saw him there, covering his face from the glass and groaning in pain from my blow. I had struck him right on the eye and ripped some skin. The conflicting part of this new thought in my head took over and I staggered up onto all fours. There was an echoing sound in the sky and I looked up. The left over sounds of a shockwave, like that of a fighter jet screaming overhead and breaking the sound barrier, rippled through the air. I could see the faint outlines of a disappearing wave. I pushed myself up to be on my knees now and I looked over to G who was stumbling back to his feet out of the car.

"G!" I screamed, gaining his attention. "What the hell was that!?" I asked him.

Panting, he threw his hands up. "I dunno bro!" He answered.

Worried, I looked around quickly. Then back to him. "Go, man!" I said. "Get the girls out of here!"

G nodded and then rushed around to the driver's side of the convertible.

I turned to Sexex who was getting up to lean his back against the Escalade again.

I got up and walked over to him.

Once the chaos had passed over the line of cops, Clare got to her feet again too. She looked all around with bewilderment all over her face. All the other cops got up too and a frenzied chatter broke out amongst them all.

I grabbed hold of Sexrex again and brought him to my face.

Suddenly—I felt a twinge in my brain and shut my eyes tight to shake it off. I glared at his evil face, wanting so badly to finish the job.

But...

Strange words were filling my thoughts.

"*Let him live?*" Where was this coming from? "*Another way?*" What!?

"John!" G's voice called behind me.

I was stuck frozen, staring at Sexrex's grinning face.

"C'mon cowboy." He whispered to me. "C'mon."

"John!" G called again.

Behind the truck, at the line. The officers and agents all looked to Clare. She was still trying to figure out what that anomaly was.

The officer who had been previously frustrated with her was staring at her angrily. He had had enough of this.

"A screw this!" He shouted. "Move forward!!" He ordered his men.

A section of the line all followed his direction and began to advance towards the cement truck.

I seethed at Sexrex, wanting to destroy him.

"*JOHN!!*" The voice of my electric ghost came to mind. This time it rang so much clearer and made so much more sense for some reason. "*DON'T DO IT!!*"

I shut my eyes to try and rid the thoughts. "*There's another way...*" A whispering thought crept in. "*Enough violence...*"

I opened my eyes suddenly and saw his smirking face.

"John, they're coming!" G said behind me from the driver seat.

Slowly and cautiously, that line of police emerged towards the truck. Confused and panicked, all the other jurisdictions looked at each other on what to do. Most of them followed suit and advanced with the first wave of cops.

I gritted my teeth as I made up my mind. I glared at Sexrex and he glared back with his one good eye. I focused on his glass eye with the clover iris and then chuckled.
"What's so funny, copper?" He asked me.
"Nothin' man." I said. "I'm not gonna kill you. You know why?"
He just laughed. "That sounds familiar." He said. "Isn't that what I said to you?"
"You don't deserve death." I hissed. "I'd rather watch you. As you watch your empire crumble!"
His face dropped immediately. "No..." He whispered.
"John!" G cried. "C'mon!!"

The advancing officers drew closer towards the cement truck. They all had their guns drawn and they slowly crept closer and closer.

"No!" Sexrex cried. "Just kill me! I can't do jail man!"
I hoisted him up by the collar and held his head in place with my forearm against his neck. I smiled and brought my face in real close to his.
And I whispered;
"It's your lucky day you Irish son-of-a-bitch!"
Then I reached in with a claw like hand—into his eye socket! He screamed and tried to get lose but I pressed him into place as I continued.

"Cmon, c'mon!" The team leader shouted to his group. "Split up, surround the truck! We'll come at 'em from both sides!"
The officers all spread out on his orders.

Behind the truck now,
G hammered the pedal to the floor and we sped away from the scene, screeching our tires and leaving a trail of smoke.
"There they go!" Someone shouted.
All the voices erupted in a panic as team leaders all began to scramble their groups. The main group focused on the truck as others double backed to their vehicles to begin pursuit
"Go! Move now!" The original team leader ordered. His group rushed the cement truck now and came around both sides of it, only to find the smashed Escalade and Sexrex slumped against the side of it.

Voices all shouted in unison for him to not move and put his hands up and so forth. He slowly raised his hands with no protest as they rushed in to secure him.

The other groups made it to their vehicles and started the pursuit of our convertible. We sped away from the scene and my eyes found Ridley's sleeping body as we rushed past. I watched him zoom past us as we sped by with regret, wishing I had more time to speak with my friend.

"He's clear!" A cop shouted, after inspecting Sexrex.
"Get him up!"
"Wait!" The team leader yelled. "What's that in his eye?"
Everyone looked at his face and squinted to see his eye. They quickly realized that he only had one, and that the other was now a gaping black hole in his face.
"Fake eye?" Someone asked.
"Well, yah, it used to be...there ain't nothin' there no more!"
"What's in there?"
One of the cops closet to him reached in and picked out the rolled up piece of paper that was placed inside the chasm. A rolled up paper, like a scroll. The cop looked at it funny and then handed it to the leader. The leader unrolled it and read the message I had scribbled;
'AN EYE FOR AN EYE'
The leader dropped his arms in frustration and made a disappointed face.

In the convertible, as we sped away, I rolled my little keepsake around in my hand. It was heavier then it looked. It was like a big cue ball, shiny and white, except the green clover in place of an iris. I chuckled to myself and gave it a little toss up to catch it quickly.
I sighed out a huge relieving breath and turned to see the girls, safe in the back seat. It was especially good to see Maggie there. Even though she was still out of it and lethargic. I smiled.
I turned back around and looked at G. He was red-lining this car to get away but he took a few side glances at me and smiled.
I looked behind us again at all the lights and sirens that were a ways back and pursuing.

At the scene, the officers hauled Sexrex up and dragged him to their cruisers at the line. The team leader approached Clare and handed her the note. She took it and opened it up. After reading the message she had to contain a smile. She looked over to watch them put the defeated kingpin into the back of a car and then she chuckled very softly.
"Only you, John." She whispered to herself.
Then she turned inwards, looking back into Baltimore now. She could see a small red dot that was our getaway car followed by a huge gap and then the

police cruisers from Baltimore PD pursuing. She let out a long sigh and then tuned in to something. Something that she felt since the blast passed through.

A tingling sensation, like pins and needles on the side of her face. With a furrowed brow, she reached up and touched her cheek.

It felt as if someone had touched it.

* * *

In the aftermath of the shockwave that swept D.C. The news was frenzied with stories of it.

"*Dr. Richter, Dr. Richter!*" One reporter caught him as he and his crew were arriving at the airport. "*Do you have any comment about the catastrophe in D.C.?*"

"*What happened in D.C yesterday,*" Richter began as they all walked. "*Was an unforeseen complication with our equipment. All I can say, is that I am sorry for damage done to the city, and that I will be working hard on rectifying the issue.*"

"*What was the issue!?*"

"*What went wrong!?*"

"*How do you answer for the destruction and the injuries!?*"

"*Is the time project going to shut down!?*"

A flurry of questions, from the crowd of reporters, bombarded him.

"*No!*" He answered. "*The project will not be shutting down! But we will be taking a bit of a hiatus, to try and figure out the cause, thank you!*"

The crowd exploded with more questions but the hired security held them all back as the entourage entered the airport doors.

"Vultures!" Ernest commented, in real time.

They were seated on their flight and had been watching this story on the news. They took a private flight back this time on Globe-X's dime.

"What are we going to do, Jay?" Ernest asked him.

Richter was sitting across from them, with his face buried into his ledger. He was going over his calculations and notes.

"I don't know what they're so upset about!" Richter said, not looking up. "The destruction isn't catastrophic like they're saying."

Ernest and Donald looked at each other.

"Mr. Richter!" Kitch whined. "There's millions of dollars of damage!"

Richter stopped for a moment and looked up from his notes. "Well, at least the window companies will be thriving this year!" He joked.

Ernest and Donald shared a chuckle at that one.

"Our insurance is going to have to fork out that money!"

"What do you want me to say, Kitch!?" Richter snapped. "I'm sorry!? Well fine, I'm sorry!!"

The room went silent. "I'm sorry..." He repeated, quieter. "But this should never have happened. Someone sabotaged us. That link should never have been turned on."

"Who would do that?" Donald asked.

"I don't know. The same person who turned China on too soon."

They all looked around at each other suspiciously. "I'm going to have some words for Chuck when I get back, let me tell ya! I'm still trying to rule out the possibility that this was an accident, but...if we can't...we'll have to start considering the obvious."

"What's that?"

"That someone inside is seriously screwing with my machine!"

In Israel.

The work site was aflutter with activity. Everyone was suited up in radiation suits and busy working. Calls from overseas demanding to know what happened had all the workers scrambling.

All but one...

The lead technician who Richter had left in charge.

Deceased, at the hands of Ranston's smokey goon.

But his name tag on the suit didn't read 'W'.

It read; 'Chuck'.

'Chuck' just calmly sat at the console in the desert and he smiled to himself.

* * *

The flashes of the camera burned his one good eye.

They told Sexrex to turn for his mug shots. Face left, face right. The cameras flashed him as he held that iconic prisoner sign.

Sounds filled this kingpin's ears over the next few days, and weeks.

The rattling and rolling sound of a steel cage closing, echoed into the dark jail as they slammed the cell door on him.

The sound of jingling handcuffs.

The pounding of a judge's gavel as his court hearing proceeded.

The sound of the prosecutor's voice laying down all the offences he was charged with...

* * *

Clare, my beautiful wife returned home from work one evening. She entered into the darkness of our loft and placed her things down. Then she flicked on the lights as the big metal door clanged closed.

She walked towards the kitchen but stopped short as something startled her. Strangely to her, there was something someone other than her had placed on the table.

A picture frame, pinning down a white envelope.

She just stared at it for a while, afraid to approach, because she knew what it was.

After a moment she did approach and saw that it was one of the pictures from our nightstands, of us during happier times. The note had her name printed on it and that was all.

She swallowed a lump in her throat and reached for the letter. Soon she was reading it...

My Dearest Clare

I don't know where to begin.

I wanted to tell you so many times. What I was planning. What I was feeling!

But I was afraid. Please don't blame yourself. This is not your fault. The world needed saving and you were doing that with Kovacs...

...Meanwhile,

In retrospect from reading this letter. Clare went back to work. She entered the mission room with a sigh as my words in the letter stuck in her head. She imagined my voice reading the letter to her...

...The way I feel about the world, Clare...it's crazy! I know it is! There's too much...

...Clare fired up her work station as she recounted my words. Images of that new terrorist group Ray had been telling her about, The Lung, appeared on her screen. She saw images of their attacks, and trail of destruction...

...It's all so evil,

My words echoed in her head.

and it's all so devastating. I couldn't live in it, knowing that behind my door, there were so many unspeakable and disgusting things. It's not right. And man was never meant to live like this! I know you agree with me, Clare. We used to stay up late talking about it...how to save the world...

...back on that same day of the car chase. The same day of the D.C. shockwave.

We had left behind a gun battle, between the police and Sexrex's goons. Ridley had left behind his rookie partner, Jimenez. Ken, Bart, and Tom had fled the scene once the shooting started.

When the fire fight had ended, leaving most of the goons dead, and a few in custody, it was Jimenez who unlatched the back door of the cargo truck I had closed. When the door sprung open, young Jimmy Jimenez looked into the back at all the girls the goons had herded back there to be shipped off to another trafficking ring. It was Maggie's face I was thinking of as I wrote the next section of my letter to Clare. Her's and the faces of all those other poor girls as the cops ushered them off the truck to safety...

...But, I was led to believe that the answer to that problem was a disturbing one.

My words read, applying to this situation.

I went down a dark path. I was a bulldozer. A car in the red, after what happened to our baby. Even a car accident is all part of the problem. I didn't want anyone else in the world to have to feel the way I felt after that night...

*...Jimenez watched each broken face of the girls as they were brought down off the truck. Knowing about human trafficking and seeing the faces of the victimized girls were two different things. Their sad and lost eyes broke his heart as much as it did mine.

I got away that day too. When the cops caught up to our red convertible, it was abandoned on the side of the road.

G and I had taken off on foot, down the hidden paths leading back to Baltimore...

...But, I'm writing you, Clare, to tell you...

The letter I wrote after that day continued.

...I've had a change of heart. I can't explain it. A piercing thought that has invaded my mind somehow. Maybe it's because I miss you so much. Maybe not having the things that once connected me to the goodness of life has made me different...

...G and I hooked a bus back to our city, along with the 2 girls. On the drive there I began to think of what to write to Clare...

...That's why I gave you Sexrex.

The letter read. Clare recounted my written words as she followed the media coverage of his demise...

...That's why I didn't kill him. Because I knew that he had an entire empire out there that wouldn't just disappear with him...

...Elsewhere, the sound of boots kicking down doors and police raid commands being shouted broke into dozens—hundreds even—of establishments under Sexrex's rule...

...Weed him out. Squeeze him...

...During all of the raids, Sexrex was a broken man...

...I know his type now. He's a proud, arrogant, vain man. Jail doesn't suit him...

...A defeated man. Once he thought he was untouchable. But now, his arrogant rule over this city was coming to an end. And he knew the truth of my words to Clare as he sat in his cell...

...He'll make a deal to get out. Even if he has to start at nothing...

...He sat humbly during all of it...

...He'll give up his entire empire and start over...

...The cops shut down his club as the investigators uncovered each one of his operations. During the trial, he gave up all his under bosses and all his cronies. He gave it all up—told the police where each one of his establishments were. He handed over the keys to his kingdom in exchange for a shorter sentence—a plea bargain deal that resulted in a more lenient punishment, and when the trial was over, Sexrex sat back in his new cell to start counting the days until his release...

...He'll get out...
My letter concluded.
...But the city will be safe, for a while. And that'll have to do...when he comes back...just leave him to me and my friends...

...G and I made it back to his house in the slums. We brought the girls in and made them comfortable. As comfortable as possible to begin their detoxing off the drugs. A knock on the door brought Ken, Bart, and Tom in to the house now too...

...At his humble home, Ridley returned from night shift. He grabbed a drink from the fridge and cracked it open as he sauntered over to the pile of mail on his counter...

...I'm sorry about your father Clare...
The letter read on...

...Ridley began sifting through the envelopes, tossing aside bills, and separating mail for his wife.

...But, you have to believe me when I say...there's more to the story...

Ridley got the bottom and stopped suspiciously. A lone white envelope with no return address and no stamps looked back at him. Only his name was printed on the face of it.
He quickly opened the envelope and reached in to take out its contents...

...One day, when this is all over, I'll tell you the story...

...He furrowed his brow and he inspected it. A small, square shaped chip. A memory drive. A note accompanied it that said; For *Clare. When she's ready.* Ridley dropped his eyes to the bottom of the page to read the last bit;
Asta Lavista, Rid.
He cracked a smile, and even chuckled at my reference.

When we were settled I spent the night on the front porch of G's place, watching this broken city. I lit the first smoke I had had in a while and enjoyed that first pull. I smoked the cigarette as I watched the neighbourhood and thought about Clare...

...*My wife. My love. I'm sorry I left you...*

...Clare sat, at our table, as she finished this last section of my letter, and tears began to well up behind her eyes...
...*I want more than anything to be with you, but...I can't right now. I promise you, I will put it right. We will be together again. Know that I am out here. Know that I am alright. Know that I love you...*
...Clare sniffed, and her tears fell on the words...
...*I need to be out here, Clare...*

...Somewhere in the city,
   A kid shook his spray can, and began a simple work of art on the faded bricks of a Baltimore city building...

...*A guy like me doesn't belong in the real world. I'm too extreme for my own good. I'm not like everyone else. I'm almost not a real person...*

...Bart started to explain excitedly about something he saw. A symbol. A writing on the wall that told us...As we were preparing to launch a whole new kind of initiative, the buzz had been building.
   The word had been spreading.
   The...feeling,
      had been growing...

...*Being out here is teaching me though...*
...Clare read on...
...*Life can be absolutely devastating. Unbearable. Unrelenting...*

...The city was talking about a mayor who had been killed because of his corruption, instead of being allowed to slip through the holes in our justice system or pay off the judges with his dirty money...

...But...if it's one thing I've learned out here...the very thing that makes life awful, also makes it so precious...

...They were talking about a daring attempt to take on a seedy underboss and free the city of the sex trade...

...I've seen it out here. It's so fragile. So delicate...

...About a man on a bus, who dared to step up and take out a major threat and menace, and a hero in the night who saved one girl and probably many more by taking out the trash...

...Which has taught me, we have to be so careful, in what we do with our own lives...

...After Bart's excited depiction of the art he saw, I sat and watched Maggie. I was deep in thought, recalling the words I had written Clare...

...I don't want to make the same mistakes as the people I'm trying to stop. I don't know what the answer is, Clare. But I need time...

...I stared into the mirror at G's once again. I took a good long look at my new face.
 The new me.

In a long stretching movement, the kid had pressed the nozzle and stained the walls red. He looped around to form a giant circle...

...just a little while longer to figure it out. Can you give that to me?...

...Then he moved to the inside of the circle and sprayed two straight lines, from top to bottom and side to side, crossing each other.

As the swoops of his hand painted the bricks, the swoops of mine sheared my head. The buzzer sliced through my hair and chunks of it fell to the floor...

...Wait for me Clare...
The letter coming to its end...
...Please wait for me...

...We all stood in a circle making our decision. The 5 of us. Myself, G, Bart, Ken and Tom...

...I'll still be out here...
I told Clare.

...*Watching over you...*

...I stared into the mirror, running my hands over the shaved sides of my head. I figured my new identity on the streets needed a new look...

...The kid stepped back from his work and smiled, shaking the can up some more. He had drawn the symbol—the doodle—from my note...

...*If there's anything you need, Clare, Just look for my mark...*

...The giant red, encircled cross now stained the wall...

...*I'll be here.*
　The Baptist.

When the kid was done, he chucked the can aside and wiped his hands.
The symbol now stood as a beacon for others, with the words written beside it;
　'MAKE WAY'.

THE BAPTIST WILL RETURN
IN PART II:
'A NEW TESTAMENT'

ACKNOWLEDGEMENTS
Special Thanks:

A lot of time and effort went into the production of this book, yet it would still not be possible without the help from many important people:

The South-town boys of Payable On Death (P.O.D.) for writing the Satellite album that became the anthem of my youth, and sparked the original ideas for this story. My parents for always encouraging my dreams. My wife who put up with my feverish typing at all hours of the day, supporting me through all of this process and allowing me the time I spent on this! Also for being the first beta reader of the book's first draft. Nancy Stewart for taking on the book as a beta read and assisting with re-structuring and re-writes, and for offering your honest and raw opinions. The book took a whole new turn based on your advice and it brought out ideals that formed the book's second drafts and went on to inspire the third, fourth and final draft—also for providing helpful resources in editing. Ella Burakowski, author of 'Hidden Gold' & Sue Klonowski. Sesadri Bell & author; Judy Powell (Judy Treasure). Chris Sarracini & Mike Story. My film crew and actors on the promo trailers; Claudio DeSantis, Josh Milrod, Jeff Mielitz, and Marvick Chan. Jodi Snitman (for letting us use your house that day, it was very last minute, thank you!). My brother; Patrick Gerard for being the voice of The Stranger, and for also encouraging me along the way. My sister; Kelly Gerard-Downey & brother-in-law; Shaun Downey, for letting us film in your studio & make-up artist hookup; Sarah London who masterfully turned my face into a bloody pulp for both the trailers and the book cover. My man; Dan Branco for recording the voice overs and producing the final mix for the trailers. Jeff Mielitz for pouring in hours of your time into making beautiful and haunting scores for some of the trailers. Mario Rizzuti on graphic design advice and marketing. Dan Fitzpatrick. John Rodgers. Steve Fedoruk. Mike Linnen & John Westenberg; when I was writing these dark worlds and characters, sometimes getting lost inside my own mind and despairing about the world, your chats with me would remind me of the goodness of who we follow and that there is in fact another way.
Last, but most certainly not the least of anything; My God and Saviour.

Made in the USA
Middletown, DE
14 May 2017